DEATH OF A HERO

BY RICHARD ALDINGTON

Death of a Hero, a novel
Roads to Glory, stories
A Dream in the Luxembourg, a poem
Medallions, translations from the
Greek and Latin
The Alcestis of Euripides, a translation
D. H. Lawrence, a study
Fifty Romance Poems, in preparation
and
Imagist Anthology, 1930
with contributions by Richard Aldington,
James Joyce, D. H. Lawrence, etc.

Chatto & Windus

DEATH OF A HERO

A NOVEL

BY

RICHARD ALDINGTON

LONDON
CHATTO & WINDUS
1930

'But here we trifle! but one can't pass one's
youth too amusingly; for one must grow old,
and that in England; two most serious circumstances, either of which makes people
grey in the twinkling of a bedstaff; for know
you, there is not a country upon earth where
there are so many old fools and so few
young ones.'   Horace Walpole

NOTE

THIS novel in print differs in some particulars from the same book in manuscript. To my astonishment, my publishers informed me that certain words, phrases, sentences, and even passages, are at present taboo in England. I have recorded nothing which I have not observed in human life, said nothing I do not believe to be true. I had not the slightest intention of appealing to any one's salacious instincts; if I had wanted to do that, I should have chosen a theme less seriously tragic. But I am bound to accept the opinion of those who are better acquainted with popular feelings than I am. At my request the publishers are removing what they believe would be considered objectionable, and are placing asterisks to show where omissions have been made. If anything ' objectionable ' remains, the responsibility is, of course, mine. In my opinion it is better for the book to appear mutilated than for me to say what I don't believe.

En attendant mieux,

R. A.

TO

HALCOTT GLOVER

MY DEAR HAL,—Remembering George Moore's denunciation of prefaces, I felt that what I wanted to say here could be best expressed in a letter to you. Although you are a little older than I, you belong essentially to the same generation—those who spent their childhood and adolescence struggling, like young Samsons, in the toils of the Victorians ; whose early manhood coincided with the European War. A great number of the men of our generation died prematurely. We are unlucky or lucky enough to remain.

I began this book almost immediately after the Armistice, in a little Belgian cottage—my billet. I remember the landscape was buried deep in snow, and that we had very little fuel. Then came demobilisation, and the effort of readjustment cost my manuscript its life. I threw it aside, and never picked it up again. The attempt was premature. Then, ten years later, almost day for day, I felt the impulse return, and began this book. You, I know, will read it sympathetically for many reasons. But I cannot expect the same favour from others.

This book is not the work of a professional novelist. It is, apparently, not a novel at all. Certain conventions of form and method in the novel have been erected, I gather, into immutable laws, and are looked upon with quite superstitious reverence. They are entirely disregarded here. To me the excuse for the novel is that one can do any damn thing one pleases. I am told I have done things as terrible as if you introduced asides and soliloquies into your plays, and came on to the stage in the middle of a scene to take part in the action. You know how much I should be interested if you did that— I am all for disregarding artistic rules of thumb. I dislike standardised art as much as standardised life. Whether I have been guilty of Expressionism or Super-realism or not, I don't know and don't care. I knew what I wanted to say, and said it. And I know I have not tried to be ' original.'

The technique of this book, if it can be said to have one, is that which I evolved for myself in writing a longish modern poem (which you liked) called ' A Fool i' th' Forest.' Some people said that was ' jazz poetry ' ; so I suppose this is a jazz novel. You will see how appropriate that is to the theme.

I believe you at least will be sympathetic to the implied or expressed idealism of this book. Through a good many doubts and hesitations and changes I have always preserved a certain idealism. I believe in men, I believe in a certain fundamental integrity and comradeship, without which society could not endure. How often that integrity is perverted, how often that comradeship betrayed, there is no need to tell you. I disbelieve in bunk and despotism, even in a dictatorship of the intelligentsia. I think you and I are not wholly un-acquainted with the intelligentsia ?

Some of the young, they who will ' do the noble things that we forgot,' think differently. According to them, bunk must be parried by super-bunk. Sincerity is superannuated. It doesn't matter what you have to say ; what matters is whether you can put it across successfully. And the only hope is to forbid everybody to read except a few privileged persons (chosen how and by whom ?) who will autocratically tell the rest of us what to do. Well, do we believe that ? I answer on your behalf as well as my own that we emphatically do not. Of course, these young men may be Swiftian ironists.

But, as you will see, this book is really a threnody, a memorial in its ineffective way to a generation which hoped much, strove honestly, and suffered deeply. Others, of course, may see it all very differently. Why should they not ? I believe that all we claim is that we try to say what appears to be the truth, and that we are not afraid either to contradict ourselves or to retract an error.

Always yours,

RICHARD ALDINGTON.

Paris 1929.

CONTENTS

PROLOGUE

PROLOGUE

MORTE D'UN ERÖE

allegretto

THE casualty lists went on appearing for a long time after
the Armistice—last spasms of Europe's severed arteries.
Of course, nobody much bothered to read the lists.
Why should they? The living must protect themselves
from the dead, especially the intrusive dead. But the
twentieth century had lost its Spring with a vengeance.
So a good deal of forgetting had to be done.

Under the heading ' Killed in Action,' one of these
later lists contained the words :
' Winterbourne, Edward Frederick George, A/Capt.,
2/9 Battn. R. Foddershire Regt.'

The small interest created by this item of news and
the rapidity with which he was forgotten would have
surprised even George Winterbourne ; and he had that
bottomless cynicism of the infantry subaltern which veiled
itself in imbecile cheerfulness, and thereby misled a good
many not very acute people. Winterbourne had rather
hoped he would be killed, and knew that his premature demise in the middle twenties would be borne
with easy stoicism by those who survived him. But
his vanity would have been a little shocked by what
actually happened.

A life, they say, may be considered as a point of light
which suddenly appears from nowhere, out of the blue.
The point describes a luminous geometrical figure in
space-time; and then just as suddenly disappears. (Interesting to have seen the lights disappearing from Space-

Time during one of the big battles—Death dowses the
glims.) Well, it happens to us all ; but our vanity is
interested by the hope that the rather tangled and not
very luminous track we made will continue to shine for
a few people for a few years. I suppose Winterbourne's
name does appear on some War Memorial, probably in
the Chapel of his Public School ; and, of course, he's
got his neat ration of headstone in France. But that's
about all. Nobody much minded that he was killed.
Unassertive people with no money have few friends ; and
Winterbourne hadn't counted much on his scanty flock,
least of all on me. But I know—because he told me
himself—that he had rather relied on four people to
take some interest in him and his fate. They were his
father and mother, his wife and his mistress. If he had
known what actually occurred with these four at the
news of his death I think he would have been a little
shocked, as well as heartily amused and perhaps a bit
relieved. It would have freed him from certain feelings
of responsibility.

Winterbourne's father, whom I knew slightly, was an
inadequate sentimentalist. Mild, with an affectation of
gentility, incompetent, selfishly unselfish (*i.e.* always
patting himself on the back for ' renouncing ' something
he was afraid to do or be or take), he had a genius for
messing up other people's lives. The amount of irre-
parable harm which can be done by a really good man
is astounding. Ten astute rogues do less. He messed
up his wife's life by being weak with her ; messed up
his children's lives by being weak and sentimentalish
with them and by losing his money—the unforgiveable
sin in a parent ; messed up the lives of his friends and
clients by honestly losing their money for them : and

messed up his own most completely. That was the one thing he ever did with complete and satisfactory thoroughness. The mess he got his life into would have baffled an army of psychologists to unravel.

When I told Winterbourne what I thought of his father, he admitted it was mostly true. But he rather liked the man, probably disarmed by the mildness, and not sufficiently hard to his father's soft, selfish sentimentality. Possibly old Winterbourne would have felt and have acted differently in his reactions to George's death, if circumstances had been different. But he was so scared by the war, so unable to adjust himself to a harsh, intruding reality—he had spent his life avoiding realities—that he took refuge in a drivelling religiosity. He got to know some rather slimy Roman Catholics, and read the slimy religious tracts they showered on him, and talked and sobbed to the exceedingly slimy priest they found for him. So about the middle of the war he was ' received,' and found—let us hope—comfort in much prayer and Mass-going and writing rules for Future Conduct and rather suspecting he was like François de Sales and praying for the beatification of the super-slimy Thérèse of Lisieux.

Old Winterbourne was in London, ' doing war work,' when the news of George's death came. He would never have done anything so positive and energetic if he had not been nagged and goaded into it by his wife. She was animated less by motives of disinterested patriotism than by exasperation with him for existing at all and for interrupting her love affairs. Old Winterbourne always said with proud, sad dignity that his ' religious convictions forbade ' him to divorce her. Religious convictions are such an easy excuse for being nasty. So she found a war

job for him in London, and put him into a position where
it was impossible for him to refuse.

The telegram from the War Office—' regret to inform
. . . killed in action. . . Their Majesties' sympathy
. . .'—went to the home address in the country, and was
opened by Mrs. Winterbourne. Such an excitement for
her, almost a pleasant change, for it was pretty dull in the
country just after the Armistice. She was sitting by the
fire, yawning over her twenty-second lover—the affair
had lasted nearly a year—when the servant brought the
telegram. It was addressed to Mr. Winterbourne, but
of course she opened it ; she had an idea that ' one of
those women ' was ' after ' her husband, who, however,
was regrettably chaste, from cowardice.

Mrs. Winterbourne liked drama in private life. She
uttered a most creditable shriek, clasped both hands to
her rather soggy bosom, and pretended to faint. The
lover, one of those nice, clean, sporting Englishmen with
a minimum of intelligence and an infinite capacity for
being gulled by females, especially the clean English sort,
clutched her unwillingly and automatically but with quite
an Ethel M. Dell appearance of emotion, and exclaimed:

' Darling, what is it ? Has *he* insulted you again ? '

Poor old Winterbourne was incapable of insulting any
one, but it was a convention always established between
Mrs. Winterbourne and her lovers that Winterbourne
had ' insulted ' her, when his worst taunt had been to
pray earnestly for her conversion to the True Faith, along
with the rest of ' poor misguided England.'

In low moaning tones, founded on the best tradition of
sensational fiction, Mrs. Winterbourne feebly ejaculated :

' Dead, dead, dead ! '

' Who 's dead ? Winterbourne ? '

(Some apprehension perhaps in the attendant Sam

Browne—he would have to propose, of course, and might be accepted.)

' They 've killed him, those vile, *filthy* foreigners. My *baby* son.'

Sam Browne, still mystified, read the telegram. He then stood to attention, saluted (although not wearing a cap), and said solemnly :

' A clean sportin' death, an *Englishman's* death.'

(When Huns were killed it was neither clean nor sportin', but served the beggars—(' *******,' among men) —right.)

The tears Mrs. Winterbourne shed were not very natural, but they did not take long to dry. Dramatically, she ran to the telephone. Dramatically, she called to the local exchange :

' Trrrunks. (Sob.) Give me Kensington 1030. Mr. Winterbourne's number, you know. (Sob.) Our *darling* son—Captain Winterbourne—has been killed by those (sob) beasts. (Sob. Pause.) Oh, thank you *so* much, Mr. Crump, I *knew* you would feel for us in our trouble. (Sob. Sob.) But the blow is so sudden. I *must* speak to Mr. Winterbourne. Our hearts are *breaking* here. (Sobissimo.) Thank you. I 'll wait till you ring me.'

Mrs. Winterbourne's effort on the telephone to her husband was not unworthy of her :

' Is that you, George ? Yes, Isabel speaking. I have just had *rather* bad news. No, about George. You must be prepared, darling. I fear he is seriously ill. What ? No. *George.* GEORGE. Can't you hear ? Yes, that 's better. Now, listen, darling, you must prepare for a *great* shock. George is seriously ill. Yes, *our* George, our *baby* son. What ? Wounded ? No, not wounded, very *dangerously* ill. No, darling, there is little hope.

(Sob.) Yes, darling, a telegram from the *King* and *Queen*. Shall I read it? You are prepared for the shock, (sob) George, aren't you? ' Deeply regret . . . killed in action. . . . Their Majesties' sympathy. . . .' (Sob. Long pause.) Are you there, George? Hullo, hullo. (Sob.) Hullo, hullo. HULLO. (Aside to Sam Browne.) He's rung off! How that man *insults* me! how can I bear it in my sorrow? After I had prepared him for the shock! (Sob. Sob.) But I have always had to *fight* for my children, while he squatted over his books—and *prayed*.'

To Mrs. Winterbourne's credit, let it be said, she had very little belief in the value of prayer in practical affairs. But then, her real objection to religion was founded upon her dislike for doing anything she didn't want to do, and a profound hatred for everything distantly resembling thought.

At the fatal news Mr. Winterbourne had fallen upon his knees (not forgetting, however, to ring off the harpy), ejaculating : ' Lord Jesus, receive his soul ! ' Mr. Winterbourne then prayed a good deal, for George's soul, for himself, for ' my erring but beloved spouse,' for his other children, ' may they be spared and by Thy Mercy brought to the True Faith,' for England (ditto), for his enemies, ' though Thou knowest, Dear Lord Jesus, the enmity was none of my seeking, sinner though I be, mea culpa, mea culpa, mea maxima culpa, Ave Maria. . . .'

Mr. Winterbourne remained on his knees for some time. But, as the hall tiles hurt his knees, he went and knelt on a hassock at the *prie-dieu* in his bedroom. On the top of this was an open Breviary in very ecclesiastical binding with a florid ecclesiastical book-marker, all lying on an ecclesiastical bit of embroidery, the ' gift of a Catholic sister in Christ.' Above, on a bracket, was a coloured B.V.M. from the Place St. Sulpice, holding a nauseating Infant Jesus dangling a bloody and sun-rayed Sacred Heart. Over this again was a large but rather cheap-looking imitation bronze Crucifix, with a reproduction (coloured) of Leonardo's *Last Supper* to the right, and another reproduction (uncoloured) of Holman Hunt's (heretical) *Light of the World* to the left. All of which gave Mr. Winterbourne the deepest spiritual comfort.

After dinner, of which he ate sparingly, thinking with dreary satisfaction how grief destroys appetite, he went round to see his confessor, Father Slack. He spent a pleasantly emotional evening. Mr. Winterbourne cried a good deal, and they both prayed ; Father Slack said perhaps George had been influenced by his father's prayers and virtues and had made an act of contrition before he died; and Mr. Winterbourne said that although George had not been ' received ' he had ' a true Catholic spirit ' and had once read a sermon of Bossuet ; and Father Slack said he would pray for George's soul, and Mr. Winterbourne left £5 for Masses for the repose of George, which was generous (if foolish), for he didn't earn much.

And then Mr. Winterbourne used to pray ten minutes longer every night and morning for George's soul, but unfortunately he went and got himself run over just by the Marble Arch as he was meditating on that blessed martyr, Father Parsons, and that other more blessed martyr, Father Garnet of Gunpowder fame. So, as the £5 was soon exhausted, there was nobody to pray for George's soul ; and for all the Holy Roman and Apostolic Church knows or cares, poor old George is in Hell, and likely to remain there. But, after the last few years of his life, George probably doesn't find any difference.

So much for George's father and George's death. The
' reactions ' (as they are called) of Mrs. Winterbourne
were different. She found it rather exciting and stimulating at first, especially erotically stimulating. She was
a woman who constantly dramatised herself and her life.
She was as avid of public consideration as an Italian
lieutenant, no matter what the quality of the praise. The
only servants who ever stayed more than a trial month
with her were those who bowed themselves to an abject
discipline of adulation for Mrs. Winterbourne, Mrs.
Winterbourne's doings and sayings and possessions and
whims and friends. Only, since Mrs. Winterbourne was
exceedingly fickle and quarrelsome, and was always
changing friends into enemies and vowed enemies into
hollow friends, a more than diplomatic suppleness was
exacted of these mercenary retainers, who only stayed
with her because she gave them presents or raised their
wages whenever the praise was really gratifying.

Although a lady of ' mature charms,' Mrs. Winterbourne loved to fancy herself as a delicious young thing
of seventeen, passionately beloved by a sheik-like but
nevertheless ' clean ' (not to say ' straight ') Englishman.
She was a mistress of would-be revolutionary platitudes
about marriage and property (rather like the talk of an
' enlightened ' parson), but, in fact, was as sordid, avari-
cious, conventional, and spiteful a middle-class woman as
you could dread to meet. Like all her class, she toadied
to her betters and bullied her inferiors. But, with her
conventionality, she was, of course, a hypocrite. In her
kittenish moods, which she cultivated with a strange lack
of a sense of congruity, she liked to throw out hints about
' kicking over the traces.' But, as a matter of fact, she
never soared much above tippling, financial dishonesty,
squabbling, lying, betting, and affairs with bounderish

young men, whom only her romantic effrontery could
have dared describe as ' clean and straight,' although
there was no doubt whatever about their being English,
and indeed sportin' in a more or less bounderish way.

She had had so many of these clean, straight young
sheiks, that even poor Mr. Winterbourne got mixed up,
and when he used to write dramatic letters beginning,
' Sir,—You have robbed me of my wife's affection like a
low hound—be it said in no un-Christian spirit,' the
letters were always getting addressed to the penultimate
or antepenultimate sheik, instead of the straight, clean one
of the moment. However, rendered serious by the
exhortations of the war Press and still more by the ever-
ripening maturity of her charms, Mrs. Winterbourne
made an instinctive and firm clutch at Sam Browne—so
successfully that she clutched the poor devil for the remainder of his abbreviated life. (She did the abbrevia-
tion.) Sam Browne, of course, was almost too good to be
true. If I hadn't seen him myself I should never have
believed in him. He was an animated—and not so very
animated—stereotype. His knowledge of life was rudi-
mentary to the point of being quadruped, and intelligence
had been bestowed upon him with rigid parsimony. An
adult Boy Scout, a Public School fag in shining armour—
the armour of obtuseness. He met every situation in life
with a formula, and no situation in life ever reached him
except in the shape imposed upon it by the appropriate
and predetermined formula. So, though he wasn't very
successful at anything, he got along all right, sliding
almost decorously down grooves which had nothing ring-
ing about them. Unless urged, he never mentioned his
wound, his decoration, or the fact that he had ' rolled up '
on August 4th. The modest, well-bred, etcetera, English
gentleman.

The formula for the death of a married mistress's son was stern heroism, and gentle consolation to the wounded mother-heart. Mrs. Winterbourne played up at first— it was the sort of thing that the sheik always did with his passionate but tender love. But the effect of George's death on her temperament was, strangely enough, almost wholly erotic. The war did that to lots of women. All the dying and wounds and mud and bloodiness—at a safe distance—gave them a great kick, and excited them to an almost unbearable pitch of amorousness. Of course, in that eternity of 1914-18 they must have come to feel that men alone were mortal, and they immortals ; wherefore they tried to behave like houris with all available sheiks— hence the lure of 'war work' with its unbounded oppor- tunities. And then there was the deep primitive physio- logical instinct—men to kill and be killed ; women to produce more men to continue the process. (This, how- ever, was often frustrated by the march of Science, viz. anti-conceptives ; for which, much thanks.)

So you must not be surprised if Mrs. Winterbourne's emotion at the death of George almost immediately took an erotic form. She was lying on her bed in an ample pair of white drawers with very long ruffles and a remark- ably florid, if chaste, chemise. And the sheik, strong, silent, restrained, tender, was dabbing her forehead and nose with eau-de-cologne, while she took large sips of brandy at increasingly frequent intervals. It was, of course, proper and even pleasant to have her grief so much respected ; but she did wish Sam hadn't to be poked always into taking the initiative. Couldn't the man see that tender nerves like hers needed to be soothed with a little Real Love *at once* ?

' He was so much to me, Sam,' she said in low, indeed tremulous tones, subtly calculated. ' I was only a child

when he was born—a child *with* a child, people used to
say—and we grew up together. I was so young that I did
not put up my hair until two years after he was born.'
(Mrs. Winterbourne's propaganda about her perennial
youth was so obvious that it would hardly have deceived
the readers of ' John Blunt '—but the sheiks all fell for it.
God knows how young they thought she was—probably
imagined Winterbourne had 'insulted' her when she was
ten.)

'We were always together, such pals, Sam, and he told
me everything.'

(Poor old George! He had such a dislike for his
mother that he hadn't seen her five times in the last five
years of his life. And as for telling her anything—why,
the most noble of noble savages would immediately have
suspected *her*. She had let George down so badly time
after time when he was a boy that he was all tight inside,
and couldn't give confidence to his wife or his mistresses
or a man.)

'But now he's gone'—and somehow Mrs. Winterbourne's voice became so erotically suggestive that even
the obtuse sheik noticed it and was vaguely troubled—
' now he's gone, I've nothing in the world but *you*, Sam.
You heard how that vile man insulted me on the telephone
to-day. Kiss me, Sam, and promise you'll always be a
pal, a *real* pal.'

Active love-making was not in the sheik's formula for
that day ; consolation there was to be, but the ' sacred-
ness ' of mother-grief was not to be profaned by sexual
intercourse ; although that too, oddly enough, was
' sacred ' between a ' clean ' Englishman and a ' pure '
woman who had only had one husband and twenty-two
lovers. But what can the Sam Brownes of the world
do against the wills, especially the will to copulate, of

the Mrs. Winterbournes ? ** **** *********** ** ***
*********. He, too, found a certain queer, perverse
satisfaction in honeying and making love over a nasty
corpse ; while, if he had been capable of making the
reflection, he would have realised that Mrs. Winterbourne
was not only a sadist, but a necrophilous one.

In the succeeding weeks George's death was the source
of other, almost unclouded, joys to Mrs. Winterbourne.
She pardoned—temporarily—the most offending of her
enemies to increase the number of artistically tear-
blotched letters of bereavement she composed. Quite a
few of the nearly gentry, who usually avoided Mrs.
Winterbourne as a particularly virulent specimen of the
human scorpion, paid calls—very brief calls—of con-
dolence. Even the Vicar appeared, and was greeted with
effusive sweetness ; for though Mrs. Winterbourne pro-
fessed herself a social rebel and an 'Agnostic' (not, however, until she had been more or less kicked out of middle-
class and Church society), she retained a superstitious
reverence for parsons of the Established Church.

Another joy was squabbling with Elizabeth Winterbourne, George's wife, about his poor little 'estate' and
military effects. When George joined up, he thought he
had to give his father as his next-of-kin. Later, he found
his mistake, and when he went out to France the second
time he gave his wife. The War Office carefully preserved both records, either under the impression that there
were two George Winterbournes, or because the original
record was never erased and so became law. At any
rate, some of George's possessions were sent to the country
address, and, although directed to his father, were un-
scrupulously seized by his mother. And the remainder
of his military kit and the pay due him went to his wife.

Old Mrs. Winterbourne was fearfully enraged at this.
Stupid red tape, she said it was. Why! wasn't her
baby son *hers*? Hadn't she borne him, and therefore
established complete possession of him and his for the
rest of her natural life? What can any woman mean to
a *Man* in comparison with his *Mother*? Therefore, it
was plain that she was the next-of-kin, and that all
George's possessions, including the widow's pension,
should come to her and her only : Q.E.D. She bothered
her harassed husband about it, tried to stimulate Sam
Browne to action—but he evaporated in a would-be
straight, clean letter to Elizabeth, who knocked him out
in the first round—and even consulted a lawyer in London.
Old Mrs. Winterbourne came back from London in a
spluttering temper. 'That man' (*i.e.* her husband) had
'insulted' her again, by timidly stating that all George's
possessions ought to be given to his wife, who would
doubtless allow them to keep a few 'mementoes.' And
the lawyer—foul brute—had unsympathetically said that
George's wife had a perfect right to sue her mother-in-
law for detaining her (Elizabeth's) property. George's
will was perfectly plain—he had left everything he had to
his wife. However, that small amount of George's property which his mother got hold of she kept, in defiance
of all the King's horses and writs. And she took, she
embraced, the opportunity of telling 'that woman' (*i.e.*
Elizabeth) what she thought of her—which, if believed,
meant that poor Elizabeth was a composition of Catherine
of Russia, Lucrezia Borgia, Mme de Brinvilliers, Moll
Flanders, a *tricoteuse*, and a hissing villainess from the
Surrey side.

But George only lasted his mother as a source of post-
humous excitement for about two months. Just as the
quarrel with Elizabeth reached stupendous heights of

vulgar invective (on her side), old Winterbourne got himself run over.   So there was the excitement of the inquest
and a real funeral, and widow's weeds and more tear-
blotched letters.   She even sent a tear-blotched letter to
Elizabeth, which I saw, saying that ' twenty years '—it
was really almost thirty—' of happy married life were
over, both father and son were now happily united, and,
whatever Mr. Winterbourne's faults, he was a *gentleman*.'
(Heavily underlined and followed by several exclamation
marks, the insinuation being apparently that Elizabeth
was no lady.)

A month later Mrs. Winterbourne married the sheik—
alas ! no sheik now—at a London registry office, whence
they departed to Australia to live a clean sportin' life.
Peace be with them both—they were too clean and sportin'
for a corrupt and unclean Europe.

George's parents, of course, were grotesques.   When,
in a mood of cynical merriment, he used to tell his friends
the exact truth about his parents, he was always accused—
even by quite intelligent people—of creating a monstrous
legend.   Unless all the accepted ideas about heredity and
environment are false—which they probably are—it is a
regular mystery of Udolpho how George managed to be
so different from his parents and the family *milieu*.
Physically he looked like them both—in every other respect, he might have dropped from the moon for all the
resemblance he had to them.   Perhaps they seemed so
grotesque because neither of them could adjust to the
tremendous revolution in everything, of which the war
was a cause or symptom.   The whole immense drama
went on in front of their noses, and they never perceived
it.   They only worried about their rations.   Old Winterbourne also worried a good deal about ' the country,' and

wrote letters of advice to the *Times* (which didn't publish
them), and then rewrote them on Club notepaper to the
Prime Minister. They were invariably politely acknowledged by a secretary. But Mrs. Winterbourne only
cared spasmodically about ' the country.' Her view of
the British Empire was that it should continue the war
as a holy crusade for the extermination of all ' filthy vile
foreigners,' making the world safe for straight, clean
sheiks and pure, sweet, kittenish Englishwomen of fifty.
Grotesques indeed, fanciful, unbelievable, like men's
fashions of 1840. To me, who only saw them a few
times, either in company with George or as his executor,
they seemed as fantastic, as ridiculous, as prehistoric as
the returning *émigrés* seemed to Paris in 1815. Like the
Bourbons, the elder Winterbournes learned nothing from
the war, and forgot nothing. It is the tragedy of England
that the war has taught its Winterbournes nothing, and
that it has been ruled by grotesques and a groaning Civil
Service of disheartened men and women, while the young
have simply chucked up the job in despair. *Gott strafe
England* is a prayer that has been fully answered—by the
insanity of retaining the old Winterbourne grotesques
and pretending they are alive. And we go on acquiescing,
we go on without even the guts to kick the grotesque Aunt
Sallies of England into the Limbo they deserve. *Pero,
paciencia. Mañana. Mañana. . . .*

I think that George committed suicide in that last
battle of the war. I don't mean shot himself, but it was
so very easy for a company commander to stand up when
an enemy machine-gun was traversing. The situation he
had got into with Elizabeth and Fanny Welford was not
inextricable, but it would have needed a certain amount
of patience and energy and determination and common

sense to put right. But by November '18 poor old George was whacked, whacked to the wide. He was a bit off his head, as nearly all the troops were after six months in the line. Since Arras (April '17) he had lived on his nerves, and when I saw him at the Divisional Rest Camp in October '18 he struck me as a man who was done for, used up. He ought to have gone to the Brigadier and got sent down for a bit. But he was so horribly afraid of being afraid. He told me that last night I saw him that he was afraid even of whizz-bangs now, and that he didn't see how he would face another barrage. But he was damned obstinate, and insisted on going back to the battalion, although he knew they were due for another battle. We lay awake half the night, and he went over Elizabeth and Fanny and himself, and himself and Fanny and Elizabeth, until it was such a nightmare, such a portentous House of Atrides tragedy, that I began to think myself that it was hopeless. There was a series of night-bombing attacks going on, and we lay in the darkness on sacking beds, muttering to each other— or rather George went on and on muttering, and I tried to interrupt and couldn't. And every time a bomb fell anywhere near the camp, I could feel George start in the darkness. His nerves were certainly all to pieces.

Elizabeth and Fanny were not grotesques. They adjusted to the war with marvellous precision and speed, just as they afterwards adapted themselves to the post-war. They both had that rather hard efficiency of the war and post-war female, veiling the ancient predatory and possessive instincts of the sex under a skilful smoke-barrage of Freudian and Havelock Ellis theories. To hear them talk theoretically was most impressive. They were terribly at ease upon the Zion of sex, abounding in inhibitions, dream symbolism, complexes, sadism, repressions, masochism, Lesbianism, sodomy, etcetera. Such wise young women, you thought, no sentimental nonsense about *them*. No silly emotional slip-slop messes would ever come *their* way. They knew all about the sexual problem, and how to settle it. There was the physical relationship and the emotional relationship and the intellectual relationship ; and they knew how to manage all three, as easily as a pilot with twenty years' experience brings a handy ship to anchor in the Pool of London. They knew that freedom, complete freedom, was the only solution. The man had his lovers, and the woman had hers. But where there was a 'proper relationship,' nothing could break it. Jealousy ? it was impossible that so primitive a passion could inhabit those enlightened and rather flat bosoms. Female wiles and underhand tricks ? insulting to make such a suggestion. No, no. Men must be 'free' and women must be 'free.'

Well, George had simple-Simonly believed all this. He 'had an affair' with Elizabeth, and then he 'had an affair' with Fanny, her best friend. George thought they ought to tell Elizabeth. But Fanny said why bother ? Elizabeth *must* know instinctively, and it was so much better to trust to the deeper instincts than to talk about things with 'the inferior intelligence.' So they said nothing to Elizabeth, who didn't know instinctively, and thought that George and Fanny were 'sexually antipathetic.' That was just before the war. But in 1914 something went wrong with Elizabeth's period, and she thought she was going to have a baby. And then, my hat, what a pother ! Elizabeth lost her head entirely. Freud and Ellis went to the devil in a twinkling. No more talk of 'freedom' *then* ! If she had a baby, her father would cut off her allowance, people would cut her, she wouldn't be asked to Lady Saint-Lawrence's dinners, she . . . Well, she ' went at ' George in a way which threw him on his beam-ends. She made him use up a lot of money on a special licence, and they were married at a Registry office in the presence of Elizabeth's parents, who were also swept bewildered into this sudden match, they knew not how or why. Elizabeth's father had feebly protested that George hadn't any money, and Mrs. Winterbourne senior wrote a marvellous tear-blotched dramatic epistle, in which she said that George was a feeble-minded degenerate who had broken his mother's tender heart and insultingly trampled upon it, in a low, sensual lust for a vile woman who was only 'after' the Winterbourne money. As there wasn't any Winterbourne money left, and the elder Winterbournes lived on tick and shifts, the accusation was, to say the least, fanciful. But Elizabeth bore down all opposition, and she and George were married.

After the marriage, Elizabeth breathed again and became almost human. Then and only then did she think of consulting a doctor, who diagnosed some minor female malady, told her to 'avoid cohabitation' for a few weeks, and poofed with laughter at her pregnancy. George and Elizabeth took a flat in Chelsea, and within three months Elizabeth was just as ' enlightened ' as before and fuller of ' freedom ' than ever. Relieved by the doctor's assurance that only an operation could enable her to have a child, she ' had an affair ' with a young man from Cambridge, and told George about it. George was rather surprised and peeved, but played the game nobly, and most gallantly yielded the flat up for the night whenever Elizabeth dropped a hint. Of course, he didn't suffer as much deprivation as Elizabeth thought, because he invariably spent those nights with Fanny.

This went on until about the end of 1915. George, though attractive to women, had a first-rate talent for the malapropos in dealing with them. If he had told Elizabeth about his affair with Fanny at the moment when she was full-flushed with the young man from Cambridge, she would no doubt have acquiesced, and the thing would have been smoothed over. Unluckily for George, he felt so certain that Fanny was right and so certain that Elizabeth was right. He was perfectly convinced that Elizabeth knew all about him and Fanny, and that if they didn't speak of it together the only reason was that 'one took such things for granted,' no need to 'cerebrise' about them. Then one night, when Elizabeth was getting tired of the young man from Cambridge, she was struck by the extraordinary alacrity George showed in 'getting out.'

'But, darling,' she said, 'isn't it very expensive always going to a hotel ? Can we afford it ? And don't you mind ?

'Oh no,' said the innocent George; 'I shall run round and spend the night with Fanny as usual, you know.'

Then there was a blazing row, Elizabeth at George, and then Fanny at George, and then—epic contest—Elizabeth at Fanny. Poor old George got so fed up, he went off and joined the infantry, fell into the first recruiting office he came to, and was whisked off to a training camp in the Midlands. But, of course, that didn't solve the situation. Elizabeth's blood was up, and Fanny's blood was up. It was Achilles against Hector, with George as the body of Patroclus. Not that either of them so horribly wanted George, but it was essential to each to come off victorious and 'bag' him, with the not improbable epilogue of dropping him pretty quickly after he had been 'bagged' away from the other woman. So they each wrote him tender and emotional and ' understanding ' letters, and sympathised with his sufferings under military discipline. Elizabeth came down to the Midlands to bag him for week-ends ; and then one week when she was ' having an affair ' with a young American in the Flying Corps, George got his ' firing leave ' and spent it with Fanny. George was a bit obtuse with women. He was very fond of Elizabeth, but he was also very fond of Fanny. If he hadn't been taken in with the ' freedom ' talk and had kept Elizabeth permanently in the dark about Fanny, he might have lived an enviable double life. Unfortunately for him, he couldn't, and never did, see that the ' freedom ' talk was only talk with the two women, although it was real enough to him. So he wrote them both the most imbecile and provocative letters, praised Elizabeth to Fanny, and Fanny to Elizabeth, and said how much he cared for them both ; and he was like Shelley, and Elizabeth was like Mary, and Fanny was like Emilia Viviani. And he went on doing that even in France, right up to the end. And he never even suspected what an ass he was.

Of course, George had not set foot on the boat which took him to the Boulogne Base-Camp for the first time, before both Elizabeth and Fanny had become absorbed in other ' affairs.' They only fought for George in a desultory way as a symbol, more to spite each other than because they wanted to saddle themselves with him.

Elizabeth was out when her telegram came from the War Office. She did not get it until nearly midnight, when she came back to the flat with a fascinating young Swedish painter she had met at a Chelsea ' rag ' that evening. She was a bit sozzled, and the young Swede—

tall, blond, and handsome—was more than a little fired
with love and whisky. The telegram was lying on the
door-mat with two or three letters. Elizabeth picked
them up, and opened the telegram mechanically as she
switched on the electric light. The Swede stood watching her drunkenly and amorously. She could not avoid
a slight start, and turned a little pale.

'What's the matter?'

Elizabeth laughed her high little nervous laugh, and
laid the telegram and letters on the table.

'The War Office regrets that my husband has been
killed in action.'

It was now the Swede's turn to be startled.

'Your husband? . . . Perhaps I'd better . . .'

'Don't be a bloody fool,' said Elizabeth sharply; 'he
went out of my life years ago. *She'll* mind, but I shan't.'

She cried a bit in the bathroom, however; but the
Swede was certainly a very attentive lover. They drank
a good deal of brandy, too.

Next day Elizabeth wrote to Fanny the first letter she
had sent her for months :

'Only a line, darling, to tell you that I have a telegram
from the W.O. to say George was killed in France on
the 4th. I thought it would be less of a shock for you
to hear it from me than accidentally. Come and see
me when you get your weeps over, and we can hold a
post-mortem.'

Fanny didn't reply to the letter. She had been rather
fond of George, and thought Elizabeth heartless. But
Elizabeth too had been fond of George ; only, she wasn't
going to give it away to Fanny. I saw a good deal
of Elizabeth while settling up George's scanty estate—

mostly furniture and books in the flat, his credit at Cox's, a few War Bonds, a little money due to him from civilian sources, and Elizabeth's pension. However, it meant a certain amount of letter-writing, which Elizabeth was glad to have me do. I also saw Fanny once or twice, and took her the trifles George had left her. But I never saw the two women together—they avoided each other; and when my duties as executor were done, I saw very little of either. Fanny went to Paris in 1919, and soon married an American painter. I saw her in the Dome one night in 1924, pretty well rouged and quite nicely dressed, with a party. She was laughing and flirting with a middle-aged American—possibly an art patron—and didn't look as if she mourned much for George. Why indeed should she?

As for Elizabeth, she rather went to pieces. With her father's allowance, which doubled and became her own income when he died, and her widow's pension, she was quite well off as poor people of the 'artistic' sort go. She travelled a good deal, always with a pretty large brandy-flask, and had more lovers than were good for her—or them. I hadn't seen her for years, until about a month ago I ran into her on the corner of the Piazzetta in Venice. She was with Stanley Hopkins, one of those extremely clever young novelists who oscillate between women and homosexuality. He had recently published a novel so exceedingly clever, so stupendously smart and up-to-date and witty and full of personalities about well-known people, that he was quite famous, especially in America, where all Hopkins's brilliantly quacking and hissing and kissing geese were taken as melodious swans and (*vide* Press) as a 'startling revelation of the corruption of the British Aristocracy.' We went and had ices together, all three, at Florian's; and then Hopkins went off to get something, and left us together for half an hour. Elizabeth chattered very wittily—you had to be witty with Hopkins or die of shame and humiliation—but never mentioned George. George was a drab bird from a drab past. She told me that she and Hopkins would not marry; they had both determined never to pollute themselves with the farce of 'legalised copulation,' but they would 'probably go on living with each other.' Hopkins, who was a very rich young man as well as a successful novelist, had settled a thousand a year on her, so that they could both be 'free.' She looked as nearly un-miserable as our cynical and battered generation can look; but she still had the brandy-flask.

Like a fool, I allowed myself to be persuaded to drink liqueur brandies after dinner that evening; and paid for it with a sleepless night. No doubt it was the unexpected meeting with Elizabeth which made me think a lot about George during those ghastly wakeful hours. I can't claim that I had set up any altar to the deceased George in my heart, but I truly believe that I am the only person left alive who ever thinks of him. Perhaps because I was the only person who cared for George for his own sake, disinterestedly. Naturally, his death meant very little to me at the time—there were eighty deaths in my own battalion on the day George was killed, and the Armistice and getting out of the blasted Army and settling my own problems and starting civilian life again and getting to work, all occupied my attention. In fact, it was not until two or three years after the war that I began to think much, if at all, about George. Then, although I didn't in the least believe in it, I got a half-superstitious, half-sentimental idea that 'he' (poor old bag of decaying bones) wanted me to think about him. I half-knew, half-guessed that the

C

George was very enthusiastic about modern painting.
His own painting, he told me, was ' pretty dud,' but in
peace time he made a good living by writing art criticism
for various papers and by buying modern pictures, chiefly
French and German, on commission for wealthy collectors.
We lent each other books from our scanty store, and
George was quite thrilled to know that I had published
one or two little books of poetry and had met Yeats and
Marinetti. I talked to him about modern poetry, and he
talked to me about modern painting ; and I think we
helped to keep each other's ' souls ' alive. In the evenings
we played chess or strolled about, if it was fine. George
didn't go square-pushing with tarts, and I didn't go
square-pushing with tarts. So on Saturday afternoons
and Sundays we took long walks over that barren but
rather beautiful Dorset down country, and had a quiet
dinner with a bottle of wine in one or other of the better
country inns. And all that kept up our own particular
' morale,' which each of us had determined not to yield to
the Army swinishness. Poor George had suffered more
than I. He had been more bullied as a Tommy, had a
worse time in France, and suffered horribly from that
' tightness ' inside, that inability to confide himself,
induced by his singular home life and appalling mother.
I feel quite sure he told me more about himself, far more,
than he ever told any one else, so that eventually I knew
quite a lot about him. He told me all about his parents
and about Elizabeth and Fanny, and about his childhood
and his life in London and Paris.

As I say, I liked George, and I'm grateful to him
because he helped me to keep alive when a legion of
the swine were trying to destroy me. And, of course,
I helped him. He had a strong dose of shyness—his
mother had sapped his self-confidence abominably—

which made him seem rather conceited and very aloof. But *au fond* he was extraordinarily generous, spontaneous, rather Quixotish. It was that which made him so helpless with women, who neither want nor understand Quixotic behaviour and scrupulousness, and who either think they mean weakness or are veils for some devilish calculation. But with another man, who wanted nothing from him but a frank exchange of friendliness, he was a charming and inexhaustible companion. I was damned glad to get my commission and leave that stinking hole of a Camp, but I was really sorry to part from George. We agreed to write, and applied for commissions in the same regiment. Needless to say, we were gazetted to completely different regiments from those we had applied for. We exchanged one or two letters while waiting in depots in England, and then ceased writing. But by an odd freak of the War Office we were both sent to different battalions in the same Brigade. It was nearly two months before we found this out, when we met by accident at Brigade Headquarters.

I was rather startled at George's appearance, he looked so worried and almost scared. I saw him on reliefs or at Brigade H.Q. or at Divisional Rest Camp several times. He looked whacked in May '18. In July the Division moved down to the Somme, but George's company front was raided the night before we left, and he was badly rattled by it. I had watched the box barrage from the top of Battalion H.Q. dugout (I was then signal officer), but I never thought that George was in it. He lost several men as prisoners, and the Brigadier was a bit nasty about it, which made George more rattled and jumpy than ever. I told him then that he ought to apply for a rest, but he was in an agony of feeling that he was disgraced and a coward, and wouldn't listen to me.

whose death no other human being has agonised.   What
can we do ?   Headstones and wreaths and memorials and
speeches and the Cenotaph—no, no, it has got to be something *in* us.   Somehow we must atone to the dead—the
dead, murdered, violently-dead soldiers.   The reproach
is not from them, but in ourselves.   Most of us don't
know it, but it is there, and poisons us.   It is the poison
that makes us heartless and hopeless and lifeless—us the
war generation, and the new generation too.   The whole
world is blood-guilty, cursed like Orestes, and mad, and
destroying itself, as if pursued by an infinite legion of
Eumenides.   Somehow we must atone, somehow we
must free ourselves from the curse—the blood-guiltiness.
We must find—where ?   how ?—the greater Pallas who
will absolve us on some Acropolis of Justice.   But mean-
while the dead poison us and those who come after us.

That is why I am writing the life of George Winterbourne, a unit, one human body murdered, but to me a
symbol.   It is an atonement, a desperate effort to wipe
off the blood-guiltiness.   Perhaps it is the wrong way.
Perhaps the poison will still be in me.   If so, I shall search
for some other way.   But I shall search.   I know what is
poisoning me.   I do not know what is poisoning you, but
you are poisoned.   Perhaps you too must atone.

PART I

George Moore an elegant scandal in a hansom ; Hardy a rural atheistic scandal, not yet discovered to be an intolerable bore ; Oscar prancing negligently, O so clever, O so lad-di-dah.

Rummy old England. Pox on you, you old bitch, you 've made worms' meat of us. (We 've made worms' meat of ourselves.) But still, let me look back upon thee. Timon knew thee.

The Winterbournes were not gentry, but nourished vague and unfounded traditions of past genteel splendours. They were, however, pretty comfortable middle-class. Worcestershire, migrated to Sheffield. Methodist on female side ; C. of E. on the Winterbourne side. Young George Augustus—father of our George—was pretty comfortable. His mother was a dominating old bitch who destroyed his initiative and courage, but in the 'eighties hardly any one had the sense to tell dominating bitch-mothers to go to hell. George Augustus didn't. At fifteen he wrote a Nonconformist tract (which was published) expressing nothing but his dear Mamma's views. He became top of his school, in conformity with dear Mamma's views also. He did not go to Oxford, as he wanted, because dear Mamma thought it unpractical. And he did pass his examinations as a lawyer, because dear Mamma thought it so eminently right that he should have a profession and that there should be a lawyer in the family. George Augustus was a third son. The eldest son became a Nonconformist parson, because dear Mamma had prayed for guidance on her marriage night and during her first pregnancy (only, she never mentioned such horrid occurrences, even to her husband, but—she had 'prayed for guidance'), and it had been revealed to her that her firstborn must take up The Ministry. And take it up, poor devil, he did. The second son had a little bit of spunk, and his dear Mamma made him a waster. Remained George Augustus, dear Mamma's darling chick, who prayed at her knee, and was flogged regularly once a month by dear Papa, because the Scripture says : Spare the rod, spoil the child. Dear Papa had never done anything in particular, lived on his ' means,' was generally rather in debt, and spent the last fifteen years of his life praying to the C. of E. God in the garden, while dear Mamma prayed to John Wesley's God in her bedroom. Dear Mamma admired dear pious Mr. Bright and grand Mr. Gladstone ; but dear Papa collected and even read all the Works of the Right Hnble. the Earl of Beaconsfield, K.G.

Still, George Augustus was pretty comfortable. The one thing he wanted in life was to be pretty comfortable. After he became a full-blown solicitor, at the age of twenty-four, a family council was held. Present: Dear Mamma, dear Papa, George Augustus. Nothing formal, *of* course, just a cosy little family gathering after tea, round the blazing hearth (coal was cheap in Sheffield then), rep curtains drawn, and sweet domestic peace. Dear Papa opened the proceedings :

' George, you are now come to man's estate. At considerable sacrifice, your dear Mamma and I have given you a Profession. You are an Admitted Solicitor, and we are proud—I think we may say " proud," Mamma ?—that we have a legal luminary in the family . . .'

But dear Mamma could not allow dear Papa even the semblance of authority, respected not even the forms of Limited Domestic Monarchy, and cut in :

' Your Papa is right, George. The question is now, what are you going to *do* in your Profession ? '

rural Kent. George Augustus met Isabel Hartly, and,
before he knew where he was, had arranged irrevocably
a marriage with her—*without* telling dear Mamma. *Hic
incipit vita nova.* Thus was George, young George,
generated.

The Hartlys must have been more fun than the Winterbournes. The Winterbournes had never done a damn
thing in their lives, and were as stuffily, frowsily, mawkish-
religiously boring as a family could be and still remain—
I won't say alive or even sentient, but—able to digest
their very puddingy meals. The Hartlys were different.
They were poor Army. Pa Hartly had chased all round
the Empire, dragging with him Ma Hartly, always in pod
and always pupping in incongruous and inconvenient
spots—the Egyptian desert, a shipwrecked troopship,
a malarial morass in the West Indies, on the road to
Kandahar. They had an inconceivable number of
children, dead, dying, and alive, of all ages and sexes.
Finally, old Hartly settled down near his wife's family in
rural Kent, with a smallish pension, a tiny ' private '
income, and the world of his swarming progeny on his
less than Atlantean shoulders. I believe he had had two
or three wives, all horribly fertile. No doubt the earlier
Mrs. Hartlys had perished of superfluous child-bearing,
' superfoetation of τὸ ἕν.'

Isabel Hartly was one—don't ask which in numerical
order, or by which wife—of Captain Hartly's daughters.
She was very pretty, in a florid, vulgarish way, with her
artful-innocent dark eyes, and flashing smiles, and pretty
little bustle and frills, and ' fresh complexion ' and
' abounding health.' She was fascinatingly ignorant,
even to the none too sophisticated George Augustus.

And she had a strength of character superior even to dear Mamma's, added to a superb, an admirable vitality, which bewitched, bewildered, electrified the somewhat sluggish and pretty comfortable George Augustus. He had never met any one like her. In fact, dear Mamma had never allowed him to meet any one but rather soggy Nonconformists of mature years, and ' nice ' youths and maidens of exemplary Nonconformist stupidity and lifelessness.

George Augustus fell horribly in love.

He abode at the village inn, which was cheap and pretty comfortable ; and he did himself well. On these holidays he had such a mood of exultation (subconscious) in getting away from dear Mamma that he felt like a hero in Bulwer Lytton. We should say he swanked ; probably the early 'nineties would have said he came the masher. He certainly mashed Isabel.

The Hartlys didn't swank. They made no effort to conceal their poverty or the vulgarity imported into the family by the third (or fourth) Mrs. Hartly. They were fond of pork, and gratefully accepted the gifts of vegetables and fruit which the kind-hearted English countrypeople force on those they know are none too well off. They grew lots of vegetables and fruit themselves, and kept pigs. They made blackberry jam and damson jam, and scoured the country for mushrooms ; and the only ' drink ' ever allowed in the family was Pa Hartly's ' drop o' grog ' secretly consumed after the innumerable children had gone to bed in threes and fours.

So it wasn't hard for George Augustus to swank. He took the Hartlys — even Isabel — in completely. He talked about ' my people ' and ' our place.' He talked about his Profession. He gave them copies of the Nonconformist tract he had published at fifteen. He gave

Ma Hartly a fourteen-pound tin of that expensive (2s. 3d. a pound) tea she had always pined for since they had left Ceylon. He bought fantastic things for Isabel—a coral brooch, a copy of the *Pilgrim's Progress* bound in wood from the door of Bunyan's parish church, a turkey, a year's subscription to the *Family Herald Supplement*, a new shawl, boxes of 1s. 6d. a pound chocolates, and took her for drives in an open landau smelling of horse-piss and oats.

The Hartlys thought he was 'rich.' George Augustus was so very comfortable and *exalté* that he too really thought he was 'rich.'

One night, a sweet rural night, with a lemon moon over the sweet, breast-round, soft English country, with the nightingales jug-jugging and twit-twitting like mad in the leafy lanes, George Augustus kissed Isabel by a stile, and—manly fellow—asked her to marry him. Isabel—she had a pretty fiery temperament even then—had just sense enough not to kiss back and let him know that other 'fellows' had kissed her, and perhaps fumbled further. She turned away her pretty head with its Pompadour knot of dark hair, and murmured—yes, she did, because she *had* read the stories in the *Quiver* and the *Family Herald* :

' O Mr. Winterbourne, this is so unexpected ! '

But then her common-sense and the eagerness to be ' rich ' got the better of her *Quiver* artificiality, and she said, oh so softly and moderately :

' *Yes !* '

George Augustus quivered dramatically, clasped her, and they kissed a long time. He liked her ever so much more than the London whores, but he didn't dare do any more than kiss her, and exclaim :

' Isabel ! I love you. Be mine. Be my wife and

build a home for me.   Let us pass our lives in a delirium
of joy.   O that I need not leave you to-night ! '

On the way home Isabel said :

' You must speak to father to-morrow.'

And George Augustus, who was nothing if not the
gent, replied :

> ' I could not love thee, dear, so much,
> Loved I not honour more.'

Next morning, according to schedule, George Augustus
called on Pa Hartly with a bottle of 3s. 6d. port and a leg
of fresh pork ; and after a good deal of hemming and
blushing and talking round the subject (as if old Hartly
hadn't heard from Isabel what was coming), formally and
with immense solemnity applied for the job of supporting
Isabel for the rest of his and her natural lives.

Did Pa Hartly refuse ?   Did he hesitate ?   Eagerly,
gratefully, effusively, enthusiastically, he granted the
request.   He slapped George Augustus on the shoulder,
which military expression of goodwill startled and slightly
annoyed the prim George Augustus.   He said George
Augustus was a man after his own heart, the man he
would have chosen to make his daughter happy, the man
he longed to have as a son-in-law.   He told two barrack-
room stories, which made George Augustus exquisitely
uneasy ;   drank two large glasses of port ;   and then
launched out on a long story about how he had saved the
British Army when he was an Ensign during the Crimea.
George Augustus listened patiently and filially ; but as
hour after hour went by and the story showed no signs of
ending, he ventured to suggest that the good news should
be broken to Isabel and Ma Hartly, who (unknown to the
gentlemen) were listening at the keyhole in an agony of
impatience.

' fellows,' whom she really loved but had jilted for George Augustus's ' riches.'

' . . . It was a cloudy day, but as we knelt at the altar a long ray of sunshine came through the church window and rested lovingly on our bowed heads. . . .'

How could they rise to such bilge ?   But they did, they did, they did.   And they believed in it.   If only they 'd had their tongues in their cheeks there might have been some hope.   But they hadn't.   They believed in the sickish, sweetish, canting bilge, they believed in it.   Believed in it with all the superhuman force of ignorance.

Can one tabulate the ignorances, the relevant ignorances, of George Augustus and Isabel when they pledged themselves until death do us part ?

George Augustus did not know how to make a living ; he did not know in the very least how to treat a woman ; he did not know how to live with a woman ; he did not know how to make love to a woman—in fact, he was all minus there, for his experience with whores had been sordid, dismal, and repulsive ; he did not know the anatomy of his own body, let alone the anatomy of a woman's body ;

*   *   *   *   *   *   *   *   *   *

he did not know that pregnancy is a nine months' illness ; he had not the least idea that childbirth costs money if the woman is not to suffer vilely ; he did not know that a married man dependent on his and his wife's parents is an abject, helpless, and contemptible figure ; he did not know that it is hard to earn a decent living even when you have 'a Profession'; he knew damn little about even his profession ; he knew very little indeed about the conditions of life and nothing about human psychology ; he knew nothing about business and about money, except how to spend it ; he knew nothing about indoor sanitation, food values, carpentry, house-furnishing, shopping, fire-lighting, chimney-sweeping, higher mathematics, Greek, domestic invective, making the worse appear the better cause, how to feed a baby, music, dancing, Swedish drill, opening sardine-tins, boiling eggs, which side of the bed to sleep with a woman, charades, gas stoves, and an infinity of other things all indispensable to a married man.

He must have been rather a dull dog.

As for Isabel—what she didn't know includes almost the whole range of human knowledge. The puzzle is to find out what she *did* know. She didn't even know how to buy her own clothes—Ma Hartly had always done that for her. Among the things she did not know were : How babies are made and come ; how to make love ; how to pretend she was enjoying it even when she wasn't ; how to sew, wash, cook, scrub, run a house, purchase provisions, keep household accounts, domineer over a housemaid, order a dinner, dismiss a cook, know when a room was clean, manage George Augustus when he was in a bad temper, give George Augustus a pill when he was liverish, feed and wash a baby and pin on its napkins, pay and receive calls, knit, crochet, make pastry, how to tell a fresh herring is stale, the difference between pork and veal, never to use margarine, how to make a bed comfortably, look after her health especially in pregnancy, produce the soft answer which turneth away wrath, keep the home fires burning, and an infinity of other things indispensable to a married woman.

(I really wonder how poor old George managed to get born at all.)

On the other hand, both George Augustus and Isabel knew how to read and write, pray, eat, drink, wash themselves, and dress up on Sundays. They were both pretty well acquainted with the Bible and Hymns A. and M.

THE baby was christened Edward Frederick George—
Edward after the Prince of Wales (later H.M. King
Edward VII.), Frederick after his grandfather, George
after his father.

Isabel wanted to call him George Hartly, but dear
Mamma saw to it that there was as little Hartly as possible
about *her* grandson.

The early years of the Isabel-George Augustus *ménage*
are really very dismal to contemplate. Largely because
it was forced upon them by their elders and social convention, they began on a basis of humbug ; unfortunately,
they continued on a basis of humbug. Not only were
they shattered by the awful experience of the wedding-
night, but they were a good deal bored by the honeymoon
generally. There wasn't much to do at Isabel's sweetly-
pretty watering-place. George Augustus wouldn't admit
even to himself that he was about as competent to be a
husband as to teach white mice to perform military evolutions. Isabel knew in herself that they had begun with
a ghastly failure, knew it with her instincts rather than
her mind, but she had her pride. She knew perfectly
well that the failure would be attributed to her, and that
she could expect no sympathy from any one, least of all
her own family. Wasn't she ' happily ' married to a man
who 'luved' her—a 'luv' match—and to a 'rich' man ?
So Isabel consoled herself with the thought that George
Augustus was ' rich,' and they both wrote ecstatic hum-
bugging honeymoon letters to families and friends. And
once they had started on the opposite road to honesty and
facing facts, they were dished for life—condemned, they

too, to the dreary landscape of humbug and ' luv.' O
that God and Luv business ! Isn't it mysterious that
Isabel didn't take warning from the wretched cat-and-dog
life of Ma and Pa, and that George Augustus hadn't
noticed the hatred which surged between dear Mamma
and dear Papa under the viscid surface of domestic peace
and religion ; and that they didn't try to break away to
something a little better ? But no, they accepted the
standards, they had *Luv* and they had *God*, so of
course all would be for the best in this best of all
possible worlds.

George Augustus continued to play at being 'rich' on
his honeymoon. A week before his wedding he was
allowed a banking account for the first time in his life.
Dear Papa paid in £200, and, by arrangement with George
Augustus, dear Mamma was made to believe it was £20.
To this dear Mamma added a generous £5 from her own
jointure, ' a little nest-egg for a rainy day '—though what
on earth you want with a ' nest-egg ' on ' a rainy day,'
God and Luv only know. So the happy young couple
started out with £205, and not the slightest chance of
earning a penny until George Augustus gave up being
' rich ' and ' pretty comfortable ' and settled down to face
facts and do a little work.

They spent a good deal—for them—on the honeymoon.
George Augustus had a purse containing a lot of sovereigns
and two £5 notes, with which he swanked intolerably.
Isabel had never seen so much money at once and thought
George Augustus was richer than ever. So she immediately began sending ' useful presents ' to the innumerable
members of the impoverished Hartly family ; and George
Augustus, though annoyed—for he was fundamentally
mean—let her. Altogether they spent £30 in a fortnight,

the hopeful life of George Augustus by seducing him into a disastrous marriage. . . .

At that moment Isabel fainted, and most unfortunately for our George the threatened miscarriage was averted— thanks more to Isabel's health and vitality than to the ministrations of her inept husband and in-laws. Only dear Papa was genuinely distressed, and used what shred of influence he had to protect Isabel. As for George Augustus, he simply collapsed, and did nothing but ejaculate :

'Dear Mamma! Isabel! Let us be loving and united. Let us bear one another's burdens ! '

But he was swept away in the torrent of genuine hatred revealed by this instructive scene. Even dear Mamma dropped her Nonconformist tract hypocrisy, and only picked it up again when Isabel fainted.

On dear Papa's suggestion George Augustus took Isabel away to the seaside on what was left of the £200 ; and thus it happened that George was born in a seaside hotel.

It was a difficult birth, clumsily doctored. Isabel suffered tortures for nearly forty hours. If she had not been as strong as a young mare, she would inevitably have died. During this agonising labour, George Augustus prayed freely, took short walks, read *Lorna Doone*, had a half-bottle of claret with his lunch and dinner, and slept tranquilly o' nights. When, finally, he was admitted on tiptoe to a glance at the half-dead woman with the horrid little packet of red infant by her side, he—raised his hand and gave them his blessing. He then tiptoed down to dinner, and ordered a whole bottle of claret in honour of the event.

ISABEL and George Augustus depress me so much that I am anxious to get rid of them. On the other hand, it is impossible to understand George unless you know his parents. And then the older Winterbourne *ménage* rather fascinates me, with a fascination of loathing and contempt. I cannot help wondering how they could have been such ignorant fools, how they came to make so little effort to break free from the humbug, how less than nothing they cared about being themselves. Of course, I tell myself that our own magnanimous nephews will ask themselves precisely the same questions about *us* ; but then I also tell myself that they must see we *did* struggle, we did fight against the humbug and the squelching of life and the worn-out formulae, as young George fought. Perhaps Isabel did fight a little, but the forces of inertia and active spite were too much for her. Perhaps the twenty-two lovers and the talk about Agnosticism and Socialism (of which Isabel at all periods of her life knew rather less than nothing) were a sort of protest. But she was beaten by the economic factor—by the economic factor *and* the child. You can say what you please, but poverty and a child will quench any woman's instinct for self-development and self-assertion—or turn it sour. It turned Isabel's sour and sharp. As for George Augustus, I doubt if he had any instincts left, except the instinct to be pretty comfortable. Whatever he achieved in and with his life was entirely the product of Isabel's will and Isabel's goading. He was a born mucker. And, since Isabel was ignorant, self-willed, and over-ambitious, and turned sour and sharp under the tender mercies of dear Mamma, she came a mucker too—through George Augustus. Yet I

The first four years of George's life passed in a welter of squabbling, incompetence, and poverty, of which he was quite unconscious, though what harm was done to his subconscious would take a better psychologist than I to determine. I imagine that the combined influence of dear Papa, dear Mamma, Ma and Pa Hartly, George Augustus, and Isabel started him off on the race of life with a pretty heavy handicap weight. I should say that George was always an outsider in the Tattersall's Ring of Life—about 100 to 7 against. However, one can but stick to the events as closely as possible, and leave the reader to form conclusions and lay his own odds.

Before George was six months old the rows had begun again in the Sheffield house, and this time more virulently and fiercely than ever. Dear Mamma felt she was fighting for her authority and John Wesley against the intruder. Isabel was fighting for herself and her child and—though she didn't know it—any vestige of genuine humanity there might have been in George Augustus.

About that time George Augustus became really intolerable. A man he had known as a law student returned to Sheffield, bought a practice, and did rather well. Henry Bulburry came it over George Augustus pretty thick. He had spent three years in a London solicitor's office, and to hear him talk you would have thought Mr. Bulburry was the Lord Chancellor, the Beau Brummell, and the Count d'Orsay of the year 1891. Bulburry patronised George Augustus, and George Augustus lapped his patronage up gratefully. Bulburry knew all the latest plays, all the latest actresses, all the latest books. He roared with laughter at George Augustus's Dickens and *Lorna Doone*, and introduced him to Morris, Swinburne, Rossetti, Ruskin, Hardy, Mr. Moore, and young Mr. Wilde. George Augustus got fearfully excited, and

became an aesthete. Once when Pater came to lecture
at Sheffield he was so much moved at the spectacle of
those wonderful moustaches that he fainted, and had to
be taken home in a four-wheeler. George Augustus at
last found his *métier*. He realised that he was a dreamer
of dreams born out of his due time, that he should have
floated Antinous-like with the Emperor Hadrian to the
music of flutes and viols on the subtly-drifting waters of
the immemorial Nile. Under a canopy of perfumed silk
he should have sat enthroned with Zenobia while trains of
naked, thewed Ethiopian slaves, glistening with oil and
nard, laid at his feet jewels of the opulent East. He was
older than the rocks among which he sat. He was subtler
than delicate music ; and there was no change of light, no
shifting of the shadows, no change in the tumultuous outlines of wind-swept clouds, but had a meaning for him.
Babylon and Tyre were in him, and he too wept for beautiful Bion. In Athens he had reclined, violet-crowned, at
the banquet where Socrates reasoned of love with Alci-
biades. But above all, he felt a stupendous passion for
mediæval and Renaissance Florence. He had never been
to Italy, but he was wont to boast that he had studied the
plan of the city so carefully and so frequently that he could
find his way about Florence blindfold. He knew not one
word of Italian, but he spoke ecstatically of Dante and
' his Circle,' criticised the accuracy of Guicciardini,
refuted Machiavelli, and was an authority—after Roscoe—
on the life and times of Lorenzo and Leo x.

One day George Augustus announced to the family that
he should abandon his Profession and WRITE.

There may be little differences in an English family, for
the best of friends fall out at times, but in all serious crises
they may be depended upon to show a united front.

who was editing an amateurish aesthetic review in London, to publish an article by George Augustus entitled 'The Wonder of Cleopatra throughout the Ages.' George Augustus got a guinea for the article, and for a week the family was hushed and awed.

But in that atmosphere of exasperation and dread of the Unknown Obscene, rows were inevitable. And, since George Augustus remained almost hermetically sealed in his cosy study, and refused to come out and be rowed with, even when dear Mamma tapped imperiously at the door and reminded him, through the panels, of his Duties to God, his Mamma, and Society, the rows inevitably took place between dear Mamma and Isabel.

One night, after George Augustus was asleep, Isabel got up and stole £5 from his sovereign-purse. Next morning, she took the baby for a walk as usual, but took it to the railway station and fled to the Hartly home in rural Kent. This was certainly not the boldest thing Isabel ever did—she afterwards did things of incredible rashness—but it was one of the most sensible, from her point of view. It was the first of her big efforts to force George Augustus to action. It reminded him that he had taken on certain responsibilities, and that responsibilities are realities which cannot always be avoided. She bombed him out of the dug-out of dear Mamma's tyranny, and eventually Archied him out of the empyrean of aestheticism and writing.

But she didn't let herself or George Augustus down to the Hartly family. She reckoned—and reckoned rightly —that George Augustus would follow her up pretty smartly, for fear of 'what people would say.' So she sent a telegram to Pa and Ma to say she was coming to see them for a few days—they were pretty well accustomed to Isabel's impulsive moves by this time—and she left a note, a dramatic and naturally (not artistically) tear-stained note

for George Augustus on the bedroom dressing-table.
She took a few inexpensive presents home, and played her
part so well that at first even Ma Hartly only vaguely
suspected that something was wrong.

The loving and united home at Sheffield was in some
consternation when Isabel did not return for lunch ; and
the consternation almost became panic—it certainly
became rage in dear Mamma—when George Augustus
found and communicated Isabel's letter.

' She must be found and brought back here at once,'
said dear Mamma decisively, already scenting carnage
from afar ; ' she has disgraced herself, disgraced her husband, and disgraced the family.   I have long noticed that
she is inattentive at family prayers.   She must be given a
good lesson.   It was an ill day for us all when Augustus
married so far beneath him.   He must go and fetch her
back from her low, vulgar family—to think of our dear
little George being in such *immoral* surroundings ! '

' Suppose she won't come ? ' said dear Papa, who had
suffered so many years from dear Mamma that he had a
fellow-feeling for Isabel.

' She must be *made* to come,' said dear Mamma.
' Augustus !   You must do your duty and assert your
authority as a *Husband*.   You must leave to-night.'

' But what will people *say* ? ' murmured George
Augustus dejectedly.

At those fatal words even dear Mamma flushed beneath
the pallor of fifty years' bad temper and cloistered malevolence.   What would people say ?   What would people
say !   What indeed !   What would the Minister say ?
What would Mrs. Standish say ?   And Mrs. Gregory ?
And Miss Stint, who was another Minister's niece ?   And
Cousin Joan, who had an eye like a brace of buzzards, and

a nose for scandal and other carrion which would have been surprising in a starving condor of the Andes ? What would they say ? Why, they would say that young Mrs. Winterbourne had run away with a ticket-collector on the G.W.R. They would say young George had turned out to have a touch of the tar-brush owing to the prolonged residence of Captain and Mrs. Hartly in the West Indies ; and that, consequently, Mrs. Winterbourne and the infant had been spirited away 'to a home.' They would say that there was a 'dreadful disease' in the Winterbourne family, and that Isabel had run away with an infected baby. They would also say things which, being nearer the truth, would be even more painful. They would say that dear Mamma had plagued Isabel beyond the verge of endurance—and so she had run away, with or without an accomplice. They would say that George Augustus was unable to support his family, and that Isabel had grown tired of thumb-twiddling and 'all this nonsense about books.' They would say—what would they not say ? And the Winterbournes, unique in this among human beings, were sensitive to ' what people said.'

So when George Augustus said dejectedly, ' What will people *say* ? ' even the ranks of Tuscany—viz. dear Mamma—were for a moment dismayed. But that undaunted spirit (which has made the Empire famous) soon rallied, and dear Mamma evolved a plan, and issued orders with a precision and clarity which may be recommended to all Brigadiers, Battalion, Company, and Platoon commanders. The maids must be told at once that Mrs. Winterbourne had been unexpectedly called home by the illness of her father—which was immediately done ; but as the maids had been listening with delighted eagerness to the conference in the parlour, that bit of camouflage was not very effective. Then dear Mamma would pay a round of visits that afternoon, and casually let drop that ' dear Isabel ' had been unexpectedly etcetera ; to which she would add negligently that an 'important conveyance' had detained her son in Sheffield until the next morning, when he would follow his wife— ' such a devoted couple, and only my daughter-in-law's earnest entreaties could prevail upon my dear son not to neglect this important business to act as her cavalier.' Then, George Augustus would leave next morning for rural Kent, and would hale Isabel home like the husband of patient Grissel, or some other hero of romance.

All of which was carried out according to schedule, with one important exception. When George Augustus unexpectedly walked into the multitudinous and tumultuous Saturday dinner of the Hartly family—loin of fresh pork, greens, potatoes, apple sauce, fruit-suet pudding, but no beer this time—he found no patient Grissel awaiting him. And his very impatient and aggrieved Grissel was backed up by an equally aggrieved family, who by now had wormed out of her by no means reticent mind something of the truth. The Hartlys were simply furious with George Augustus for not being 'rich.' The way he had come it over them ! The way he had mashed Isabel with his 1s. 6d. a pound chocolates ! The way dear Mamma had put on her airs of righteous disapproval at Captain Hartly's little jokes about a fellah in India (Ha ! ha !) and a couple of native women (He ! he !) ! The intolerable way in which dear Papa had come it about '64 port and Paris and the Plains of Waterloo ! And after the Hartlys had endured all those humiliations, to find that George Augustus was not 'rich' after all ! O, horrible, most horrible !

So when George Augustus, still half-armed with the bolts of thunder-compelling dear Mamma, walked in dramatically to that agape of roast pig, he found he had a tougher job to deal with than he had imagined.

He was greeted with very constrained and not very polite reticence by the elder Hartlys, and gazed at by such an inordinate number of round-O-eyed youthful Hartlys that he felt all the reproachful juvenile eyes in the world must be directed upon him, as he struggled with an (intentionally) tough and disagreeable portion of the meal.

Need it be said ? George Augustus was defeated by Isabel and the Hartlys, as he would have been defeated by any one with half an ounce of spunk and half a dram of real character.

He capitulated.

Without the honours of war.

He apologised to Isabel.

And to Ma Hartly.

And to ' the Captain.'

An Armistice was arranged, the terms of which were :

George Augustus surrendered unconditionally, and all the honours of war went to Isabel.

Isabel was not to return to dear Mamma or to Sheffield, not ever again.

They were to take a cottage in rural Kent, not far from the Hartlys.

George Augustus was to return to Sheffield and bring to rural Kent his precious aesthetes and as much furniture as he could cadge.

He was to sell his 'practice' in Sheffield, and to start to 'practise' in rural Kent.

As a concession to George Augustus, he was to be allowed to WRITE—for a time. But if the Writing proved unremunerative within a reasonable period—such period to be determined by Isabel and the Other High Contract-

ing Powers—he was to ' practise ' with more assiduity—
and profit.

Failing which, George Augustus would hear about it,
and Isabel would apply for a maintenance order for herself
and child.

Signed, sealed, and delivered over a quart bottle of East
Kent Pale Ale.

Poor old George Augustus ! the shadows of the prison
were rapidly closing round *him*, though he didn't know it.
He had a hell of a time with dear Mamma when he went
home with his tail between his legs and without Isabel,
and announced that they had determined to take a cottage
in rural Kent and—WRITE.   At the word ' write,' dear
Mamma sniffed :

' And who, pray, will pay your washing-bills ? '

In a spirit of loving-kindness and forbearance, George
Augustus ignored this taunt, which was just as well, since
he could think of nothing to say in reply.

Well, dear Papa came to the rescue again. He gave
George Augustus as much of the furniture as he dared,
and another gift of £50 he hadn't got. And Bulburry
got George Augustus orders for an article on The Friends
of Lorenzo the Magnificent, and another article on My
Wanderings in Florence. Bulburry also advised George
Augustus to write a book, either a history of The Decline
and Fall of the Florentine Republic, or a novel on the un-
hackneyed topic of Savonarola. In addition, Bulburry
gave him an introduction to one of those enterprising
young publishers who are always arising in London to
witch the world with noble publishing, and then, after
two or three years, always disappear in the bankruptcy
court, leaving behind a sad trail of unpaid bills and disappointed authors and wrecked reputations.

So George Augustus set up in rural Kent as a WRITER, in a pleasant little cottage which Isabel had found for them.

(I do wish you could have seen the 'artistic' ties George Augustus wore when he was a WRITER ; they would have given you that big feeling.)

But—let us be just—George Augustus really worked— three hours a day, like all the great authors—at writing. He produced articles and he produced stories and he began the Decline and Fall of the Florentine Republic and the most blood-curdling novel about Savonarola, beginning : ' One stormy night in December 14—, two black-cloaked figures might have been observed traversing the Piazza della Signoria in Florence on their way from Or San Michele to the private residence of Lorenzo the Magnificent, now known as the Palazzo Strozzi.'

Poor George Augustus ! Take it for all in all, we shall look upon many like him again. He had a lot to learn. He had to learn that the only books which have the least importance are those which are made from direct contact with life, which are built out of a man's guts. He had to learn that every age pullulates with imitators of the authors who have done this, and created a fashion—which in time and for a time kills them and their influence.

But still, for a year or so he had his cottage in rural Kent and was a Writer. He dreamed his dream, though it was a pretty silly and castrated dream. If he hadn't married Isabel and gotten her with child, he might have made quite a reasonably good literary hack. But, oh ! those hostages given to Fortune ! **** ***** **** *****, and your life will look after itself.

As for Isabel, she was happy for the first, and perhaps the last, time in her life. She adored her cottage in rural

Kent. What did it matter that George Augustus wasted his time Writing ? He still had about £170 and earned a few guineas a month by articles and stories. But for her the thrill was having a real home of her own. She furnished the cottage herself, partly with the heavy mahogany 1850 stuff George Augustus had brought from Sheffield, partly with her own atrocious taste and bamboo. George urged her to furnish ' artistically,' and the resultant chaos of huge, solid, stodgy, curly mahogany and flimsy bamboo, palms, cauliflower chintzes, and framed photographs would have rendered the late Mr. Oscar Wilde plaintive in less than fifty seconds. Never mind ; Isabel was happy. She had her home and she had George Augustus under her eye and thumb, and she had her baby —whom she adored with all the selfishness of a pure woman—and, best of all, she did NOT have dear Mamma pestering and sneering and praying at her through every hour of the day and at every turn. Dear Isabel, how happy she was in her hum-ble little ho-o-ome ! Put it to yourself, now. Suppose you had been one of an innumerable family, enduring all the abominable discomforts and lack of privacy in that elementary Soviet System. And suppose you had then been uncomfortably impregnated and most painfully delivered, and then bullied and pried into and domineered over and tortured by dear Mamma : wouldn't you be glad to have a home of your own, however humble, and however flimsily based on sandy foundations of WRITING and arty ties ? Of course you would. So Isabel looked after the baby, *tant bien que mal*, and cooked abominable meals, and was swindled by the tradesmen, and ran up bills which frightened her, and let young George catch croup and nearly die, and didn't interrupt George Augustus's wooing of the Muse more than half a dozen times a morning and—was happy.

But in all our little arrangements on this satellite of the Sun, we are apt to forget—among a multitude of other things—two important facts. We are the inhabitants of a planet who keep alive only by a daily consumption of the material products of that planet ; we are members of a crude collective organisation which distributes these essential products in accordance with certain bizarre rules painfully evolved from chaos by primitive brains. George Augustus certainly forgot these two facts—if he had ever recognised them. A man, a woman, and a brat cannot live for ever on £170 and a few odd guineas a month. They couldn't do it even in the eighteen-nineties, even with extraordinary economy. And Isabel was not economical. Neither, for that matter, was George Augustus. He was mean, but he liked to be pretty comfortable, and his notions of the pretty comfortable were a bit extravagant. Torn between his respect for the Right Hnble. the Lord Tennyson's well-known predilection for port and Mr. Algernon Charles Swinburne's less notorious but undisguised preference for brandy neat, George Augustus finally became original, and fell back on his favourite claret. But, even in the 'nineties, claret was not cheap ; and three dozen a month rather eat into an income of four to six guineas. And then Isabel was inexperienced. In housekeeping inexperience costs money ! So a time arrived when the £170 was nearly at zero, and the few guineas a month became fewer instead of more numerous. Then George, young George, developed some infant malady ; Isabel lost her head, and insisted on a doctor ; the doctor, like all the English middle classes, thought a Writer was a harmless fool with money, to be bled ruthlessly, called far more often than was necessary, and sent in a much bigger bill than he would have dared send a stockbroker or a millionaire.

Then George Augustus had the influenza and thought he was going to die. And after that Isabel was stricken with haemorrhoids in her secret parts, and had to be treated. Consequently, the bank balance of a few guineas was turned into a deficit of a good many pounds ; and the affable Bank Manager rapidly became strangely unaffable when his polite references to the overdraft remained unsatisfied with the manna of a few cheques.

It became obvious to Isabel—and would long ago have become obvious to almost any one but George Augustus —that Luv and WRITING in a cottage were hopelessly bankrupt.

Well, dear Papa pungled once more—with a pound a week ; and Pa Hartly weighed in with a weekly five shillings. But that was misery, and Isabel was determined that, since she had married George Augustus for his 'riches,' 'rich' he should be or perish in the act of trying to acquire riches. So she brought into play all the feminine arsenal, reinforced with a few useful underhand punches and jabs in the moral kidneys, learned from dear Mamma. George Augustus tried to keep high above these material and degrading necessities, but, as I said, Isabel finally Archied him down. When they could no longer get credit even for meat or bread, George Augustus capitulated, and agreed to ' practise ' once more. He wanted to go back to Sheffield and be pretty comfortable again, under the talons of dear Mamma. But Isabel was —quite rightly — adamant. She refused to return to Sheffield. George Augustus had got her on false pretences, i.e. that he was ' rich.' He was not rich. He was, in fact, damn poor. But he had taken on the responsibility of supporting a woman, and he had got that woman with child. He had no business to be pretty comfortable any longer under the wings of dear Mamma. His business was to get rich as quickly as possible ; at any rate, to provide for his dependants. Inexorable logic, against which I can find no argument even in sophistry.

So they went to a middling-sized, dreary coast town just then in the process of 'development' (Bulburry's suggestion), and George Augustus put up another brass plaque. With no results. But then, just as the situation was getting desperate, dear Papa died. He did not leave his children a fortune, but he did leave them £250 each—and strangely enough he actually had the money. Dear Mamma was left in rather 'straitened circumstances,' but she had enough to be unreservedly disagreeable to the end of her days.

That £250—and the Oscar Wilde case—just saved the situation. The £250 gave them enough to live on for a year. The Oscar Wilde case scared George Augustus thoroughly out of aestheticism and writing. What! They were hanging men and women for wearing of the green? Then, George Augustus would wear red. After ' The Sentence,' George Augustus, like most of England, decided that art and literature were niminy-piminy, if not greenery-yallery. I don't say he burned his books and arty ties, but he put them out of sight with remarkable alacrity. The Great Voice of the English People had spoken in no Uncertain Tones, and George Augustus was not deaf to the Message. How could he be, with Isabel pouring it into one ear by word of mouth, and dear Mamma—un-expected but welcome ally—into the other by letter ? A nation of Mariners and Sportsmen naturally excel in the twin arts of leaving a sinking ship and kicking a man when he is down. Three months after The Sentence you would never have suspected that George Augustus had ever dreamed of Writing. His clothes were of exemplary Philistinism—indeed, the height of his starched collars and

the plainness of his ties had an almost Judas touch in
their unaesthetic ugliness. Urged on by Isabel he became
a Freemason, an Oddfellow, an Elk, a Heart of Oak, a
Buffalo, a Druid, and God knows how many other
mysterious things. He himself abandoned Florence,
forgot even the blameless Savonarola, and prayed for
Guidance. They attended the ' best Church ' twice on
every Sunday.

Slowly at first, then more and more rapidly, George
Augustus increased his practice ; and the lust of earning
money came upon him. They ceased to live in one room
behind the office, and took a small but highly respectable
house in the residential quarter of the town. Two years
later they took a country cottage in a very high-class
resort, Martin's Point. Two years after that they bought
a large country-house at Pamber, and another smaller
house just outside the ' quaint old ' town of Hamborough.
George Augustus began to buy and to build houses.
Isabel, whose jointure had been less than nothing when
she married, now began to complain because her allowance was ' only £1200 a year.' In short, they prospered,
and prospered greatly—for a time.

They had another child, and another, and another, and
another. A man and a woman who can do nothing else
can always have children, and, if they are legally married
and are able to support their progeny, there seems no end
to the amount of begetting they may do and the laurel
crowns of virtue to which they are thereby entitled.
Isabel put her vitality into child-bearing, boosting George
Augustus to profitable action, thrusting herself ever onward and upward financially and socially, buying and
furnishing houses, quarrelling with her friends, acquiring
sheiks, malforming her children's minds, capriciously

interfering with their education, swanking to the Hartlys
with her money, patronising the now aged and less
venomous dear Mamma, and other lofty and inspiring
activities. Was she happy ? What a question ! We are
not placed here by a benevolent Providence to be happy,
but to make ourselves unpleasant to our neighbours and
to impose the least amiable portions of our personalities
on as many people as possible. Was George Augustus
happy ? Which I parry with—did he deserve to be
happy ? He made money, anyway, which is more than
you and I can do. He dropped claret for whisky, and
the aesthetes for the 'English Classics,' all those 'noble'
authors who have ' stood the test of time,' and thereby
become so very dull that one prefers to go to the cinema,
which has not stood any such test. He had a brougham,
in which he drove daily to his office. He became a
Worshipful Grand Master, and possessed any amount of
funny little medals and coloured leather *caches-sexe*,
which are apparently worn in the Mysteries of the Free-
masons. He framed his certificates as a Solicitor, a
Buffalo, a Druid, and all the other queer things, and
hung them in various places to surprise and awe the inexperienced. He had a great many bills. For about ten
years he was so prosperous that he was able to give up
attending Church on Sundays.

GEORGE, the younger, liked Hamborough best, perhaps, Martin's Point next, Pamber hardly at all, and he detested Dullborough, the town which contained his father's offices and the minor public school which he attended.

The mind of a very young child is not very interesting. It has imagination and wonder, but too unregulated, too bizarre, too 'quaint,' too credulous. Does it matter very much that George babbled o' white lobsters, stirred up frogs in a bucket, thought that the word 'mist' meant sunset, and was easily persuaded that a sort of milk pudding he detested had been made from an ostrich's egg? Of course, a good deal of adult imagination consists in people's persuading themselves that they can see white lobsters, just as their poetry consists in persuading themselves that the milk pudding *did* come out of the ostrich's egg. The child at least is honest, which is something. But on the whole the young child-mind is boring.

The intellect wakes earlier than the feelings, curiosity before the passions. The child asks the scientist's Why? before he asks the poet's How? George read little primers on Botany and Geology and the Story of the Stars, and collected butterflies, and wanted to do chemistry, and hated Greek. And then one evening the world changed. It was at Martin's Point. All one night the South-West wind had streamed over the empty downs, sweeping up in a crescendo of sound to a shrill ecstasy of speed, sinking into abrupt sobs of dying vigour, while underneath steadily, unyieldingly, streamed and roared the major volume of the storm. The windows rattled. Rain pelted on the panes, oozed and bubbled through the joints of the woodwork. The sea, dimly visible at dusk, rolled furiously—tossing the long breakers on the rocks, and made a tumult of white horses in the Channel. Even the largest ships took shelter. In the irregular harmony of that storm George went to sleep in his narrow, lonely child's bed, and who knows what Genius, what Puck, what elfin Spirit of Beauty came riding on the storm from the South, and shed the juice of what magic herb on his closed eyes ? All next day the gale blew with ever-diminishing violence. It was a half-holiday, and no games on account of the wet. After lunch, George went to his room, and sank absorbed in his books, his butter-flies, his moths, his fossils. He was aroused by a sudden glare of yellow sunlight. The storm had blown itself out. The last clouds, broken in lurid, ragged-edged fragments, were sailing gently over a soft blue sky. Soon even they were gone. George opened the window and leaned out. The heavy, dank smell of wet earth-mould came up to him with its stifling hyacinth-like quality ; the rain-drenched privet was almost over-sweet ; the young poplar leaves twinkled and trembled in the last gusts, shaking down rapid chains of diamonds. But it was all fresh—fresh with the clarity of air which follows a great gale, with the scentless purity of young leaves, the drenched grasses of the empty downs. The sun moved majestically and imperceptibly downwards in a widening pool of gold, which faded, as the great ball vanished, into pure, clear, hard green and blue. One, two, a dozen blackbirds and linnets and thrushes were singing ; and as the light faded they dwindled to one blackbird tune of exquisite melancholy and purity.

Beauty is in us, not outside us. We recognise our own beauty in the patterns of the infinite flux. Light, form, movement, glitter, scent, sound, suddenly apprehended as givers of delight, as interpreters of the inner vitality, not as the customary aspect of things. A boy, caught for the first time in a kind of ecstasy, brooding on the mystery of beauty.

A penetrating voice came up the stairs :

' Georgie ! Georgie ! Come out of that stuffy room at once ! I want you to get me something from Gilpin's.'

What perverse instinct tells them when to strike ? How do they learn to break the crystal mood so unerringly ? Why do they hate the mystery so much ?

Long before he was fifteen George was living a double life—one life for school and home, another for himself. Consummate dissimulation of youth, fighting for the inner vitality and the mystery. How amusingly, but rather tragically, he fooled them ! How innocent-seemingly he played the fine, healthy, barbarian schoolboy, even to the slang and the hateful games! Be ye soft as doves and cunning as serpents. He 's such a *real* boy, you know—viz. not an idea in his head, no suspicion of the mystery. ' Rippin' game of rugger to-day, Mother. I scored two tries.' Upstairs was that volume of Keats, artfully abstracted from the shelves.

A double row of huge old poplars beside the narrow brook swayed and danced in the gales, rustled in the late spring breeze, stood spirelike heavy in July sunlight—a stock-in-trade of spires without churches left mysteriously behind by some mediæval architect. Chestnut trees hung over the walks built on the old town walls. In late May after rain the sweet musty scent filled the lungs and nostrils, and sheets of white and pink petals hid the asphalt. In summer the tiled roofs of the old town were soft deep orange and red, speckled with lemon-coloured lichens. In winter the snow drifted down the streets and formed a tessellated pattern of white and black in the cobbled market-place. The sound of footsteps echoed in the deserted streets. The clock bells from the Norman tower, with its curious bulbous Dutch cupola, rang so leisurely, marking a fabulous Time.

Said the gardener :
' It 's a rum thing, Master George, them rabbits don't drink, and they makes water ; and the chickens don't make water, but they drinks it.'
Insoluble problem, capricious decrees of Providence.

Confirmation classes.
' You 'll have to go and see old Squish.'
' What 's he say to you ? '
' Oh, he gives you a lot of jaw, and asks you if you know any smut.'
In the School Chapel. Full-dress Preparation Class for Confirmation. The Head in academic hood and surplice entered the pulpit. Whispers sank to intimidated silence, dramatically prolonged by the hawk-faced man silently bullying the rows of immature eyes. Then in slow, deliberate, impressive tones :
' Within ten years one half of you boys will be DEAD ! '
Moral : prepare to meet thy God, and avoid smut.
But did he know, that blind prophet ?
Was he inspired, that stately hypocrite ?
Like a moral vulture he leaned over and tortured his palpitating prey. Motionless in body, they writhed within, as he painted dramatically the penalties of Vice and Sin, drew pictures of Hell. But did he know ? Did he know the hell they were going to within ten years, did he know *how* soon most of their names would be on the

Chapel wall ?   How he must have enjoyed composing
that inscription to those 'who went forth unfalteringly,
and proudly laid down their lives for King and Country'!

One part of the mystery was called SMUT.   If you were
smutty you went mad and had to go into a lunatic asylum.
Or you 'contracted a loathsome disease' and your nose
fell off.

The pomps and vanities of this wicked world, and all
the sinful lusts of the flesh.   So it was wicked, like being
smutty, to feel happy when you looked at things and read
Keats ?   Perhaps you went mad that way too and your
eyes fell out ?

' That's what makes them lay eggs,' said the little girl,
swinging her long golden hair and laughing, as the cock
leaped on a hen.

O dreadful, O wicked little girl, you're talking smut to
me.   You'll go mad, I shall go mad, our noses will drop
off.   Oh, please don't talk like that, please, please !

From fornication and all other deadly sins . . .   What
is fornication ?   Have I committed fornication ?   Is that
the holy word for smut ?   Why don't they tell me what it
means ?   why is it the foulest thing a decent man can
commit ?   When that thing happened in the night it must
have been fornication ;   I shall go mad and my nose will
drop off.

Hymn Number . . .   A few more years shall roll.

How wicked I must be !

Are there two religions ?   A few more years shall roll,
in ten years half of you boys will be dead, Smut, nose
dropping off, fornication and all other deadly sins.   Oh,
wash me in Thy Precious Blood, and take my sins away.
Blood, Smut.

And then the other—a draught of vintage that has been cooled a long age in the deep-delved earth, tasting of Flora and the country green, dance and Provençal song, and sunburned mirth ? Listening to the sound of the wind as you fell asleep ; watching the blue butterflies and the Small Coppers hovering and settling on the great scented lavender bush ; taking off your clothes and letting your body slide into a cool, deep, clear rock-pool, while the grey kittiwakes clamoured round the sun-white cliffs and the scent of seaweeds and salt water filled you ; watching the sun go down and trying to write something of what it made you feel, like Keats ; getting up very early in the morning and riding out along the white empty lanes on your bicycle ; wanting to be alone and think about things and feeling strange and happy and ecstatic—was that another religion ? Or was that all Smut and Sin ? Best not speak of it, best keep it all hidden. I can't help it if it is Smut and Sin. Is *Romeo and Juliet* smut ? It 's in the same book where you do parsing and analysis out of *King John*. Seize on the white wonder of dear Juliet's hand and steal immortal blessing from her lips. . . .

But more than words about things were things themselves. You looked and looked at them, and then you wanted to put down what they looked like, rearrange them in patterns. In the drawing-class they made you look at a dirty whitish cube, cylinder, and cone, and you drew and re-drew hard outlines which weren't there. But for yourself you wanted to get the colours of things and how they faded into each other and how they formed themselves — or did you form them ? — into exciting patterns. It was so much more fun to paint things than even to read what Keats and Shakespeare thought about them. George spent all his pocket-money on paints and

drawing-pencils and sketch-books and oil-sketching paper
and water-colour blocks. For a long time he hadn't
much to look at, even in reproductions. He had Cruik-
shank and Quiz illustrations which he didn't much care
for; and a reproduction of a Bouguereau which he hated;
and two Rossetti pictures which he rather liked; and a
catalogue of the Tate Collection which gave him photographs of a great many horrible Watts and Frank Dicksees.
Best of all, he liked an album of coloured reproductions
of Turner's water-colours. Then, one spring, George
Augustus took him to Paris for a few days. They did an
'educative' visit to the Louvre, and George simply leaped
at the Italians and became very Pre-Raphaelite and adored
the Primitives. He was quite feverish for weeks after he
got back, unable to talk of anything else. Isabel was
worried about him : it was so *unboyish*, so—well, really,
quite *unhealthy*, all this silly craze for pictures, and spending hours and hours crouching over paint-blocks, instead
of being in the fresh air. So much nicer for the boy to be
manly. Wasn't he old enough to have a gun licence and
learn to kill things ?

So George had a gun licence, and went out shooting every morning in the autumn. He killed several
plovers and a wood-pigeon. Then one frosty November
morning he fired into a flock of plovers, killed one, and
wounded another, which fell down on the crisp grass with
such a wail of despair. ' If you wing a bird, pick it up
and wring its neck,' he had been told. He picked up the
struggling, heaving little mass of feathers, and with
infinite repugnance and shut eyes tried to wring its neck.
The bird struggled and squawked. George wrung
harder and convulsively—and the whole head came off in
his hand. The shock was unspeakable. He left the
wretched body, and hurried home shuddering. Never

again, never, never again would he kill things. He oiled
his gun dutifully, as he had been told to do, put it away,
and never touched it again. At nights he was haunted by
the plover's wail and by the ghastly sight of the headless,
bleeding bird's body. In the daytime he thought of
them. He could forget them when he went out and
sketched the calm trees and fields, or tried to design in his
tranquil room. He plunged more deeply into painting
than ever, and thus ended one of the many attempts to
' make a man ' of George Winterbourne.

The business of ' making a man ' of him was pursued
at School, but with little more success, even with the aid
of compulsion.

' The type of boy we aim at turning out,' the Head used
to say to impressed parents, ' is a thoroughly manly
fellow. We prepare for the Universities, of course, but
our pride is in our excellent Sports Record. There is an
O.T.C., organised by Sergeant-Major Brown (who served
throughout the South African War) and officered by the
masters who have been trained in the Militia. Every boy
must undergo six months' training, and is then competent
to take up arms for his Country in an emergency.'

The parents murmured polite approval, though rather
tender mothers hoped the discipline was not too strict and
' the guns not too heavy for young arms.' The Head was
contemptuously and urbanely reassuring. On such occa-
sions he invariably quoted those stirring and indeed
immortal lines of Rudyard Kipling which end up, ' You'll
be a man, my son.' It is *so* important to know how to
kill. Indeed, unless you know how to kill you cannot
possibly be a Man, still less a Gentleman.

' The O.T.C. will parade in the Gymnasium for drill

and instruction at twelve. Those who are excused will take Geography under Mr. Hobbs in Room 14.'

George hated the idea of the O.T.C.—he didn't quite know why, but he somehow didn't want to learn to kill and be a thoroughly manly fellow. Also, he resented being ordered about. Why should one be ordered about by thoroughly manly fellows whom one hates and despises ? But then, as a very worthy and thoroughly manly fellow (who spent the War years in the Intelligence Department of the War Office, censoring letters) said of George many years later : ' What Winterbourne needs is discipline, *Discipline*. He is far too self-willed and independent. The Army will make a Man of him.' Alas ! it made a corpse of him. But then, as we all know, there is no price too high to pay for the privilege of being made a thoroughly manly fellow.

So George, feeling immeasurably guilty, but immeasurably repelled, sneaked into the Geography class, instead of parading like a thoroughly manly fellow in embryo. In ten minutes a virtuous-looking but rather pimply prefect appeared :

' Captain James's compliments, sir, and is Winterbourne here ? '

As George was walked over to the Gymnasium by the innocent-looking, rather pimply, but thoroughly manly prefect, the latter said :

' Why couldn't you do what you 're told, you filthy little sneak, instead of having to be ignominiously *fetched* ?'

George made no answer. He just went hard and obstinate, hate-obstinate, inside. He was so clumsy and so bored—in spite of infinite manly bullyings—that the O.T.C. was very glad indeed to send him back to the Geography class after a few drills. He just went hate-obstinate, and obeyed with sullen, hate-obstinate docility.

He didn't disobey, but he didn't really obey, not with anything inside him. He was just passive, and they could do nothing with him.

He wrote a great many impositions that term and lost a number of his precious half-holidays, the hours when he could sketch and paint and think about things. But they didn't get at the inside vitality. It retreated behind another wall or two, threw up more sullen, hate-obstinate walls, but it was there all right. It might be all Smut and Sin ; but if it was, well, Smutty and Sinful he would be. Only, he wouldn't say ' turd ' and ' talk smut ' with the others, and he kicked out fiercely when any of the innocent-looking, rather pimply prefects tried to put their arms round him or make him a 'case.' He just wouldn't have it. He was more than hate-obstinate then, and blazed into fearful white rages, which left him trembling for hours, unable even to hold a pen. Consequently, the prefects reported that Winterbourne had 'gone smutty' and was injuring his health, and he was 'interviewed' by his House Master and the Head—but he baffled them with the hate-obstinate silence, and the inner exultation he felt in being Sinful and Smutty in his own way, along with Keats and Turner and Shakespeare.

The prefects gave him a good many ' prefects' lickings ' on various pretexts, but they never made him cry, even, let alone break down the wall between his inner aliveness and their thorough manliness.

He got a very bad report that term, and no remove. For which he was duly lectured and reprimanded. As the bullying urbane Head reproved, did he know that the sullen, rather hard-faced boy in front of him was not listening, was silently reciting to himself the Ode to a Nightingale, as a kind of inner Declaration of Independence ? ' Magic casements '—that was when you opened the window wide at sunset to listen to the birds, or at night-time to look at the stars, or first thing in the morning to smell the fresh sunlight and watch the leaves glittering.

' If you go on like this, Winterbourne, you will disgrace yourself, your parents, your House, and your School. You take little or no interest in the School life, and your Games record is abominable.   Your set-captain tells me that you have cut Games ten times this term, and your Form Master reports that you have over a thousand lines of impositions yet to work off.   Your conduct with regard to the O.T.C. was contemptible and unmanly to a degree we have never experienced in *this* School.   I am also told that you are ruining your health with secret abominable practices against which I warned you—unavailingly, I fear —at the time I endeavoured to prepare you for Confirmation and Holy Communion.   I notice that you have only once taken Communion since your Confirmation, although more than six months have passed.   What you do when you cut Games and go running off to your home, I do not know.   It cannot be anything good.'   (Magic casements, opening on the foam.)   ' It would pain me to have to ask your parents to remove you from the School, but we want no wasters and sneaks here.   Most, indeed all, your fellow-boys are fine manly fellows ; and you have the excellent example of your House Prefects before you.   Why can you not imitate them ?   What nonsense have you got into your head ?   Speak out, and tell me plainly.   Have you entangled yourself in any way ? '

No answer.

' What do you do in your spare time ? '

No answer.

' Your obstinate silence gives me the right to suspect the worst.   *What* you do I can imagine, but prefer not to mention. Now, for the last time, will you speak out honourably and manfully, and tell me what it is you do that makes you neglect your work and Games and makes you conspicuous in the School for sullen and obstinate behaviour ? '

No answer.

' Very well. You will receive twelve strokes from the birch. Bend over.'

George's face quivered, but he had not shed a tear or made a sound as he turned silently to go.

' Stop. Kneel down at that chair, and we will pray together that this lesson may be of service to you, and that you may conquer your evil habits. Let us together pray GOD that He will have mercy upon you, and make you into a really manly fellow.'

They prayed.

Or rather, the Head prayed, and George remained silent. He did not even say ' Amen.'

After that the School gave him up and let him drift. He was supposed to be dull-minded as well as obstinate and unmanly, and was allowed to vegetate vaguely about the Lower Fifth. Maybe he picked up more even of the little they had to teach than they suspected. But as the silent, rather white-faced, rather worried-looking boy went mechanically through the day's routine, hung about in corridors, moved from classroom to classroom, he was busy enough inside, building up a life of his own. George went at George Augustus's books with the energy of a fierce physical hunger. He once showed me a list in an old notebook of the books he had read before he was sixteen. Among other things, he had raced through most of the poets from Chaucer onwards. It was not the amount that he read which mattered, but the way in which he read. Having no single person to talk to openly, no one to whom he could reveal himself, no one from whom he could learn what he wanted to know, he was perforce thrust back upon books. The English poets and the foreign painters were his only real friends. They were his interpreters of the mystery, the defenders of the inner vitality which he was fighting unconsciously to save. Naturally, the School was against him. They set out to produce 'a type of thoroughly manly fellow,' a 'type' which unhesitatingly accepted the prejudices, the 'code' put before it, docilely conformed to a set of rules. George dumbly claimed to think for himself, above all to *be* himself. The 'others' were good enough fellows, no doubt, but they really had no selves to *be*. They hadn't the flame. The things which to George were the very *cor cordium* of life meant nothing to them, simply passed them by. They wanted to be approved and be healthy barbarians, cultivating a little smut on the sly, and finally dropping into some convenient post in life where the 'thoroughly manly fellow' was appreciated—mostly, one must admit, minor and unpleasant and not very remunerative posts in unhealthy colonies. The Empire's backbone. George, though he didn't realise it then, wasn't going to be a bit of any damned Empire's backbone, still less part of its kicked backside. He didn't mind going to hell, and disgracing himself and his parents and his House and The School, if only he could go to hell in his own way. That's what they couldn't stand—the obstinate passive refusal to accept their prejudices, to conform to their minor-gentry, kicked-backside-of-the-Empire code. They worried him, they bullied him, they frightened him with cock-and-bull yarns about Smut and noses dropping off; but they didn't get him. I wish he hadn't been worried and bullied to death by those

two women. I wish he hadn't stood up to that
machine-gun just one week before the Torture ended.
After he had fought the swine (*i.e.* the British ones)
so gallantly for so many years. If only he had hung
on a little longer, and come back, and done what he
wanted to do ! He could have done it, he could
have 'got there'; and then even 'The School'
would have fawned on him. Bloody fool ! Couldn't he
see that we have only one duty—to hang on, and smash
the swine ?

Once, only once, he nearly gave himself away to The
School. At the end of the examinations, as a sort of after-
thought, there was an English Essay. One of the subjects was : What do you want to do in Life ? George's
enthusiasm got the better of his caution, and he wrote a
crude, enthusiastic, schoolboyish rhapsody, laying down
an immense programme of life, from travel to astronomy,
with the beloved Painting as the end and crown of all.
Needless to say, he did not get the Prize or even any
honourable mention. But, to his amazement, on the last
day of term, as they went to evening Chapel, the Head
strolled up, put an arm round his shoulders, and pointing
to the planet Venus said :
'Do you know what that star is, my boy ? '
'No, sir.'
'That is Sirius, a gigantic sun, many millions of miles
distant from us.'
'Yes, sir.'
And then the conversation languished. The Head
removed his arm, and they entered the Chapel. The last
hymn was 'Onward, Christian Soldiers,' because ten of
the senior boys were going to Sandhurst.
George did not join actively in the service.

The summer holidays were the only part of the year when he was really happy.

The country inland from Martin's Point is rather barren. But, like all the non-industrialised parts of England, it has a character, very shy like a little silvery-grey old lady, which acts gently but in the end rather strongly on the mind. It was the edge of one of the long chalk downs of England, with salt marshes to left and right, and fertile clay land far behind—too far for George to reach even on a bicycle. In detail it seemed colourless and commonplace. From the crest of one of the high ridges, it had a kind of silvery-grey, very old quality, with its great, bare, treeless fields making faint chequer-patterns on the long, gentle slopes, with always a fringe of silvery-grey sea in the far distance. The chalk was ridged in long parallels, like the swell of some gigantic ocean arrested in rock. The ridges became more abrupt and violent near the coast, and ended in a long, irregular wall of silvery-grey chalk, poised like a huge wave of rock-foam for ever motionless and for ever silent, while for ever at its base lapped the petty waves of the mobile and whispering sea. The sheep-and-wind-nipped turf of the downs grew dwarf bee-orchis, blue-purple bugloss, tall ragged knapweed, and frail harebells. In the valleys were tall thistles and foxgloves. Certain nooks were curiously rich with wild-flowers mixed with deep rich-red clover and marguerite-daisies. In the summer these little flowery patches—so precious and conspicuous in the surrounding barrenness—were a flicker of butterfly wings : the creamy Marbled Whites, electric blue of the Chalkhill Blue, sky-blue of the Common and Holly Blue, rich tawny of the Fritillaries, metallic gleam of the Coppers, cool drab of the Meadow Browns. The Peacock, the Red Admiral, the Painted Lady, the Tortoise-

shell wheeled over the nettles and thistles, poised on the
flowers, fanning their rich mottled wings. In a certain
field in August you could find Clouded Yellows rapidly
moving in little curves and irregular dashes of flight over
swaying red-purple clover, which seemed to drift like a
sea as the wind ran over it.

Yet with all this colour the 'feel' of the land was silvery-
grey. The thorn-bushes and the rare trees were bent at
an angle under the pressure of the South-West gales.
The inland hamlets and farms huddled down in the
hollows behind a protecting wall of elms. They were
humble, unpretentious, but authentic, like the lives of the
shepherds and ploughmen who lived in them. The three
to ten miles which separated them from the pretentious
suburbanity of Martin's Point might have been three
hundred, so unmoved, so untouched were they by its golf
and its idleness and tea-party scandals and even its in-
creasing number of 'cars.' In hollows, too, crouched its
low, flint-built Norman churches, so unpretentious, for
all the richness of dog-toothed porches and Byzantine-
looking tympanums and conventionalised satiric heads
sneering and gaping and grimacing from the string-courses.
Hard, satiric people those Norman conquerors must have
been—you can see the hard, satiric effigies of some of their
descendants in the Temple Church. They must have
crushed the Saxon shepherds and swineherds under their
steel gauntlets, smiling in a hard, satiric way. And even
their piety was hard and satiric, if you can judge from the
little flinty, satiric churches they scattered over the land.
Then they must have pushed on westward to richer lands,
abandoning those barren downs and scanty fields to the
descendants of the oppressed Saxon. So the land seemed
old ; but the hard, satiric quality of the Normans only
remained in odd nooks of their churches—all the rest had

grown gentle and silvery-grey, like a rather sweet and gentle silvery-grey old lady.

All this George struggled to express with his drawing-and paint-blocks. He tried to absorb—and to some extent did absorb—the peculiar quality of the country. He attempted it all, from the twenty-mile sweeps of undulating Down fringed by the grey-silver sea, to the church doors and little patient photographic, semi-scientific painting of the flowers and butterflies. From the point of view of a painter, he was always too literal, too topographical, too minutely interested in detail. He saw the poetry of the land but didn't express it in form and colour. The old English landscape school of 1770-1840 died long before Turner's body reached St. Paul's and his money went into the pockets of the greedy English lawyers instead of to the painters for whom he intended it. The impulse expired in painstaking topography and sentimental prettiness. There wasn't the vitality, the capacity to struggle on, which you find in the best work of painters like Friesz, Vlaminck, and even Utrillo, who can find a new sort of poetry in tossing trees or a white farmhouse or a *bistro* in the Paris suburbs. George, even at fifteen, knew what he wanted to say in paint, but couldn't say it. He could appreciate it in others, but he hadn't got the power of expression in him.

Hitherto George had been quite alone in his blind instinctive struggle—the fight against the effort to force him into a mould, the eager searching out for life and more life which would respond to the spark of life within. Now he began to find unexpected allies; discovered at first almost with suspicion, then with immense happiness, that he was not quite alone, that there were others who valued what he valued. He discovered men's friendship and the touch of girls' lips and hands.

First came Mr. Barnaby Slush, at that time a 'most famous novelist,' who had hit the morbid-cretinish British taste with a sensational, crude-Christian moral novel which sold millions of copies in a year and is now forgotten, except that it probably lies embalmed somewhere in the Tauchnitz collection, that mausoleum of unreadable works. Mr. Slush was a bit of a boozer and highly delighted with his notoriety. Still, he did occasionally look around him ; he was not wholly blinkered with prejudice and unheeding blankness like most of the middle-class inhabitants of Martin's Point. He noticed George, laughed at some of the pert but acute schoolboyish remarks George made and for which he was invariably squelched, was 'interested' in his passion for painting and the persistence he gave to it.

' There 's something in that boy of yours, Mrs. Winterbourne. He 's got a mind. He 'll do something in the world.'

' Oh, do you think so, Mr. Slush ? '—Isabel, halfflattered, half-bristling with horror and rage at the thought that George *might* ' have a mind '—' he 's just a healthy, happy schoolboy, and only thinks of pleasing his Mummie.'

' Umph,' said Mr. Slush. ' Well, I 'd like to do something for him. There 's more in him than you think. *I* believe there 's an artist in him.'

' If I thought that,' exclaimed Isabel viciously, ' I 'd flog him till all such nonsense was flogged out of him.'

Mr. Slush saw he was doing George more harm than good by this well-meant effort, and was discreetly silent. However, he gave George one or two books, and tried to talk to him on the side. But George was still too suspicious of all grown-ups, particularly those who came and

drank whisky in the evening with George Augustus and
Isabel. Besides, poor, flabby, drink-sodden, kindly Mr.
Slush rather repelled his hard, intolerant youthfulness ;
and they got nowhere in particular. Still, Mr. Slush was
important to the extent that he prepared George to give
some confidence to others. He broke down the first outer
wall built by George against the world. The way in
which Isabel got rid of Mr. Slush, whose possible influence
on George she instinctively suspected, was rather amusing. George Augustus and Mr. Slush went to a Free-
masons' dinner together. Now that Freemasonry had
served its purpose, Isabel was intensely jealous of its
mysteries—poor mysteries !—which George Augustus
honourably refused to reveal to her, and she hated those
periodical dinners with a bitter hatred. That night there
arose one of the most terrific thunderstorms which had
ever been known in that part of the country. For six
hours forked and sheet lightning leaped and stabbed at
earth and sea from three sides of the horizon ; crash after
crash of thunder broke over Martin's Point and rumbled
terrifically against the cliffs, while desperate drenching
sheets of rain beat madly on roofs and windows and
gushed wetly down the steep roads. It was impossible
for the men to get home. They remained—drinking a
good deal—at the hotel until nearly four, and then drove
home sleepily and merrily. Isabel put on her tragedy-
queen air, sat up all night, and greeted George Augustus
with horrid invective.

' Think of poor Mrs. Slush out there in that lonely
farm, and me and the children crouching here in terror,
while you men were guzzling, and besotting yourselves
with whisky ' . . . etcetera, etcetera.

Poor George Augustus attempted a feeble defence—it
was swept away. Mr. Slush innocently walked over next

day to see how things were after the storm, was insulted, and
driven from the house in amazed indignation. He 'put'
Isabel a little vindictively 'in his next novel,' but, as she
said and said truly, he never 'darkened their doors' again.

In one way George loved the grey sea and barrenness, in
another way he hated them. To get away to the lush
inland country was a release, an ecstasy, the more precious
in that it happened so rarely. When he was a small child,
a maid-servant took him 'down home' to the hop-picking.
Confused and fantastic memories of it remained with him.
He never forgot the penetrating sunlight, the long dusty
ride in the horse-bus, the sensation of hot-sharp-scented
shadow under the tall vines, the joy of the great rustling
heaps falling downward as the foreman cut the strings,
the tenderness of the rough women hop-pickers, the taste
of the smoky picnic tea and heavy soggy cake (so delicious!)
they gave him. Later—in the fourteen-sixteen years—it
was a joy to visit the Hambles. They were retired professional people, who lived in a remote country-house
among lush meadows and rich woods. Mr. Hamble was
a large, freckly man who collected insects, and was a
skilled botanist ; and thus charmed that side of George.
But the real delight was the lush countryside — and
Priscilla. Priscilla was the Hambles' daughter, almost
exactly George's age, and between those two was a curious,
intense, childish passion. She was very golden and
pretty—much too pretty, for it made her self-conscious
and flirtatious. But the passion between those two
children was a genuine thing.

     *   *   *   *   *   *   *   *   *   *

For quite three years George was under the influence of
his passion for Priscilla, never really forgot her, always in

a dim, dumb, subconscious way felt the frustration.
Like all passions it was something fugitive, the product of
a phase, but it ought not to have been frustrated.   It was
a pity they were so often separated, because that meant
infinite letter-writing and so made him always tend to
too much idealising and intellectualising in love affairs.
But when they were together it was pure happiness.
Priscilla was a very demure and charming little mistress.
They played all sorts of games with other children, and
went fishing in the brook, picked flowers in the rich water-
meadows, hunted bird-nests along the hedges.   All these
things, great fun in themselves, were so much more fun
because Priscilla was there, because they held hands and
kissed, and felt very serious, like real lovers.   Sometimes
he dared to touch her childish breasts.   And the feeling
of friendliness from the clasp of Priscilla's hands, the
pleasure of her short childish kisses and sweet breath, the
delicate texture of her warm childish-swelling breasts,
never quite left him ; and to remember Priscilla was like
remembering a fragrant English garden.   Like an English
garden, she was a little old-fashioned and self-consciously
comely, but she was so spring-like and golden.   She was
immensely important to George.   She was something he
could love unreservedly, even if it was only with the maw-
kish love of adolescence.   But far more than that temporary service, she gave him the capacity to love women,
saved him from the latent homosexuality which lurks in so
many Englishmen and makes them for ever dissatisfied
with their women.   She revealed to him—all unconsciously
—-the subtle inexhaustible joys of the tender companionate
woman's body.   Even then he felt the delicious contrast
between his male nervous muscled hands and her tender
swelling breasts, opening flowers to be held so delicately
and affectionately.   And from her too he learned that the

most satisfactory loves are those which do not last too long, those which are never made thorny with hate, and drift gently into the past, leaving behind only a fragrance—not a sting—of regret. His memories of Priscilla were few, but all roses. . . .

You see, they cannot really kill the spark if it is there, not with all their bullyings and codes and prejudices and thorough manliness. For, of course, they are not manly at all, they are merely puppets, the products of the system —if it may be dignified by that word. The truly manly ones are those who have the spark, and refuse to let it be extinguished ; those who know that the true values are the vital values, not the £ s. d. and falling-into-a-good-post and the kicked-backside-of-the-Empire values. George had already found a sort of ally in poor Mr. Slush, and an exquisite child-passion in Priscilla. But he needed men too, and was lucky enough to find them. How can one estimate what he owed to Dudley Pollak and to Donald and Tom Conington ?

Dudley Pollak was a mysterious bird. He was a married man in the late fifties, who had been to Cambridge, made the Grand Tour, lived in Paris, Berlin, and Italy, known numbers of fairly eminent people, owned a large country-house, appeared to have means, possessed very beautiful furniture and all sorts of *objets d'art*, and was a cultivated man—in most of which respects he differed exceedingly from the inhabitants of Martin's Point. Now what do you suppose was the reason why Pollak and Mrs. Pollak let their large house furnished, and spent several years in a small cottage in a rather dreary village street a couple of miles from Martin's Point ? George never knew, and nobody else ever knew

The fantastic and scandalous theories evolved by Martin's
Point to explain this mystery were amusing evidence of
the vulgar stupidity of those who formed them, and have
no other interest. The Pollaks themselves said that they
had grown tired of their large house and that Mrs. Pollak
was weary of managing servants. So simple is the truth
that this very likely was the real explanation. At any rate,
there they lived together in their cottage, crowded with
furniture and books; cooking their own meals, very often—
they were both excellent cooks—and waited on by a couple
of servants who ' lived out.' Now, although Pollak was
forty years older than George, he was in a sense the boy's
first real friend. The Pollaks had no children of their own,
which may go to explain this odd but deep friendship.

Pollak was a much wilier bird than poor old Slush. He
sized Isabel up very quickly and accurately, and just
politely refused to let her quarrel with him, and just as
politely refused to receive her. But he was so obviously
a gentleman, so obviously a man of means, that no reasonable objection could be made when he proposed to George
Augustus that ' Georgie' should come to tea once a week
and learn chess. Martin's Point was a very chessy place;
it was somehow a mark of respectability there. Before
this, George had gone to play chess with a very elderly
gentleman, who put so much of the few brains he had
into that game that he had none left for the preposterous
poems he composed, or indeed anything else. So every
Wednesday George went to tea with the Pollaks.

They always began, most honourably and scrupulously,
with a game of chess; and then they had tea; and then
they talked. Although George never suspected it until
years afterwards, Pollak was subtly educating him, at the
same time that he tried to give him the kind of sympathy
he needed. Pollak had many volumes of Anderson's

photographs, which he let George turn over while he talked negligently but shrewdly about Italian architecture, styles of painters, della Robbia work ; and Mrs. Pollak occasionally threw in some little anecdote about travel. By the example of his own rather fastidious manners he corrected schoolboy uncouthnesses. He somehow got George riding lessons, for in Pollak's days horse-riding was an indispensable accomplishment. Pollak always worked on the boy by suggestion and example, never by exhortation or patronage. He always assumed that George knew what he negligently but accurately told him. The manner in which he made George learn French was characteristic of his methods. One afternoon Pollak told a number of amusing stories about his young days in Paris, while George was looking through a volume of autograph letters of Napoleon, Talleyrand, and other Frenchmen—which, of course, he could not read. Next week, when George arrived he found Pollak reading.

' Hullo, Georgie, how are you ? Just listen to this lovely thing I 've been reading, and tell me what you think of it.'

And Pollak read, in the rather chanting voice he adopted in reading poetry, André Chénier's ' L'épi naissant mûrit, de la faux respecté.' George had to confess shamefacedly that he hadn't understood. Pollak handed him the book, one of those charming large-type Didot volumes ; but André Chénier was too much for George's public-school French.

' Oh, I *do* wish I could read it properly,' said George. ' How did you learn French ? '

' I suppose I learned it in Paris. " 'Tis pleasing to be schooled in a strange tongue by female eyes and lips," you know. But you could learn very soon if you really tried.'

' But how ?   I 've done French at school for ages, and I simply can't read it, though I 've often tried.'

' What you learn at school is only to handle the tools— you 've got to learn to use them for yourself.   You take *Les Trois Mousquetaires*, read straight through a few pages, marking the words you don't know, look them up, make lists of them, and try to remember them.   Don't linger over them too much, but try and get interested in the story.'

' But I 've read *The Three Musketeers* in English.'

' Well, try *Vingt Ans Après*.   You can have my copy and mark it.'

' No, there 's a paper-backed one at home.   I 'll use that.'

In a fortnight George had skipped through the first volume of *Vingt Ans Après*.   In a month he could read simple French prose easily.   Three months later he was able to read *La Jeune Captive* aloud to Pollak, who afterwards turned the talk on to Ronsard, and opened up yet another vista.

The Coningtons were much younger men, the elder a young barrister.   They also talked to George about books and pictures, in which their taste was more modern if less sure than Pollak's urbane Second Empire culture.   But with them George learned companionship, the fun of infinite, everlasting arguments about ' life ' and ideas, the fun of making *mots* and laughing freely.   The Coningtons were both great walkers.   George of course had the middle-class idea that five miles was the limit of human capacity for walking.   Like Pollak, the Coningtons treated him as if he were a man, assumed also that he could do what they were showing him now to do.   So when Donald Conington came down for a week-end, he assumed that George would want to walk. That day's walk had such an effect upon George that he could even remember the date, 2nd of June. It was one of those soft, cloudless days that do sometimes happen in England, even in June. They set out from Hamborough soon after breakfast and struck inland, going at a steady, even pace, talking and laughing. Donald was in excellent form, cheery and amusing, happy to be out of harness for a few hours. Four miles brought them beyond the limits of George's own wanderings, and after a couple of hours' tramp they suddenly came out on the crest of the last chalk ridge and looked over a wide, fertile plain of woodland and tilth and hop-fields, all shimmering in the warm sunlight. The curious hooked noses of oast-houses sniffed over the tops of soft round elm-clumps. They could see three church spires and a dozen hamlets. The only sound came from the larks high overhead.

'God!' exclaimed Donald in his slightly theatrical way, 'what a fair prospect!'

A fair prospect indeed, and an unforgettable moment when one comes for the first time to the crest of a hill and looks over an unknown country shimmering in the sun, with the white coiling English lanes inviting exploration. Donald set off down the hill, singing lustily: 'O mistress mine, where are you roaming?' George followed a little hesitatingly. His legs were already rather tired, it was long past eleven—how would they get back in time for lunch, and what would be said if they were late? He mentioned his fears timidly to Donald.

'What! Tired? Why, good God, man, we've only just started! We'll push on another four miles to Crockton, and have lunch in a pub. I told them we shouldn't be in until after tea.'

The rest of the day passed for George in a kind of

golden glory of fatigue and exultation. His legs ached bitterly—although they only walked about fifteen miles all told—but he was ashamed to confess his tiredness to Donald, who seemed as fresh at the end of the day as when he started. George came home with confused and happy memories—the long talk and the friendly silences, the sun's heat, a deer-park and Georgian red-brick mansion they stopped to look at, the thatched pub at Crockton where he ate bread and cheese and pickles and drank his first beer, the elaborately carved Norman church at Crockton. They sat for half an hour after lunch in the churchyard, while Donald smoked a pipe. A Red Admiral settled on a grey flat tombstone, speckled with crinkly orange and flat grey-green lichens. They talked with would-be profundity about how Plato had likened the Soul—Psyche—to a butterfly, and about death, and how one couldn't possibly accept theology or the idea of personal immortality. But they were cheerful about it— the only sensible time to discuss these agonising problems is after a pleasant meal accompanied with strong drink; and they felt so well and cheery and animal-insouciant in the warm sunlight, they didn't really believe they would ever die. In that they showed considerable wisdom; for you will remember that the wise Montaigne spent the first half of his life preparing for death, and the latter part in arguing that it is much wiser never to think about dying at all—time enough to think of *that* when it comes along.

For Donald that was just a pleasant day, which very soon took its place among the vague mists of half-memory. For George it was all extraordinarily important. For the first time he felt and understood companionship between men—the frank, unsuspicious exchange of goodwill and talk, the spontaneous collaboration of two natures. That was really the most important gain. But he also discovered the real meaning of travel. It sounds absurd to speak of a fifteen-mile walk as ' travel.' But you may go thousands of miles by train and boat between one international hotel and another, and not have the sensation of travelling at all. Travel means the consciousness of adventure and exploration, the sense of covering the miles, the ability to seize indefatigably upon every new or familiar source of delight. Hence the horror of *tourism*, which is a conventionalising, a codification, of adventure and exploration—which is absurd. Adventure is allowing the unexpected to happen to you. Exploration is experiencing what you have not experienced before. How can there be any adventure, any exploration, if you let somebody else—above all, a travel bureau—arrange everything beforehand ? It isn't seeing new and beautiful things which matters, it's seeing them for yourself. And if you want the sensation of covering the miles, go on foot. Three hundred miles on foot in three weeks will give you infinitely more sense of travel, show you infinitely more surprising and beautiful experiences, than thirty thousand miles of mechanical transport.

George did not rest until he went on a real exploration walk. He did this with Tom Conington, Donald's younger brother—and that walk also was unforgettable, though they were rained upon daily and subsisted almost entirely upon eggs and bacon, which seems to be the only food heard of in English country pubs. They took the train to Corfe Castle, and spent a day in walking over to Swanage through the half-moor, half-marsh country, with its heather and gorse and nodding white cotton-grasses. Then they went along the coast to Kimmeridge and Preston and Lulworth and Lyme Regis, sleeping in cottages and small pubs. From Lyme Regis they turned inland, and went by way of Honiton, Collumpton, Tavistock, to Dulverton and Porlock, along the north Devon coast to Bideford, and back to South Molton, where they had to take the train, since they had spent their money and had only enough to pay their fares home. The whole walk lasted less than a fortnight, but it seemed like two months. They had such a good time, jawing away as they walked, singing out of tune, finding their way on maps, getting wet through and drying themselves by taproom fires, talking to every one, farmer or labourer, who would talk to them, reading and smoking over a pint of beer after supper. And always that sense of adventure, of exploration, which urged them on every morning, even through mist and rain, and made fatigue and bad inns and muddy roads all rather fun and an experience.

One gropes very much through all these ' influences ' and ' scenes ' and fragmentary events in trying to form a picture of George in those years. For example, I found the date of the Crockton walk and a few disjointed notes about it on the back of a rough sketch of Crockton church porch. And the itinerary of the walk with Tom Conington, with a few comments, I found in the back of a volume of selected English essays, which George presumably took with him on the walk. The heart of another is indeed a dark forest, and, however much I let my imagination work over these fragments of his life, I find it hard to imagine him at that time, still harder to imagine what was going on in his mind. I imagine that he more or less adjusted himself to the public-school and home hostility ; that, as time passed and he began to make friends, he felt more confidence and happiness. Like most sensitive people he was subject to moods, affected by the weather and the

season of the year. He could pass very rapidly from a
mood of exuberant gaiety almost to despair. A chance
remark—as I myself found—was enough to effect that
unfortunate change. He had a habit always of implying
more or less than he said, of assuming that others would
always jump with the implied, not with the expressed,
thought. Similarly, he always expected the same sort of
subtle obliquity of expression in others, and very seldom
took remarks at their face value. He could never be
convinced or convince himself that there were not im-
plications under the most commonplace remark. I
suppose he had very early developed this habit of irony
as a protection and as a method of being scornful with
seeming innocence. He never got rid of it.

But for a time he was very happy. At home there was
a kind of truce—ominous, had he only known—and he
was left much to himself. Priscilla awoke and satisfied
the need for contact with the feminine, fed the awakening
sensuality. Then, when Priscilla somehow drifted away,
there was another, much slighter, more commonplace
affair with a girl named Maisie. She was a slightly
coarse, dark type, a little older than George and much
more developed. They used to meet after dark in the
steep lanes of Martin's Point, and kiss each other. George
was a little scared by the way she gobbled his mouth and
pressed herself against him ; and then felt self-reproach-
ful, thinking of Priscilla and her delicate, English-garden
fragrance. One night, Maisie drew them along a different
walk to a deserted part of the down, where a clump of
thick pines made a close shadow over coarse grass. They
had to climb up a steep hill-side.

'Oh, I'm tired,' said Maisie ; 'let's sit down.'

She lay down on the grass, and George lay beside her.

He leaned over her and felt the low warm mounds of her breasts through his thin summer shirt.

' The touch of your mouth is beautiful,' said George. ' Honey and milk is under her tongue.'

*   *   *   *   *   *   *   *   *   *

She lay passive and let him kiss her for a few minutes, and then sat up abruptly.

' I must go home.'

' Oh, but why ?   We were so happy here, and it 's still early.'

' Yes, but I promised mother I 'd be home early to-night.'

George walked back to the door of Maisie's house, and wondered why her good-night kiss was so un-tender, so perfunctory.

A few nights later George went out—on the pretext of ' mothing '—in the hope of finding Maisie.   As he came silently round a corner, he saw about twenty yards ahead, in the dusk, Maisie walking away from him with a young man of about twenty.   His arm was round her waist, and her head was resting on his shoulder as she used to rest it on George's.

*   *   *   *   *   *   *   *   *   *

When a great liner came round the Foreland, you ran to the telescope to see whether it was a P. & O., a Red Star, or a Hamburg-Amerika.   You soon got to recognise the majestic, four-funnelled *Deutschland* as she moved rapidly up or down the Channel.   The yellow-funnelled boats for Ostend, the white-funnelled boats for Calais and Boulogne, were daily events, hardly to be noted—and yet how they seemed to lure one to that unknown life across the narrow seas ! On clear days you could see the faint shining of the cliffs of France. On foggy nights the prolonged anapaest of the Foreland Lightship foghorn answered the hoarse spondees of the passing ships, groping their way up Channel. Even on the most rainy or most moonlit night the flash of the lighthouse made dabs of yellow light on the walls of George's bedroom. There were no nightingales at Martin's Point, but morning and evening thrushes and blackbirds.

Hamborough was so different, lying off the chalk downs on the edge of the salt marshes, the desolate, silent, unresponsive salt marshes, so gorgeous at sunset. The tidal river ran turbid and level with its banks, or deep between walls of sinister mud. Little flocks of fleet-winged grey-white birds—called ' oxey-birds '—flickered rapidly away in front of you on sickle-moon wings. A brown-sailed barge, far inland, seemed to be gliding over-land through the flat, green-brown marsh land. Behind, far across the flat, desolate ex-sea-bottom ran the old coastline, and on a bluff stood the solid ruins of a Roman fort. ' Pe-e-e-wit,' said the plunging plovers, ' pee-e-ee-wit.' No other sound. The white clouds, dappled English clouds, moved so silently over the cool blue English skies ; such faint blue, even on what the English call a ' hot ' day.

You went to the marshes by way of the Barbican, the Barbican through which the old English kings and knights had ridden with their men-at-arms, when they made one of their innumerable descents on more civilised France. There stood the mediæval Barbican, on the verge of the commonplace little money-grubbing town, like a stranded vestige from some geological past. What was the Barbican to early twentieth-century Hamborough ? An obstacle to the new motor road, whose abolition was always being discussed in the Town Council, and whose destruction was only postponed because the thickness of the walls made it too expensive. On the other side you walked out into flat, fertile country, past almshouses and the hoary stone-mullioned Elizabethan Grammar School, over the level crossing, to Saxon Friedasburg, where tradition said a temple to Freya had once stood. How silver-grey the distant sea-fringe, how silver-grey the lines of rippling poplars ! How warmly golden—like Priscilla —the wheat-fields under the late August afternoon sunshine !

These are the gods, the gods who must endure for ever, or as long as man endures, the gods whom the perverse, blood-lustful, torturing Oriental myths cannot kill. Poseidon, the sea-god, who rules his grey and white steeds, so gentle and playful in his rare moods of tranquillity, so savage and destructive in his rage. With a clutch of his hand he crumples the wooden beams or steel plates of the wave-wanderers, with a thrust of his elbow he hurls them to destruction on the hidden sandbank or the ruthless sharp-toothed rocks. Selene, the moon-goddess, who flies so swiftly through the breaking clouds of the departing storm, or hangs so motionless-white, so womanly-waiting, in the cobalt night-sky among her attendant stars. Phoebus, who scorns these silvery-grey northern lands, but whose golden light is so welcome when it comes. Demeter, who ripens the wheat and plumps the juicy fruit and sets cordial bitterness in the hop and trails ragged flower and red hip and haw along the hedges. And then the lesser humbler gods—must there not be gods of sunrise and twilight, of bird-singing and midnight silence, of ploughing and harvesting, of the shorn fields and the young green springing grass, gods of lazy cattle and the uneasily bleating flocks and of the wild

creatures—(hedgehogs and squirrels and rabbits, and
their enemies the weasels)—tenuous Ariel demi-gods of
the trembling poplars and the many-coloured flowers and
the speckled fluttering butterflies ? In ever-increasing
numbers the motor-cars clattered and hammered along
the dusty roads ; the devils of golf leaped on the acres and
made them desolate ; sport and journalism and gentility
made barren men's lives. The gods shrank away, hid
shyly in forgotten nooks, lurked unsuspected behind
bramble and thorn. Where were their worshippers ?
Where were their altars ? Rattle of the motors, black
smoke of the railways. One—perhaps only one—wor-
shipper was left them. One alone saw the fleet limbs
glancing through the tree-trunks, saw the bright faun-eyes
peering anxiously from behind the bushes. Hamadryads,
fauns, do not fly from me ! I am not one of ' them,' one
of the perverse life-torturers. I know you are there ; come
to me, and talk with me ! Stay with me, stay with me !

Then the blow fell.

' WHAT can have happened ? What can have happened ? O my God, what can have happened ? '

Isabel paced up and down the room, uttering this and kindred exclamations to nobody in particular, while an outwardly calm, inwardly very much perturbed George silently echoed the question. George Augustus had gone to London on his usual weekly trip, and as usual George had met the six o'clock train. No George Augustus. He met the seven-ten, the eight-fifty, and the eleven-five, the last train : and still no George Augustus. No telegram, no message. A feeling of impending calamity hung over the house that night, and there was not much sleep for Isabel and George. Next morning a long rambling letter, emotional and vague, arrived from George Augustus. The gist was that he was ruined, and in flight from his creditors.

It was a bitter enough pill for George, bitterer still for Isabel. She had schemed and boosted George Augustus for years, she thought they were well off and getting better off. And she had taken pride in it as her own work. She had George Augustus so much under her thumb that whatever he did was through her influence. But the very perfection of her system was its ruin. He was so afraid of her that he dared not confess when a speculation went wrong. To keep up the standard of expense he began to mortgage ; to redeem the situation he plunged deeper into speculation and neglected his practice. Rumours began to get about. Then suddenly he was taken with panic, and fled. Later investigation showed that his affairs were not so compromised as he had imagined ; but the sudden mad flight ruined everything.

In a day the Winterbournes dropped from comparative affluence to comparative poverty.

The effect on George was really rather disastrous. After the almost sordid distress of his early adolescence, he had succeeded in saving the spark, had built up a life for himself, had created a positive happiness. But all that rested, in fact, on the family money. The distrust of himself and others which had gradually disappeared, the sense of suspicion and frustration, came flooding back with renewed bitterness. And the whole calamity was aggravated by circumstances of peculiar and unnecessary suffering, which made distrust and bitterness not unjustifiable. Demented apparently by that madness which afflicts those whom the gods wish to destroy, George Augustus had ' had a little talk ' on the subject of a career with the boy not three months before, when he must have known he was hopelessly involved.

' Now, Georgie, you have only a few months longer, and you will be leaving school. You must think of a career in life. Have you thought about it ? '

' Yes, father.'

' That 's right. And what career do you want to take up ? '

' I want to be a painter.'

' I rather expected you 'd say that. But you must remember that you can hardly expect to make money by painting. Even if you have the talent, which I 'm sure you have, it takes many years to establish a reputation, and still more years before you can hope to make an adequate income.'

' Yes, I know that. But I 'm convinced that if I had a small income and could do what I wanted, I should be far

happier than if I made a great deal of money doing what
I hated.'

' Well, my boy, I 'm really rather glad that you don't
take the purely money point of view. But think it over.
If you take your examinations and qualify, there is a
regularly established practice in which you can take your
place as my partner and, in due course, as my successor.
Think it over for a few months. And if you finally decide
to take the course you mention, I daresay I can allow you
two or three hundred a year, which will be four hundred
when I die.'

Now all this was very fatherly and kindly and sensible.
In an outburst of quite genuine affection and gratitude
George protested first of all that he could not bear to think
of his father's dying and that it was odious to think of
profiting by his death.

' But,' he added, ' I am quite determined to be a painter
in spite of everything. If you can help me as you say, it
will all be perfect.'

Nothing more was said on the subject, but in the following weeks George drew and painted hard, went twice to
London to look at the galleries and get materials, and
thought he was making progress. But what strange weakness permitted George Augustus to yield to the cruelty of
raising these hopes which he must have known would be
speedily wrecked ? The thought of this was constantly
in George's mind, as he moved about silently, rather
scared, in the morning hours following the receipt of
the letter. It was a problem he never solved, but
the incident did not increase his trust in the world or
himself.

Other incidents confirmed this mood. Both Isabel and
George Augustus rather pushed George forward to take
the brunt of the calamity. Isabel's first suggestion to

George was that he should go as a grocer's errand-boy at three shillings a week, a proposition which George indignantly and properly rejected. Whereupon she called him a parasite and a graceless spendthrift. Probably the suggestion was only hysteria, but it hit hard and rankled. Then, it was George do this, and George do that. It was George who had to interview insolent tradesmen and creditors, and plead for further credit and 'time.' It was George who recovered £90 in gold which had been stolen by the office boy, and was refunded. It was George who was sent to persuade his father to come back and face out the storm. It was George who was made to go and collect rents from suspicious and uneasy tenants. It was George who had to see solicitors and try to get a grasp of the situation. They even accepted his offer of the few pounds (birthday gifts saved up) which he had in the Post Office Savings Bank. Rather a shock for a boy not seventeen, who had been living an *exalté* inner life, and who had been led to suppose that his material future was assured. It is not wholly surprising that he was very unhappy, a bit resentful, and that his mistrust became permanent, his modesty diffidence.

Things went on in this joyless way for about a year. 'Disgrace' was avoided, but it was obvious that the Winterbourne opulence was gone, and George Augustus had lost his nerve. It was from this period that the beginnings of his subsequent conversion dated. In defeat he returned to the beliefs of childhood, but some latent unrecognised hostility to the influence of dear Mamma finally led him to the form of Christianity most opposed to hers. As for George, he brooded a great deal and oscillated between moods of hope and exultation and moods of profound depression. They moved nearer to

London, and he tried, with very little success, to sell some of his paintings. They were too ambitious and too youthful, with no commercial value. He was all the time uneasily conscious that he ought to 'get out' and that his family were anxious for him to 'do something.' Kind friends wrote proposing the most dreary and humiliating jobs they could think of. Even Priscilla—a bitter blow—thought that 'George should do something *at once*, and in a few years might be earning two pounds a week as a clerk.' Then George made the acquaintance of a journalist, a very uneducated but extremely kindly and good-natured man. Thomas had some sort of sub-editorship in Fleet Street, and generously offered to allow George to do some minor reporting for him, an offer which was jumped at. George did his first job—which was passed —and returned home, naturally very late, in a glow of virtuous exultation, thinking how he would surprise his parents next morning with the news, like a good little boy in a story-book. The surprise, however, was his. He was met at the door by an angry Isabel, who, without awaiting his explanation, demanded to know what he meant by coming home at that hour, and accused him of 'going with a vile woman.' George was too disgusted to make any reply, and went to bed. Next morning there was a glorious row, in which Isabel played the part of a broken-hearted mother and George Augustus came out very strong as a *père noble* of the Surrey melodrama brand. George was upset, but his contempt kept him cool. George Augustus was perorating :

'If you continue in this way you will break your mother's heart ! '

It was so ludicrous—poor old George Augustus !—that George couldn't help laughing. George Augustus raised his hand in a noble gesture of paternal malediction :

' Leave this house !   And do not return to it until you have learned to apologise for your behaviour.'

' You mean it ? '

' I solemnly mean it.'

' Right.'

George went straight upstairs and packed his few clothes in a suit-case, asked if he might have the volume of Keats, and left in half an hour—with elevenpence in his pocket, humming :

' Now of my threescore years and ten, twenty will not come again.'

So that was that.

END OF PART I

PART II

PART II

1

BANK pass-books and private account-books are revealing documents, strangely neglected by biographers. One of the most useful things to know about any hero is the extent of his income, whether earned or unearned, whether crescendo or diminuendo. Complicated *états d'âme* are the luxury of leisured opulence. Those who have to earn their living must accept Appearances as Reality, and have little time for metaphysical woes and passions. I once thought of beginning this section with an accurate facsimile of George's private account, and pass-books. But that would be *vérisme*. It is enough to say that his unearned income was nil, and his earned income small but crescendo. Like most people who are too high-spirited to work for stated hours at a weekly wage, he drifted into journalism, which may be briefly but accurately defined as the most degrading form of that most degrading vice, mental prostitution. Its resemblance to the less reprehensible form is striking. Only the more fashionable cocottes of the dual trade make a reasonable income. The similarity between the conditions of the two parallel prostitutions becomes still more remarkable when you reflect that on the physical side you pretend to be a milliner, or a masseuse, or a clergyman's daughter, or a lady of quality, or even a lady journalist in need of a little aid for which you are prepared to make suitable acknowledgment; and on the mental side you pretend to be a poet, or an expert in something, or a lady of quality, or a duke. Both require suppleness in a supreme degree, and in both the fatal handicaps are honesty, modesty, and independence.

All of which George discovered very rapidly, and acted accordingly. But his powers of simulation were inadequate, and consequently he failed at all times to conceal the fact that he possessed some vitality and beliefs, and held to them. This, of course, for a long time prevented his obtaining work from any but crank periodicals, of which London before the war possessed about three, which believed in allowing contributors to say what they thought. Needless to say, they have since perished ; and London journalism is now one compact sun of sweetness and light. If this, or indeed anything, much mattered, one might be tempted to deplore it.

In the course of his *naïf* peregrinations George became temporarily acquainted with numerous personages, whom he classified as morons, abject morons, and queer-Dicks. The abject morons were those editors and journalists who sincerely believed in the imbecilities they perpetrated, virtuous apprentices gone to the devil, honest boot-blacks out of a job. The morons were those who knew better but pretended not to, and who by long dabbling in pitch had become pitchy. The queer-Dicks were more or less honest cranks, or at least possessed so much vanity and obstinacy that they seemed honest. After a few vague and awkward struggles, George found himself limited to the queer-Dicks. Of these there were three, whom for convenience sake I shall label Shobbe, Bobbe, and Tubbe. Mr. or Herr Shobbe ran a literary review, one of those 'advanced' reviews beloved by the English, which move rapidly forward with a crab-like motion. Herr Shobbe was a very great man. Comrade Bobbe ran a Socialist weekly which was subsidised by a demented eugenist and a vegetarian Theosophist. Since Marxian economics, eugenics, pure food, and theosophy did not wholly fill its columns, the organ of the intellectual and wage-weary worker permitted regular comments on art and literature. And since none of the directors of the journal knew anything whatever about these subjects, they occasionally and by accident allowed them to be treated by some one with ideas and enthusiasm. Comrade Bobbe was a very great man. As for Mr. Waldo Tubbe, who hailed (why 'hailed'?) from the Middle Western districts of the United States, he was an exceedingly ardent and patriotic British Tory, standing for Royalism in Art, Authority in Politics, and Classicism in Religion. Unfortunately, there was no dormant peerage in the family; otherwise he would certainly have spent all his modest patrimony in endeavouring to become Lord Tubbe. Since he was an unshakeable Anglo-Catholic, there were no hopes of a Papal Countship; and Tory Governments are proverbially shabby in their treatment of even the most distinguished among their intellectual supporters. Consequently, all Mr. Waldo Tubbe could do in that line was to hint at his aristocratic English ancestry, to use his (possibly authentic) coat-of-arms on his cutlery, stationery, toilet articles, and book-plates, and know only the 'best' people. How George ever got to know him is a mystery; still more how he came to write for a periodical which once advertised that its list of subscribers included four dukes, three marquesses, and eleven earls. The only explanation is that Mr. Tubbe's Americanised Toryism was a bit more lively than the native brand, or that he leaned so very far to the extreme Right that without knowing it he sometimes tumbled into the verge of the extreme Left. But, in any case, Mr. Waldo Tubbe was also a very great man.

Upon the charity of these three gentlemen our hero chiefly but not extravagantly subsisted, skating indeed upon very thin ice in his relations with them, and expending treasures of diplomacy and dissimulation which might have been employed in the service of his Country. It subsequently transpired (why ' transpired ' ?) that his Country did not want his brains, but his blood.

Sunday in London. In the City, nuts, bolts, infinite curious pieces of odd metal, embedded in the black shiny roads, frozen rivers of ink, may be examined without danger. The peace of commerce which passes all desolation. Puritan fervour relapsed to negative depression. Gigantic wings of Ennui folded irresistibly over millions. Vast trails of automobiles hopelessly hooting to escape. Epic melancholy of deserted side-streets where the rhythmic beat of a horse's hoofs is an adagio of despair. Horrors of Gunnersbury. The spleen of the railway line between Turnham Green and Hammersmith, the villainous sordidness of Raynes Park, the ennui which always vibrates with the waiting train at Gloucester Road station, emerge triumphant when the Lord is at rest and possess the streets. The rain is one melancholy, and the sun another. The supreme insult of pealing bells morning and evening. Dearly beloved brethren, miserable sinners, stand up, stand up for Jesus. Who will deliver us, who will deliver us from the Christians ? O Lord Jesus, come quickly, and get it over !

It was a merry Sunday evening of merry England in the month of March 1912. After a long day of unremitting but not very remunerative toil, George had gone to call on his friend, Mr. Frank Upjohn. The word ' friend ' is here, as nearly always, inexact, if by friend is meant one who feels for another a disinterested affection unaccompanied by sexual desire. (Friendship accompanied by sexual desire is love, the phoenix or unicorn of passions.) In the case of George and Mr. Upjohn there was at least a

truce to the instinctive hostility and grudging which
human beings almost invariably feel for one another.
Ties of mutual self-interest bound them. George made
jokes and Mr. Upjohn laughed at them : and vice versa.
Mr. Upjohn desired to make George a disciple, and
George was not averse from making use of Mr. Upjohn.
Mutual admiration, implied if not expressed and perhaps
not wholly insincere, enabled them to form a small protective nucleus against the oceanic indifference of mankind, and thus feel superior to it. They ate together,
and even lent each other small sums of money without
security. The word ' friend ' is therefore justified *à
peu près*.

Needless to say, Mr. Upjohn was a very great man. He
was a Painter. Since he was destitute of any intrinsic and
spontaneous originality, he strove much to be original,
and invented a new school of painting every season. He
first created a sensation with his daring and brilliant
'****** ** * ********** *******,' which was denounced
in no unmeasured terms by the Press, **** ****** ***
*** ****** ** ****** ****** *** *** **********
********** ** *** ****. ' The Blessed Damozel in
Hell ' passed almost unnoticed, when fortunately the
model most unjustly obtained an affiliation order against
Mr. Upjohn and thus drew attention to a neglected
masterpiece, which was immediately bought by a man
who had made a fortune in ******** ****** *****.
Mr. Upjohn then became aware of the existence of modern
French art. One season he painted in gorgeous Pointil-
liste blobs, the next in monotone Fauviste smears, then
in calamitous Futuriste accidents of form and colour. At
this moment he was just about to launch the Suprematist
movement in painting, to which he hoped to convert
George, or at any rate to get him to write an article about

I

it.   Suprematist painting, which has now unfortunately
gone out of fashion, was, as its name implies, the supreme
point of modern art.   Mr. Upjohn produced two pictures
in illustration (the word is perhaps inaccurate) of his
theories.   One was a beautiful scarlet whorl on a background of the purest flake white.   The other at first sight
appeared to be a brood of bulbous yellow chickens, with
thick elongated necks, aimlessly scattered over a grey-
green meadow ; but on closer inspection the chickens
turned out to be conventionalised phalluses.   The first
was called Decomposition-Cosmos, and the second Op. 49,
Piano.

Mr. Upjohn turned on both electric lights in his studio
for George to study these interesting productions, at which
our friend gazed with a feeling of baffled perplexity and
the agonised certainty that he would have to say something about them, and that what he would say would
inevitably be wrong.   Fortunately, Mr. Upjohn was
extremely vain and highly nervous.   He stood behind
George, coughing and jerking himself about agitatedly.

' What I mean to say is,' he said, puncturing his dis-
course with coughs, ' there you 've got it.'

' Yes, yes, of course.'

' What I mean is, you 've got precise expression of
precise emotion.'

' Just what I was going to say.'

' You see, when you 've got that, what I mean is, you 've
got something.'

' Why, of course ! '

' You see, what I mean to say is, if you get two or three
intelligent people to *see* the thing, then you 've got it.   I
mean you won't get those damned block-headed sons of
bitches like Quijasso and Caesar Frank to see it, I mean,
it simply smashes them, you see.'

' Did you expect them to ? '

' You see, what you 've got is complete originality *and* The Tradition.   One doesn't worry about the hacks, you see, but what I mean to say, one does *mildly* suppose Quijasso had a few gleams of intelligence, but what I mean is they won't *take* anything new.'

' I get the originality, of course, but I admit I don't quite see the traditional side of the movement.'

Mr. Upjohn sighed pettishly and waved his head from side to side in commiserating contempt.

' Of course, you *wouldn't*.   What intelligence you have was ruined by your lack of education, and your native obtuseness makes you instinctively prefer the academic. I mean, can't you SEE that the proportions of Decomposition-Cosmos are exactly those of the Canopic vase in the Filangieri Museum at Naples ? '

' How could I see that,' said George, rather annoyed, ' since I 've never been to Naples ? '

' That 's what I mean to say,' exclaimed Mr. Upjohn triumphantly, ' you simply have no education *what-so-ever* ! '

' Well, but what about the other ? ' said George, desiring to be placable; ' is that in the Canopic vase tradition ? '

' Christ-in-petticoats, NO !   I thought even you 'd see *that*.   What I mean is, can't you *see* it ? '

' They might be free adaptations of Greek vase painting ? ' said George tentatively, hoping to soothe this excitable and irritated genius.   Mr. Upjohn flung his palette knife on the floor.

' You 're *too* stupid, George.   What I mean is, the proportion and placing and colour-values are exactly in the best tradition of American-Indian blankets, and what I mean is, when you 've got that, well, I mean, you 've got something ! '

' Of course, of course, it *was* stupid of me not to see.
Forgive me, I 've been working at hack articles all day, and
my mind 's a bit muzzy.'

' I mildly supposed so ! '

And Mr. Upjohn, with spasmodic movements, jerked
the two easels round to the wall.   There was a short pause
in the conversation.   Mr. Upjohn irritatedly cast himself
at full length upon a sofa, and spasmodically ate candied
apricots.   He placed them in his mouth with his fore-
finger and thumb, holding his elbow at an angle of ninety
degrees to his body, with his chin far extended, and
bit them savagely in half.   George watched this impressive
and barbaric spectacle with the interest of one who at last
discovers the meaning of the mysterious rite of Urim and
Thummim.   A timid effort at making conversation was
repelled by Mr. Upjohn, with a gesture which George
interpreted as meaning that Mr. Upjohn required complete silence to digest and sweeten with candied apricots
the memory of George's treasonable obtuseness.   Suddenly George started, for Mr. Upjohn, after coughing
once or twice, swung himself from his couch with incredible swiftness, hawked vigorously, flung open a
window with unnecessary violence and spat voluminously
into the street.   He then turned and said calmly :

' You 'd better come along to fat Shobbe's.'

George, who was young enough to enjoy going to mis-
cellaneous parties, gratefully acquiesced ; and was still
further gratified by being allowed to witness the strange
and complex ablutions performed by Mr. Upjohn from
a wash-basin startlingly concealed in a veneered mahogany
tallboy.

Mr. Upjohn was evidently a very clean man, at least in
those portions of his body exposed to the public gaze.
He washed and rinsed his face thoroughly, brushed his

teeth until George apprehended lest the bristles be worn
to the bone, gargled and spat freely. He soaped and
pumiced his hands, which were large, yellow, and slightly
spatulate ; and excavated his nails with singular industry
and pertinacity. He then sat down before a folding table-
mirror in three parts, which reflected both profiles as well
as full-face, and combed and brushed and re-brushed and
re-combed his coarse hay-like hair until it crackled with
induced electricity. When Mr. Upjohn judged that
hygiene and beauty-culture had received their full due,
he arrayed himself in a clean collar, a tie of remarkable
lustre and size, and a narrow-waisted rather long coat
which, taken in conjunction with the worn but elegant
peg-top trousers he had on, gave him a pleasantly rake-
helly and Regency look. This singular scene, which
occupied the better part of an hour, was conducted by
Mr. Upjohn with great gravity, varied by the emission
of a singular and discordant chant or hum, and wild
petulant oaths whenever any object of the toilet or of
his apparel did not instantly present itself to his hand.
Oddly enough, Mr. Upjohn was not a sodomist. He was
a professedly ardent admirer of what our ignorant fore-
fathers called the soft sex. Mr. Upjohn often asserted
that after the immense toils of Suprematist painting
nothing could rest him but the presence of several beautiful women. While gallantly and probably necessarily
discreet as to his conquests, he was always prepared to
talk about love, and to give subtle erotic advice, which led
any man who had actually lain with a woman to suspect
that Mr. Upjohn was at best a fumbler and probably still
a virgin.

Mr. Upjohn then endued a very Regency thin grey
overcoat, stuck a long ebony cane with no handle under
his left armpit, tossed a soft grey hat rakishly on to his

hair, and made for the door. George followed, half-impressed, half-amused by this childish swagger and self-conscious bounce.

In the street the Sabbath ennui of London emerged from its lair like a large, dull grey octopus, and shot stealthy feelers of depression at them. Mr. Upjohn, safe as Achilles in the Stygian dip of his conceit, strode along energetically with an inward feeling that he had gone one better on James McNeill Whistler. The boredom of Mr. Upjohn came from within, not from without. He was so absorbed in Mr. Upjohn that he rarely noticed what was going on about him.

George fought at the monster and plunged desperately into talk.

' What about this coal strike ?   Will it ruin the country as the papers say ?   Isn't it a foolish thing on both sides ? '

This strike was George's first introduction to the reality of the 'social problem' and the bitter class-hatred which smoulders in England and at times bursts into fierce crises of hatred, restrained only by that mingling of fear and 'decency' which composes the servile character of the British working-man.

' Well, what I mean to say is,' said Mr. Upjohn, who very rarely managed to say what he meant but always meant to say something original and startling, ' it ain't our affair.   But what I mean is, if the miners get more money it 'll be all the better for us.   They 're more likely to buy our pictures than sons of bitches like Bond and Pittsquith.'

George was a bit staggered at this.   In the first place, he had been looking at the problem from a national, not a personal, point of view.   And, in the second place, he knew just a little about working-men and their conditions. He could not see how five shillings a week more would

convert the miners to collecting the Suprematist school
of painting, or make them abandon their cultivated
amusements of coursing, pigeon-flying, gambling, wife-
beating, and drinking. But Mr. Upjohn delivered his
obiter dicta with so much aplomb that a boy of twenty
might be excused for failing to see their complete
absurdity.

They were walking up Church Street, Kensington, that
dismal communication trench which links the support line
of Kensington High Street with the front line of Notting
Hill Gate. How curious are cities, with their intricate
trench systems and perpetual warfare, concealed but as
deadly as the open warfare of armies! We live in
trenches, with flat revetments of house-fronts as parapet
and parados. The warfare goes on behind the house-
fronts—wives with husbands, children with parents, em-
ployers with employed, tradesmen with tradesmen,
banker with lawyer, and the triumphal doctor rooting out
life's casualties. Desperate warfare—for what? Money
as the symbol of power; power as the symbol or affirma-
tion of existence. Throbbing warfare of men's cities!
As fierce and implacable and concealed as the desperate
warfare of plants and the hidden carnage of animals. We
walk up Church Street. Up the communication trench.
We cannot see 'over the top,' have no vista of the immense
no-man's-land of London's roofs. We cannot pierce
through the house-fronts. What is going on behind
those dingy, unpierceable house-fronts? What tortures,
what contests, what incests, what cruelties, what sacrifice,
what horror, what sordid emptiness? We cannot pierce
through the pavement and Belgian blocks, see the sub-
terranean veins of electric cables, the arteries of gas- and
water-mains, the viscera of underground railways. We

cannot feel the water filtering through London clay ; do not perceive the relics of ruined Londons waiting for archæologists from the antipodes ; do not see, far, far down, the fossiled bones of extinct animals and their coprolites. Here in Notting Hill the sabre-toothed tiger roared and savagely devoured its victims ; the huge-horned deer darted in terror ; wolves howled ; the brown bear preyed ; overhead by day screamed the eagles and by night flitted huge bats. Mysterious forest murmurs, abrupt yells and threatening growls, and the amorous hatred of female beasts, were vocal when the Channel was the Rhine's estuary.

'Time passes,' said George ; 'what do we know of Time ? Prehistoric beasts, like the ichthyosaurus and ***** ********, have laired and copulated and brought forth . . .'

A motor-bus roared by, like a fabulous noisy red ox with fiery eyes and a luminous interior, quenching his words.

'Eh ?' said Mr. Upjohn. '***** !'

'Now, look at these simian bipeds,' George pursued, pointing to an inoffensive pair of lovers and a suspicious cop, 'more foul, more deadly, more incestuously blood-lustful . . .'

'You see, what I mean is, nothing matters to these people but our conversation. . . . Now, what I mean is, you get fat Shobbe to let you write an article on me and Suprematism.'

'We should go to the Zoo more often, and watch the monkeys. The chimpanzee leaps with the dexterity of a politician. The Irish-looking ourang smokes his pipe as placidly as a Camden Town murderer. The purple-bottomed mandrils on heat will initiate you into love. And the perpetual chatter of the small monkeys—how

like ourselves ! What ecstatic clicking about nothing !
Go to the ape, thou poet.'

Mr. Upjohn laughed abruptly and spat with a raucous
cough :

' An old idea, but what 's it got to do with *le mouve-
ment* ? Still, what I mean is, I might do something with
it. . . .'

Poor old George ! He was a bloody fool. He never
learned how fatally unwise it is to express any sort of an
idea to a brother—still less to a sister—artist.

Mr. Upjohn discoursed on Suprematism and himself.

At Notting Hill Gate, George halted. The Sabbath
ennui shot its tentacles at him, and enlaced his spirit,
dragging him down into the whirlpool of wanhope. Why
go on ? Why affront the veiled hostility of people ?
Why suffer those eyes to search and those nimble unerring tongues to wound ? Oh, wrap oneself in solitude,
like an armoured shroud, and bend over the dead words
of a dead language ! A simian biped ! O gods, gods !
And Plato talks of Beauty.

' Come along,' shouted Mr. Upjohn, a few paces ahead,
' this way. Holland Park. Old Shobbe 'll be waiting
for me in that mob. What I mean is, he knows I 'm the
only other intelligent person in London.'

George still hesitated. He sank deeper in the mael-
strom of unintelligible and causeless despair. Why go
on ? The adolescent love of death and suicide—corollary
to youth's vitality and vivid energy—swept over him in
choking waves. To cease upon the midnight with no
pain. . .

' I think I shan't come,' he shouted after the retreating
Mr. Upjohn.

Mr. Upjohn hurried back and seized George's arm :

' What 's the matter with you ?   The best way to get an article out of Shobbe is to go and see him on his Sunday evenings.   Come on.   We shall be late.'

No Euripidean chorus uttered gnomic reflections on the inevitable and irresistible power of Ananke, the Destiny which is above the gods.   No bright god warned him, no oracular voice spoke to him.   Conflict of freewill and destiny !   But is there a conflict ?   Whether we move or are still, whether we go to the right or the left, hesitate or rush blindly forward, the thread is inexorably spun. Ananke, Ananke.

George yielded reluctantly to the tug at his arm
' All right, I 'll come."

As they were shown into Mr. Shobbe's large studio they encountered an indescribable babble of human voices, which gave strange point to George's zoological remarks, since it sounded as if all the macaws at the Zoo had got into the monkey-house to argue with its inhabitants about theology. Mr. Shobbe's studio (or ' stew-joe,' as his humbler Cockney contributors called it) was already dim with cigarette smoke. The excited and elevated babble of voices was due to the fact that this was one of Mr. Shobbe's rare caviar and champagne evenings, and not one of the ordinary beer and ham-sandwich *débâcles*. George and Mr. Upjohn were still in the doorway, hidden by the opening door, when a couple of champagne corks popped. George noticed a look of horror and perplexity, mingled with the satisfaction always produced by the prospect of free alcohol, in Mr. Upjohn's countenance. George wondered vaguely why, and followed the ebullient swagger of Mr. Upjohn into the large room. It was not until long afterwards that he realised the cause of this rapid and subtle flash of horror in Mr. Upjohn. The champagne and caviar evenings were reserved for the ' better ' contributors to, and the wealthier guarantors of, Mr. Shobbe's periodical. Upjohn was County and Cambridge, with a small income and prospects of a large inheritance from a senile aunt—he was therefore one of the ' better ' contributors. George, on the other hand, was merely middle-class, talented, and penniless. Mr. Upjohn had thus committed a social error of hair-raising enormity by bringing George to the champagne reception under the false impression that it was merely a beer ' do ' for the common mob.

With genial bonhomie Mr. Shobbe greeted in Mr.
Upjohn the potential inheritance from the senile aunt.
Upon George he turned a coldly languid blue eye, and for
a moment lent him a hand even limper, flabbier, and
clammier than usual.   George noticed the difference, but
ingenuously assumed that it was because he was younger
than Mr. Upjohn and incapable of producing ' ****** **
* ********** ******* ' or the doctrines of Suprematism.
But Mr. Upjohn, with more acute social ambitions, was
aware of his *gaffe*.   He mumbled his apology, which was
almost lost in the surrounding babble :

' Brought 'm 'long discuss 'n article on Me 'n S'prem-
atism.'

Mr. Shobbe only half-heard, and nodded vaguely.
The slight awkwardness of the situation was ended by the
appearance of Mrs. Shobbe, who greeted them both ; and
they passed into the room.   George attributed the feeling
of strain to his own shyness and aloofness.   He was still
naïf enough to suppose that people are welcomed for their
own sake.

In justice to the distinguished gathering in Mr. Shobbe's
studio (two 'social' journalists were present) it must be
said that the babble and the excitement were not wholly
due to the champagne.   Pre-war London was comparatively sober.   Numbers of women did not even drink
at all, and cocktails and communal copulation had not
then been developed to their present state of intensity.
Whether the art of scandal-mongering has suffered by
this new social activity is hard to say, but as ever it remains
the chief diversion of the British intelligentsia.   Serious
conversation is of course impossible, on account of the
paper-pirates who are always hovering about to snatch up
an idea.   One definite improvement is that the *bon mot*,

the *recherché* pun, the intentional witticism, are definitely discouraged. Indeed, one of the brightest of the post-war reputations was created by a young man who had the self-restraint to sit through forty-five literary parties without saying a word. This frightened everybody so much that when this modern lay Trappist departed you heard on all sides :

' Brilliant young man.'

' Extraordinarily clever.'

' I hear he 's writing a book on metaphysics in the Stone Age.'

' No, really ? '

' They say he 's the greatest living authority on pre-Columbian literature ! '

' How quite too marvellous.'

But in those distant pre-war days people strove to chatter themselves into notice through a chaos of witticisms. On this particular evening, however, witticisms were in the background, for an event had occurred to stagger this small cosmos of affectation into sincerity. With the exception of George (who was too young and unknown to matter) and a few women, almost everybody present had been connected with a publishing firm which had suddenly gone bankrupt. On Mr. Shobbe's recommendation some of his wealthier guarantors had put money into the firm ; the painters were ' doing ' illustrated editions or writing books on the Renaissance artists still popular in those unenlightened days ; and the writers had received contracts for an almost unlimited number of works. Money had been lavishly spent and some rather amusing things had been begun. Then suddenly the publisher vanished with the lady typist-secretary and the remainder of the cash. Hence the excited babble.

George stood, a little dazed, beside a small group of

youngish men and women. A dark, rather sinister-looking young man kept saying :

'Le crapule !   Ah ! le crapule ! '

George wondered vaguely who was a crapule and why, and half-listened to the conversation.

'He was paying me three hundred a year and . . .'

'My last novel did so well that he gave me a five years' contract and an advance of . . .'

'Yes, and I was getting twenty per cent. . . .'

'Yes, but do let me tell you this.   Shobbe says that the lawyers told him four thousand pounds of the money came from the diocesan funds of . . .'

'Yes, I know.   Shobbe told us.'

'Le crapule ! '

'What 'll the archbishop say ? '

'Oh, they 'll smother that up.'

'Yes, but look here—do shut up for a minute, Bessie—what I want to know is, how do we stand ?   What about our copyrights ?   Shobbe told me the legal position is . . .'

'Hang the legal position.   What do we get out of it ? '

'Crapule ! '

'Nothing, probably.   *You* won't get much, anyhow. He hadn't even published your book, and I was to get three hundred a year and . . .'

'It isn't so much the money I mind as having my book off the market when it was going so well—did you see the long article on me in last week's . . .'

'Crapule ! '

George glanced almost affectionately at the sinister-looking young man.   It struck him that the repeated 'crapule' was addressed as much to his present audience as to the unknown perpetrator of these calamities.   At that

moment Mr. Upjohn came along, and George took him
aside.

'I say, Frank, what 's all this talk about ? '

'Dear Bertie has eloped with Olga and the cash.'

'Dear Bertie ? Oh, you mean . . But the firm
will go on, won't it ? '

'Go on the streets. You see, there isn't a cent left.
What I mean is, I shall have to find some one else to do
my Suprematist book. What I mean to say is, Bertie
had a glimmering of intelligence . .'

'Who 's Olga ? '

But at that moment a lady with two unmarried daughters
and private information about the senile aunt's fortune
plunged sweetly at Mr. Upjohn.

'Oh, Mr. Upjohn, how *nice* to see you again ! How
are you ? '

'Mildly surviving.'

'You *never* came to my last at-home. Now you *must*
come and have dinner next week. Sir George was *so*
much impressed last week by what you said about the new
school of painting you have founded—what *is* the name ?
I 'm so *stupid* about remembering names.'

Mr. Upjohn introduced them :

'Lady Carter—George Winterbourne. He 's a painter
—of sorts.'

Lady Carter took in George at a glance—shabby
clothes, old tie carelessly knotted, hair too long, abstracted
gaze, poor, too young anyway—and was politely insolent.
After a few words, she and Mr. Upjohn walked away.
She pretended to be amused by Mr. Upjohn's conversation.

George went over to the table and took a sandwich and
a glass of champagne. The ceaseless babble of petty talk

about petty interests irritated and bored him. He felt isolated and hate-obstinate. So this was Upjohn's 'only intelligent group in London'! If this is 'intelligence,' then let me be a fool for God's sake. Better the great octopus ennui outside than these jelly-fish tentacles stinging with conceit, self-interest, and malice.

He went over to talk to Comrade-Editor Bobbe. Mr. Bobbe was a sandy-haired, narrow-chested little man with spiteful blue eyes and a malevolent class-hatred. He exercised his malevolence with comparative impunity by trading upon his working-class origin and his indigestion, of which he had been dying for twenty years. Nobody of decent breeding could hit Mr. Bobbe as he deserved, because his looks were a perpetual reminder of his disease, and his behaviour and habits gave continual evidence of his origin. He was the Thersites of the day, or rather that would have been the only excuse for him. Intellectually he was Rousseau's sedulous and somewhat lousy ape. His conversation rasped. His vanity and class-consciousness made him yearn for affairs with upper-class women, although he was obviously a homosexual type. Admirable energy, a swift and sometimes remarkable intuition into character, a good memory and excellent faculty of imitation, a sharp tongue and brutal frankness, gave him power. He was a little snipe, but a dangerous one. Although biassed and sometimes absurd, his weekly political articles were by far the best of the day. He might have been a real influence in the rapidly growing Socialist Party if he could have controlled his excessive malevolence, curbed his hankering for aristocratic alcoves, and dismissed his fatuous theories of the Unconscious, which were a singular mixture of misapprehended theosophy and ill-digested Freud. George admired his feverish energy and talents, pitied him for his ill-health and agonised sense of class inferiority, disliked his malevolence, and ignored his theories.

' What are *you* doing here, Winterbourne ?   I shouldn't have thought Shobbe would invite *you*.   You haven't any money, have you ? '

' Upjohn brought me along.'

' Upjohn-and-at-'em ?   What 's he want of you ? '

' An article on his new school of painting, I think.'

Mr. Bobbe tittered, screwing up his eyes and nose in disgust, and flapping his right hand with a gesture of take-it-away-it-stinks.

' Suprematist painting !   Suprematist dung-bags ! Suprematist conceit and empty-headed charlatanism ! Did you see him toady to that Carter woman, *Lady* Carter ?   Puh ! '

There was such vindictiveness in that ' puh ' that George was disconcerted.   True, he himself suspected Mr. Upjohn was a bit of a charlatan, and knew he was odiously conceited ; at the same time, there was something very kind-hearted and generous in poor Upjohn-and-at-'em, who had received that nickname for his furious onslaughts on any one who was established and successful, in alleged defence of any one who was struggling and neglected.   Unfortunately, these vituperative efforts of poor Mr. Upjohn did no good to his friends and served only to bring himself advertisement—the advertisement of ridiculousness.   But George felt he ought to say something in defence.

' Well, of course he 's eccentric and sometimes offensive, but he 's got a streak of curious genius and real generosity.'

Mr. Bobbe snarled rather than tittered.

' He 's an insignificant, toadying little cheese-worm. That 's what he is, a toadying little *cheese-worm*.   And you won't be much better, my lad, if you let yourself drift with these people. You'll go to pieces, you'll just go *com-plete-ly* to pieces. But humanity's rotten. It's all rotten. It stinks. It's worm-eaten. Look at those mingy fellows prancing round those women on the tips of their toes. Cold-hearted, ****-*********, mingy sneaks! Look at the women, pining for a bit o' real warm-hearted man's love, and what do they get ? Mingy cold-hearted ********! I know 'em, I know 'em. Curse the mingy lot of 'em. But it won't last long, it can't. The workers won't stand it. There'll be a revolution and a bloody one, and soon too. Mingy sons of spats and eye-glasses ! '

George was amazed and embarrassed by this outburst. He did indeed feel repelled by most of the gathering, particularly by persons like Mr. Robert Jeames, the Poets' Friend, who made anthologies of all the worst authors, wore a monocle and spats, and lisped through a wet tooth. But after all Mr. Jeames was harmless and quite amiable. One might not agree with his taste ; one might not feel attracted by him, or indeed by most of the people present. But there was certainly a wide difference between such a feeling and 'mingy sneaks' and 'cheese-worms.' Moreover, George was a little offended by Mr. Bobbe's proletarian vocabulary, while he failed to see exactly why the sexual frigidity of a few men in dinner-jackets should cause the workers to rise in bloody revolution.

' I shouldn't think the workers care a hoot. If it's as you say, the women are more likely to join the suffragettes.'

' Faugh ! ' said Mr. Bobbe, ' puh ! Suffragettes ? Take them away. They smell. They're unclean. They're obscene. Women and votes ! It's the last stage of decomposition of the mingy world. When the women start to get power, it's the end. It means the men are done for, mingy cold-hearted sneaks. Once let the women in, and nothing can save the world. Socialism, perhaps, and a genuine out-reaching of the inward unconscious Male-life to the dark Womb-life in Woman. But no, they 're not worthy of it. Let 'em go. You 'll see, my lad, you 'll see. Within five years there 'll be a . . .'

' Oh, Mr. Bobbe,' said Mrs. Shobbe's voice, and a timid little greyish lady, all in grey and silver, appeared, gentle and fluttering beside them, like a large gentle grey moth. ' Oh, Mr. Bobbe, do forgive me for interrupting your *interesting* conversation. Lady Carter is *so* anxious to meet you and admires you *so* much. I 'm sure you 'll like her and her two daughters—such *beautiful* girls.'

George watched Mr. Bobbe as he bowed servilely to Lady Carter and entered into an animated conversation with that living rung in the social ladder. He watched the scene for several minutes, and was just thinking of leaving when Mr. Waldo Tubbe came near him.

' Well, Winterbourne,' he remarked in his neat, mincing English, ' you appeared sunk in thought. What was the precise object of your contemplation ? '

' Bobbe was inveighing against Upjohn for toadying to Lady Carter, and then as soon as Mrs. Shobbe came and asked him to be introduced, he rushed off and you can see him there sitting at Lady Carter's feet with clasped hands.'

Mr. Tubbe looked unnecessarily grave.

' O-oh,' he said, with a very genteel roll to the ' o,' and an air of suggesting unutterable things. This was a very great asset to Mr. Tubbe in social intercourse. He found that an interrogative silence on his part forced other people to talk, and made them slightly ill at ease, so that they betrayed what they did not always wish to express. He

would then gravely remark ' Oe-oh ' or ' In-deed ? ' or
' Really ? ' with a deportmental air which was highly
impressive and somehow slightly reproving.　It was reported that Mr. Tubbe spent hours practising in private
the exact intonation of his ' Oe-ohs,' ' Reallys,' and ' In-
deeds.'　He had certainly brought them to a high pitch
of gentility and suppressed significance.　Mr. Tubbe
drank a good deal—gin mostly ; but it must be said for
him that the drunker he gôt, the more genteel and darkly
significant he became.

There was a pause after Mr. Tubbe's ' Oe-oh.'　His
interrogative silence did its work.　George plunged into
talk, saying the first thing which came into his head.

' I came along with Upjohn, after seeing his new
pictures.'

' In-deed ? '

' He would like me to write an article on them, but it 's
very difficult.　Honestly, I don't understand them and
think they 're rather nonsense ; don't you ? '

' Oe-oh.'

' Have you seen them ? '

' Noe-o.'

Say something, blast you !

Another long pause.

' Well, my dear Winterbourne, I am very happy to
have had some conversation with you.　Come in and
see me soon, quite soon.　Will you excuse me ?　I must
ask Lord Congreve a question.　Good-bye.　*Good*-bye ! '

George observed the greeting between Mr. Waldo
Tubbe and Lord Congreve.

' Hullo, Waldo ! '

' My *dear* Bernard ! . . .'

Mr. Tubbe shook hands with an air of restrained but

very considerable emotion. He treated Lord Congreve with a kind of dignified familiarity, rather like Phélypeaux playing billiards with Louis Quatorze. Mr. Shobbe, who was the third party to this interesting reunion, behaved more easily, with a *puissance-à-puissance* geniality. George could not hear what they were saying, and did not want to. He was watching Mrs. Shobbe, who was talking gently with two younger women on a couch in one corner of the studio. Poor Mrs. Shobbe, of whom one always thought as a soft, kind grey moth, for ever fluttering with kindly intent and for ever fluttering wrong. She had that sweet exasperating gentleness and refined incompetence which marked so many women of the wealthier class whose youth was blighted by Ruskin and Morris. Her portrait had been painted by Burne-Jones—there it was on the wall, over-sweet, over-wistful, stylised to look like one of his Arthurian damosels. And there she was grey and moth-like, the sweetness gone insipid, the wistfulness become empty and regretful. Had she ever looked like that portrait ? No one would have known it was she, unless they had been told.

Poor Mrs. Shobbe ! In turns one pitied, almost loved, despised, and was exasperated by her. Such crushed in-sipidity. And yet such a gallant effort to do ' what is right.' But she somehow disgusted one with refinement and trying to do what is right, and made one yearn sym-pathetically towards a hard-swearing, hard-working, hard-drinking motor mechanic. Her life must have been very unhappy. Her well-off Victorian parents (wholesale wine trade, retired) had given her a good education of travel and accomplishments, and had systematically and gently crushed her. It was chiefly the mother, of course, that abominable mother-daughter ' love ' which is compact of bullying, jealousy, parasitism, and baffled sexuality. With what ghastly pertinacity does a disappointed wife ' take it out ' on her daughter ! Not consciously, of course ; but it is the unconscious cruelty and oppression of human beings which seem the most dreadful. To escape, she had married Shobbe.

Nothing can be more fatal for a girl than to marry an artist of any kind. Have affairs with them, my dears, if you like. They can teach you a great deal about life, human nature, and sex, because they are directly interested in these matters, whereas other men are cluttered with prejudices, ideals, and literary reminiscences. But do not marry them, unless you have a writing of divorcement in the pocket of your night-gown. If you are poor, life will be horrid even though there are no children ; and if you have children, it will be hell. If you have money, you may be quite sure that it is not you but your money which has been espoused. Every poor artist and intellectual is looking for a woman to keep him. So you look out too. Of course, not only are there no delicious marriages, there are not even any good ones—Rochefoucauld was such an optimist. And in any case marriage is a primitive institution bound to succumb before the joint attack of contraceptives and the economic independence of women. Remember, artists are not seeking tranquillity and legitimate posterity, but experience and an income. So look out !

Poor Mrs. Shobbe did not look out ; she had never been allowed to do anything so unmaidenly. She became the means whereby Mr. Shobbe avoided the dismal but common fate of working for a living. He snubbed her, he patronised her, he neglected her, he was unfaithful to her, but hung on to her like a sloth to a tree-branch—she had three thousand a year, most of which he spent. As for Shobbe, he was a plump and talented snob of German origin. His aquiline nose was the one piece of evidence, apart from his bad manners, which supported his claim to aristocratic birth. Before the Great War he was always talking about his year's service in an aristocratic German regiment, or beginning a sentence, 'When I was last with the Kaiser,' or talking voluble German whenever there was an audience, or saying 'Of course, you English . . .' After the war he discovered that he was and always had been a patriotic English gentleman. Be it said to his credit, he 'rolled up' himself and did not only 'give' a few cousins. But then, there was Mrs. Shobbe to get away from on a legitimate excuse—how many patriotic English gentlemen in the war armies were rather avoiding their wives than seeking their country's enemies? Shobbe was an excellent example of the artist's amazing selfishness and vanity. After the comfort of his own person he really cared for nothing but his prose style and literary reputation. He was also an amazing and very amusing liar—a sort of literary Falstaff. As for his affairs with women—my God! Yet, after all, were they really so lurid? Probably they were grossly exaggerated because Shobbe had talent, and everybody was jealous of it. . . .

George suddenly became aware that Mrs. Shobbe was beckoning to him from the couch. Some of the noisier guests had departed—probably to drink more freely—and a wide-opened window had carried away much of the tobacco smoke. George emerged from his reverie and went quickly over to her.

'You know Mrs. Lamberton, don't you, Mr. Winterbourne? And this is Miss Paston, Elizabeth Paston.'

How-do-you-do's.

'And, oh, Mr. Winterbourne, will you get us some iced

lemonade, please ? We 're all dying of thirst in this smoky room.'

George brought the drinks, and sat down in a chair facing the women. They chatted aimlessly. Soon Mrs. Shobbe went away. She saw a lonely old maid in the opposite corner of the room, and felt it 'right' to talk to her. Mrs. Lamberton sighed.

' Why does one come to these intellectual agapes ? An expense of spirit in a waste of time.'

' Now, Frances !' said Elizabeth, with her hard, nervous little laugh, ' you know you 'd hate it if you weren't asked.'

' Besides, it 's one place where you 're sure not to meet your husband,' said George.

' Oh, but then I *never* see him. Only last week I had to ask the servants where Mr. Lamberton was. I didn't know whether he was still alive or only preoccupied with a new conquest.'

' And was he ? '

' What ? '

' Alive. I didn't know he ever had been.'

They laughed, though the paltry jest was near the truth.

' And yet,' George pursued, with the ruthless clumsiness of youth, ' you must have liked him once. Why ? Why do women like men ? And on what singular principle do they choose their husbands ? Instinct ? Self-interest ? '

Neither answered. Women do not like these questions, especially from young men whose duty it is to be dazzled by charms they cannot analyse. Of course, the questions were impertinent ; but if a young man is not impertinent, what on earth is the use of him ?

The women lit cigarettes. George looked at Elizabeth Paston. A slender figure in red silk ; black, glossy hair drawn back from a high, intellectual forehead ; large, very intelligent dark eyes ; a rather pale, rather Egyptian-looking face with prominent cheek-bones, slightly sunken cheeks, and full red lips ; a nervous manner. She was one of those 'near' virgins so common in the countries of sexual prohibition. Her hands were slender, the line from her ear to her chin exquisitely beautiful, her breasts too flat. She smoked cigarettes too rapidly, and had a way of sitting with a look of abstraction in a pose which showed off the lovely line of her throat and jaw. Her teeth were a little irregular. The delicate ear was like a frail pink shell under the dark sea-fronds of her hair. Her calves and ankles, such important indications of female character and temperament, were hidden under the long skirts of those days ; but the bared arms and wrists were slender and a little sensual as they lay along her clothed thighs. George was greatly attracted. Apparently she also liked him, and Mrs. Lamberton noticed it with that swift, rather devilish intuition of women. She rose to leave.

' Oh, Frances, don't go yet ! ' exclaimed Elizabeth. ' I only came to see you, and you were so surrounded by men I have scarcely seen you.'

' Yes, don't go.'

' I must. You don't know the duties awaiting a careful wife and good mother.'

She slipped away, leaving them alone.

' Isn't she a dear ? ' said Elizabeth.

' Something very lovely and precious. Even when she talks nonsense in that slightly affected way she seems to be saying something valuable.'

' Do you think she is beautiful ? '

' Beautiful ? Yes, in a way, but she isn't one of those horrid regular beauties. You notice her at once in a room, but you 'd never see her on the walls of the Academy. It isn't her beauty so much as her personality, and that you feel more by intuition than by observation. And yet the effect is beauty.'

' Are you very much in love with her ? '

' Why, aren't you ? Isn't every one ? '

' In love with her ? '

George was silent. He was not sure whether the question was *naïf* or very much the reverse. Elizabeth changed the conversation.

' What do you " do " ? '

' Oh, I 'm a painter, and I write hack articles for Shobbe and such people to earn a living.'

' But don't you sell your pictures ? '

' I try to; but you see, people in England aren't much interested in modern art, not as they are on the Continent or even in America. They want the same old thing done over again and done with more sugar. One thing about the British bourgeois—he doesn't know anything about pictures, but very stoutly stands for what he likes, and what he likes is anything except art. The newest historians say that the Anglo-Saxons come from the same race as the Vandals, and I can well believe it.'

' Surely there are some up-to-date collectors in England.'

' Why, yes, of course, probably as many as anywhere else, but too many of them collect pictures as an investment and so only take what the dealers advise them to buy ; others are afraid to touch English art, which has gone soggy with Pre-Raphaelitism and touched imbecility with the anecdotal picture. There are people with taste and enthusiasms, but they 're nearly all poor. It 's much the same in Paris. The new painters there are having a terrific struggle, but they 'll win. The young

are with them.   And then in Paris it 's rather chic to know
the latest movements and to defend the rebel artists
against the ordinary mass ignorance and hostility.   Here
they 're still terrified by the fate of Oscar, and it 's chic to
be a sporting imbecile.   The English think it 's virile to
have no sensibilities.'

' Are you English or American ? '

' English, of course.   Should I care about them if I
were not ?   In a way, of course, it doesn't really matter.
The nationalist epoch of painting is over—it 's now an
international language centred in Paris and understood
from Petersburg to New York.   What the English think
doesn't matter.'

George was excited and talking volubly.   Elizabeth
encouraged him.   Females know instinctively or by bitter
experience that males like to tell them things.   It is so
very curious that we talk of vanity as if it were almost
exclusively feminine, whereas both sexes are equally vain.
Perhaps males are vainer.   Women are sometimes plainly
revolted by really inane compliments, while there is no
flattery too gross for a male.   There simply isn't.   And
not one of us is free from it.   However much you may be
on your guard, however much you may think you dislike
it, you will find yourself instinctively angling for female
flattery—and getting it.   Oh yes, you 'll get it, just as long
as that subtle female instinct warns them there is potency
in your loins. . . .

' Mother of the race of Aeneas, voluptuous delight of
gods and men, sacred Aphrodite '—how does it go ?   But
the poet is right.   She, the sacred one, the imperious
reproductive instinct, with all Her wiles and charms, is
indeed the ruler over all living things, in the waters, in the
air, on land.   Over us Her sway is complete, for it is not

seasonal but permanent. (Who was the lady who said that if the animals don't make love all the time the reason is that they are *bêtes* ?) Priests, with all weapons from circumcision to prudery, have warred with Her ; legislators have laid down rules for Her ; well-meaning persons have tried to domesticate Her. Useless ! ' At thy coming, goddess,' the celibate hides his shaved crown and sneaks to a brothel, the clerk in holy orders enters into holy matrimony, the lawyer visits the little shopgirl he ' helps,' domestic peace is shaken alive with adulteries. For man is an ambulatory digestive tube which wants to keep alive, and Death waits for him. Descartes was a fool in these matters, like so many philosophers. ' I think, therefore I am.' Idiot ! I am because others loved ; I love that others may be. Hunger and Death are the realities, and between those great chasms flits a little Life. The enemy of Death is not Thought, not Apollo with gold shafts of light, useless against the Foe of gods and men, as you see him in the prologue to *Alkestis*. It is She, the Cyprian, who triumphs, woman-like, with her wiles. Generations She yields Him, the Devourer, as His prey, and unwearyingly raises up new races of men and women.

*　*　*　*　*　*　*　*　*　*

It is She who plumps the flat white belly and then, treacherous and cruel to Her instrument once Her purpose is achieved, with intolerable anguish tears forth from shaking mother-flesh the feeble fruit of Man. All the thoughts and emotions and desires of adult men and women circle about Her, and Her enemies are but Death's friends. You may elude Her with asceticism, you may thwart Her purpose (who shall write a new myth of the rubber-tree, Death's subtle gift ?), but if you love Life you must love Her, and if you puritanically say She is not, you are both a fool and Death's servant. If you hate Life, if you think the suffering outweighs the pleasure, if you think it the supreme crime to transmit life, then you must indeed dread Her as the author of the supreme evil—Life.

Elizabeth and George talked and found each other delightful. They thought it was their interest in art and ideas. Delightful error! All the arts of mankind are the Cyprian's handmaids, and even the chaste and tweeded spectre Sport has unwittingly been made Her pander—for with no grudging hand does the Goddess scatter Her gifts, smiling upon the amorous play of children and not disdaining even those who desire their own sex. She is beneficent and knows there are only too many ready to propagate, and is not anxious to create too many victims for Hunger, and therefore patronises even the heretics of Sparta and Lesbos. . . .

We should turn churches into temples to Venus, and set up a statue to Havelock Ellis, the moral Hercules who has partially succeeded in cleansing the Augean stable of the white man's mind. . . .

Under the benign influence of the Cyprian they talked, they went on talking. They had drifted on to the topics of Christ and Christianity, that interminable *pons asinorum* of youthful discussions.

' But I think Christ is wonderful,' Elizabeth was saying with an air of having discovered something, ' because he completely ignored social values and considered people only for what they really were in themselves. It is so strange to think of his being made the pretext for the world's most elaborate system of priestcraft when the whole of his life and teaching is a protest against it. And then I like his going about with fishermen and prostitutes.'

'The bohemian Christ? But have you noticed what a Proteus he is? Everybody interprets the historical Jesus to please himself. He is a whole mythology in himself. If you really try to discover the historical Jesus, you find you keep stripping away veil after veil, and then just as you think you are coming to the real figure you find there's nothing there. But, I grant you, Christ is a very sympathetic figure. What I cannot endure is Christianity and the harm it has done Europe. I detest its system of values, its persecution, its hatred of life (it worships a tortured and expiring god), its cult of self-sacrifice and sexual aberrations like sadism, masochism, and chastity. . . .'

Elizabeth laughed, a little shocked.

'Oh, oh! Now you are exaggerating!'

'Not at all. I think I could prove what I say, at the expense of some time and boring you. Consider the lives of Saints like Catherine of Siena, Sebastian and all the infinite martyrs; look at their representation in art; and then ask yourself what instincts are really satisfied by the cult of these personalities and images.'

'That sounds like good Protestant prejudice.'

'There are lots of things I detest in Protestantism—its smugness and aridity, for instance—but I like its honesty. And we owe it a great deal. It was because of the political inconveniences resulting from a multitude of sects that Holland and England reintroduced religious tolerance, which had disappeared with the triumph of the Christians. Of course, the tolerance is not complete, because the Christians are still persecutors at heart and have a thousand ways of vexing and maligning those who disagree with them or are merely indifferent. Hence the extraordinary defensive puritanism of English rationalists. But something has been achieved. After all, during many centuries I should have been arrested, tortured, and probably murdered for what I have just said to you, and you would have thought me a carbonised monster. Now any alleged truth or moral proposition or belief which has to be enforced by torture or defended by sophistry stands self-condemned.'

Was ever woman in this manner wooed ! But George had mounted one of his hobby-horses and was careering away through a dust of words. Elizabeth, with practical instinct, stopped him.

' Where do you live ? '

' In Greek Street. I 've got a large room there, big enough to paint in. Where do you live ? '

' In Hampstead. It 's rather horrid and the place is full of old maids. But anything is better than being at home. I don't mind my father, but my mother makes me so nervous when I 'm at home that I feel I shall just die if I have to be any longer with her.'

' I 'm glad you hate your parents, at least one of them. It 's so important to recognise these antipathies, which are after all perfectly natural. Most animals hate their mature young. I remember I used to watch the young robins exterminating their fathers, and think how right it was. But it ought to be the mothers. Men sometimes leave each other alone.'

' Oh, it 's partly due to the awful domestic-den family life. They can't really help it, poor dears. The den was forced on them, and they had to live in it.'

' Not really. They must have wanted it. It 's all part of people's amazing cowardice, their panic terror of life. It 's a device of governments, an official cheat.'

George was off again. ' All states are founded on the obligation of a man to provide for the child he begets and the woman who produces it. The State wants children, wants more and more "citizens" for various reasons. The State exploits the love of a man for a woman and his tenderness towards her children—even she may not know whether they are his or not. And so she 's taught to say : " Be careful, step warily, don't offend any one, remember your first duty is to provide for me and the children, you mustn't let us starve, oh, do be careful," with the result that the poor man very soon becomes a member of the infinite army of respectable season-ticket holders. . . .'

' Oh! Oh!' Elizabeth laughed again. 'Why are you so full of moral indignation ? '

' I'm not. Only, I live a great deal alone. I 'm always thinking about things and rarely have a chance of speaking about them. Most of my brilliant acquaintances, like Upjohn, have so much to say about themselves that I never seem to get a chance of discussing anything else. And my non-brilliant acquaintances are simply shocked and reproving. They think I 'm utterly damned because I read Baudelaire, for instance. Have you noticed the British middle-class superstition that anything they can label " Gallic " must necessarily be libidinous and depraved ? I get tired of telling them that the beauty of Baudelaire's verse is infinitely more spiritual and " uplifting "—to use their damned cant—than all the confounded nonconformist - baptist - cum - Salvation Army . . .'

But the end of George's denunciation was never uttered, for at that moment they were interrupted by the gentle Mrs. Shobbe.

' Excuse me for interrupting you, Mr. Winterbourne. Elizabeth dear, do you know how late it is ? I 'm afraid

you 'll miss the last bus, and you know I promised your
dear mother I would look after you. . . .'

Both George and Elizabeth saw with surprise and some
embarrassment that the studio was nearly empty. Almost
every one else had gone and they hadn't noticed it, absorbed in their delightful exploration of each other. Of
course, in these cases it isn't what is said that matters, but
all that remains unsaid. The talk is mere 'parade,' a
rustling out of the peacock's tail, a kind of antennae
delicately fumbling. Lovers are like mirrors—each gazes
rapturously at himself reflected in the other. How
delicious the first flashes of recognition !

Elizabeth jumped nervously to her feet, almost up-
setting a small table.

' Oh my ! I 'd no idea it was so late. I must go.
Good-bye, Mr.—, Mr.—'

' Winterbourne,' said George. ' But if you 're going
to Hampstead, let me take you back as far as Tottenham
Court Road and put you on the Hampstead bus. It 's
not out of my way at all.'

' Yes, do, Elizabeth. I feel so nervous at your being
alone in London at night like this. Whatever should we
do if anything happened to you ? '

' Why, what 's likely to happen ? ' said George contemptuously, ever ready to defend the cause of female
emancipation; 'she 's got sense enough not to let herself
be run over, and if any one tries to rape her she can yell
for a policeman.'

' Such a violent and rude young man,' Mrs. Shobbe
lamented as they went for Elizabeth's things. ' But
they 're all like that now. They seem to have *no* respect
for *anything*, not even the purity of womanhood. I don't
know if I ought to let him take you home, Elizabeth.'

'Oh, that's all right; besides, I rather like him. He's quite amusing. I shall ask him to come and have tea with me at my studio.'

'*Elizabeth!*'

But Elizabeth was already at the door, where George was waiting. All the guests had departed except Mr. Upjohn and Mr. Waldo Tubbe. A last whiff of their conversation reached George's ears:

'You see, what I mean is, you take Suprematism, what I mean is, you see, there you 've got something . . .'

And like the toll of Big Ben over the sleeping city came Mr. Tubbe's last, deep-breathed, significant, deport-mental:

'Oe-oh.'

THIS banal party and banal conversation with Elizabeth were of capital importance in George's life. The party, with its revelations of character and general tedium, confirmed George in his growing dislike for the intellectual banditti. Self-interest, though universal, is less tolerable in those who are supposed to be above it—there is, of course, no reason why a good artist should not be successful; but when one considers the intrigues now necessary for success, there is a natural prejudice in favour of those who do not elbow in the throng. Vanity is none the less odious even when there is some reason for it, though why any one should feel vain of publishing books and exhibiting pictures is a mystery, when you reflect that two thousand novels a year are published in England alone and that tens of thousands of canvases are showed annually in Paris. Gossip and scandal are none the less scandal and gossip even when witty and when the victims are more or less conspicuous in the small world which receives, or haughtily disdains to receive, Press-cuttings. George felt it rather unimportant to know which talented lady was 'with' which famous gentleman. His interest was comparatively so languid that he forgot most of the scandal he was told ten minutes after he heard it, and rarely bothered to repeat what little he remembered. Somehow people are frightfully offended if you say ' Does it matter ? ' when they tell you with sparkling eyes that somebody you know has run away with the mistress of Snooks, the painter, or that Pocock, the eminent impresario, has just celebrated the birth of his twenty-fifth illegitimate child. Does it matter, indeed ! Why this fascinated delight in the private

lives of the great? They're just as sordid as everybody else's.

The artist, anyway, is not nearly so important as he
thinks himself It's all poppycock and swagger for
Baudelaire to say that a man can live three days without
food but not a day without poetry. It may have been
true of Baudelaire ; it certainly isn't true of the world
in general. In any nation only a comparatively small
minority are interested in the arts, and most of those
merely want to be amused. If all the artists and writers
of a nation were suddenly obliterated by some plague of
Egypt, some legitimately vengeful angel, most people
would be totally unaware that they had suffered any loss,
unless the newspapers made a fuss about it. But let the
journeymen bakers go on strike for a fortnight. . . . If
I were a millionaire it would amuse me to go about giving
high-minded artists five hundred pounds a year to shut
up. The suggestion is not copyright.

Our young friend was, of course, filled with numerous
high-falutin delusions about the supreme importance of
art and the dazzling supremacy of artists over the rest of
mankind. But he had two fairly sound ideas. One was
that the artist should do his job, like any one else, as well
as he could, without making too much fuss about it ; the
other was that knowledge of the arts and practice of any
art are chiefly important for sharpening the intelligence
and perceptions, extending one's experience and intensifying life. These objects are not furthered by scandal,
preposterous vanity, and arrivism. He was therefore
perfectly right in feeling a certain amount of contempt for Mr. Shobbe's guests. The life of Rousseau
the Douanier is infinitely more respectable than that
of a fashionable portrait-painter, touting socially for
orders.

Elizabeth and George continued their conversation on the bus from Holland Park to Tottenham Court Road. Like most bright young things they abounded in their own sense. As George said, it was perfectly obvious that they were an immense improvement on their predecessors, that they knew exactly how to avoid the lamentable errors and absurdities of former generations, and that they were going to have most interesting and delightful lives. Anybody who has not felt these pleasing delusions at the age of twenty must, I fear, be ranged in George's category of abject morons. Youth is so much more valuable than experience ; it is also far more intelligent. Few things are more astounding and touching than the kindly tolerance of the young for their imbecile elders. For, have no doubts about it, even the greatest minds degenerate annually, and the finest moral character is repulsive at forty. Think of the fire and flash and inspiring genius of young General Bonaparte and the stupid degeneracy of the Emperor who had to retreat ignominiously from Moscow. A nation which relies on the alleged wisdom of sexagenarians is irrevocably degenerate. Attila was only thirty when he sacked sexagenarian Rome—at least, he ought to have been.

Elizabeth and George were very young, and hence, on *a priori* grounds, extremely intelligent. Probably the highest intensity of life ever reached by man or woman is in the early stages of their first real love affair, particularly if it is not thwarted by insane social and religious prejudices inherited from the timid and envious aged, and not contaminated by marriage.

They emerged from the stuffy, smoke-heavy room into the broad avenue, and walked towards Notting Hill tube station. A warm south-westerly wind was blowing, moisture-laden, the kindly courier of Spring. Gone was the raw, acrid damp of Winter, and they imagined they could taste in the air the faint, salt flavour of southern seas and the earthy English acres.

' We shall have rain to-morrow,' said George, instinctively looking up at the cloudy sky invisible beyond the glare of street lamps. ' It is Spring at last. The crocuses will be nearly over. I must go and look at the flowers at Hampton Court. Will you come ? '

' I 'd love to, but isn't Hampton Court full of trippers ? '

' Not if you go at the right time. I have walked there in the early morning as solitary as ever King Charles when the Privy Garden was really private. I should rather like to live in King William's summer-house.'

' I like wilder and more primitive country, the Downs and those great round empty Exmoor hills. And I like the clear rough waves dashing against the rocks in Cornwall.'

' I don't know Cornwall, but I love the Downs above Storrington, and I 've walked over Exmoor twice. But now I 'm rather in revolt against mere country—" Nature," as they used to call it. Nature-worship is a sort of Narcissus-worship, holding up Nature's mirror to ourselves. And how abominably selfish these Nature-worshippers are ! Why ! they want a whole landscape to themselves, and they complain bitterly when farm-labourers want modern grocery stores and w.c.s. Whole communities apparently are to live in static ignorance and picturesque decay in order to gratify their false ideas of what is beautiful.'

' Of course, I hate the Simple-Lifers too. There was a set of them near the place at the seaside where we went for the holidays as children . . .'

' Oh ! Have you got brothers and sisters ? '

' A sister and two brothers. Why, haven't you ? '

' Yes, I believe so, but I never think about it.   Relatives are awful—they contribute absolutely nothing to your interest in life, and think that gives them a perpetual right to interfere in your affairs.   And they have the monstrous impudence to pretend that you ought to love them. " Blood is thicker than water," they say sententiously. So it may be, but I don't want to dabble in thick blood.   I hate proverbs—don't you?   I 've always noticed that any-thing absurd or tyrannical or fatuous can always be supported by a proverb—the collective stupidity of the ages.   But, I say, I 'm so sorry I interrupted you.   I go on talking and talking, and don't give you a chance to say a word.'

' Oh, I like it.   I think your ideas are amusing.'

' Not amusing, merely common-sense.   But you mustn't let me talk all the time.   You see, I find most people rather oppress my spirits, and keep me from saying what I really think.   So as a rule I 'm silent, but when I find a sympathetic victim—well, you 've already had a bitter experience of how I chatter nineteen to the dozen. There I 'm off again !   Now tell me what you were going to say about the Simple-Lifers.'

' The Simple-Lifers ?   Oh, yes, I remember.   Well, there was a set of people down there who had fled from the horrors of the mechanical age—you know, the usual art-y sort, Ruskin-cum-William Morris . . .'

' Handlooms, vegetable diet, long embroidered frocks, with home-spun tweed trousers from the Hebrides ?   I know them.   " News from Nowhere " people.   What a gospel to lead nowhither ! '

' Yes.   Well, they were to lead the simple life, work with their hands part of the time, and do arts and crafts and write the rest of the time.   They were also to show the world an example of perfect community life.   They used to make the farm-girls dance round a Maypole—the boys wouldn't come, they stood in the lane and jeered.'

' And what happened ? '

' Well, those who hadn't private incomes got very hard up, and were always borrowing money off the two or three members who had money. The arts and crafts didn't sell, and the toiling on the land had very meagre results. Then they got themselves somehow into two or three cliques, always running down the people in the other cliques, talking scandal about them, and saying they were ruining everything by their selfish behaviour. Then the wife of one of the rich members ran away with one of the men, and the other rich members were so scandalised that they went away too, and the whole community broke up. The village was very glad when they went. The farmers and gentry were furious because they talked Socialism and the ideal State to the labourers. And all the labourers' wives were furious because the Simple-Life women tried to brighten up their lives and make them furnish their cottages " artistically." . . .'

They had missed two buses outside the tube station in their excited chatter. A third came along. George grabbed Elizabeth's arm :

' Come on, here 's our bus. Let 's go on top.'

The bus-top was empty except for a couple spooning on a back seat. George and Elizabeth a little haughtily went to the very front.

' Other people's love-affairs are very tedious,' said George sententiously.

' Oh, very.'

' Rather primitive and humiliating.'

' Why humiliating ? '

' Oh, because . . .'

' Fares, please ! '

The conductor lurched skilfully against the front of the bus as it made a cow-like leap forward. George raked in his pocket for the pennies.

' Let me pay my share.'

Elizabeth produced a sixpence.

' Oh no, please.   Look, let me take you back to Hampstead, and you can pay from Tottenham Court Road.'

' All right.'

The conductor and the fare-paying had interrupted the rhythm of their communication.   They were silent.   The bus ran noisily along the wave-furrowed, shiny, tarred street, with the dark mystery of Kensington Gardens to the right and the equally mysterious boarding-houses of Bayswater to the left.   Near the street-lamps the grass behind the railing was a vivid artificial green, as if some one had splashed down a bucketful of bright paint.   Like savages in some primitive dance, the ancient trees swayed slowly, irregularly, and mysteriously in the strong wind. A red apocalyptic glow from the lights of Oxford Street stained luridly and uneasily the low rolling clouds before them.   The grey monster Ennui of Sunday-in-London had vanished.   George took his hat off and let the wind rumple his hair.   Their young cheeks were fresh with driving moist wind.

' Don't you really like the Pre-Raphaelites ? ' asked Elizabeth, as the bus slowed down near Lancaster Gate.

' I used to.   About three years ago I was quite cracked about Rossetti and Burne-Jones and Morris.   Now I simply hate them.   I can still read Browning and Swinburne—Browning for his sense of life, Swinburne for his intoxicating rhetoric.   But after spending three months in Paris I got frightfully excited about modern painting. Do you know Apollinaire ? '

' No, who 's he ? '

' Oh, he 's a Polish Jew who has written some quite good poems and does amusing word-pictures he calls Calligrammes. He lives by writing and editing obscene books, and he 's the great defender of the new painters like Picasso and Braque and Léger and Picabia.'

' The Cubists ? '

' Yes.'

' I 've only heard of them. I never saw any of their work. I thought they were just " wild men " and *fumistes* ? '

' You wait ten years, and see then if you dare to say that Picasso is a *fumiste* ! But haven't you been to Paris ? '

' Yes, I was there last year, in September.'

' We must have been there together. How curious ! I wish I 'd seen you.'

' Oh, it was very dull. I was with father and mother, and everybody we met kept talking about the coming war with Germany. A friend of father's in the Admiralty told him in confidence that it was absolutely certain to happen.'

' What nonsense ! ' said George explosively, ' what absolute nonsense ! Haven't you read Norman Angell's *Great Illusion* ? He shows quite conclusively that war does nearly as much damage to the victor as the conquered. And he also says that the structure of modern international commerce and finance is so delicate and widespread that a war couldn't possibly last more than a few weeks without coming to an end automatically, because all the nations would be ruined. I 'll lend you the book if you like.'

' I don't know anything about such things, but father's friend said the Government were very worried about the position.'

' I can't believe it. What ! A war between European

nations in the twentieth century? It's quite unthink-
able. We're far too civilised. It's over forty years
since the Franco-Prussian War . . .'

'But there's been a Russo-Japanese War and the
Balkan Wars . . .'

'Well, yes, but they're different. I can't believe any
of the big European nations would start a war with another.
Of course, there are Chauvins and Junkers and Jingoes,
but who cares a hang about them? The people don't
want war.'

'Of course, I don't know, but I heard Admiral
Partington telling father that the navy is bigger, newer,
and more efficient than it's ever been. And he said the
German army is huge and most efficient, and the French
are so frightened they've made the period of conscription
three years. And he said, look out when the Kiel Canal
is opened.'

'Good Lord, you surely don't believe what stodgy old
Admirals say, do you? It's their job to frighten people
with war scares so that they can go on getting money out
of the country and building their ridiculous Dread-
noughts. I met a coastguard officer last summer, who
got drunk and said he'd sealed orders as to what to do in
case of war. I told him I thought that seal would not be
broken until the angels in the Apocalypse arrived.'

'And what did he say to that?'

'He just shook his head, and ordered another whisky.'

'Well, it doesn't concern us. It's not our business.'

'No, thank God, it doesn't and can't concern us.'

They were in Oxford Street, rolling past the shuttered
shop-fronts. A good many people were on the pave-
ments, but the street was comparatively empty of vehicles,
empty and sonorous. As they ran down past Selfridge's,

the curved line of lights in the centre of the street looked like an uncoiled necklace of luminous, glittering beads. At Oxford Circus they gazed down the old Regent Street with its long lines of *café-au-lait* Regency houses, broken only at the Quadrant by the new Piccadilly Hotel.

'Isn't that like us?' said George. 'We have an attempt at town-planning, and, dull as Nash is, at any rate his design is simple and dignified, and then we go and ruin the Quadrant with a horrid would-be-modern hotel.'

'But I thought you believed in modernity in art.'

'So I do, but I don't believe in mucking up the art of the past if it can be avoided. Besides, I don't call these pastiches of Renaissance palaces modern architecture. The only people who have got a live modern architecture are the Americans, and they don't know it.'

'Those awful sky-scrapers!'

'They're awful in one way, but they're original. I saw some photographs of New York from the harbour recently, and I thought it the most beautiful city in the world, a sort of gigantic and stupendous Venice. I'd like to go there—wouldn't you?'

'No, I'd like to go to Paris and live in the real students' quarter, and to Italy and Spain.'

The bus stopped at the end of Tottenham Court Road. They got down, and crossed the street to wait for the Hampstead bus.

'Look here,' said Elizabeth: 'why do you bother to come all the way out to Hampstead? I'm perfectly used to going about alone. I shall be all right.'

'Of course, you would be. But I'd like to come most awfully. I hope I shall see a good deal of you, and we haven't arranged where and when to meet again.'

' But there won't be a bus back.'

' Oh, I shall walk. I like walking. And it 'll be an antidote to the fug and idiotic talk at Shobbe's. Here 's the bus. Come on.'

They clambered on to the top of the bus, and again got the front seat. Elizabeth took off her right-hand glove to pay the fare, and after the conductor had gone George gently and rather timidly put his hand on hers. She did not withdraw it. Having established this delicious and dangerous contact, they sat silent for a while. The firm, cool male hand gently espoused her slim, glove-warmed fingers. In them both was the exaltation of the Cyprian, potential desire recognised only as a heightening of vitality. The first step along the primrose path—how delightful ! But whither does it lead ? To what everlasting bonfires of servitude or ashy wastes of indifference ? Neither of them thought of the future. Why should they ? The young at least have the sense to live only in the present moment.

Preceded by the silver dove-drawn chariot of the Paphian, the heavy bus lumbered northward. Sweet is the smile of Cypris, but ironic and a little terrifying, enigmatic as the fixed smile of the Veian Apollo.

Like all imaginative and sensitive men, George was not what is called an enterprising lover. He had too much male modesty, the inherent *pudor* which is so much stronger and more genuine than the induced modesty of women, that coquettish flight of the nymph who casts a rosy apple at her pursuer to encourage him to continue. Odd, but perhaps in the nature of things, that those men who have most contempt for women are generally the most successful with them. There must be a vast amount of latent masochism in women, ranging from the primitive delight in being knocked down, to the subtle enjoyment of

complex jealousies. How ghastly—if you think about it
—their passion for soldiers! To breed babes by him
who has slain men—puh! there's too much spilt blood
in the world; one sickens at it. Give me some civet. . . .

Once more they fell into talk—eager, excited, more
intimate talk. They were calling each other 'George'
and 'Elizabeth' before they reached the stately homes
of Camden Town. By the time they passed Mornington
Crescent they had admitted that they liked each other
'frightfully' and would see a good deal of each other. In
their excitement they talked rather incoherently, jumping
from one topic to another in their eagerness to say something of all that seemed to clamour for expression, reck-
lessly wasting their emotional energy. Their laughter
had the ring of pure happiness. George slipped his arm
through Elizabeth's and held her fingers more amorously.
Their natures expanded in a sudden delicious efflores-
cence; great coloured plumes of flowers seemed to sway
and nod above their heads. They were enclosed in a
nimbler air, the clear oxygen of desire, so light, so compact, so resistant to the grey monster Ennui of Sunday-
in-London.

'Isn't it strange!' George exclaimed, with that fatuity
peculiar to lovers; 'I only met you this evening and yet I
feel as if I had known you all my life!'

'So do I!'

He gratefully squeezed her fingers in silence, caught in
a sudden panic of bashfulness, unable to pursue further.

'Do let's meet often. We can go to the galleries and
Queen's Hall and Hampton and Oxshott. I can get you
tickets for the new picture shows. Do you know the
Allied Artists?'

'Yes, I belong.'

' Do you ? Why ever didn't you tell me you are a painter too ? '

' Oh, I 'm such a bad painter; besides, you didn't ask me.

' *Touché* ! How self-absorbed one is ! I apologise.'

' You must come and have tea at my studio and look at my—what I call my pictures. But you mustn't be too critical. When can you come ? '

' Any time. To-morrow if you like.'

Elizabeth laughed.

' Oh ! Oh ! You are impatient. Can you come on Friday ? '

' So long ? It seems ages away ! '

' Well, Thursday, then.'

' All right; what time ? '

' About four.'

Elizabeth was probably not acquainted with Stendhal's ingenious theory of crystallisation, but she acted instinctively in accordance with it. Three days and four nights made exactly the right period. To-morrow was too soon, the crystals would be in process of formation. A week would be rather too long, they would be tending to disintegrate. . . . Infinite subtlety of females ! One must admit they need it.

George accompanied Elizabeth to the boarding-house where she lived and took the address of her studio. She held out her hand, after putting the latch-key in the Yale lock.

' Till Thursday, then, good-night.'

' Good-night.'

He held her hand a moment, and then awkwardly and timidly kissed it. In her turn she felt a sudden panic, opened the door swiftly, and disappeared inside, with a last hasty ' Good-night, good-night ! '

George stood for several moments irresolutely on the step. He was desolated, thinking he had offended her.

Inside Elizabeth was murmuring silently to herself : ' He kissed my hand, he kissed my hand ! I 've a lover, a lover ! '

The sudden panic and flight were a masterpiece of erotic strategy—they left that feeling of uncertainty, of mingled hope and fear, so valuable to the production of a powerful crystallisation.

George walked back to Greek Street, enclosing in himself a small chaos of emotions and thoughts. He went by way of Fitzjohn's Avenue and St. John's Wood. The infinite debate in a lover's mind—did she or didn't she, would she or wouldn't she ?—moved in those curious arabesques where a mind continually wanders away from a main stem of thought, and perpetually comes back to it. Upjohn's ridiculous conceit, Shobbe's party, never go to that sort of thing again, Bobbe's acrid offensiveness, how delicate that line from her ear to her throat, I should like to paint her, now, in that article to-morrow I must try to show clearly and definitely what the new painters are attempting, I wonder if she was really offended when I kissed her hand, but I must think about that article, let me see, begin with an explanation of non-representational, yes, that 's it, I must get a new tie for Thursday, this one 's worn out. . . . And thus, with merciless iteration.

Under a gas-lamp near Marlborough Road Station he stopped and tried to write his first poem, and was surprised to find how difficult it was and what nonsense he wrote. A policeman came out of a side-street, and looked a little suspiciously at him. George moved on. A little later he began to sing ' Bid me to live,' interrupted himself half-way through to make a note for a study in analysis of form. He walked rapidly and absorbedly, unconscious of his physical fatigue. Just before he crossed Oxford Street, he stopped and clapped his hands together. My God! I was a fool to kiss her hand the first time I met her, she 'll think I do that to every girl and won't want to speak to me again. Oh well, it 's done. I wish I could kiss her mouth. I must remember to tell her on Thursday about that show at the Leicester Gallery. . . .

He lay awake long that night, unable to sleep for very love of living. So much to see, so much to experience, so much to achieve, so much to be and do ! How wonderful to do things with Elizabeth ! It would be fun to go to New York, of course, but perhaps one ought to see the Old World first ? She said something about Paris and Spain. We might go together. Cursed money difficulty. Never mind, if one wants to do a thing hard enough, one always manages to do it. I suppose I 'm in love with her ? It would be divine to kiss her and touch her breasts and . . . Of course, one mustn't have a baby, that would be too ghastly. I must find out. I wish we could go to Paris, the trees will be leafing in the Luxembourg. . . .

In the night-silence, water dripped with insistent melody in some hidden tank. From outside came the shrill distant notes of train whistles, rather silvery and exquisite, bringing the yearning for travel, ' the horns of elf-land faintly blowing.' Where had he read that ? Oh, of course, Stevenson. Funny how the Coningtons thought Stevenson a good author. . . .

Good-night, Elizabeth, good-night, sweet, sweet Elizabeth, good-night, good-night.

M

BEFORE our eyes we have the regrettable examples of George Augustus and Isabel, Ma and Pa Hartly, dear Mamma and dear Papa—eponyms of sexual infelicity.

Are we more intelligent than our ancestors ? What a question for the British Press or for those three musketeers of publicity cheap and silly, of tattered debates on torn topics—Shaw, Chesterton, and Belloc ! Shaw, yes, the puritan Beaumarchais—*un coup de chapeau* ; but the others ! To the goddess Ennui sung by Pope, the groans of the Britons. Who will deliver us from the R.C. bores ?

The problem may be stated thus :

Let X equal the ménage dear Mamma-dear Papa, or a typical couple of the 'seventies and 'eighties ;

And let Y equal the ménage George Augustus and Isabel, or a typical couple of the 'nineties and 'noughts ;

And further, let Z equal Elizabeth and George, or a typical bright young pair of the Georgian or European War epoch ;

Then, it remains to be proved whether Z is equal to, or greater than, or less than X and/or Y.

A pretty theorem, not to be solved mathematically— too many unknown quantities involved.

I am naturally prejudiced in favour of Z, because I belong to their generation, but what do *les jeunes*, the sole competent authority, think ? For, after all—let us be perfectly frank—dear Papa expired peacefully in his bed ; George Augustus was unhappily but accidentally slain in the performance of his religious duties ; whereas George, if you accept my interpretation of the facts, virtually committed suicide at the age of twenty-six.

But then dear Papa and George Augustus did not have to fight the European War. . . .

The problem, you see, is almost insoluble, no doubt because it is wrongly stated. Let us examine it in different terms.

Without going back to Horace's egg, may we not assume that he and she have lived well who have lived with felicity?

This not only involves the problem of the *summum bonum* or sovereign good, so much debated by the ancient philosophers, but the awful difficulty of knowing who is to decide whether another person has lived with felicity. Is there such a thing as a happy life? And, if there is, would it be the most desirable life? Would you like to be Claudian's old man of Verona? Or Mr. John D. Rockefeller? Or Mr. Michael Arlen? Or any other type of unabridged felicity?

There are, of course, lots of things and people who will eagerly or dogmatically tell you exactly what you have to do to be happy. There is, for instance, the collective wisdom of the ages, as embodied in our religions, philosophies, laws, and social customs. What a mess! What a junk-shop of dusty relics! And in any case, ' the collective wisdom of the ages ' is merely one of the innumerable devices of government by which the Anglo-Saxon peoples are humbugged into thinking themselves free, enlightened, and happy.

But let us abandon these abstruse and arid speculations. . . . The point is, did George and Elizabeth (consider them for the moment, please, rather as types than individuals) come better prepared to the erotic life than their predecessors, were they more intelligent about it, did

they make a bigger mess of things ? Does the free play
of the passions and intelligence make for more erotic
happiness than the taboo system ? Liberty versus Restraint. Wise Promiscuity versus Monogamy. (This is
becoming a Norman Haire tract.)

* * * * * * * *
* * * * * * * *

Mother of the race of Aeneas, voluptuous delight of
gods and men, sacred Aphrodite, who from the recesses
of Thy divine abode lookest in pity upon the sorrowing
generations of men and women, and sheddest upon us
rose-petals of subtle and recurrent pleasure and the
delicious gift of Sleep, do Thou, Goddess, be ever with
us, and neglect not the felicity of Thy worshippers ! Do
Thou, alone beautiful, daughter of the Gods, drench us
with loveliness !

From which to the lives of Pa and Ma Hartly *et al.*
is indeed a staggeringly long step. . . .

I hold a brief for the war generation. J'aurais pu
mourir ; rien ne m'eût été plus facile. J'ai encore à
écrire ce que nous avons fait. . . . (Bonaparte à Fontaine-
bleau—admirez l'érudition de l'auteur.)

Yet why should we mourn, O Zeus, and why should we
laugh ? Why weep, why mock ? What is a generation
of men that we should mourn for it ? As leaves, as leaves,
says the poet, spring, bourgeon, and fall the generations of
Man—No ! but as rats in the rolling ship of the Earth as
she plunges through the roar of the stars to the inevitable
doom. And like rats we pullulate, and like rats we
scramble for greasy prey, and like rats we fight and

murder our kin. . . . And—O gigantic mirth !—the
voice of the Thomiste is heard !

Peace be to you, O lovers, peace unto Juliet's grave !

At the time of which I am writing—the three or four
years preceding 1914—young men and women were just
as much interested in sexual matters as they are now, or
were at any other time. They were in revolt against the
family or domestic-den ethic, that 'ordained for the pro-
creation of children' attitude whereby the State turns its
adult members into a true proletariat, mere producers
of *proles*. And they were almost as much in revolt
against Tennysonian and Pre-Raphaelite 'idealism,'
which made love a sort of hand-holding in the Hesperides.
But, let it be remembered, Freudianism (as distinct from
Freud, that great man whom every one talks about and
nobody reads) had scarcely begun to penetrate. All
things were not interpreted in terms of sexual symbolism :
and if one had the misfortune to slip on a banana-peel in
the street, he was not immediately told that this implied
repressed desire to undergo the initiatory mutilating rite
of the Mohammedans. They thought they were re-
discovering the importance of the physical in love ; they
hoped they were not neglecting the essential tenderness,
and the mythopœic faculty of lovers which is the source
of much beauty.

Late in April, George and Elizabeth went to Hampton
Court. They met at Waterloo about nine, went by train
to Teddington, and walked through Bushey Park. Each
had brought a frugal lunch, half because of poverty,
half from some Pythagorean delusion about austerity
in diet.

They walked on the grass through the long elm naves.

'How blue the sky is!' said Elizabeth, throwing back her head and breathing the soft air.

'Yes, and look how the elms make long Gothic arches!'

'Yes, and do look at the young leaves, so shrill, so virginal a green!'

'Yes, and yet you can still see the beautiful tree skeleton—youth and age!'

'Yes, and the chestnut blossom will be out soon!'

'Yes, and the young grass is—Oh, Elizabeth, look, look! The deer! There's two young ones.'

'Where? Where are they? I can't see them. I *want* to see them!'

'There they are! Look, look, running across to the right.'

'Oh yes! How funny the little ones are! But how graceful! How old are they?'

'Only a few days, I should think. Why are they so beautiful and young babies so hideous?'

'I don't know. They're always supposed to look like their fathers, aren't they?'

'*Touché*—but I should think that would make the mothers hate them, and they love the little beasts.'

'Not always. A friend of mine had a baby last year, and she didn't want it when it was coming, but kept thinking she would love it when it came. And when she saw it, she simply loathed it, and they had to take it away. But she simply *made* herself look after it. She says it's ruined her life and she doesn't find it a bit interesting, but now she's fond of it and couldn't bear it to die.'

'Perhaps she didn't love her husband.'

'Oh yes, she does. She simply dotes on him.'

'Well, maybe it wasn't his child.'

'Oh! Oh!' Elizabeth slightly shocked. 'It *was*

his child. But one reason why she didn't like it was because it separated them.'

'How long had they been married when the child was born?'

'Oh, I don't know—less than a year.'

'Idiotic!' said George, banging the end of his walking-stick on the ground; 'ab-so-lute-ly idiotic! Why the devil did they go and have a child bang off like that? Of course, she's unhappy and they're "separated." Serves 'em right.'

'But could they help it? I mean—well, you know—it just happens, doesn't it?'

'Good Lord, Elizabeth, what a prehistoric notion! Of course it doesn't "just happen." There are several ways . . .'

'It seems a bit revolting?'

'Not a bit! You may feel so because you've had mushy ideas about maidenly modesty and such twaddle instilled into you. That's all part of the taboo. Now, I think the really civilised thing is *not* to let such things happen to us like animals, but to control them. It's all most frightfully important, and perhaps the one really important problem for our generation to solve.'

'But you surely don't think everybody should give up having children?'

'Why, of course not! I do say so sometimes when I feel discouraged and disgusted with the poor scarecrows of humanity we are now. Fewer and better babies. Isn't it insane that we exercise over animals the control they haven't got themselves, and yet resolutely refuse even to discuss it about human beings? How can you have a fine race if you breed insensately like white mice?'

'Well, but, George dear, you can't interfere with other people's lives like that!'

' I didn't say one should.   But I believe that if people
have the necessary knowledge and we get rid of the taboo,
they will for their own sakes come to breed more eugenic-
ally.   Of course, it 's an intimate and private matter—no
need for Sir Thomas More's insane regulations and naked
exhibitions before modest matrons and discreet old
gentlemen.   It 's not for the old to interfere with the
lusts of youth !   Damn the old !   But here 's another
point.   Like most intelligent women and a few men,
you 're indignant at the way women have been treated
in the past and at the wicked mediæval laws of this
country.   You want women to be free to live more interesting lives.   So do I.   Any man who isn't an abject
moron would rather see women becoming more intelligent
and magnanimous instead of having them kept ignorant
and timid and repressed and meekly acquiescent, and
therefore sly and catty and wanting to get their own back.
But you won't achieve that with Suffrage.   Of course, let
women have votes if they want them.   But who the devil
wants a vote ?   I 'd gladly give you mine if I had one.
But the point is this—when women, all women, know how
to control their bodies, they 'll have an enormous power.
They 'll be able to choose when and how they 'll have a
child and what man they want as its father.   Over-
population causes wars as much as commercial greed and
diplomatic deceit and imbecile patriotism.   Talk about
the miners' strike !   What I want to see is a universal
strike of women.   They could bring all the governments
of the world to their knees in a year.   Like the Lysistrata,
you know, but not a failure this time.'

' Oh, George, you are amusing with your fancies !   You
make me laugh ! '

' Laugh away !   But I 'm serious.   Of course, it isn't
possible to have such a concerted action all over the world.

For one thing, it wouldn't be politic to announce it, because the unscrupulous governments will always go to any extent of force and fraud to sustain their infamous régimes. . . .'

They had crossed the road outside Bushey Park and entered the palace gates. Between the wall which backs the Long Border, the Tudor side of the palace, and another long high wall, is the Wilderness, or old English garden, composed on the grandiose scale advocated by Bacon. It is both a garden and a 'wilderness,' in the sense that it is planted with innumerable bulbs (which are thinned and renewed from time to time), but otherwise allowed to run wild. George and Elizabeth stopped with that sudden ecstasy of delight felt by the sensitive young—a few of them—at the sight of loveliness. Great secular trees, better protected than those in the outer Park, held up vast fans of glittering green-and-gold foliage which trembled in the light wind and formed moving patterns on the tender blue sky. The lilacs had just unfolded their pale hearts, showing the slim stalk of closed buds which would break open later in a foam of white and blue blossoms. Underfoot was the stouter green of wild plants, spread out like an evening sky of verdure for the thick-clustered constellations of flowers. There shone the soft, slim yellow trumpet of the wild daffodil ; the daffodil which has a pointed ruff of white petals to display its gold head ; and the more opulent double daffodil which, compared with the other two, is like an ostentatious merchant between Florizel and Perdita. There were the many-headed jonquils, creamy and thick-scented ; the starry narcissus, so alert on its long, slender, stiff stem, so sharp-eyed, so unlike a languid youth gazing into a pool ; the hyacinth-blue frail squilla almost lost in the lush herbs ; and the hyacinth, blue and white and red, with its firm, thick-set stem and innumerable bells curling back their open points. Among them stood tulips—the red, like thin blown bubbles of dark wine ; the yellow, more cup-like, more sensually open to the soft furry entry of the eager bees ; the large parti-coloured gold and red, noble and sombre like the royal banner of Spain.

English spring flowers ! What an answer to our ridiculous ' cosmic woe,' how salutary, what a soft reproach to bitterness and avarice and despair, what balm to hurt minds ! The lovely bulb-flowers, loveliest of the year, so unpretentious, so cordial, so unconscious, so free from the striving after originality of the gardener's tamed pets ! The spring flowers of the English woods, so surprising under those bleak skies, and the flowers the English love so much and tend so skilfully in the cleanly wantonness of their gardens, as surprisingly beautiful as the poets of that bleak race ! When the inevitable ' fuit Ilium ' resounds mournfully over London among the appalling crash of huge bombs and the foul reek of deadly gases while the planes roar overhead, will the conqueror think regretfully and tenderly of the flowers and the poets ? . . .

When George, on one of our walks, told me the gist of this conversation with Elizabeth, I was at once more amused and more interested than I allowed him to see. There are certain aspects of people's bodies, certain things they say and do, which not only determine one's attitude towards them but seem to explain them. And more, in some cases they seem to reveal an epoch. Every one has experience of attraction or repulsion caused by another's body. For instance, there was once a poet whose work I admired ; but the first time I met him he tried to hold a girl's hand.   I didn't mind *that*—au contraire.   What I minded was the awful spectacle of his large, ugly, raw-red hand, with knotty fingers and gnawed mourning nails, trying to enclose the washed and chubby hand of my little friend. . . . I could never read his poems again without thinking of that Mr. Hyde-like hand, the Barry-more film hand of Mr. Hyde.

Now, I had a reason for dwelling at some length on these preliminary conversations of George and Elizabeth with George much in the foreground.   They seem to explain a great deal, at least to me.   They reveal him and at the same time ' throw more light ' (as the learned say) on the state of mind of a generation of young men who mostly perished in their twenties.   As a rule, George was very silent.   Like most people who think at all, he had very little of the small change of conversation and disliked aimless babbling.   But when he was with somebody he liked, he talked.   My God, how much he talked !   He was passionately interested in ideas, passionately inter-ested in his own reactions to the appearances of things, comparatively little interested in the lives of other people except in a general and abstract way.   He noticed in a flash the girl at a party who looked like a Botticelli (people still admired Botticelli in those days, and girls lived up to it), but he would never see, for example, the look on the face of the rather plain woman whom one guessed to be in love with the handsome host uxoriously devoted to his new wife.   Consequently his talk was all ideas and impressions.   He had an almost indecent love of ideas. If you threw George a new idea he caught it with a skilled and grateful snap, like a seal at the Zoo catching a fish jerked at it by the keeper.

Of course, it is very natural that young men and women should be interested in ideas which are new to them

though probably stale enough to those a bit older.   But
the young War Generation seem to me to have been
abnormally swayed by ideas of grandiose 'social reform.'
England swarmed with Social Reformers.   I don't pretend to know why.   Perhaps it was due to the political
idealism of Ruskin and Morris, aided by the infinitely
more sensible work of the Fabians.   Everybody was the
architect of a New Jerusalem, and a rummy assortment
of plans they provided.   This passion has now reached
the disinterested and noble-minded trade unionist and
to some extent even the agricultural labourer.   Consequently, you may now hear, at Hyde Park Corner or in
pubs or third-class carriages, beautifully garbled versions
of the highbrow talk of about twenty years ago.   You thus
have the encouraging and delightful spectacle of a proletariat eagerly expecting a millennium, impossible at any
time, but particularly impossible after a catastrophe which
has plunged the intellectuals into Spenglerian pessimism
and hurled the weaker or more cynical into the ironic
bosom of Mother Church. . . .

George was pretty much affected by this Social Reform
bunk.   He was always looking at things from ' the point
of view of the Country,' and far more frequently from
' the point of view of humanity.'   This may have been
a result of his Public School, kicked-backside-of-the-
Empire training.   I know he resisted it with commend-
able contempt and fury, but where so much pitch was
flying about he could scarcely avoid some of it.   Perhaps
the young are always like that, although one does not seem
to notice it.   As I pointed out to George years afterwards,
he was quite right to discuss the matter frankly and openly
with Elizabeth before they proceeded further, but all this
bunk about eugenics and women's rights and preventing
wars by birth-control would have discouraged any girl

who had not fully made up her mind already that she wanted him. It was appallingly bad strategy as seduction —though, *en passant*, let it be noted that ' seduction ' is one of those primitive notions which could only inhabit the degenerate minds of lawyers and social uplifters, since in nine cases out of ten the ' seducer,' if any, is the woman. I thought that George ought to have imparted a little elementary information, and have pointed out that in the present state of human affairs it is not quite right for people to have a child without being legally married because it 's so hard on the child, although in some cases it should be done deliberately as a protest against a foolish prejudice. He ought then to have explained how it may spoil a sexual relationship to have a child too soon and unthinkingly. And he should then have demonstrated by example and precept that love is an art, and a very difficult art, and one most dismally and disastrously neglected, especially by ' well-bred ' Englishmen. It sounds incredible, but it is true, that there are thousands of such men, perfectly decent, humane persons, who despise a woman if they think or know that she experiences any sexual pleasure. And then they wonder vaguely why women are shrewish and discontented. . . .

All this will sound very elementary to some people and very reprehensible to others. I am simply trying to explain these people. Of course, there is always the superior person who veils puritanism by saying : ' I 'm so bored with all this talk about sex. Why can't people go to bed with the person they want to, and stop talking about it ? ' Well, why shouldn't we talk about what interests us, and what, after all, is extremely important to adult life and happiness ? Maybe we can learn something from the adulteries of others. It seems to me that the error of the Elizabeth and George generation was that they were far too absolute, too general, too dogmatic in their 'ideas' about sex. They *would* let the Social Reform bunk distort their view. They had seen in their own homes the dreadful unhappiness and suffering caused by Victorian, and indeed Edwardian, ignorance and domestic dennery and swarming infants; and they reacted violently against it. So far, good. But they failed to see that in the way they went about it they were merely setting up another tyranny—the tyranny of free love. Why shouldn't people be monogamous if they want to be? Maybe it suits them. Don't be dragooned into it, of course, but don't be frightened out of it if you're made that way. There are certain elementary precepts which always hold good—for instance, Balzac's 'Never begin marriage with a rape'; but this is a wholly personal and very complex and delicate relation which people must work out for themselves. All one asks is that they shall not be interfered with by law and busybodies. It is an interesting comment on the sadism latent in communities that the cruelty and misery of the Victorian home are legally protected and held up as shining examples of behaviour, whereas any attempt to make people a little more natural and happy and tolerant is supposed to be wicked. How men destroy their own happiness! How they hate happiness and pleasure! Think of the insane delusion of female chastity which holds that any woman who has 'had' more than one man is 'impure,' whereas in fact many women soon come to dislike profoundly their first lover, and most are only really happy and satisfied with a fourth or sixth or tenth.

Alas! 'with human nature what it is,' the love-lives of most people will always alternate between brief periods of happiness and long periods of suffering. The 'sexual problem' will only be solved with the millennium which produces a perfect humanity. Until then we can only look on and sigh at the ruined lives ; and reflect that men and women might be to each other the great consolation while in fact they do little but torment each other. . . .

I do not pity Elizabeth and George. They were very happy that day—and on other days—and to be quite happy even for one day is sufficient sanction for the misfortune of existence.

They went from the Wilderness into the large garden and walked slowly beside the Long Border, where the gardeners were busily potting out spring flowers. The crocuses were almost over, and the large motor lawnmower was smoothly humming over the delicate green turf of the great lawns. They looked at the trimmed yews and wondered if they had been planted by Cardinal Wolsey. They criticised, somewhat adversely, the lead statue of the three Graces, and, walking under the trees by the canals, noticed the cold green lily-leaves just beginning to unfold under water. They stood at the end of the Long Border and for a long time in silence watched the swirl and eddy of the Thames, the house-boats being freshly painted for the season, the exquisite swaying fronds of the young willows. In the Privy Garden, on the raised walk and under the lime-tree avenue where the great clumps of crocuses lay sprawled and dying and overgrown at the foot of each tree, they talked of King Charles, and fought over the age-old contest of King and Parliament. Elizabeth was romantically for the handsome, melancholy King ; George, Whiggish and all for political freedom, though gravely disapproving of Puritan vandalism. They went through the Fountain Court and the beautiful Tudor Courts, and walked along the river, and sat under a tree to eat their lunch. They talked and argued and laughed and made plans and reformed the world and felt important (God knows why !) and held hands and kissed when they thought no one was looking. . . . And yes, they were very happy.

Dear Lovers ! If it were not for you, how dreary the world would be ! Never shall a pair of you pass me without a kindly discreet glance and a murmured wish, ' Be happy.' How my heart warmed to an old French poet as we walked slowly on the Boulevard, and the lovers in the soft evening air passed us by, hand so close in hand, bodies so amorously near, eyes so sparkling and alive ! Now and then, in the intoxicating air of the spring and the tolerant kindliness of the Parisians, a pair would feel so exuberant and so enthusiastic and so moved with each other's perfections, that they would have to stop and exchange a long kiss, perfunctorily hidden by a quite inadequate tree-trunk. Nobody interrupted them, nobody scowled, no policeman arrested them for indecency. And the old poet paused, and laid his hand on my arm, and said : ' Mon ami, I grow old ! I am nearly sixty. And sometimes as I pass along the streets and see these warm young people I find myself thinking : " How impudique ! Why is this permitted ? Why do they intrude their passions on me ? " And then I remember that I too was young, and I too passed eagerly and happily with one or other of my young mistresses whom I thought so beautiful, each of whom I loved with so immortal a love ! And I look at the lovers passing and I say to myself : " Allez-y, mes enfants, allez-y, soyez heureux ! " '

Dear Lovers ! Let us never forget that you are the sweetness of the bitter world.

And Elizabeth and George lingered through the sunny

hours ; and before the afternoon became too chill—for April is cold in England—they went back slowly through the long glades of the Park, they too hand in hand like the lovers on the Boulevard, they too with bodies amorously near, they too with eyes sparkling and alive, they too pausing to join their lips when the loveliness of life and the ecstasy of loving drew them together in a kiss.

They were so happy they did not know they were tired.

IT is fascinating to observe how people organise and disorganise their lives, fascinating to see how an impulse of vitality sends them off on a certain line, how they wobble, err, suffer, recover themselves. What is the most banal street, the most tedious place you know? Think how fascinating if only you knew the real lives of those tedious people!

There are two centres or poles of activity in every adult life—the economic and the sexual. Hunger and Death, the enemies. Your whole adult life depends on how you deal with the two primitive foes, Hunger and Death. Never mind how much the conditions of collective human life seem to have altered them, they are there; you can never really get away from Hunger and Death, from the need to eat and the will to live again.

Thus, two problems are created—the economic and the sexual. There is no cut-and-dried solution of either. Existence is tolerable—I will not say 'happy,' though I believe in happiness—to the extent that as an individual you are successful in solving these two problems. Certain traditional solutions are presented to us all in youth, and the swiftness with which we see their foolishness is an almost unerring test of intelligence. When we have seen through them, a new and delicate problem presents itself —we have to create our own happiness underneath or in despite of the Laws (or rules for collective life) and at the same time preserve intact the sense of Justice, or that which is due to each.

The primitive, the proletarian, the common man and woman solution is merely one of *quantity*. Get all the grub and copulation you want and more than you want, and *ipso facto* you will be happy. Put money in thy purse. Excellent Iago, what a fool you are! Noble Caliban, what a silly beast! Savages, the heroes of Homer, and working-men gorge on the flesh of beeves. To sack a town and rape all the women was the sexual ideal of centuries of civilised savages. To do the same thing with money sneakingly, instead of with the sword openly, is the actual ideal of Dr. Frank Crane's world-famous business men. The judgment of the wiser world is upon them all. Let them join the megatherium and the wild ass.

Then you have the Rudyard Kipling or British Public School solution. Not so far removed from the other as you might think, for it is a harnessing of the same primitive instincts to the service of a group—the nation—instead of to the service of the individual. Whatever is done for the Empire is right. Not Truth and Justice, but British Truth and British Justice. Odious profanation! You are the servant of the Empire; never mind whether you are rich or poor, do what the Empire tells you, and so long as the Empire is rich and powerful you ought to be happy. Woman? A rag, a bone, and a hank of hair. Get rid of the sexual problem by teaching men to despise women, either by open scorn or by putting them on the pedestal of chastity. Of course, they 're valuable as possessions. Oh, quite! There can be no world peace because the man who has the most money gets the best woman, as the German Kaiser said at the gathering of the nations. As if the nations were a set of Kiplingesque characters bidding against each other for an expensive tart! How despicable, how odious!

No, each of us has to work out the problems for himself,

and, I repeat, on the correct solution of both depends
happiness in life. I do not pretend to be able to teach
what is your solution. I think I know what is mine ; but
that is not necessarily yours. But I am quite sure that
the quantitative and the British Public School solutions
are wrong. . . .

The struggle with Hunger, or the economic problem,
leads to situations of astonishing ' human interest,' as
Balzac recognised. But we are not much concerned with
it here. It was highly important in the case of Isabel :
very little in the case of Elizabeth and George. They
were content with very little, which they obtained quite
easily—Elizabeth from her parents, George by various
odd jobs which occupied only a comparatively small part
of his time. Each wanted to avoid the slavery of working
eight hours a day at a stated wage, for some one else,
though both were willing to work sixteen hours a day on
their own, at what they wanted to do. Neither had the
slightest ambition to dominate others through wealth.
Of course, you may say they solved the economic problem
by dodging it. However, as far as they are concerned as
individuals, that *was* a solution.

But this ' dodging solution ' (if you like to call it such)
involved the sexual problem too. It was quite obvious
that George was incapable of supporting a woman and
children on his perfunctorily performed jobs, while
his painting was rather a liability than an asset. On
the other hand, it was equally obvious that Elizabeth
was not rich enough to afford the luxury of an artist
husband and a family. It therefore followed that
they could not afford children ; and since they didn't
want them, this was a misfortune they contemplated
with calm. But, since they didn't want children, it
followed that there was no need to get married. Why

get married, except for the sake of the unfortunate little bastard ?

All of which they talked out very fully before they ever lay together. You may say, of course, that this is very wicked and 'unnatural,' that if every one acted in this way the human race would soon come to a full stop. I shall not make the obvious retort of 'a good job, too,' but merely say that I observe no danger of under-population in Europe. Since the population of England is about three times the amount which the land of England can feed, I am inclined to think that George and Elizabeth should be regarded as a national hero and heroine in this respect. . . .

If you are as quick-witted as you ought to be, you will already have noticed one big difference between the George-Elizabeth ménage (I don't mean the legal ir-regularity, which is of no importance) and the ménages of George Augustus-Isabel, Dear Mamma-dear Papa, Ma-and-Pa Hartly. 'They talked it out very fully before they ever lay together.' You get the point ? They used their intelligence, they actually used their intelligence, *before* embarking on a joint sexual experience. That's the great break in the generations. Trying to use some intelligence in life, instead of blindly following instincts and the collective imbecility of the ages as embodied in social and legal codes. Isabel 'married for money' and got what she deserved, viz. bankruptcy. But she had been obliquely taught that it was a girl's duty to use men's sexual passion as a means of acquiring property. Whoring within the law. The Trade Union of married women. George Augustus was greatly attracted by Isabel and wanted to lie with her. Why not ? My God! why not ? But he had never thought about the problems. He didn't want children ; Isabel didn't want children. Not really.

But they had been taught that if a man and woman wanted to lie together it was horribly wicked to do so unless they were 'married.' The parson, the public ceremonies, and the signatures made 'sacred' what was otherwise inexpressibly wrong and sinful. But in the code on which George Augustus and Isabel were reared, 'marriage' meant 'a dear little baby' nine months after the wedding bells. All right for those who go into it with open eyes. Perfect. Charming. I'll be godfather every ten months. *J'adore les enfants.* But all wrong, all so rottenly wrong, if you go into it like a couple of ninnies, mess up your sexual life, disappoint the man, disgust the woman, and produce an infant you can't look after properly. . . .

Which is precisely what George Augustus and Isabel did, and what their parents did before them. . .

Now, the marriage of Molière's time was jolly sensible so far as it went. You, Eraste, love Lisette ? Good. You, Lisette, love Eraste ? Admirable. You wish to crown your flame ? Most natural and delightful. But you know that means infants ? Perfect. How much money have you got, Eraste ? Nothing ? Ah ! . . . But your father approves ? Will give ten thousand crowns if Lisette's father will give another five thousand ? Delicious. *Quite* a different situation. Your father approves, Lisette ? Yes ? Quick, a notary. Bless you, my children !

That was blunt, bluff common-sense. I'm sorry for Lisette, but not for Lisette's children.

The only trouble was that Lisette and Eraste were not very happy sexually—hence the *amants* of Lisette and the *amies* of Eraste. So you dropped into promiscuity, and Eraste didn't know if Lisette's later brats were his ; and Lisette didn't know how many dear little bastards Eraste was scattering about the world. All of which made for nastiness, cantankerousness, and hypocrisy.

The simple process of dissociating sex life from the philoprogenitive instinct was performed by the War Generation—at least on the grand scale, for isolated practitioners had long existed. The march of Science (how delightful clichés are !) had brought certain engines within the reach of all ; and sensible people profited by them. The old alternative of burning or marrying disappeared. And the following, far better, proposition arose. It was perfectly possible for man or woman to live a satisfactory sex life without having children. Hence, by the scientific process of trial and error, it became possible for each to seek the really satisfactory lover ; while those who were philoprogenitively inclined might marry (*en attendant mieux*) for the sake of the children. Thus there was a return to the wise promiscuity of the Ancients (if the Ancients ever did anything so sensible, which I greatly doubt), which was a great advance on humbug, domestic tyranny, furtive promiscuity, and whoring. One definite result, which we see to-day, is an undeniable decline in the number of whores—the first time this has occurred since the Edict of Milan.

Unfortunately the pre-war ' engines ' were rather crude and not wholly reliable. . . .

George and Elizabeth, then, were either extremely sensible or disgustingly immoral—I don't mind what your judgment is, I am recording facts. I don't, however, attempt to disguise my own prejudice, which is that intelligence makes for a far better life than ' Luv ' and ' God,' those euphuisms for stupidity and ignorance. In a manner of speaking they were pioneers. At any rate, they thought they were, which is all that matters here.

They really thought they had worked out a more sensible, more intelligent, more humane relationship between the sexes. But there were certain rather important little snags they overlooked. Like most bright young things, they were very cocksure of themselves, a good bit too cocksure. And then, while one doesn't at all deny that they were pretty bright, and on the right track, their knowledge was unhappily theoretical, chiefly derived from George's reading and meditations. It 's a confoundedly dangerous thing for two virgins to take on the job of initiating each other into a complicated art they only know theoretically. Dangerous, in that high hopes may be dashed, rather lovely emotions sadly frustrated, and a beautiful relationship spoiled. There are dangers in meeting the undeniably right person too soon in life. Two handsome young married people, obviously deeply in love—what a charming spectacle, how delightful! . . . Wait ! You wait ! Not very long, either. . . .

You haven't forgotten Fanny and the young man from Cambridge. . . .

Well, Elizabeth and George worked out their scheme, and for a considerable time it all worked admirably. But for the war and the upset of every one's mind and life and character, it might have weathered the small storms of Fanny and the young man—and perhaps other Fannies and other young men—and still have gone on working. Elizabeth abandoned her Hampstead boarding-house and found a large room, which did as a studio, in Bloomsbury. She wrote her parents in Manchester that she did this for the sake of economy and to be nearer her ' work '—whatever that might mean. The economy consisted in the fact that when she spent the night with George at his 'studio' she was obviously not wearing out her own bed-clothes. Elizabeth's mother paid her a surprise visit. Most luckily George had gone away for the week-end, and Elizabeth was 'discovered' calmly painting by herself. She behaved with the admirable dissimulation which comes so naturally to women, swiftly whipped away one or two objects (such as a tobacco pipe and pouch, *The Psychology of Sex* inscribed 'To darling Elizabeth from George') which might have betrayed a certain intimacy with a male, and sent George a long warning telegram. Mrs. Paston stayed three days. Of course, she suspected 'something.' Elizabeth looked about ten times prettier, was much more smartly dressed, talked differently, used all sorts of new phrases, and was obviously very happy, so happy that even three days of her mother failed to depress her completely. Elizabeth treated her char-lady with reasonable humanity, so when Mrs. Paston severely cross-examined her in secret about Elizabeth, the char-lady just went beautifully stupid and stood by Elizabeth nobly. 'Oh no, ma'am, I never seen nothin' wrong.' 'Oh yes, ma'am, Miss Elizabeth's such a nice young lady.' 'I'm only here of mornings, ma'am.' So Mrs. Paston, baffled but somewhat suspicious—what right had Elizabeth to look so well and happy and pretty away from her dear parents?—had to return home and present a blank report.

So that alarm died down.

Elizabeth became inordinately proud of being no longer a virgin. You might have thought she was the only devirginated young woman in London. But, like King Midas, she burned to share her secret, to make some-body else envious. So one week when George had run over to Paris about some pictures, she invited Fanny to tea, and after a tremendous amount of preparation confessed the lovely secret. Partly to Elizabeth's disappointment and partly to her relief, Fanny took the news as something very ordinary.

' I 'm really surprised you waited so long, my dear.'

' But you 're nearly as old as I am ! '

' Oh, but, darling, didn't you *know* ? I 've had two or three affairs. Only, I didn't say anything to *you*. I thought you 'd be shocked.'

' Shocked ? ' Elizabeth laughed scornfully, though she *was* a bit surprised. ' Why on earth should *I* be shocked ? *I* think people should be free to have all the love affairs they want.'

' Do tell me who he is ! '

Elizabeth blushed slightly and hesitated.

' No, I won't tell you now, but you 'll meet him soon.'

' But, Elizabeth, I hope you 're careful ? You won't go and have a baby ? '

Elizabeth laughed scornfully again.

' Have a baby ? Of course not ! Why ever do you think I 'm so silly ? George and I talked it——'

' Oh ! His name 's " George," is it ? '

' Yes. Did I let that out ? Yes, George Winterbourne. Well, we talked it all out, and we 've got a perfectly good arrangement. George says we 're too young to have children, so why get married ; and anyway we 're too poor. If we want children later on, we can always *get* married. I said I wouldn't tie myself down with *any* man—I don't want anybody else's name. I told George that if I wanted other lovers I should have them, and if he wanted any one else he was to have her. But, of course, when there 's a relationship as firmly established as ours, one doesn't *want* any one else.'

Fanny smiled.

As a matter of fact, Elizabeth had not said anything of the sort, when George drew up his Triumphal Scheme of the Perfect Sex Relationship. She had been rather timid and uncertain at first. But George's discourses and the books on physiology and psychology and sex which he made her read, and her own exultation at being no longer a virgin, had sent her spinning in the other direction. She had, in a few months, far out-distanced George in ' freedom.' Her argument was rational and quite defensible ; indeed, it was a corollary to George's own views, though he hadn't seen it. Because you were very fond of one person, she argued, that was no reason why you shouldn't be attracted by others. Monogamy was established to tyrannise women and to make sure offspring were ' legitimate ' and to provide for them and the mother. But where women are free and there is no offspring, what on earth is the good of an artificial and forced fidelity ? Directly one has to *promise* fidelity, directly an effort of will is made to ' remain faithful,' a false position is set up. The effort of keeping such a promise is the surest assurance that it will be broken sooner or later. On the other hand, while you are in love with some one, well, you 're in love, and you either don't want any one else, or if you do, you 're probably only too happy to get back speedily to the person you do really care for.

There was logic, and a good deal of sense, in this, George had to admit. But he also had to admit to himself that he didn't altogether like the idea of Elizabeth ' going with ' somebody else. Nor, for that matter, would Elizabeth have liked George ' going with ' another girl. But she deceived herself unknowingly. At that time she was very much under the influence of a Swedish book she had read, a book devoted to the Future of the Race. This was the work of an earnest-minded virgin of fifty who laid it down as an indisputable axiom that there must be complete frankness between the sexes. ' The old notion of sexual fidelity must go,' declared this enthusiastic writer, ' and only from the golden sun-bath of divinely nude freedom can rise the glorious new race,' etc. etc. Elizabeth didn't know the authoress was an old maid, and she was annoyed with George for making fun of the ' golden sun-bath of divinely nude freedom.'

' But, Elizabeth,' George had said, when she propounded this argument, ' of course I believe that people should be free, and it 's disgusting for them to stay together when they don't any longer love each other. But suppose I happened to want some one else, just a sort of whim, and went on loving you, wouldn't it be better if I said nothing about it ? And the same with you ? '

' And tell each other lies ? Why, George, you yourself have said time and again that there can be no genuine relationship which involves deceit. The very essence and beauty and joy of our relation depend upon its being honest and frank and accepting facts.'

' Why, yes, but . . .'

' Look at the lives of our parents, look at all the sneaking adulteries going on at this very moment in every suburb of London. Don't you see—why, you *must* see—that what 's wrong about adultery is not the sexual part of it at all, but the plotting and sneaking and dissimulation and lies and pretence. . . .'

' That 's true,' said George slowly and reflectively, that 's true. But—suppose I told you that when I was last in Paris I spent the nights with Georgina Harris ? '

' Did you ? '

' No, of course not. But, you see . . .'

' What would it have mattered if you had ? My Swedish woman you make fun of is very sound about

that. She says that two people should spend a few days
or more away from each other every few weeks, and that
it may be a very good thing for them to have other sexual
experience. It prevents any feeling of sameness and
satiety, and often brings two people together more closely
than ever, if only they 're frank about it.'

' I wonder,' said George, ' I wonder. Is there any one
you 're interested in, Elizabeth ? '

' Of course not. You 're really rather unintelligent
about this, George. You know perfectly well I love you
passionately and shall never love any one else so much.
But there mustn't be any lying and dissimulation, and no
artificial fidelity. If you want to go off for a night or a
week-end or a week with some charming girl or woman,
you must go. And if I want to do the same with a man,
I must. Don't you see that by thwarting a mere *béguin*
you may turn it into something more serious, whereas by
enjoying it you get rid of it ? Probably, as my Swedish
woman says, one is so much disappointed that a single
night is more than enough, and one returns to one's love
eagerly, cured of wandering fancies for the next six
months.'

' Yes, I daresay there 's something in that. It seems
sound. And yet if the original relationship is so secure
and if the other affair is so slight and unimportant and
merely physical, it seems unnecessary to hurt one's love
by speaking about it. I don't tell you every day what I
had for lunch. Besides, even if one spends only one
night with another person, that implies at least a one-
night's preference, which might hurt.'

' Which might hurt ! ' Elizabeth mocked. ' George,
you 're being positively old-fashioned. Why, when you
go to Paris, isn't that a preference ? And when I go to
Fanny's cottage in the country for a week-end, isn't that

a preference ?   How do you know we 're not Sapphic friends ? '

' I 'm jolly sure you 're not !   You 're neither of you in the least bit Lesbian types.   Besides, you 'd have told me.'

' You see !   You know quite well I 'd have told you.'

' Yes, but going to Paris or the country for a few days isn't the same sort of " preference." '

The argument tailed off in a futile attempt to define ' preference.'   Ultimately Elizabeth carried her point. It was definitely established that ' nothing could break ' a relationship such as theirs ; but that ' love itself must have rest,' and therefore there was wisdom in occasional short separations ; that so far from breaking up such a relationship, occasional ' slight affairs ' elsewhere would only strengthen and stimulate it.   George allowed himself to be convinced.   The snag here lay in the fact that he had definitely sensed the possible danger of arousing jealousy ; whereas Elizabeth, confident in herself and the theories of her Swedish old maid, scorned the idea that so base a passion could even enter *their* relation.

About two months after this, George and Elizabeth were cheerfully dining in a small Soho restaurant when Fanny came in with a young man, the ' young man from Cambridge,' Reggie Burnside.

' Oh, look ! ' exclaimed Elizabeth, ' there 's Fanny and a friend with her.   Fanny !   Fanny ! ' signalling across the room.   Fanny came across.

' This is George Winterbourne.   You 've often heard of Fanny, George.   I say, Fanny, do come and have dinner with us.'

' Yes, do.'

' But I 've got Reggie Burnside with me.'

' Well, bring him along too.'

The young man was introduced, and they sat down at the table. In most respects Fanny was curiously different from Elizabeth ; each was not so much the antithesis as the complement to the other. Fanny was just a little taller than Elizabeth (George disliked short women); and where Elizabeth was dark and Egyptian-looking and pale, Fanny was golden and English (not chocolate-box English) and most delicate white and red. She was a bit like Priscilla, George thought, but with the soft gold of Priscilla made hard and glittering, like an exquisite metallic flower. There was something both gem-like and flower-like in Fanny. Perhaps that was due to her eyes. With other women you are conscious almost immediately of all sorts of beauties and defects, but with Fanny you were instantaneously absorbed by the eyes. When you thought about her afterwards, you just saw a mental image of those extraordinary blue eyes, disassociated from the rest of her, like an Edgar Poe vision. But, unlike so many vivid blue eyes, they were gem-like rather than flower-like ; they were not soft or stupid or sentimental or languid, but clear, alert, and rather hard. You may see exactly their shade of colour in the deeper parts of Lake Garda on a sunny day. Yet the quality was not aqueous, but vitreous. Venetian glass, perhaps ? No, that is too opaque. It is very hard to say what was the quality which made them so remarkable. Men looked at them once and fell helplessly in love, one might say almost noisily in love—Fanny didn't mind, it was obviously her *métier* to have men fall in love with her. Perhaps Fanny's eyes were simply made a symbol in the imagination of that mysterious sexual attraction which radiated from her, or perhaps they conformed to some unwritten but instinctively recognised canon of the perfect eye, the Platonic ' idea ' of eyes. . . .

With Elizabeth you saw not the eyes alone, but the whole head.   You would have liked to keep Fanny's eyes, magnificently set in gold, in an open jewel-casket, to look at when you doubted whether any beauty remained in the dull world.   But with Elizabeth you wanted the whole head, it was so much like one of those small stone heads of Egyptian princesses in the Louvre.   So very Egyptian. The full, delicately-moulded lips, the high cheek-bones, the slightly oblique eye-sockets, the magnificent line from ear to chin, the upward sweep of the wide brow, the straight black hair.   Oddly enough, on analysis Elizabeth's eyes proved to be quite as beautiful as Fanny's, but somehow less ostentatiously lovely.   They were deeper and softer, and, which is rare in dark eyes, intelligent. Fanny's blue eyes were intelligent enough, but they hadn't quite the subtle depths of Elizabeth's, they hadn't the same reserve.

Elizabeth lived very much in and on herself ; Fanny was a whole-hearted extravert.   Where Elizabeth hesitated, mused, suffered, Fanny acted, came a cropper, picked herself up gaily and started off again with just the same zest for experience.   She was more smartly dressed than Elizabeth.   Of course, Elizabeth was always quite charming and attractive, but you guessed that she had other things to think about beside clothes.   Fanny loved clothes, and, with no more money than Elizabeth, contrived to look stunningly fashionable where Elizabeth merely looked O.K.   Oddly enough, Fanny was not devoured by the Scylla of clothes, the monster of millinery which is never satiate with its female victims.   Her energy saved her from that.   She and Elizabeth were both restlessly energetic;   but whereas Elizabeth's energy went into

dreaming and arguing and trying to paint, Fanny's went
into all sorts of activities with all sorts of persons. She
did not 'do' anything, having sense enough to see that
in most young women 'art' is merely a kind of safety-
valve for sex. Fanny, I 'm glad to say, did not need a
safety-valve for her sex ; the steam-pressure was kept
regulated and the engine worked perfectly, thank you
very much. She was emotionally and mentally far less
complicated than Elizabeth, less profound ; therefore to
her the new sexual régime, where perfect freedom has
happily taken the place of service, presented fewer
possible snags. I 've said, of course, that Fanny sometimes came a cropper ; she did, but she hadn't Elizabeth's
capacity for suffering, Elizabeth's desolate despair when
her silk purse turned out to be a sow's ear—which every
one else had known long before.

Perhaps the remarkable quality of Elizabeth's mind
and character is best showed by the fact that she never
said or implied anything mean or nasty about Fanny's
clothes. . . .

Reggie Burnside was a rich young man engaged in
some mysterious 'research work' at Cambridge, something connected with the structure of the atom, and highly
impressive because the nature of his work could only be
explained in elaborate mathematical symbols. He wore
spectacles, talked in a high intellectual voice with the
peculiar intonation and blurred syllables favoured by
some members of that great centre of learning, and appeared exceedingly weary. Even Fanny's impetuous
dash never galvanised him into a spontaneous action or a
natural remark. He also was extremely modern, and
was devoted to Fanny. He was always at hand when
nothing better presented itself—the permanent second

string to the fiddle, or, as Fanny put it, one of her *fautes*, adding *sotto voce*, my *faute-de-mieux*.

The talk at first was the usual highbrow chatter of the period—Flecker and Brooke and Mr. Russell, referred to as ' Bertie ' in a casual way by Fanny and Reggie, to the mystification of George. This is one of the charming traits of the English intelligentsia. Every one they don't know is an outsider, and they love to keep the outsider outside by a gently condescending patronage. A most effective method is to talk nonchalantly about well-known people by their Christian names :

' Have you read Johnny's last book ? '

' No-oh. Not yet. The last one was a dreadful bore. Is this any better ? '

' No-oh, I don't think so. Tommy dislikes it profoundly. Says it reminds him of sports on the village green.'

' How a*mus*ing ! '

' Oh, Tommy can be quite a*mus*ing at times. I was with him and Bernard the other day, and Bernard said . . .'

And if the outsider is silly enough to bite, and to say timidly or bluntly, ' Who 's Johnny ? ' the answer comes swift and sweet :

' O-oh ! Don't you *know* . . . ! '

And then the dazzled outsider is condescendingly informed who ' Johnny ' is, and, especially if a mere American or Continental, is crushed to learn that ' Johnny ' is Johnny Walker or some other enormously brilliant light in the firmament of British culture. . . .

George got sick of hearing about ' Bertie ' without being told who the devil Bertie was, and began to talk about

Ezra Pound, Jules Romains, and Modigliani. But he soon
learned by sweet implication that such people might be
all very well in their way, but after all, well, you know
what I mean, Cambridge *is* Cambridge. . . . So George
shut up and said nothing. Then Reggie began to talk to
Elizabeth about Alpine climbing, the sport of Dons—and
a very appropriate one too, if you think about it. And
Fanny talked to George.

Now Fanny was quite a subtil little beast of the field,
and saw that George was a bit sulky, and guessed why.
Vapourish airs were indifferent to her. She had been
brought up among such people, and unconsciously
adopted their tone when speaking to them. But when
she was among other sorts of people she just as unconsciously dropped the vapourish airs and let her natural self
respond to theirs. She had a foot, one might almost say
a leg, in several social worlds ; and got on perfectly well
in any of them. There was a sort of physical indifference
in Fanny which at first sight looked like mere hardness,
and wasn't. In fact, she wasn't nearly as hard as Elizabeth, who could be quite Stonehengey at times. And
then suddenly crumble. But Fanny's physical indifference carried her through a lot ; one felt that her
morning bath had something Lethean about it, and
washed away the memory of last night's lover along
with his touch.

So Fanny began to talk to George quite naturally and
gaily. He was suspicious, and gave her three verbal bangs
in quick succession. She took them with unflinching
good-humour, and went on talking and trying to find out
what he was interested in. George pretty soon melted to
her gaiety—or perhaps it was the gem-like eyes. He
looked at them, and wondered what it felt like to possess
natural organs which were such superb *objets d'art*. They

must, he reflected, cause her a good deal of annoyance. Every man who met her would feel called upon to inform her that she had wonderful eyes, as if he had made an astounding discovery, hitherto unrevealed by any one. George decided that it would be well *not* to comment upon Fanny's eyes at a first meeting.

Reggie had failed to interest Elizabeth in Alpine climbing, and switched off to '*amus*ing' anecdotes, which were more successful. Under the mild influence of a little wine and a sympathetic listener Reggie shed some of his worst mannerisms and became almost human. He liked Elizabeth. She might not be wholly '*amus*ing,' but she was '*refresh*ing.' (She was a good listener.) And when the talk once again became general, George began to think that Reggie was not such a bad fellow after all ; there was a sort of ' niceness ' about him, the genuine English pride and good-nature under a screen of affectation.

They sat over coffee and cigarettes until the fidgeting of the waiter and ' Madame's ' little games with the electric switches warned them that their money and absence would now be more welcome than their company. It was well after ten—too late for the cinema. They walked down Shaftesbury Avenue, George with Reggie, and Elizabeth with Fanny.

' I like your George,' said Fanny.

' Do you ? I 'm so glad.'

' He 's a bit *farouche*, but I like the way he enthuses about what interests him. It 's not put on.'

' I think Reggie 's rather nice.'

' Oh ! Reggie . . .' and Fanny waved her hand with a little shrug.

' But he *is* nice, Fanny You know you like him.'

' Yes, he 's all right.   I 'm not wild about him.   You can have him, if you want.'

' Oh!   Oh!' Elizabeth laughed; ' wait till I ask you ! '

They separated at Piccadilly Circus.   Fanny and Reggie went off somewhere in a taxi.   Coming down Shaftesbury Avenue, George had noticed that it was a clear night with a full moon, and insisted on going to the Embankment to see the moonlight on the Thames.   They turned into the Haymarket.

' What do you think of Fanny ? ' asked Elizabeth.

' I think she has most marvellous eyes.'

' Yes, that 's what every one says.'

' I was trying to be original !   But she 's a nice girl, too.   At first, when she and Burnside began talking, I thought she was hopelessly infected by his sort of affectation.'

' Why !   Don't you like him ?   I thought he was charming.'

' Charming ?   I shouldn't say that.   I think he 's not a bad sort of fellow really, but you know how exasperating I find the Cambridge bleat.   Ah 'd much raver lis'n to a muckin' Cawkn'y, swop me bob, I would.'

' But you know he 's a very important young scientist, and supposed to be doing marvellous research work.'

' Do you know what it is ? '

' No.   Fanny couldn't tell me.   She said you had to be a specialist yourself to understand what he 's doing.'

' Well, I must say I 'm a bit suspicious of these mysterious " specialists," who can't even tell you plainly what they 're doing.   I think Boileau 's right—what's accurately conceived can be clearly expressed.   When Science begins to talk the language of mystic Theology and superstition, I begin to suspect it vehemently. Besides, only the feeble sections of any aristocracy take on vapourish airs and affected ways of talk. Well-bred people haven't any affectations. And men with really fine minds haven't any intellectual vanity.'

' Oh, but Reggie isn't vain. He didn't even mention his work to me. And he told such *amusing* stories.'

' That 's just another form of insolence—they assume you 're too ignorant and stupid to understand their great and important labours, so they never condescend even to mention them, but tell " *amusing* stories," as I see you 've already learned to call Common-Room gossip.'

Elizabeth was silent, ominously silent. She was more used to the Cambridge manner than George was, and thought he fussed too much about it. Besides, she had been really attracted by Reggie. She thought George was making a jealous scene. There she did him a wrong ; it never occurred to George that Elizabeth might fall in love with Reggie. (Oddly enough, it never *does* occur to a husband or a lover *in esse* to suspect his probable coadjutor—until it is too late. He suspects plenty of wrong people, but rarely the right one. The Cyprian undoubtedly has artful ways.) As a matter of fact, George had not the slightest feeling of jealousy. He was merely saying what he felt, as he would have done about any other chance acquaintance. He respected Elizabeth's silence. It was one of their numerous pacts—to respect each other's silence. So they walked mutely down Whitehall, while George thought vaguely about Fanny and his next day's work, and cocked his head up to try to see the moon, and watched the occasional buses bounding along like rapid barges in the empty light-filled river of Belgian blocks ; and Elizabeth brooded over the supposed revelation of a hitherto unsuspected tendency to silly jealousy in George. But just as they approached the Abbey, George slipped his arm through hers so naturally, affectionately, and unsuspiciously that Elizabeth's ill-humour vanished, and in two minutes they were chattering as volubly as ever.

They walked along the Embankment from Westminster Bridge towards the City. A serene sky hung over London, transposed to an astonishing blue by the complementary yellow of the brilliant street lights. A few trams and taxis were still moving on the Embankment, but after the ceaseless roar of day traffic the air seemed almost silent. At times they could hear the lap and gurgle of the swift river water, as the strong flood tide ran inland, bearing a faint flavour of salt. The river was beautifully silver in the soft, steady moonlight which wavered into multitudes of ripples as soon as it touched the broken surface of the Thames. Blocks of moored barges stood black and immovable in the silver flood. The Southern bank was dark, low, and motionless, except for the luminous announcements of the blessings of Lipton's Tea and the *Daily Mail*. The Scotchman in coloured moving lights pledged the bonny Highlands in countless sparkling glasses of electric whisky. Hungerford Railway bridge seemed filled with the red eyes of immense dragons, whose vast bulk lay coiled somewhere invisibly on either bank. Occasionally a red eye would wink green, a brightly-lit train would crawl cautiously and heavily over the vibrating bridge. The lighted windows of the Cecil and the Savoy aroused no envy in them. Nor did they pine to inspect the records of a great people lying behind the darkened and silent façade of Somerset House.

Opposite the quiet Temple Garden they paused by the parapet and looked up and down that magnificent sweep of river, with its amazing mixture of dignified beauty and almost incredible sordidness.   They stood for some time, talking in quiet tones, comparing the Thames with the Seine, and wondering what dreamlike city would have arisen by those noble curves if London had been inhabited by a race of artists.   Elizabeth wanted to set Florence or Oxford on either side of the Thames between West-minster and St. Paul's.   George agreed that that would be lovely, but thought the buildings would be dwarfed by the width of the river, the long bridges, and the length of façade.   And they finally agreed that with all its sordid-ness and hugger-mugger and strange contrast of palaces abutting on slums, the Embankment had a beauty of its own which they would not exchange even for the dream-city of a race of artists.

Midnight boomed with majestic, policeman-like slow-ness from Big Ben ; and as the last deep vibrations faded from the air, the great city seemed to be gliding into sleep and silence.   They lingered a little longer, and then turned to go.

Then, for the first time they noticed what they knew would be there but had forgotten in their absorbed delight in the silvery water and moon-washed outlines of the city —that on every bench sat crouched or huddled one or more miserable, ragged human beings.   In front of them ran the mystically lovely river ; behind them the dark masses of the Temple rose solidly and sternly defensive of Law and Order behind the spear-front of its tall sharp-pointed iron fence.   And there they crouched and huddled in rags and hunger and misery, free-born members of the greatest Empire the earth has yet seen, citizens of Her who so proudly claimed to be the wealthiest of cities, the exchange and mart of the whole world.

George gave what change he had in his pockets to a noseless syphilitic hag, and Elizabeth emptied her purse into the hand of a shivering child which had to be awakened to receive the gift, and cowered as if it thought it was going to be struck.

Ignoring the hag's hoarse 'Thank yer kindly, Sir, Gord bless yer, Lidy,' they fled clutching each other's hands. They did not speak until they said good-night outside Elizabeth's door.

DURING 1913 life ran on very pleasantly and happily for George and Elizabeth. As in the cases of the fortunate nations without a history, there appears to be very little to record about this year. I make no doubt that it was the happiest in George's life. He was, as they say, 'getting on,' and had less need to worry about money. In the spring they went to Dorsetshire and stayed at an inn. Elizabeth did a certain amount of painting, but apart from a few sketches George did not attempt landscape, especially the picturesque landscape—he wanted his painting to be urban, contemporary, and hard. They walked a good deal over Worbarrow Down and the rather desolate heath land round about. On more than one occasion they traversed the very same piece of land where George was afterwards in camp with me, a coincidence which seemed to make a great impression upon him. Certain aspects of a familiar landscape always call up the same train of thought ; and as people are never weary of telling us what particularly strikes them, so George rarely failed to convey this piece of stale news to me as we walked out of camp by what had once been the rough cart-track he and Elizabeth had followed in less desolate days. He seemed to think it remarkable that he should be so miserable in exactly the same place where he had once been so happy. As I pointed out, that showed great ignorance of the ironic temper of the gods, who are very fond of such genial contrasts. They delight to lay a corpse in a marriage bed, and to strike down a great nation in the fullest flush of its pride and power. One might think that happiness was 'hubris,' the excess which calls down the vengeance of Fate.

They returned to London for a few weeks, and then went to Paris. Elizabeth adored Paris, and wanted to live there permanently ; but George was against it. He had got some bug about the best art being ' autochthonous,' and declared that an artist ought to live in his own country. But the real reason was that Parisian life seemed so pleasant and the town so full of artists more gifted and more advanced than himself, that he found it almost impossible to work there. It was easier to feel important in the comparative desert of London. So they returned to London ; and in the autumn George had his first ' show,' which was not altogether such a failure as he had expected.

When autumn turned to winter, and the yellow leaves of the plane-trees drifted down into heaps in the London squares, lying miserably sodden under the rain, the ever-lasting London drizzle, Elizabeth got very restless. She wanted to get away, anywhere under blue skies and sun. Her throat and lungs were rather sensitive, and when the weather turned foggy she nearly choked in the heavy, soot-laden, stifling air. They talked about going to Italy or Spain, but George knew only too well that he could not afford it. He might indeed get assurances from various impresarios he frequented that ' work could go on as usual,' but he knew only too well that a month's absence would mean a decline and that after three months he would be practically forgotten and dropped. It 's a dangerous thing to have a national reputation for honesty —people get to trading upon it and seem to think it absolves them from individual obligations. So George, after forming various vague plans for a delightful winter in Sicily or the island of Majorca, had to admit to Elizabeth that he simply dared not go. He begged her to go alone, or to find some friend to go with her. But Elizabeth flatly

refused to go without him. So they stayed in London,
and worked and coughed together. Perhaps it might
have been better to take the risk, for as things turned out
George never saw either Spain or Italy, which he had
wanted so much to see.

Fanny came to London for a week in November, before
going South for the winter ; and they saw her nearly every
day. Fanny and George were by this time on a footing of
pretty friendly familiarity. That is to say, they always
kissed each other on meeting and parting—after Fanny
had kissed Elizabeth—and held hands in taxis whether
Elizabeth was there or not. Elizabeth didn't object at
all. Not only because of her theory of freedom. She
was at that time rather deeply involved in some theory of
' erogenous zones ' in women, and men's reaction to them.
And she had got it firmly into her mind that Fanny was
' sexually antipathetic ' to George, because he had one day
innocently and casually remarked that he thought Fanny
rather flat-chested. Elizabeth leaped on this—it confirmed her theory so nicely. George had known Fanny
for over a year and ' nothing had happened ' between
them, and therefore it was plain that Fanny's ' erogenous
zones ' awoke no response in him.

' Most peculiar,' said Elizabeth, when she discussed the
matter with a demure-looking but mighty ironical Fanny.
' *I* should have thought you 'd be the very type of woman
to attract him. But he only talks about your " marvellous
eyes," and they aren't erogenous zones at all. That means
he only likes you as a human being. . . .'

So Elizabeth took no notice when Fanny kissed George ;
or when she said : ' George darling, do go and get some
cigarettes for me,' and George departed with alacrity ; or
when George called Fanny ' My love ' or ' Fanny darling.'
People throw these endearments about so liberally nowa-

days, how on earth is one to know ? And, in fact, all this
went on for a long time, and nothing did ' happen.'
George was quite devoted to Elizabeth, and then they
were away when Fanny was in London, and Fanny was
away when they were in London. Both George and
Fanny begged Elizabeth to ' go South ' with Fanny, but
Elizabeth wouldn't. She was very loyal, and wouldn't
take a holiday George couldn't share. But by this time
Fanny had become fond of George, very fond indeed.
She was weary of Reggie, who was sometimes so absorbed
in atoms that he neglected his functions as Fanny's *faute-
de-mieux*. She thought it might be an excellent plan if
she and Elizabeth swopped riders, so to speak. Not
that she wanted to ' take George away ' from his mistress.
Oh ! not at all. Fanny didn't want him as a *permanence*
—Elizabeth was welcome to that. But she felt he might
do excellently as a *locum tenens*, while Elizabeth was
widening her experience with Reggie. So there was an
unusual warmth in her farewell kiss to George, who had
gone down to see her off at Victoria, and a lingeringly soft
pressure of her hand, and a particularly inviting look in
her beautiful eyes.

' Good-bye, darling ! ' and she leaned from the
window and to his surprise kissed him again on the lips.
' Of course, I 'll write—often. And mind you write to
me. I shall be back in March at latest.'

Fanny did write—occasionally to Elizabeth, once or
twice to them both, frequently to George. Her letters
to George were much longer and more amusing than the
others. George showed some of them to Elizabeth and
forgot to show others. He replied punctually and
affectionately.

Just before Christmas, Reggie Burnside passed through
London on his way to Mürren. He dropped into Eliza-

beth's studio for tea, and finding her alone asked her to
marry him, in a casual, offhand way, rather as he might
have suggested their going to Rumpelmeyer's instead
of having tea in the studio. Elizabeth was surprised,
flattered, and fluttered. They had quite a long discussion.
Elizabeth was amazed that Reggie should want to marry,
and above all to marry her. If she hadn't been so flattered,
she would have been offended at any one's thinking she
would do such a thing. She had almost the 'thank-you-
I'm-not-that-sort-of-girl' sniffiness about it.

' Is this a new brand of joke, Reggie ? '

' Good God, no ! I'm perfectly serious.'

' But why in heaven's name do you want to *marry* ? '

' It's more convenient, you know, addressing letters
and meeting people and all that.'

' But why want to marry *me* ? '

' Because I'm in love with you.'

Elizabeth pondered a little over this.

' Well,' she said slowly, ' I don't believe I'm in love
with you. I'm sure I'm not. I like you most awfully,
but I'm not in love with you, I'm in love with
George.'

' Oh, George ! ' Reggie waved a contemptuous hand.
' What's the good of your wasting your time with a
man like that, Elizabeth ? He won't do anything. He
doesn't know anybody worth mentioning, except ourselves, and nobody at Cambridge thinks anything of his
painting.'

Elizabeth was on the defensive immediately.

' Don't talk nonsense, Reggie ! George is a dear, and
I won't have you say things like that about him. And as
if anybody cares a hang what mouldy young Cambridge
thinks about a painter ! '

Reggie changed his tack.

' All right, if you don't want to marry me, don't. But, look here. You oughtn't to spend the winter in London with that cough and your chest. I 'll give up Mürren if you 'll come for a month with me to some small place on the Riviera. We can easily find a place where there aren't any English.'

This was a far more gratifying and dangerous proposal to Elizabeth than matrimony. She was heartily sick of London fog and cold and drizzle and mire and soot and messy open fires which fill the room with dust but don't warm it. More than once she had regretted not having gone away with Fanny. Moreover, a ' month's affair ' with Reggie would perfectly well fit into the arrangement with George, whereas they hadn't thought of and hadn't discussed the possibility of either marrying some one else. Elizabeth hesitated, but she had a feeling that it would be rather mean to leave George suddenly alone in London and go off on her own with Reggie, if only for a month. She certainly was extraordinarily fond of George.

' No, Reggie, I can't come this time. Go to Mürren, and when you come back, perhaps . . . well, we 'll see.'

Elizabeth made toast and tea, and they sat on a large low divan in front of the fire. The dingy light soon faded from the soiled sky ; but they sat on in the firelight, holding hands.

She let Reggie kiss her as much as he wanted, but for the time being resisted any further encroachments.

Elizabeth's resistance, at that precise moment, to the advances of Mr. Reginald Burnside seems to me a striking example of George's infelicity. I mean that I see a direct link between it and the sudden inexplicable standing up of a man in khaki before a murderous machine-gun fire, not long after dawn, on the morning of the 4th

of November 1918. . . . Not that I wish melodramatically 'to set the brand of Cain' upon Elizabeth or upon
Fanny or upon both jointly. Far from it. *They* didn't
make the war. *They* didn't give George the jumps.
And after all there is a doubt, almost a mystery, involved
in George's death. Did he really commit suicide ? I
don't know. I 've only got circumstantial evidence and
my own hunch about it, a sort of intuition, a something
haunting in my memory of the man, an Orestes-like feeling
of some inexpiated guilt. Who is to say whether a man
can really commit suicide on a battlefield ? Desperate
recklessness and looking for trouble may be the very
means of his escaping the death which finds the prudent
coward crouching in a shell-hole. And suppose he did
deliberately get himself killed, ought we, ought I, to
attach any blame to Elizabeth and Fanny ? I don't
think so. There were plenty of other things to disgust
him with life. And even supposing that he realised the
war was ending, realised that in his state of mind he
simply could not face the problem of his relation with
those two women, still I think them utterly blameless.
The mess was as much his fault as theirs. It was really
quite an easy mess to clear up. What made it impossible
was George's shattered nerves, and for that they were not
to blame. Oh, not in the least. Perhaps I 'm as much
to blame as anybody. I ought to have done something
to get George sent out of the line. I think I might have
gone to the Brigadier and have told him in private what
I knew about George's state of mind—or perhaps to his
Colonel. But I didn't go. At that time I was not
persona grata with those in authority, for I happened to
sympathise then with the young Russian Revolution, and
had foolishly argued hotly about it. So perhaps my
effort would have been wasted. And anyhow it was a

very difficult and ticklish thing to do, and I was tired,
very, very tired. . . .

At any rate, just about a fortnight after Reggie went to
Mürren, the abominable winter climate of London gave
Elizabeth some sort of a chill inside and upset her interior
economy. Within four or five days she became quite
demented. She insisted that she was with child, and
insisted that the only solution was for George to marry
her—at once. Perhaps the afternoon with Reggie had
somehow inserted the idea of marriage into her 'subconscious.' At all events, her extraordinary energy was
suddenly concentrated upon attaining a state which she
had hitherto utterly scorned. It was a silly thing to do,
but one really cannot blame her. Men are oddly callous
about these mysterious female maladies and demoniacal
possessions. They get peevish and pathetic enough if
something goes wrong with their own livers, but they are
strangely unsympathetic about the profounder derange-
ments of their yoke-fellows in iniquity. Perhaps they
might feel a little more humane if they too had a sort of
twenty-eight-day clock inside them, always a nuisance,
often liable to go wrong and set up irregular blood-
pressure and an intolerable poisoning of the brain.
George ought to have hiked her off to a gynecologist at
once. Instead of which, he behaved as stupidly as any
George Augustus would have done under the circumstances. He did nothing but gasp and stare at Elizabeth's
whirling tantrums, and worry, and offer exasperating
comfort, and propose remedies and measures which, as
Elizabeth told him, with a stamp of her foot, were impossible, impossible, *impossible*. Of course, by the
Triumphal Scheme for the Perfect Sex Relation, it was
duly enacted that under such circumstances there was
nothing to do but marry the girl. But elementary

prudence would suggest that it might be sensible to make
certain the circumstances *had* arisen, a precaution which
they entirely overlooked in the mental disarray caused by
Elizabeth's regrettable dementia.

The change wrought in Elizabeth's outlook in a few
days was amazing.   If she hadn't felt so tragically about
it, she would have been ludicrous in her mental manœuvres.   The whole Triumphal Scheme was scrapped
almost instantaneously, and by a rapid and masterly series
of evolutions her whole army of arguments was with-
drawn from the outpost line of Complete Sexual Freedom,
and fell back upon the Hindenburg line of Safety First,
Female Honour, and Legal Marriage.   It was, of course,
ridiculous for them to marry at all, either of them.   They
weren't the marrying sort.   They were adventurers in
life, not good citizens.   Neither of them was the kind of
person who exults in life insurance and buying a house
on the hire-purchase system and mowing the lawn on
Saturday afternoon and taking the ' kiddies ' (odious
word) to the seaside.   Neither of them looked forward
to the ' Old Age Will Come ' summit of felicity, with an
elderly and imbecilely contented-looking George sitting
beside a placid and motherly white-haired Elizabeth in
the garden of a dear little home, contemplating together
with smug beatitude the document from the insurance
company guaranteeing a safe ten pounds a week for the
remainder of their joint lives.   I am glad to say that
George and Elizabeth would have shuddered at any such
prospect.   But Elizabeth insisted upon marriage, and
married they duly were, despite the feeble protests of
Elizabeth's family and the masterly denunciations of
Isabel, already recorded.

In all outward respects the legal marriage made no difference whatever to their lives and relationship.   Elizabeth

retained her studio, and George his.   They met no more
frequently and on exactly the same terms of affectionate
sensuality, into which their first exultant passion had
long ago evolved.   One of the terms of the Triumphal
Scheme emphatically laid down the axiom that it was most
undesirable and dangerous for two lovers to inhabit the
same flat or small house.   If they were rich enough to
live in separate wings of a large house, all well and good ;
but if not, then they should live no nearer than neigh-
bouring streets.   The essence of freedom is the disposal
of one's own time in one's own way, and how can two
people do that if they are living on top of each other ?
Moreover, a daily absence of several hours is quite indispensable to the avoidance of the domestic-den atmosphere.   It is far better for two lovers to be happy together for three or four hours a day than to be indifferent
or miserable for twenty-four.   The joint marriage-bed,
Elizabeth used to state impressively, is destructive of all
self-respect and sexual charm, and blunts the finer edges
of sensibility. . . .

Soon after the legal formalities were irrevocably accom-
plished and Elizabeth's social anxieties somewhat calmed,
it occurred to her that she ought to consult a doctor, in
order to learn how to behave during these months of
' expecting,' as the modest working-class matron calls it.
So she got the address of a ' modern ' physician, who was
supposed to have all the latest and most enlightened
methods of dealing with pregnancy and its distresses.   To
Elizabeth's amazement she found she was not pregnant
at all !   With the not unnatural suspicion that most
doctors are more or less charlatans imposing on the ignorance of the public, she refused to believe him until he told
her flatly that in her present condition she might wait till
doomsday for the appearance of an infant, but that if she

neglected her present slight disorder it might become
serious and permanent. She then condescended to
accept his diagnosis and advice. George had accompanied her, and was sitting in the specialist's waiting-
room. A serious, concentrated, rather pi-jaw Elizabeth
had left him to enter the consulting-room, and George
fidgeted over the imbecilities of *Punch*, wondering how
on earth they would deal with the problem of an infant,
and feeling that he would probably have to take a job and
'settle down' into the horrible morass of domestic life.
To his amazement, as the consulting-room door opened,
he heard Elizabeth laugh with her old merry gaiety which
was so attractive, and caught the words :

'Well, if it's twins, doctor, you shall be godfather.'

To which the doctor replied with a laugh George
thought rather ribald and heartless under the circumstances. Elizabeth rushed into the room exclaiming :

'It's all right, darling, a false alarm. I'm no more
pregnant than you are.'

George, who was wool-gathering, might have remained
indefinitely perplexed, if the doctor had not taken him
aside and told him briefly the situation, adding that for a
little time it would be well if Elizabeth refrained from
sexual relations.

'How long do you advise ?' asked George.

'Oh, let her follow the treatment prescribed for about
a month, and then let me examine her again. I've no
doubt whatever that she'll be perfectly all right again.
As a matter of fact, she couldn't have a child without a
slight operation. Only, in the future she must avoid
chills. She ought not to spend the winter in England.'

George wrote out a cheque for three guineas (which
Elizabeth insisted on repaying afterwards), and they
celebrated the event with a dinner.

' Let us drink,' said George, ' to this happy occasion when we have NOT committed the unforgivable sin of thrusting an unwanted existence upon one more unfortunate human being.'

But perhaps the most amazing circumstance in this peculiar episode was the speed with which Elizabeth once more evacuated the old familiar Hindenburg line, and reoccupied the most advanced positions of Sexual Freedom. But, of course, she did so with a difference. Though she wouldn't admit it even to herself, and though George tried not to see it, in her case the Triumphal Scheme had broken down badly under its first stern test. Directly that test had come, she had fallen back in panic on the old cut-and-dried solution ; she hadn't had the courage to go through with it. In a way one could excuse her by saying that the interior trouble had temporarily deranged her brain, that she wasn't really responsible for her actions. But that 's only a quibble—the fact remains that she did fly in a panic to social safety and the registrar. And then the legal tie introduced a subtle difference in their relation. You may say, of course, that it needn't ; that since they continued to live in exactly the same way and to profess exactly the same attitude towards each other and ' freedom,' it made no difference whether they were legally married or not. But it did. And it does. You can see that perfectly well if you watch people. Somehow the mere fact of marriage introduces the sense of possession, and hence jealousy. Lovers, of course, may be and frequently are just as possessive and quite as jealous. But there is a difference. As a rule lovers are not first occupants, so to speak ; and they are generally willing to grant each other more liberty and to ' forgive.' But you will see married people who have become totally

indifferent to each other rise in a fury of possessiveness
and jealousy when they happen to find out that the wife
or husband, as the case may be, is in love with some one
else. This indeed may be only another aspect of that
peculiar vindictiveness bred by marriage. And another
curious modification of their relationship arose. When
Elizabeth reoccupied the Sexual Freedom line, without
knowing it she did so for herself alone, and not for George.
If George liked to accept the subsequent Elizabeth-Reggie
affair, in accordance with the provisions of the Triumphal
Scheme, all well and good ; that was his look-out. But
when it came to Elizabeth's accepting the Fanny-George
affair in the same spirit, that was a very different matter.
Elizabeth now felt somehow responsible for George, and
feeling responsible translated itself into keeping possession of. . . .

However, three months after the false alarm Elizabeth
seemed more ' advanced ' and full of ' freedom ' than
ever. Her position as a married woman enabled her to
talk with greater liberty on all sorts of topics which are
now discussed in every nursery but at that time were
considered highly improper and not to be named before
Citizens of the Empire. She got hold of a book on the
woes of the Uranians, and was deeply affected by it.
She wanted to start a crusade on their behalf, and was
greatly disappointed by the coolness with which George
met her enthusiasm.

' It is ridiculous,' said Elizabeth, ' that these unfortunate people should be persecuted by obsolete laws
derived from the prejudices of the Jewish prophets and
mediæval ignorance.'

' Of course it is, but what can one do about it ? Per-
secution-mania has always existed. It 's a very curious
coincidence that the vulgar English word for one sort of

intermediate sexual type originally meant a heretic.   But there's nothing to be done.'

' I think something ought to be done.'

' Well, I think it's too soon to do anything.   You've got to allow time for knowledge to percolate into rock-like heads, and for ignorance and superstitions to be dispelled. Let's get the ordinary relations of men and women on to a decent basis first, and then it'll be time to think about the heretics in love.'

' But, George darling, these people are hunted and exiled and despised for something which is not their " fault " at all, some difference in their physiological or psychological structure.   There probably isn't any such thing as a perfectly " normal " sexual type.   Simply because we're " normal," why should we hate and despise these people ? '

' I know, I know.   Theoretically, I agree with you absolutely.   But it's no good my mind trying to defend what my instincts and feelings reject.   Frankly, I don't like homosexuals.   I respect their freedom, of course, but I don't like them.   As a matter of fact, I don't know any, at least so far as I am aware.   No doubt some of our friends are homosexual ; but as I'm not personally interested in it, I never notice it.'

' Yes, but because you don't notice it doesn't mean that it doesn't exist.   Don't be narrow-minded, George. There are probably tens of thousands of people living miserable lives . . .'

' Oh, I know all about that !   But you can't break down the inherited prejudices of ages in five minutes.   I personally don't object to such people doing as they want. There's no tort to person or property.   But my advice to them would be to keep jolly quiet about it, and not try to make themselves martyrs, and flaunt themselves publicly.'

' Oh, oh !' Elizabeth laughed; ' Grandpa George for-
gathering with the Victorians ! '

' All right, but I 'm not going to say what I don't feel.
In this matter you must look upon me as a neutral.'

' Well, I think you ought to look into it more carefully
and sympathetically, and get Bobbe to let you write some
articles on it.'

' Thanks very much. You ask him to do it himself ;
it 's far more likely to attract *him*. If I wrote such
articles I should immediately be suspect. It 's a damned
dangerous thing to do in England ; in most cases the
suspicion is far too likely to be true ! '

And they left it at that.

All this time the war was drawing steadily nearer.
Probably it had become certain since 1911, though most
people were taken quite unawares. Why did it happen ?
Who was responsible ? Questions which have been interminably debated already and will furnish exultant historians with controversial material for generations to
come. Already one foresees the creation of Chairs in the
History of the First World War, to be set up in whatever
civilised countries remain in existence after the next one.
But for us the debate is vain, as vain as the pathetic and
reiterated enquiry, ' *Where* did I catch this horrible
cold ? ' If any body or bodies engineered this catastrophe
they must have been gratified by its shattering success.
Few lives indeed in the belligerent countries remained
unaffected by it, and in most cases the effect was unpleasant. Adult lives were cut sharply into three sections
—pre-war, war, and post-war. It is curious—perhaps
not so curious—but many people will tell you that whole
areas of their pre-war lives have become obliterated from
their memories. Pre-war seems like pre-history. What

did we do, how did we feel, what were we living for in those incredibly distant years ? One feels as if the period 1900-14 has to be treated archæologically, painfully re-created by experts from slight vestiges. Those who were still children at the Armistice, who were so to speak born into the war, can hardly understand the feeling of tranquil security which existed, the almost smug optimism of our lives. Especially in England, for the French retained uncomfortable memories of 1870 ; but still, even in France life seemed established and secure. Since Water-loo, England had engaged in no great war. There were frontier and colonial skirmishes, and the reputation of the country for military organisation and efficiency was im-mensely strengthened in the world's eyes by the conduct of the Crimean and Boer Wars. But there had been nothing on a really big scale. The Franco-Prussian War was just one of those unfortunate occurrences one must expect from backward Continental nations, and the huge struggle of the War of Secession was observed through the wrong end of the telescope. In some quarters, indeed, that war had been considered as a peculiar mercy of God to His Chosen People, enabling the British Merchant Marine to re-establish an indisputable primacy at the expense of a regrettable upstart among nations.

Talleyrand used to say that those who had not known Europe before 1789 had never known the real pleasure of living. No one would dare to substitute 1914 for 1789 in that sentence. But such a wholesale shattering of values had certainly not occurred since 1789. God knows how many governments and rulers crashed down in the earthquake, and those which remain are agitatedly trying to preserve their existence by the time-honoured methods of repression and persecution. And yet 1914 was greeted as a great release, a purgation from the vices supposed to be engendered by peace! My God! Three days of glory engender more vices and misery than all the alleged corruptors of humanity could achieve in a millennium. *Les jeunes* would be amazed if they read the nauseous poppycock which was written in 1914-15 in England, and doubtless in all the belligerent countries, except France, where practically nothing was printed at all. (However, the French have made up handsomely for the loss since then.) 'Our splendid troops' were to come home—oh, very soon—purged and ennobled by slaughter and lice, and were to beget a race of even nobler fellows to go and do likewise. We were to have a great revival in religion, for people's thoughts were now turned from frivolities to great and serious themes. We were to have a new and greater literature—hence the alleged vogue for 'war poets,' which resulted in the parents of the slain being asked to put up fifty pounds for the publication (which probably cost fifteen) of poor little verses which should never have passed the home circle. We were to have . . . but really I lack courage to continue. Let those who are curious in human imbecility consult the newspaper-files of those days. . . .

But we are still lingering in the golden calm of the last few months preceding August 1914.

Fanny had followed Elizabeth's amazing evolutions with considerable surprise and that feeling of 'something not displeasing' with which we contemplate the misfortunes of our best friends. She chiefly felt rather sorry for George. . . .

'You have a vendetta of the dead against the living.' Yes, it is true, I have a vendetta, an unappeased longing for vengeance. Yes, a vendetta. Not a personal vendetta.

What am I ?   O God, nothing, less than nothing, a husk, a leaving, a half-chewed morsel on the plate, a reject. But an impersonal vendetta, an unappeased conscience crying in the wilderness, a river of tears in the desert. What right have I to live ?   Is it five million, is it ten million, is it twenty million ?   What does the exact count matter ?   There they are, and we are responsible. Tortures of hell, we are responsible !   When I meet an unmaimed man of my generation, I want to shout at him : ' How did you escape ?   How did you dodge it ?   What dirty trick did you play ?   Why are you not dead, trickster ? '   It is dreadful to have outlived your life, to have shirked your fate, to have overspent your welcome. There is nobody upon earth who cares whether I live or die, and I am glad of it, so glad of it.   To be alone, icily alone.   You, the war dead, I think you died in vain, I think you died for nothing, for a blast of wind, a blather, a humbug, a newspaper stunt, a politician's ramp.   But at least you died.   You did not reject the sharp, sweet shock of bullets, the sudden smash of the shell-burst, the insinuating agony of poison gas.   You got rid of it all. You chose the better part.   ' They went down like a lot o' Charlie Chaplins,' said the little ginger-hair sergeant of the Durhams.   Like a lot of Charlie Chaplins.   Marvellous metaphor !   Can't you see them staggering on splayed-out feet and waving ineffective hands as they went down before the accurate machine-gun fire of the Durhams sergeant ?   A splendid little hero—he got the Military Medal for it.   Like a lot of Charlie Chaplins. Marvellous !   But why weren't we one of them?   What right have we to live ?   And the women ?   Oh, don't let 's talk about the women.   They were splendid, wonderful.   Such devotion, such devotion !   How they comforted the troops !   Oh, wonderful, beyond all praise !

They got the vote for it, you know. Oh, wonderful! Steel-true and blade-straight. Yes, indeed, wonderful, wonderful! What ever should we have done without them? White feathers, and all that, you know. Oh, the women were marvellous. You can always rely upon the women to come up to scratch, you know. Yes, indeed. What would the Country be without them? So splendid, such an example.

On Sundays the Union Jack flies over the cemetery at Etaples. It 's not so big as it was in the old wooden-cross days, but it 's still quite large. Acres and acres. Yes, acres and acres. And it 's too late to get one's little lot in the acres. Too late, too late. . . .

Yes, Fanny was sorry for George, and showed it with practical feminine sympathy. In the late spring Elizabeth 'had' to go and spend a fortnight with her parents in the north. Mrs. Paston—who never failed in any of her duties, and took jolly good care to let you know it—was accustomed to write every week to Elizabeth. This weekly letter was supposed to be a nice, chatty, affectionate record of the little home circle and friends, something to keep Elizabeth in touch with their purer lives (of pure boredom) and preserve her from the decadents and degenerates she frequented in London. In fact the letter was almost invariably a perfidious and insinuating effort to make Elizabeth uncomfortable and to discourage her with her own life. Under the endearing words of conventional family affection lurked a curious resentment and hatred. If Mrs. Paston could think of anything likely to worry Elizabeth she never failed to convey it, in the strain of 'Isn't it a pity, dear! . . .' Sometimes Elizabeth answered these letters, sometimes she did not. Recently, they had been filled with discouraging hints about the

state of Mr. Paston's health. ' Your dear father ' could
not shake off his ' bronchitis ' (*i.e.* a cold in the head), he
was very ' languid ' (*i.e.* bored, the golf links were under
water), he ' scarcely ever went out ' (he hardly ever had
done, except to play golf), he was ' getting so frail and
white-haired, poor darling daddy ' (he 'd been grey for
fifteen years and still ate four hearty meals daily), he
' seemed to be failing fast '—a pure piece of mythology.
Elizabeth was rather fond of her father, and began to get
alarmed, although she was more or less aware of her
mother's strategy. But it is the misfortune of youth
never really to credit the aged with their full meed of
perfidy and dislike. She felt she ought to go and see
her father for herself—it would be awful if he suddenly
died without her seeing him. She told George she
was going.

' All right, of course, if you want to. I 'll take you to
the station. When are you going ? '

' I wish you 'd come with me, George. Father and
mother would like to see you, and they 'd appreciate it
so much.'

' Now look here, Elizabeth, don't let 's have any humbug here. I don't ask you to meet my parents and I don't
see why I should have to stay with yours. I think your
mother 's quite awful, one of those nagging martyr women
who 're always taking on unnecessary jobs and worries,
and then grumbling about how much they have to do and
how little they 're appreciated. Your father 's all right.
He 's a decent sort, with a human respect for other people.
But after I 've feigned an interest I don't feel in golf and
we 've shaken our heads over the wickedness of Liberal
Governments, we 've really nothing left to say to each
other.'

' But it 's so much easier for me if you 'd come too.'

' No, it wouldn't.   We 'd be shown off as the happy married pair to your mother's friends, and our sufferings would be dreadful.   Besides, it 'll be easier for you to adjust yourself temporarily to their prejudices if you don't have the sensation of a satirical me watching you.'

So Elizabeth went by herself, and George remained alone in London.   He always missed Elizabeth frightfully when she went away, but instead of going out and amusing himself he stayed in and tried to pass the time by over-working.   By the evening of the fifth day he was thor-oughly fed up.   He decided to go out and ring up various friends in turn, until he found some one to have dinner with him.   He had just finished washing and was putting on a clean collar, when some one knocked at the door of his studio.

' Half a minute,' shouted George ; ' I 'm dressing. Who is it ? '

The door opened, and in came Fanny, wearing a charming new dress and a gay wide-brimmed hat with a large feather in it.

' Why, Fanny !   How good to see you, and how lovely you look ! '

They kissed affectionately.   Fanny sat down on the bed.

' I 've come to be taken out to dinner.   If you think you 're doing anything else, you 're mistaken.   You 'll have to ring up and say you can't come.'

' As a matter of fact, I was on the point of going out to find somebody to dine with me, so your coming is a godsend.'

' How 's Elizabeth ? '

' She 's all right.   I got a letter from her this morning. She 's with her parents, you know.'

' Yes, I know.   How long 'll she be away ? '

' Another ten days.   Poor darling, she sounds awfully bored already.'

' And what are you doing ? '

' Oh, fighting the lone hand here.   Do you want to see the picture I 'm finishing ? '

And George dragged round an easel with a large canvas on it, into the light.

' But it 's good, George !   It 's got great qualities of energy and design.'

' You don't think it 's too hard and angular ? '

' No, not a bit.   It 's excellent.   By far the best thing you 've done.'

And Fanny jumped up from the bed, put her arm round George, and kissed him again.   For the first time her lips were not cool, shut and sisterly, but warm and open and delicious—the lips of an accomplice.   The sudden flicker of warm desire awoke in George's flesh, and he felt his heart leap and the blood flush to his face.   He held her to him, and pressed eager firm lips to her soft yielding mouth.   For a few seconds she seemed to resist, and made as if to thrust him from her.   He held her more closely, and suddenly her stiffened body yielded delicately, moulded itself to his, her head moved slowly backwards with closed eyes.   ******* *** ***** ****** ** *** **** ** **** ** *** *** ********* ****** ** * ****** ******-***.   George gently laid his hand on her left breast, and felt the rapid beating of her heart.   She softly drew away her lips and looked at him.

' Fanny !   Fanny ! '

Her gem-like eyes, now all flower-like, looked at him.

' Fanny !   Most dear Fanny !   I must have loved you a long time without knowing it.'

Fanny spoke slowly, still watching him :

' You 're such a nice man, George, and yet such a boy.'

' And you are divine and inexpressibly lovely and thrilling and adorable. . . .'

They kissed again, and stood there embraced until George felt dizzy with the blood beating in his brain. He pulled her gently towards the bed, and they lay down, clothed, in each other's arms. George's hand moved tenderly and delicately over her uncorseted girl body, so warm and firm and fragile under the thin, cool silk dress. The incoherent words of lovers gave place to silence, and they lay trembling in each other's arms, almost like frightened children comforting each other

Fanny sighed, and opened her eyes.

' What time is it ? '

George fumbled for his watch.

' Nearly half-past eight ! '

' Heavens ! We shall be too late for dinner if we don't hurry.'

George went to get his coat, and returned to find Fanny unconcernedly drawing her silk stockings tight and trim.

' Where can we go that 's near ? '

' There 's a new place just started in Frith Street— we can go there.'

George watched her as she smoothed her mussed hair and absorbedly fitted on the large hat before the mirror. He was still trembling a little, and noticed how steady her hands were. Only a few minutes before they had been so close, all the barriers down, each existence melted in the other. That had been perfect, complete happiness. ' Had been.' Already the current of ordinary life was sweeping them apart again. Oh, not very far really, still within hailing distance. But very far, compared with

that wonderful nearness. Such an ecstasy could not last.
But why not ? Perhaps one of the many bitter jests of the
gods—to show us for an hour what happiness might be
if we were gods. None can possess another, none can be
possessed. Is it possible to give, is it possible to take ?
Does one existence really melt into another for a few
minutes, or does it only seem to ? What is she thinking
now ? Her mind is as remote from mine as if she had
slipped into another dimension. Romantically we ask
too much. It is much that she is lovely and finds me
desirable. Let us not ask too much. Enjoyment is
enough. Yet how fragile even that is ! It is as if one
tried to carry a small flickering light in a thin glass vessel
through a tumultuous, hostile crowd. How earnest is the
world to suppress the delight of lovers ! How bitterly
wrong all that is !

They went down into the warm, airless street, where the
lamps were already lighted. Dirty children still played
noisily and screamed on the side-walks. An Italian
woman slip-slopped past them in felt slippers, carrying
a jug of beer. Soho smelled frowzy and stale. Fanny
noticed this.

' Why do you and Elizabeth live in this horrid
district ? It must be awfully unhealthy, especially for
Elizabeth.'

' Oh, one gets used to it. Hampstead 's too far out,
Kensington 's too dear, Chelsea 's both dear and un-
getatable. When I 'm in town I like to be in the middle
of it. Suburbs are beastly. We all suffer from the
English " home " system of building—one hut, one family.
And from our peculiar desire to be in a town and the
country simultaneously, we don't seem able to live the
purely urban life of the Latins. But London 's too big
and frowzy.'

They dined in the small restaurant, which had been
' decorated ' with rather feeble pictures by young artists,
to give it that Latin Quarter air.   It was somehow in-
effectual.   A bit amateurish.   However, they didn't
care about that.   Since they were comparatively old
friends, they did not suffer the haunting and disagreeable uneasiness and strangeness which fall between
those who suddenly become lovers.   The spontaneity
of their passion absorbed any possible feeling of
remorse.   They talked quietly, but without any strain
and effort.   Fanny gave some amusing descriptions
of the odd freaks among the British ' colonies ' on
the Riviera.   Why is it that one sees such curious
and freakish specimens of one's countrymen abroad,
types one never sees at home ?   Do the foreign
surroundings bring out the freakishness, or were such
people destined to emigration by their very oddity ?
. . . But there could be no doubt—Fanny and George
were on a new footing with each other.   There was
a new and delicious intimacy between them.   Strange
that a few kisses and caresses should make such a
difference.

As they were leaving the restaurant, Fanny was hailed
by some friends at a table near the door.

' Hullo, Fanny !   How are you ?   I say, why don't you
come along with us ?   We 're all going to Marshall's
chambers at ten.   There 'll be lots of people there.   It
ought to be amusing.'

' No, I want to see that new film at the Shaftesbury.'

' But you can see that any time.'

' No, this is the last week, and I 'm going to Dieppe
to-morrow for a week.'

' Oh, all right.   Sorry you won't come.   Look us up
when you get back.   Good-bye, good-bye.'

They got into a taxi, and Fanny gave the address of her flat.

' Did you really mean that you are going to Dieppe to-morrow ? ' asked George a little wistfully.

Fanny squeezed his arm, and kissed him briefly and skilfully as the taxi lurched them together.

' Of course not, goose ! We 're going to be together, unless you piously decide not to. But it 's useful to have an alibi. People are still fussy about one's " reputation," you know.'

' But suppose we meet them, or some one else who knows you ? '

' I shall say I changed my mind, or that I got bored and came straight back.'

Fanny's flat was small, but pleasantly clean and modern. After the picturesque but rather dingy antiquity of his large eighteenth-century panelled room, George found it delightful to be in bright-painted, clean rooms with a white-tiled bathroom. Among Fanny's many remarkable efficiencies was the genius of discovering excellent flats at a fabulously cheap rental, furnishing them charmingly for about five pounds, and running them perfectly without the slightest fuss. She generally shifted her quarters about every six months, and invariably for the better. How pleasant is efficiency in others, especially when you are rather inefficient yourself ! I wouldn't exactly say that George was inefficient, but the details of material life rather bored him. When you had so much else to do and so little time to do it in, he thought it rather a waste of life to be too pernickety about one's surroundings and fixings. However, he decided then and there that he and Elizabeth would have to get out of Soho. It was too disgustingly frowzy.

Fanny was a marvellous lover. Or, at least, George thought so. It was not only that she was golden and supple and lithe, where Elizabeth was dark and rather stiff and virginal, but she really cared about love-making. It was her art. It was for her neither a painful duty nor a degrading necessity nor a series of disappointing experiments, but a delightful art which gave full expression to her vitality, energy, and efficiency. Like all great artists, she was entirely disinterested—art for art's sake. She chose her lovers with great care, and rather preferred them to be poor, to avoid any suspicion of commercialism or arrivism. She knew she had the genius of touch, and was unwilling that it should be wasted. If she hadn't been a great lover, she might have been a good sculptor. But like all artists she was exacting, and had her vanity. She would not waste her talents. If a subject was not profoundly responsive and appreciative, she put him aside at the earliest possible moment. No clumsy, inhibited Englishman for her ! No, thank you. Perhaps that is why she spent so much of her time abroad.

But this particular Englishman was not inhibited or ineradicably clumsy. Crude perhaps, rather lacking in style and finish, but capable of rapid progress under expert guidance. Fanny, with the artist's unerring glance, had long ago perceived that there were considerable possibilities in George. He had natural aptitudes and, what is far more important, the sense of delicate artistry which finds its highest satisfaction in bestowing delight. He was neither a bull nor a turkey gobbler. Fanny was satisfied ; she had not made a mistake. . . .

For the remaining days of Elizabeth's absence George did no work whatever. And a very good thing, too, for

he needed a holiday. He stayed at Fanny's flat. They
made picnic meals in the flat, or ate out at places where
they were pretty certain not to meet friends—City stock-
brokers' taverns, or curious pubs with sawdust and spittoons
on the floors, where you sat on stools at the bar and had
a cut from the joint and two veg. with beer. They went
to 'low' music-halls and saw all the primitive films of the
day—Charlie's were the only good ones—and for a lark
went to see what the inside of the Abbey looked like,
a place no Londoner ever visits. They agreed that it
looked like the atelier of an incredibly bad academic
sculptor installed in an overcrowded but rather beautiful
Gothic barn. Fanny rather hated Gothic architecture—
she said all those points and squiggles gave her the
creeps ; but George said that if you wanted to see the
real spirit of mediæval sculpture you ought to look underneath the seats of the canons' stalls. But they didn't
quarrel about that. They were far too happy.

Nothing more was said about Elizabeth, until the day
before she returned.

'You 'll meet her, of course ? ' said Fanny.

'Of course.'

'Well, give her my love.'

'I suppose I ought to tell her about us,' said George,
reflectively.

Fanny saw the danger in a flash. Her 'freedom' was
of a different kind from Elizabeth's rather theoretical and
idealising kind. Fanny's was light-hearted and practical ;
moreover, she had observed human beings and knew her
Elizabeth far better than George did. She also knew her
George. If George told Elizabeth, she knew quite well
there would be a bust-up, that Elizabeth's theories would
be abandoned as speedily as on the former occasion. But

she knew it was useless to reveal the truth to George. On the other hand, she didn't want to lose him and didn't want to 'take him away' from Elizabeth—not until much later when Elizabeth started the struggle. Fanny knew that George had to be managed within the limits of masculine stupidity.

'Oh, tell her if you like. But I shouldn't discuss it with her, if I were you. She must have long ago felt subconsciously the attraction between us, and you can see by her attitude that she accepts it. I don't see the need for all this talk and re-hashing of what's a private and personal matter between two people. We're so hypnotised by words, that we think nothing exists until we have talked about it. How can you interpret all these deep feelings and sensations in words ? It's because words don't suffice that we need touch. Tell Elizabeth by loving her better.'

'Then you really think she knows ? '

Fanny was a little annoyed. Why couldn't he *see*, why couldn't he take a hint ?

'If she's as acute and experienced as she tells us, she ought to have seen the possibility long ago. No doubt, if she's said nothing about it to you, the reason is that she just doesn't want to discuss it. If she accepts, that's enough.'

'But she always believes that two people should be perfectly open and frank with each other about their other affairs.'

'Does she ? Well, I advise you to say nothing until she asks you.'

'All right, darling, if you think so.'

George duly met Elizabeth at Euston. She was delighted to be back in London, away from the stuffiness of

family and the solemn boredom of middle-class existence.
She leaned out the window of the taxi and sniffed the
air.

' How lovely to smell dirty old London mud again !
It means I 'm free, free, free again ! '

' Was it very awful ? '

' Oh, awful, interminable.'

' I 'm so glad you 're back.'

' It 's wonderful.   And lovely to be with you again !
How well you look, George !— quite handsome and
Italian ! '

' That 's because you haven't seen me for a fortnight.'

' How 's Fanny ? '

' Oh, very well.   Sent her love to you.'

' Dear old beastly, ugly Tottenham Court Road !' said
Elizabeth with her nose out the window again.

' By the way, it was awfully frowsty in Soho while you
were away.   Don't you think we might move to somewhere more modern ? '

' What, to a suburb ?   Why, George ! you know you
hate suburbs, and always said you liked to live in the
middle of London.'

' Yes, I know.   But we might find something at
Chelsea.'

' But we couldn't possibly afford two places at Chelsea
rents.'

' Well, why not share a fairly large one ? '

' What, and live in the same flat ?   George ! '

' Oh, all right, if you don't want to, but Fanny thinks
Soho is unhealthy for you.'

' Well, we 'll see.'

Whether, as the Swedish old maid hinted in her book,

it was the stimulus of another affair, or whether George was anxious to display the artistries of Fanny, or whether it was merely remorse, Elizabeth found George peculiarly charming and ardent.

She attributed this to the happy effect of a brief absence.

In a few weeks they duly moved to Chelsea. Fanny found them an excellent apartment, with two large rooms, a kitchen, and a modern bathroom, for less than the combined rental of their two ramshackle rooms in Soho. Elizabeth developed an unexpected talent for ' home-making,' and fussed a good deal over the installation in spite of George's light satire. But they were both only too happy to get away from the frowstiness of Soho to a clean modern flat.

This was in June 1914. They did not go away when the hot weather arrived, intending to stay the summer in London and go to Paris for September and October. Elizabeth spent a good deal of her spare time with Reggie Burnside, and George was absorbed in his painting. He wanted to get enough good canvases for a small show in Paris in the autumn.

One day towards the end of July he left his painting early, to meet Reggie and Elizabeth for lunch somewhere near Piccadilly. It was a benign day, with fine white fleecy clouds suspended in a blue sky, and a light wind ruffling the darkened foliage of summer trees. Even the King's Road looked pleasant. George noticed, and afterwards remembered vividly, because these were the last really tranquil moments of his life, how the policeman's gloves made a clear blotch of white against a plane-tree as he regulated the traffic. A little band of sparrows were squabbling and twittering noisily in the lilacs of one of the gardens. The heat was reflected, not unpleasantly, from the warm white flag-stones of the sidewalk.

As he waited for the No. 19 bus, George did what

he very rarely did—bought a newspaper.   He always said
it was a waste of life to read newspapers—if something
really important happened, people would tell you about it
soon enough.   He didn't know why he bought a paper
that morning.   He had been working hard for two or
three weeks without seeing any one but Elizabeth, and
perhaps thought he would see what was going on in
the world.   Perhaps it was only to see if there was any
new film.

George clambered to the top of the bus, with the paper
under his arm, and paid his fare.   He then glanced
casually at the headlines and read : ' Serious Situation in
the Balkans, Austro-Hungarian Ultimatum to Servia,
Servian Appeal to Russia, Position of Germany and
France.'   George looked up vaguely at the other people
on the bus.   There were four men and two women ;
each of the men was intently reading the same special
early edition of the evening paper.   He read the de-
spatches eagerly and carefully, and grasped the seriousness
of the situation at once.   The Austrian Empire was on
the verge of war with Serbia (Servia it was then called,
until the country became one of our plucky little allies) ;
Russia threatened to support Serbia ;   the Triple Alliance
would bring in Germany and Italy on the side of Austria ;
France would be bound to support Russia under the
Treaty of Alliance, and the Entente Cordiale might involve
England.   There was a chance of a European War, the
biggest conflict since the defeat of Napoleon.   The event
he had always declared to be impossible—a war between
the ' civilised ' nations—was threatened, was at hand.   He
refused to believe it.   Germany didn't want war, France
would be mad to want it, England couldn't want it.   The
' Powers ' would intervene.   What was Sir Edward Grey
doing ?   Oh, suggesting a conference. . . .   The man on

the seat opposite George leaned towards him, tapping the
newspaper with his hand :

'What do you say to that, sir ? '

'I think it looks confoundedly serious.'

'Chance of a war, eh ? '

'I sincerely hope not. The newspapers always
exaggerate, you know. It would be an appalling
catastrophe.'

'Oh, liven things up a bit. We 're getting stale, too
much peace. Need a bit of blood-letting.'

'I don't think it 'll come to that. I . . .'

'It 's got to come sooner or later. Them Germans,
you know. They 'd never be able to face our Navy.'

'Well, let 's hope it won't be necessary.'

'Ah, I dunno. Shouldn't mind 'avin' a go at the
Germans myself, and I reckon you wouldn't either.'

'Oh, I 'm a neutral,' said George, laughing ; 'don't
count on me.'

'Umph ! ' said the man, as he got up to leave the bus,
casting a suspicious look at this foreign-looking and un-
patriotic person. 'Yes, that 's it, a foreigner, a bloody
foreigner. Umph ! What 's he doing in England, I 'd
like to know ? Umph ! '

George was back in the newspaper, unaware of the
turmoil he had excited in that elderly but patriotic bosom.

'I say,' exclaimed George, as soon as he met Elizabeth
and Reggie, ' have you two seen the newspaper to-day ? '

'Why ? ' said Elizabeth ; 'what 's in it ? Something
about you ? '

'No, there 's a war threatened in the Balkans, and it
may apparently involve every one else.'

Reggie sneered.

'Oh, piffle ! How absurd you are, George, to believe

a newspaper sensation ! Why, we were talking about it last night in the Common Room, and every one agreed that the conflict would have to be localised and that Grey would probably make a statement in a day or two. It 'll all blow over.'

Elizabeth had grabbed the newspaper, and was trying to find her way through the unfamiliar mazes of sensational rhetoric.

' So you don't think it 'll come to anything ? ' said George, hanging up his hat, and sitting down at the restaurant table.

' Of course not ! ' said Reggie contemptuously

' What do you think, Elizabeth ? '

' I don't know,' she said looking up bewildered from the paper ; ' I can't understand this curious language. Are all newspapers written like that ? '

' Mostly,' said George ; ' but I 'm glad you think it 's only a scare, Reggie. I admit I was startled when I read those headlines. That 's what comes of living absorbed in one's own life, and neglecting the fountain-heads of truth.'

All the same, he was not quite reassured, and on the way home left an order with a local newsagent for the delivery of a daily paper until further notice. He hoped the next morning's news would be better. It wasn't. Neither was the next day's. Then came the news that Russia was mobilising, and that the Grand Fleet had sailed from Spithead ' on manœuvres,' but under sealed orders. George remembered the coastguard officer who got drunk and let slip that he had sealed orders in case of war. Perhaps the man would be opening those orders in a few days, perhaps he had already opened them. He tried to paint, and couldn't ; picked up a book, and found himself thinking : Austria, Russia, Germany, France, England perhaps—good God, it's impossible, impossible ! He fidgeted about, and then went into Elizabeth's room. She was delicately painting a large blue bowl of variegated summer flowers. The room was very quiet. One of the windows was opened on to a large communal garden surrounded by the backs of houses. A wasp came in through the striped orange-and-black curtain and buzzed towards a bunch of grapes on a large Spanish plate.

' What is it, George ? '

The room was so peaceful, so secure, Elizabeth so unperturbed and as usual, that George felt half-surprised at his own agitation.

' I 'm worried about this war situation.'

' Really, George ! What *is* the good of getting into such a fuss ? You know Reggie told you there was nothing in it, and he hears all the latest news at Cambridge.'

' Yes, darling, but it isn't a matter of Cambridge now, but of Europe. The Tsar and the Kaiser won't consult the Dons before launching a war.'

Elizabeth, rather annoyed, went on painting.

' Well,' she said through the brush between her teeth, ' I can't help it. Anyway, it won't concern us.'

It won't concern us ! George stood irresolute a moment.

' I think I 'll go out and see what 's the latest news.'

' Yes, do. I 'm dining with Reggie to-night.'

' All right.'

George spent the first few days of August wandering about London, taking buses, and buying innumerable editions of newspapers. London seemed perfectly calm and as usual, and yet there was something feverish about it. Perhaps it was George's own feverishness exteriorised ;

perhaps it was the unwonted number of special editions, with shouting newsboys in unusual places handing out copies as fast as they could to little groups of impatient people. His memories of those days were confused, and he couldn't remember the chronological order of events. Two or three scenes stood out vividly in his mind—all the rest became a blur, the outlines obliterated by more dreadful scenes.

He remembered dining with Elizabeth and some other friends in a private suite of the Berkeley as the guests of a wealthy American. The talk kept running on the possibility of war, and the positions of England and America. George still clung to the great illusion that wars between the highly industrialised countries were impossible. He elaborated this view to the American man, who agreed, and said that Wall Street and Threadneedle Street between them could stop the universe.

' If there *is* a war,' said George, ' it will be a sort of impersonal, natural calamity, like a plague or an earthquake. But I think that in their own interests all the governments will combine to avert it, or at least limit it to Austria and Servia.'

' But don't you think the Germans are spoiling for a war ? ' said another Englishman.

' I don't know, I simply don't know. What does any of us know ? The governments don't tell us what they 're doing or planning. We 're completely in the dark. We can make surmises, but we don't *know*.'

' It 's probably got to come sooner or later. The world 's too small to hold an expanding Germany and a non-contracting British Empire.'

' The irresistible force and the immovable mass. . . . But it 's not a question of England and Germany, but of Austria and Servia.'

' Oh, the murder of the Archduke's just a pretext—probably arranged beforehand.'

' But by which side? I can't see the situation as a stage scene, with villains on one side and noble-minded fellows on the other. If the Archduke's murder was the result of an intrigue, as you suggest, it was a damned despicable one. Now, either the various governments are all despicable intriguers ready to stoop to any crime and duplicity to attain their ends, in which case we shall certainly have a war, if they want it; or they're more or less decent and human men like ourselves, in which case they'll do anything to avert it. We can do nothing. We're impotent. They've got the power and the information. We haven't. . . .'

The white-gloved, immaculate Austrian waiters were silently handing and removing plates. George noticed one of them, a young man with close-cropped golden hair and a sensitive face. Probably a student from Vienna or Prague, a poor man who had chosen waiting as a means of earning his living while studying English. They both were about the same age and height. George suddenly realised that he and the waiter were potential enemies! How absurd, how utterly absurd! . . .

After dinner they sat about and smoked. George took his chair over to the open window and looked down on the lights and movement of Piccadilly. The noise of the traffic was lulled by the height to a long continuous rumble. The placards of the evening papers along the railings beside the Ritz were sensational and bellicose. The party dropped the subject of a possible great war; after deciding that there wouldn't be one, there couldn't. George, who had great faith in Mr. Bobbe's political acumen, glanced through his last article, and took great comfort from the fact that Bobbe said there wasn't going to be a war. It

was all a scare, a stock-market ramp. . . . At that
moment three or four people came in, more or less
together, though they were in separate parties. One of
them was a youngish man in immaculate evening dress.
As he shook hands with his host, George heard him say
rather excitedly :

' I 've just been dining with Tommy Parkinson of the
Foreign Office. He had to leave early and go back to
Downing Street. It seems there are Cabinet meetings
all the time. Tommy was frightfully depressed and
pessimistic about the situation.'

' What did he say ? ' asked three or four eager voices.

' He wouldn't commit himself at all. He was simply
very gloomy and *distrait*, and wouldn't say anything
definite.'

' Why didn't you ask him whether Germany is mobilising ? '

' I did, but he wouldn't tell me anything.'

' Oh, well, perhaps he only has a liver.'

Among the other guests was a tall, very erect, rather
sunburned man of about forty, who had taken no part in
the conversation. He was sitting on a couch in silence
beside a woman younger than himself—his wife—who
was also silent. George heard him introduced to another
man as Colonel Thomas. After a few minutes George
went over and spoke to him.

' My name 's Winterbourne. You 're Colonel Thomas,
aren't you ? '

' Yes.'

' What do you think of the situation we 've all been
discussing so intelligently ? '

' I don't think anything. A soldier mustn't have
political " views," you know.'

' Well, but do you think the Germans are mobilising ? '

' I don't know.   I believe they are.   But that doesn't
necessarily mean war.   They may be mobilising for
manœuvres.   We 're mobilised for manœuvres on Salis-
bury Plain.'

' Mobilised !   The British Army mobilised ! '

' Only for manœuvres, you know.'

' Are you mobilised too ? '

' Yes, I leave to-morrow morning.'

' Good God ! '

' Oh, it 's only manœuvres.   They always happen at
this time of the year.'

Another day—it must have been the Sunday before the
4th of August—George went down to Trafalgar Square
to attend a Socialist peace meeting.   The space round
the Nelson Column was so crowded that he could not get
near enough to hear the speakers, who were standing on
the plinth above the heads of the crowd.   An eager-faced
man with white hair and an aristocratic voice made a
speech, directed at mob prejudices.   He apparently took
the view that the threatened war was the work of Imperial
Russia.   George caught repeatedly the words ' knout,'
' Cossacks,' and the phrase ' the eagles of war are spreadin'
their wings.'   Some of the listeners at a rival war meeting
started an attack on the peace party.   There was a scuffle,
which was very soon dispersed by mounted police.   The
crowd surged away from Trafalgar Square.   George
found himself carried towards the Admiralty Arch and
up the Mall.   He thought he might as well go back that
way, and try to get a bus at Victoria.   But opposite
Buckingham Palace the road was blocked by a huge
crowd, which was continually reinforced from all three
roads.   The Palace Gates were shut, with a cordon of
police in front of them.   The red-coated Guardsmen in

their furry busbies stood at ease in front of the sentry-boxes.

' We want King George !   We want King George ! ' chanted the mob.

' We want King George ! '

After several minutes a window was opened on to the centre balcony, and the King appeared.   He was greeted by an immense ragged cheer, and acknowledged it by raising his hand to his forehead.   The crowd began another chant :

' We want War !   We want War !   We want WAR ! '

More cheering.   The King made no gesture of approval or disapproval.

' Speech ! ' shouted the mob, ' speech !   WE WANT WAR ! '

The King saluted again, and disappeared.   A roar of mingled cheering and disappointment came from the crowd.   There were several of the inevitable humorous optimists to cry :

' Are we down-hearted ? '

' No-ooo ! '

' Is Germany ? '

' Yuss ! '

' Do we care for the Germans ? '

' No-oooo ! '

There could be no doubt about the feelings of that small section of the English population. . . .

Even then George still clung to hopes of peace, bought only the more pacific Radical papers, and believed that Sir Edward Grey would ' do something.'   Touching faith of the English in the omnipotence of their rulers ! After all, Sir Edward was not God Almighty, but merely a harassed Secretary of State for Foreign Affairs in a difficult position, with a divided Cabinet behind him. What on earth could the man have done ? Possibly a frank statement in July that if France or Belgium were attacked, England would 'come in' ? People say so now, but then it might have looked like a gesture of provocation. . . . Who are we to pass judgments ? And the nations cannot altogether pose as the victims of their rulers. It is certain that the mobs in the capitals were howling for war. It is certain that the largest popular demonstrations in favour of peace occurred in Germany. . . .

When the news came that France had mobilised, and that the Germans had crossed the Belgian frontier, George abandoned all hope immediately. He knew that one of the cardinal points of British policy is never to allow Antwerp to rest in the possession of a Great Power. The principle is as old as the reign of Queen Elizabeth or older. Who was it said, ' Antwerp is a pistol pointed at England's head ' ? All Europe was in arms, and England would join. The impossible had happened. They were in for three months of carnage and horrors. Yes, three months. It couldn't last longer. Probably less. Oh, much less. There would be an immense financial collapse, and the governments would have to cease fighting. Why, Bank rate was ten per cent. already. He jumped on a bus at Hyde Park Corner and sat just inside the entrance.

' What 's the news ? ' said the conductor.

' Very serious : the French have mobilised.'

' What abaht us ? '

' We 've done nothing yet. But it looks inevitable.'

' Wy, we ain't declared war, 'ave we ? '

' No, not yet.'

'Well, there's still 'opes, then. I reckon we'd best mind ah own business, and keep aht of it.'

Mind our own business ! How quickly that unselfish sentiment was crystallised in the national slogan : Business As Usual !

The long, unendurable nightmare had begun. And the reign of Cant, Delusion, and Delirium. I have shown, with a certain amount of excusable ferocity, how devilishly and perniciously the old régime of Cant affected people's sexual lives, and hence the whole of their lives and characters and those of their children. The subsequent reaction was, at least in its origin, healthy and right. There simply *had* to be a better attitude, the facts had to be faced. And nobody with any courage will allow himself to be frightened out of saying so, either by the hush-hush partisans of the old régime or the doing-what-grandpa-did-and-let's-pretend-it's-all-lovely, or by the fact that numerous congenital idiots have prattled and babbled and slobbered about 'sex' until the very word is an exacerbation. But the sexual life *is* important. It is in so many cases the dominant or the next to dominant factor in people's lives. We can't write about their lives without bringing it in ; so for God's sake let's do so honestly and openly, in accordance with what we believe to be the facts, or else give up pretending that we are writing about life. No more Cant. And I mean free-love Cant just as much as orange-blossoms and pealing church bells Cant. . . .

If you're going to argue that Cant is necessary (the old political excuse), then for Heaven's sake let's chuck up the game and hand in our checks. But it isn't necessary. It can only be necessary when deceit is necessary, when people have to be influenced to act against their right

instincts and true interests.   If you want to judge a man,
a cause, a nation, ask : Do they Cant ?   If the War had
been an honest affair for any participant, it would not have
needed this preposterous bolstering up of Cant.   The
only honest people—if they existed—were those who said :
' This is foul brutality, but we respect and admire brutality, and admit we are brutes ; in fact, we are proud of
being brutes.'   All right, then we know.   ' War is hell.'
It is, General Sherman, it is, a bloody, brutal hell.   Thanks
for your honesty.   You, at least, were an honourable
murderer.

It was the régime of Cant *before* the War which made the
Cant *during* the War so damnably possible and easy.   On
our coming of age the Victorians generously handed us a
charming little cheque for fifty guineas—fifty-one months
of hell, and the results.   Charming people, weren't they ?
Virtuous and far-sighted.   But it wasn't their fault ?
They didn't make the War ?   It was Prussia, and Prussian
militarism ?   Right you are, right ho !   Who made
Prussia a great power and subsidised Frederick the
Second to do it, thereby snatching an empire from
France ?   England.   Who backed up Prussia against
Austria, and Bismarck against Napoleon III. ?   England.
And whose Cant governed England in the nineteenth
century ?   But never mind this domestic squabble of
mine—put it that I mean the ' Victorians ' of all nations.

One human brain cannot hold, one memory retain, one
pen portray the limitless Cant, Delusion, and Delirium let
loose on the world during those four years.   It surpasses
the most fantastic imagination.   It was incredible—and
I suppose that was why it was believed.   It was the
supreme and tragic climax of Victorian Cant, for after all
the Victorians were still in full blast in 1914, and had
pretty much the control of everything.   Did they appeal

to us honestly, and say : ' We have made a colossal and tragic error, we have involved you and all of us in a huge war ; it 's too late to stop it ; you must come and help us, and we promise to take the first opportunity of making peace and making it thoroughly ' ?   They did not.   They said they didn't want to lose us, but they thought WE ought to go ; they said our King and Country needed us ; they said they 'd kiss us when we came home (merci ! effect of the Entente Cordiale ?) ; they said one of the most civilised races in the world were ' Huns ' ; they invented Cadaver factories ; they asserted that a race of men notorious during generations for their kindliness were habitual baby-butchers, rapers of women, crucifiers of prisoners ; they said the ' Huns ' were sneaks and cowards and skedaddlers, but failed to explain why it took fifty-one months to beat their hopelessly outnum-bered armies ; they said they were fighting for the Liberty of the World, and everywhere there is less liberty ; they said they would Never sheathe the Sword until etcetera, and this sort of criminal rant was called Pisgah-Heights of Patriotism. . . .   They said . . .   But why continue ? Why go on ?   It is desolating, desolating.   And then they dare wonder why the young are cynical and despairing and angry and chaotic !   And they still have adherents, who still dare to go on preaching to us !   Quick !   A shrine to the goddesses Cant and Impudence. . . .

I don't know if George was aware of all this, because we never discussed it.   There were numbers of things you prudently didn't discuss in those days ; you never knew who might be listening and ' report.'   I myself was twice arrested, as a civilian, for wearing a cloak and looking foreign, and for laughing in the street ; I was under acute suspicion for weeks in one battalion because I had a copy of Heine's poems and admitted that I had been abroad ; in another I was suspected of not being myself, God knows why.   That was nothing compared with the persecution endured by D. H. Lawrence, probably the greatest living English novelist, and a man of whom—in spite of his failings—England should be proud.

I do know that George suffered profoundly from the first day of the War until his death at the end of it.   He must have realised the awfulness of the Cant and degradation, for he occasionally talked about the yahoos of the world having got loose and seized control, and, by Jove! he was right.   I shan't attempt to describe the sinister degradation of English life in the last two years of the War: for one thing, I was mostly out of England; and for another, Lawrence has done it once and for all in the chapter called 'The Nightmare' in his book *Kangaroo*.

In George's case, the suffering which was common to all decent men and women was increased and complicated and rendered more torturing by his personal problems, which somehow became related to the War.   You must remember that he did not believe in the alleged causes for which the War was fought.   He looked upon the War as a ghastly calamity, or a more ghastly crime.   They might talk about their idealism, but it wasn't convincing.   There wasn't the *élan*, the conviction, the burning idealism which carried the ragged untrained armies of the First French Republic so dramatically to Victory over the hostile coalitions of the Kings.   There was always the suspicion of dupery and humbug.   Therefore, he could not take part in the War with any enthusiasm or conviction. On the other hand, he saw the intolerable egotism of setting up oneself as a notable exception or courting a facile martyrdom of *rouspetance*.   Going meant one more little brand in the conflagration ; staying out meant that

some other, probably physically weaker, brand was substituted. His conscience was troubled before he was in
the Army, and equally troubled afterwards. The only
consolation he felt was in the fact that you certainly
had a worse and a more dangerous time in the line than
out of it.

As a matter of fact, I never really 'got' George's position. He hated talking about the subject, and he had
thought about it and worried about it so much that he was
quite muddle-headed. It seemed to involve the whole
universe, and his attempts to express his point of view
would wander off into discussions about the Greek city-
states or the principles of Machiavelli. He was frankly
incoherent, which meant a considerable inner conflict.
From the very beginning of the War he had got into the
habit of worrying, and this developed with alarming
rapidity. He worried about the War, about his own
attitude to it, about his relations with Elizabeth and
Fanny, about his military duties, about everything. Now,
'worry' is not 'caused' by an event ; it is a state which
seizes upon any event to 'worry' over. It is a form of
neurasthenia, which may be induced in a perfectly healthy
mind by shock and strain. And for months and months
he just worried and drifted.

When Elizabeth decided, somewhere towards the end
of 1914, that the time had come when the principles of
Freedom must be put into practice in the case of herself
and Reggie, and duly informed George, he acquiesced at
once. Perhaps he was so sick at heart that he was indifferent ; perhaps he was only loyally carrying out the
agreement. What surprised me was that he did not take
that opportunity of telling her about Fanny. But he was
apparently quite convinced that she knew. It was therefore an additional shock when he found out that she

didn't know, and a still greater shock to see how she behaved. He suffered an obnubilation of the intellect in dealing with women. He idealised them too much. When I told him with a certain amount of bitterness that Fanny was probably a trollop who talked 'freedom' as an excuse, and that Elizabeth was probably a conventional-minded woman who talked 'freedom' as in the former generation she would have talked Ruskin and Morris politico-aestheticism, he simply got angry. He said I was a fool. He said the War had induced in me a peculiar resentment against women—which was probably true. He said I did not understand either Elizabeth or Fanny—how could I possibly understand two people I had never seen and have the cheek to try to explain them to *him*, who knew them so well ? He said I was far too downright, over-simplified, and *tranchant* in my judgments, and that I didn't—probably couldn't—understand the finer complexities of people's psychology. He said a great deal more, which I have forgotten. But we came as near to a quarrel as two lonely men could, when they knew they had no other companion. This was in the Officers' Training Camp in 1917, when George was already in a peculiar and exacerbated state of nerves. After that, I made no effort at any sort of ruthless directness, but just allowed him to go on talking. There was nothing else to do. He was living in a sort of double nightmare—the nightmare of the War and the nightmare of his own life. Each seemed inextricably interwoven. His personal life became intolerable because of the War, and the War became intolerable because of his own life. The strain imposed on him—or which he imposed on himself—must have been terrific. A sort of pride kept him silent. Once when it was my turn to act as commander of the other cadets, I was taking them in company drill. George was right-hand man in the front rank of No. 1 Platoon, and I glanced at him to see that he was keeping direction properly. I was startled by the expression on his face—so hard, so fixed, so despairing, so defiantly agonised. At mess—we ate at tables in sixes—he hardly ever spoke except to utter some banality in an effort to be amiable, or some veiled sarcasm which sped harmlessly over the heads of those for whom it was intended. He sneered a little too openly at the coarse, obscene talk about tarts and square-pushing, and was too obviously revolted by water-closet wit. However, he wasn't openly disliked. The others just thought him a rum bloke, and left him pretty much alone.

Probably what had distressed him most was the row between Elizabeth and Fanny. With the whole world collapsing about him, it seemed quite logical that the Triumphal Scheme for the Perfect Sex Relation should collapse too. He did not feel the peevish disgust of the reforming idealist who makes a failure. But in the general disintegration of all things he had clung very closely to those two women; too closely, of course. But they had acquired a sort of mythical and symbolical meaning for him. They resented and deplored the War, but they were admirably detached from it. For George they represented what hope of humanity he had left; in them alone civilisation seemed to survive. All the rest was blood and brutality and persecution and humbug. In them alone the thread of life remained continuous. They were two small havens of civilised existence, and alone gave him any hope for the future. They had escaped the vindictive destructiveness which so horribly possessed the spirits of all right-thinking people. Of course, they were persecuted; that was inevitable. But they remained detached, and alive. Unfortunately, they did not quite realise the strain under which he was living, and did not perceive the widening gulf which was separating the men of that generation from the women. How could they? The friends of a person with cancer haven't got cancer. They sympathise, but they aren't in the horrid category of the doomed. Even before the Elizabeth-Fanny row he was subtly drifting apart from them against his will, against his desperate efforts to remain at one with them. Over the men of that generation hung a doom which was admirably if somewhat ruthlessly expressed by a British Staff Officer in an address to subalterns in France : ' You are the War generation. You were born to fight this War, and it 's got to be won—we 're determined you shall win it. So far as you are concerned as individuals, it doesn't matter a tinker's damn whether you are killed or not. Most probably you will be killed, most of you. So make up your minds to it.'

That extension of the Kiplingesque or kicked-backside-of-the-Empire principle was something for which George was not prepared. He resented it, resented it bitterly, but the doom was on him as on all the young men. When ' we ' had determined that they should be killed, it was impious to demur.

After the row, the gap widened, and when once George had entered the army it became complete. He still clung desperately to Elizabeth and Fanny, of course. He wrote long letters to them trying to explain himself, and they replied sympathetically. They were the only persons he wanted to see when on leave, and they met him sympathetically. But it was useless. They were gesticulating across an abyss. The women were still human beings ; he was merely a unit, a murder-robot, a wisp of cannon-fodder. And he knew it. They didn't. But they felt the difference, felt it as a degradation in him, a sort of failure. Elizabeth and Fanny occasionally met after the row, and made acid-sweet remarks to each other. But on one point they were in agreement—George had degenerated terribly since joining the army, and there was no knowing to what preposterous depths of Tommydom he might fall.

' It 's quite useless,' said Elizabeth ; ' he 's done for. He 'll never be able to recover. So we may as well accept it. What was rare and beautiful in him is as much dead now as if he were lying under the ground in France.'

And Fanny agreed. . . .

END OF PART II

PART III

PART III

1

THE draft, under orders to proceed overseas on Active Service without delay, paraded again, in full marching order, at three-thirty.

Number two in the front rank was 31819, Private Winterbourne, G.

They had been 'sized' that morning, so each man knew his number and place. They fell in rapidly, without talking, and stood easy, waiting for the officers, on the bleak gravelled parade-ground inside the bleak isolated citadel. Their view was rectangularly cut short either by the damp grey masonry of the fortress walls or by the dirty yellow brick frontals of the barracks built under the ramparts.

They numbered one hundred and twenty, and had been under orders to proceed overseas for more than a week, during which period they had been forbidden to leave the citadel under threat of court-martial. All sentry duties were performed by troops not in the draft, and five rounds of ball ammunition were issued to each sentry. These exceptional measures were the result of nervousness on the part of the Colonel, who had been censured for what was not his fault—two men had deserted on the eve of the departure of the last draft, and two others had to be substituted at the last moment. ' Does the old mucker think we 're going to run away ? ' was the comment of the draft, wounded in their pride, when they accidentally found this out.

A stiff, coldish wind was blowing soiled-looking ragged clouds and occasional gusts of chilly rain over a greyish

winter sky. The men fidgeted in the ranks, some bend-
ing forward to ease the strain of straps, some throwing
their packs a fraction higher with a jerk of their shoulders
and loins ; one or two had taken the regulation step
forward and were adjusting their puttees or the fold in
their trouser legs. Winterbourne stood with his weight
on his right leg, holding the projecting barrel of his
obsolete drill rifle loosely in his right hand ; his head was
bent slightly forward as he gazed at the gravel expres-
sionlessly.

The draft had been parading for various purposes all
through the day, when they thought they would be free
to idle and write letters. The canteen had been put out
of bounds to prevent a possible drunken departure. The
parades had included two kit inspections and several
visits to the Quartermaster's stores to draw new winter
clothing and other objects for use overseas. Consequently, in their mood of restrained excitement, they had
become rather irritated and impatient. The fidgeting
increased under the reproving gaze of the N.C.O.'s and
the rather boiled-looking glare of the Regimental Sergeant-
Major, a military pedant of exacting standards ; nothing,
however, was said, since movement is permitted at the
' stand easy.'

The mood of the draft was not improved by a sudden
flurry of cold rain which swept across the parade-ground
in a long moaning gust, at the moment when three or
four officers came out of their Mess.

' Draft ! ' came the R.S.M.'s warning bellow.

The hundred and twenty hands slipped automatically
down the rifles, and the men stood silent and motionless,
looking to the front, and trying not to sway when the
pressure of the rising gale suddenly increased or suddenly
relaxed.

' Stand still there ! Stand *steady* ! '

There was a slight bulge in the front of each of the short service-jackets, where two field dressings in a water-proof case and a phial of iodine had been thrust into the pocket provided for them, inside the right-hand flap.

' Draft !—Draft ! 'Tenshun ! '

Two hundred and forty heels met smartly in one collective snap at the same time that the rifles were sharply brought to the sides. The draft stood to atten-tion, gazing fixedly to the front. A man unconsciously turned his head slightly in trying to catch a glimpse of the approaching officers out of the corner of his eye.

' Stand still, that man ! Look to your front, can't you ? '

Silence, except for the moaning wind and the crunch of gravel under the officers' boots. The Colonel and the Adjutant wore spurs, which jingled very slightly. The Colonel acknowledged the R.S.M.'s salute and his ' All present and c'rect, sir.'

' Rear rank—one pace step back—March ! '

One—two. The hundred and twenty legs moved mechanically like one man's.

' Rear rank—stand-at—Ease ! '

The Colonel inspected the front rank, and took a long time, fussing over various details. A man with cold fingers dropped his rifle.

' Ser'ant 'Icks, take that man's name and number, and forward the charge with his Crime Sheet ! '

' Very good, sir.'

The front rank stood at ease while the Colonel in-spected the rear rank less minutely. It was beginning to get dark, and he had to make a speech. He stood about thirty yards in front of the draft with the other officers behind him. The youthful Adjutant held his riding crop against his right thigh like a field-marshal's baton. The Colonel, an eccentric but harmless half-wit who had been returned with thanks from France early in his first campaign, was speaking :

' N.C.O.'s and Men of the 8th Upshires ! Er—you are—er—proceeding overseas on Active Service. Er. Er. I—er—trust you will do your—er—duty. We have wasted—er—spared no pains to make you efficient. Remember to keep yourselves smart and clean and—er— walk about in a soldierly way. You must always—er— maintain the honour of the Regiment which—er—er— which stands high in the records of the British Army. I— . . .'

A very faint murmur of 'Muckin' old fool,' 'Silly old mucker,' ' 'Struth ! ' came from the draft, too faint to reach the officers' ears, but the alert R.S.M. caught it, though without distinguishing the words, and cut short the Colonel's peroration with his stentorian :

' Stand still, there ! Stand *steady* ! Take their names, Ser'ant 'Icks ! '

A short pause, and the R.S.M. shouted :

' P'rade again at four-fifteen outside the Armoury, in clean fatigue, to hand in rifles. Mind they 're properly clean and pulled-through. An' no talking as you walk off p'rade.'

The Adjutant had been talking to the Colonel, and saluted as his superior departed. He walked over to the R.S.M.

' All right, Sergeant-Major, you and the other N.C.O.'s not in the draft may fall out. I 'll dismiss the men.'

' Very good, sir.'

The Adjutant walked over to the draft and stood with his right hand on his hip. He spoke slowly but without hesitation :

'Stand at ease.   Stand easy.   You can wash out what the R.S.M. just said.   Leave your rifles in the racks, but try to leave 'em clean or I shall get strafed. . . . I 'm afraid we 've chased you about a bit under the new intensive scheme of training, but it 's all in the day's work, you know.   I 'm sorry we 're not going out as a unit, but battalions are being broken up everywhere for drafts. When you get out, don't forget to look after your feet— you get court-martialled for trench feet nowadays—and don't be in a hurry to shove your heads over the top ! I 'm due to follow you myself soon, so I expect we 'll all be in the next push.   Good-bye.   And the very best of luck to you all.'

'Good-bye, sir.   Thank you, sir.   Same to you, sir. Good-bye, sir.'

'Good-bye.   Draft, 'shun.   Slope arms.   Dis-miss.'

Simultaneously their hands tapped the rifle-butts in salute, as they turned right.

The draft confusedly moved over the darkened ground to the barrack-room, chattering excitedly :

'What 's the next thing ? '

'P'rade at eight-thirty to move off at nine.'

'Who said so ? '

'It 's in B'ttalion orders.'

'Silly ole mucker old Brandon is, give me the fair pip he did with 'is "walk about soldierly"—yes ! up to yer arse in mud.'

'Bloody old ****.'

'Yes, but the Adjutant was all right.'

'Oh, 'e 's a gentleman, 'e is.'

'Makes all the difference when they 've bin in the ranks theirselves.'

'Wonder what it 'll be like in the line ? '

' Wait till y' get there and see.'

' I reckon we 'll be there this time to-morrow night.'

' Shut up, Larkin, and don't get the wind up.'

' I ain't got the wind up.'

' I say, Corporal, Corp'ral ! What time do we p'rade to-night ? '

' Ask the Ord'ly Sergeant.'

' Tea 's up, boys. Come on ! '

They fell in again at eight-thirty. The night was very dark, with a cold, damp, gusty wind from the west. All the N.C.O.'s were on parade, carrying lighted hurricane lanterns which moved and flitted and stood still in the darkness like will-o-th'-wisps. The draft were in full marching order, without rifles and side-arms, wearing their greatcoats. Their excitement occasionally broke through the military restraint and rose from a whisper to a loud hum, which would cringe abruptly under the R.S.M.'s ' Stop talking, there ! ' It took a long time to read the roll-call by the flicker of the lantern. At the sound of his name each man clicked his heels, ' Here, sir.'

' 31819, Winterbourne, G.'

' Here, sir.'

' That 's the lot, Ser'ant-Major, isn't it ? '

' That 's the lot, sir.'

' Move off in five minutes.'

' Very good, sir.'

The draft stirred restlessly in the darkness. Winterbourne looked to his left and noticed how the line of shadowy figures disappeared into the night—he might have been at one end of a line stretching to infinity for all he could see.

' Draft ! Draft ! 'Tenshun ! Move to the right in

column of fours—form fours ! Form two deep ! Form
fours ! Right ! By the right—Quick march ! '

They found themselves immediately behind the regimental band, which struck up one of the Mark III. marches
supplied to Army musicians. The draft knew it well—
' How can I draw rations—if I 'm not the ord'ly man ? '
They marched over the familiar parade-ground, out
through the postern, over the swaying drawbridge, where
the sentry presented arms.

' By the left. March at—ease. March easy.'

The band had ceased playing. They were descending
the long, winding hill road to the village and the station.
As they went along they were joined by civilians, mostly
girls, who were waiting in ones and twos. The girls
called to their men in the ranks, and they, emboldened
by excitement and this momentous change in their lives,
dared to answer back. March discipline relaxed, and
the draft was already marching raggedly as it passed the
first houses of the village. After the dense blackness of
the hillside, the light from the few gas-lamps was dazzling.

The band struck up again. Although it was past ten,
the whole village was awake and in the street to watch
them go by. The loud brass music reverberated from
the house fronts. The draft were amazed to find themselves for a moment the centre of public interest ; for so
long they had learned to consider themselves fatally
insignificant and subordinate. Voices came from all
sides : ' 'Ullo, Bert ! Good-bye, 'Arry ! Hullo, Tom !
Good-bye, Jack ! ' Winterbourne, in the front rank,
looked behind ; he noticed that some of the girls had
broken into the ranks and were marching with their men,
clinging to their arms. They appeared to be enjoying
themselves greatly. An exceedingly ragged company
surged excitedly through the village, intoxicated by the

sounding brass and the cheers and other attentions of the inhabitants.

The civilians were not allowed on the station platform. As the draft marched through the open gate, with a picket of military police on either hand, there was another chorus of ' Good-bye, Bert ! Good-bye, 'Arry ! Good-bye, Tom. Good-bye, Jack ! Good luck. Come 'ome soon. Good-bye. Good luck. Good-bye.'

They piled into the waiting troop-train, which was to pick up other drafts on the way. Twelve to a carriage. Winterbourne managed to get the window-seat next the platform. The Adjutant came up.

' Winterbourne ! Winterbourne ! '

' Sir ? '

' Oh, there you are. Looking for you. The R.T.O. says you go to Waterloo, and then proceed to Folkestone, he thinks.'

' Thanks very much, sir. It 's so much less tedious when you know what you 're doing and why and where you 're going.'

' You ought to have a commission. You 'll easily get one in France.'

' Yes, but you know why I wanted to stay in the ranks, sir.'

' Yes, I know, but men like you are needed as officers. The casualties among officers are terrifically high.'

' All right, I 'll think about it, sir.'

' Well, good-bye, old man, the very best of luck to you.'

' Thank you. And to you.'

They shook hands, to the impressed horror of the N.C.O.'s.

The crowd had gathered outside the railings by the fore part of the train, where they were not masked by the station buildings. The band were drawn up in front of them, on the platform. The train gave a warning whistle. The band struck up the Regimental March, and then ' Auld Lang Syne,' as the train slowly steamed out of the station ; they played their instruments with one hand, and ludicrously waved the other hand to the draft crowded in the moving windows. A long wavering cheer went up. The red faces of the soldiers on the platform were all turned slightly upwards, and their mouths were open. Their right arms were raised above their heads. In a blare of band music, cheering, and shouting, the cheering draft drew out of the station.

Good-bye, Bert. Good-bye, Harry. Good-bye, Tom. Good-bye, Jack. Good-bye.

The last person Winterbourne saw was the little Colonel, standing at the extreme end of the platform under a gas-lamp, standing very erect, standing rather tense and emotional, standing with his right hand raised to his cap, standing to salute his men proceeding on Active Service.

He wasn't a bad little man ; he believed intensely in his Army.

In fifteen minutes the excited chatter over fags dwindled
to the monotony of an ordinary railway journey. The
men were tired, for it was already long after Last Post.
They began to drowse. One man in the far corner from
Winterbourne was already asleep. The racks were full
of overcoats and equipment. Under the Anti-Aircraft
Regulations the curtains of the train windows were closely
drawn.

Winterbourne felt entirely unsleepy. He ceased talking
to the man beside him, and drifted into a reverie. His
mind slid backwards and forwards from one theme of
thought to another. Already he found it difficult to read
or to think consecutively. He had reached the first expressionless stage of the war soldier, which is followed by
the period of acute strain ; and that in turn gives place
to the second expressionless stage — which is pretty
hopeless.

The real test was beginning. Like everybody who had
not been there, he was almost entirely ignorant of life in
the trenches. Newspapers, illustrated periodicals, almost
useless. He had heard a lot of tales from returned
wounded soldiers. But many of them either blathered
or were quite inarticulate. Here and there a revealing
detail or memory. ' And all the time I was delirious after
I was wounded, I kep' seein' them aeryplanes goin' round
and round and then makin' a dive at me.' And the little
Cockney : ' 'Struth ! I got me tunic and me trowses all 'ung
up in Fritz's wire, an' I couldn't get orf. Got me pockets
full o' bombs, I 'ad, as well as them stick-bombs in paniers.
One of the paniers was 'ung up too, an' I ses to myself, I
ses, " If you drop them muckin' bombs, Bert, you 'll

blow yer muckin' 'ead orf." And there was old Fritz's machine-gun bullets whizzin' by, *zip*, *zip*. I could see 'em cuttin' the wire—and me cursin' and blindin'. Blimey ! I wasn't arf afraid. But I got me muckin' blighty, anyway.'

Where did he meet that amusing little Cockney ? Ah, yes, in the depot the day after he joined. There had been several soldiers just out of the hospital in the barrack-room, all swopping yarns. Winterbourne's mind reverted to himself and the past dreary months. He had been unfortunate in the N.C.O.'s of his training battalion—old regulars, who had been bullied and driven in their time, and thought they 'd escape being sent out to France by zealously bullying and driving the new drafts. No doubt they were paying off some of the old Army grudge against civilian contempt for the mercenary soldier. They particularly hated any educated or well-bred man in the ranks, and delighted to impose painful or humiliating tasks on him. George remembered the man who ' took particulars ' of his religion.

' What are yer ?   C. of E., Methodist, R.C. ? '

' I haven't any official religion. You 'd better put me down as a rationalist.'

' Garn ! What 's a muckin' rationalist ? Yer in the Army now.'

' Well, I haven't got one.'

' Bloody well find one, then. Yer 'll want suthin' over yer muckin' grave in France, won't yer ? An' yer 'll bloody well be in it in six months. No religion ! Strike me muckin' pink ! '

An amiable hero. In his zeal for religion he got Winterbourne sent on all the dirtiest and longest Sunday fatigues, until in self-defence he had to put himself down Church of England. There was, of course, no religious compulsion in the Army ; that was why Church Parade was a parade.

Winterbourne smiled as he thought of the ludicrous scene. It had been none the less painful. His gorge rose at the memory of the filth he had tried to remove from the Officers' Mess Kitchen—filth which had been left there untouched by fifty less scrupulous 'fatigues.' The kitchen was inspected every day.

He looked at his hands in the concentrated light of the railway carriage. They were coarsened and chapped, ingrained with dirt impossible to remove with ice-cold water. He thought of the delicate hands of Fanny and Elizabeth's slender fingers.

On parade the officers never swore at the men, the N.C.O.'s rarely, whatever they might do off parade. It was an offence under King's Regs. The Physical Training Instructors were, however, an exception. They sometimes displayed an uncouth humour in their objurgations. There were time-honoured pleasantries, such as ' Yer may break yer muckin' mother's 'eart, but yer won't break mine ! ' There was the Bayonet Instructor, a singularly rough diamond from Whitechapel, who in mimic bayonet-fighting at the stuffed bags loved to give the command :

' At 'is stummick an' goolies—Point ! '

This gentleman, offended at the awkward posture of a rather plump recruit doing the ' double knee bend,' had apostrophised the unfortunate man :

' 'Ere, you, Frost. ***'* *** *** **** **** * ******' *******, *** *** **** * ****** ***** ***** *** '* ****' ******* ? '

Winterbourne smiled again to himself. The road to glory was undoubtedly devious in our fair island story.

From Reveille at five-thirty until Lights Out they had

been driven and harassed and bullied for weeks to the
strain of : ' Look to yer front, there ! ' ' 'Old yer 'eads
up, can't yer ? all them tanners was picked up on first
p'rade.' ' Smith, yer got them straps crossed wrong—if
yer do it again, I 'll crime yer.' And over the voices of
the various sergeant-instructors shouting to their squads,
boomed the R.S.M.'s inevitable ' Stand still, there !
Stand *steady*.' Just like the South Foreland lightship
in a fog. The fatigue of continual over-exercise and of
the physical and mental strain was severe to men fresh
from sedentary lives, or stiff from the plough and the
workshop. For the first weeks especially they were sore
all over, and sank into heavy, unrefreshing sleep at night.
Winterbourne bore it better than most. His long walks
and love for swimming had kept him supple. He could
not raise weights like the draymen or dig like the navvies,
but he could out-march and out-run them all, learn every
new movement in half the time, dismount a Lewis gun
while they were wondering which way the handle came
off, score four bulls out of five, and saw immediately why
you made head-cover first when digging in. But he too
felt the fatigue. He remembered one perfectly awful day.
They had been drilled and marched and drilled and
inspected from dawn to evening of a baking autumn day ;
then at seven there had been three hours of night opera-
tions. At twelve they were all awakened by a false Fire
Alarm, and had to turn out in trousers and boots. Winterbourne had taken over his shoulder the arm of a man who
was too exhausted to run unassisted on to the parade-
ground. The N.C.O.'s yelped them on like sheep-dogs.

It was not the physical fatigue Winterbourne minded,
though he hated the inevitable physical degradation—the
coarse, heavy clothes, too thick for summer ; the hobnailed boots ; the plank bed ; horribly cooked food. But

he accepted and got used to them. He suffered mentally ;
suffered from the shock of the abrupt change from surroundings where the things of the mind chiefly were
valued, to surroundings where they were ignorantly
despised. He had nobody to talk to. He suffered from
the communal life of thirty men in one large hut, which
meant that there was never a moment's solitude. He
suffered because he brooded over Elizabeth and Fanny,
over the widening gulf he knew was dividing him from
them, and suffered abominably as month after month of
the war dragged on with its interminable holocausts and
immeasurable degradation of mankind. The world of
men seemed dropping to pieces, madly cast down by men
in a delirium of homicide and destructiveness. The very
apparatus of killing revolted him, took on a sort of sinister
deadness. There was something in the very look of his
rifle and equipment which filled him with depression.
And then, in the imagination, he was already facing the
existence for which this was but a preparation, already
confronting the agony of his own death. Horrific tales
—alas ! only too true—were told of companies and
battalions wiped out in a few instants. N.C.O. after
N.C.O., as Winterbourne got to know them better,
assured him that they were the only men—or almost the
only men—left alive from their platoons or companies.
And it was the truth. The proportion of casualties was
undoubtedly high in infantry units. It was, perhaps,
selfish of Winterbourne to worry about his own extinction
when so many better men had already been obliterated.
He felt rather ashamed and apologetic about it himself.
But it is human to recoil from a violent death, even at
twenty-two or three. . . .

The train began to slow down at a large junction, and he
returned to his present surroundings with a start. The

other men were asleep. Well, all the training and pre-
senting arms and saluting by numbers were over and in
the past. They were on Active Service. It was an
immense relief. Now henceforth he would be facing
dread realities, not Regular Army pedants and bullies.
As Winterbourne once remarked, one of the horrors of
the War was not fighting the Germans, but living under
the British.

After picking up more drafts, the train went on, grind-
ing its way heavily through the silent darkness. The men
were all asleep. He noticed the carriage was getting
stuffy and headachey with foul air. Some one had shut
the windows and ventilators while he was day-dreaming.
That was the old bother—whether in huts or barracks,
they *would* try to sleep in foul air. He softly slipped the
window open a couple of inches—better already. Wonder
why they like a fug ? Mental and moral fug, too. Poor
devils ! All brought up to touch their hats to the gentry,
do what they 're told, and work. Sort of helots. Yet
they 're decent enough, got character, but no intelligence.
That 's the real war, the only war worth fighting, the
battle of the intelligence against inertia and stupidity
and . . . Still, the intelligence is not always defeated ;
we 've got here somehow. Yes ! and look where we are !
His mind half-sleepily ran off along a familiar track.
What 's really the cause of wars, of this War ? Oh, you
can't say one cause ; there are many. The Socialists are
silly fanatics when they say it 's the wicked capitalists. I
don't believe the capitalists wanted a war—they stand to
lose too much in the disturbance. And I don't believe
the wretched governments really wanted it—they were
shoved on by great forces they 're too timid and too unintelligent to control. It 's the superstition of more babies

and more bread, more bread and more babies. Of course, all wars haven't been mere population wars. 'Course not—Greek city-states, mediæval Italian republics, wars of petty jealousy ; naval wars for commercial advantages —Pisa, Genoa, Venice, Holland, England ; the sport of kings, eighteenth-century diversion of the aristocracy ; wars of fanaticism, Moslems, the Crusades ; emigration wars like the irruption of the barbarians. . . . There may be commercial motives behind this War, jolly short-sighted ones—they 've already lost more than they can possibly gain. No, this is fundamentally a population War—bread and babies, babies and bread. It 's all oddly mixed up with the sexual problem we were battling with so brightly when this little packet of trouble was dumped on us by our virtuous forebears. It 's the babies-and-bread super-stition. You encourage, you force people to have babies, lots of babies, millions of babies. As they grow up, you 've got to feed 'em. You need bread. We all live from the land. England, and the rest of the world after it, went crazy with the Industrial Revolution—thought you could eat steel and railways. You can't. The world of men is an inverted pyramid based on the bowed shoulders of the ploughman—or the steel tractor—on the land. It 's the hunger-and-death business again. ' In-crease and multiply.' Damned imbecility of applying to over-populated and huge nations the sexual taboos forced on a little crowd of unhygienic Semitic nomads by sheer force of circumstance. Think of their infantile death-rate ! Breed like rabbits or vanish. Doesn't apply to us. We 're a sacrifice to over-breeding. Too many people in Europe. A damn sight too many babies. The people could be made to see, are beginning to see it—but the hurray-for-our-dear-Fatherland people, and the priests and the fanatics and the timid and the conservative, won't

see it. Go on, breed, you beauties—breed in column of
fours, in battalions, brigades, divisions, army corps. Wait
till the population of England is five hundred million and
we're all packed like herrings in a tub. Lovely. Wonderful. England über alles ! But there comes a time when
there isn't enough bread for the growing babies. Colonise.
Why ? Either grow more food or produce more things
to exchange for food. England's got huge colonies.
Germany very small ones. The Germans breed like
tadpoles. The British breed like rather slower tadpoles.
What are you going to do with them ? Kill 'em off in a
war ? Kind. Humane. Kill 'em off, and grab land and
commercial advantages from the defeated nation ? Right.
And what next ? Oh, go on breeding. Must be a great
and populous nation. And the defeated nation ? Suppose they start breeding harder than ever ? Oh, have
another war, go on having 'em, get the habit. Europe's
decennial picnic of corpses. . . .

Yes, but why so sentimental ? Why all this fuss over a
few million men killed and maimed ? Thousands of
people die weekly and somebody's run over in London
every day. Does that argument take you in ? Well, the
answer is that they're not *murdered*. And your 'thousands who die weekly' are the old and the diseased ; here
it's the young and the strong and the healthy, the physical
pick of the race. All men, too, and no women. That'll
set up a pretty nice resentment between the sexes—more
sodomy and lesbianism. Loud cheers—we're winning.
Yes, but, going back to murder—people are murdered all
the time ; look at Chicago. Look at Chicago ! We're
always patting ourselves on the back and looking smugly
at wicked Chicago. When there's a shoot-up between
gangs, do you approve of it, do you give the winning side
medals for their gallantry, do you tell 'em to go to it and

you 'll kiss them when they come back, do you march 'em
by with a brass band and tell 'em what fine fellows they
are ? Do you take the gunman as the high ideal of
humanity ? I know all about military grandeur and
devotion to duty—I 'm a soljer meself, marm. Thanks
for all you 've done for us, marm. If violence and
butchery are the natural state of man, then let 's have no
more of your humbug. Violence and butchery beget
violence and butchery. Isn't that the theme of the great
Greek tragedies of blood ? Blood will have blood. All
right, now we know. It doesn't matter whether murder
is individual or collective, whether committed on behalf
of one man or a gang or a state. It 's murder. When
you approve of murder you violate the right instincts of
every human being. And a million murders egged on,
lauded, exulted over, will raise a legion of Eumenides
about your ears. The survivors will pay bitterly for it
all their lives. Never mind, you 'll go on ? More babies,
soon make up the losses ? Have another merry old war
soon, sooner the better. . . .

O my son Absalom, my son, my son Absalom ! Thank
God I have no son, O Absalom, my son, my son !

Winterbourne nodded uneasily asleep. He started
awake as the train slowed down at London Bridge and
not at Waterloo. Where am I ? Railway station. Oh,
of course, on a draft going out to France. . . .

The draft were turned out at London Bridge, and
collected in two ranks on the platform, yawning, stretching, and adjusting their equipment. The draft-conducting
officer, a mild, brown-eyed young man on home service
after being wounded, explained that they had nearly
three hours to wait. Would they like to go to a Soldiers'
Canteen and get some food ?

' Yes, sir ! '

They marched through the empty, muddy streets. It was about midnight. Some one began to sing one of the inevitable marching songs. The officer turned round :

' Whistle, but don't sing. People asleep.'

They began to whistle ' Where are the lads of the village to-night ? '

Winterbourne found himself crossing the Thames, and looked once more at the familiar townscape. He noticed that the street-lamps had been dimmed further since he had left London, and that the once brilliantly-lighted capital now lay cowering in darkness. The dome of St. Paul's was just faintly visible to an eye which knew exactly where to look for it. The man next to Winterbourne was a Worcestershire ploughman who had never been to London and was most anxious to see St. Paul's. Winterbourne tried hard to show him where it was, but failed. The ploughman never did see St. Paul's—he was killed two months later.

Curious to march through this unfamiliar London— everything the same, but everything so different. The dimmed street-lights, the carefully blinded windows, the rather neglected streets, the comparative absence of traffic, the air of being closed down indefinitely, all gave him an uneasy feeling. It was as if a doom hung over the great city, as if it had passed its meridian of power and splendour, and was sinking back, back into the darkened past, back into the clay hills and marshes on which it stands. That New Zealander sketching the ruins from a broken pile of London Bridge seemed several centuries nearer.

> ' *Where are the lads of the village to-night?*
> *Where are the lads we knew?*

> *In Piccadilly or Leicester Square?*
> *No, not there!   No, not there!*
> *They're taking a trip on the Continong. . . .'*

The foolish words ran in Winterbourne's brain as the men whistled the tune with exasperating pertinacity. It was curious to be so near to Fanny and Elizabeth. He wondered vaguely what they were doing.

> ' *No, not there!   No, not there!* '

He had sent Elizabeth a telegram from a station on the way up, but probably it had not reached her.

They crowded into the Canteen, and ate sandwiches and eggs and bacon, and drank ginger-beer. It was too late for beer. Our temperate troops didn't need beer at that hour of the night.

About 2 A.M. they marched back to the station. To Winterbourne's surprise and delight, Elizabeth and Fanny were there. Elizabeth had received his telegram although it was after hours. She had rung up Fanny, and they had gone to Waterloo together, only to find that the train with the Upshires draft was not there. Fanny had used her charms upon a susceptible R.T.O., and he had told them where to go, so there they were. All this Elizabeth poured out in a rapid, nervous, jerky way. While Fanny just clutched Winterbourne's left hand and pressed it hard, saying nothing. They had about ten minutes before the train left. The draft-conducting officer noticed that Winterbourne was speaking to two women, ' obviously ladies,' and came up.

' Get in anywhere you like, Winterbourne, only don't miss the train.'

' Very good, sir, thank you,' and saluted smartly.

' D' you always have to do that ? ' asked Elizabeth with a little giggle.

' Yes, it 's the custom. They seem to attach great importance to it.'

' How absurd ! '

' Why absurd ? ' said Fanny, feeling that Winterbourne was somehow hurt by the contempt in her voice. ' It 's only a convention.'

The whole train was filled with different drafts of soldiers who had been ordered into the carriages. Only Winterbourne and the two girls were left on the platform, except for the R.T.O. and one or two other officers. As often happens in railway partings, they seemed embarrassed, with nothing to say to each other. Winterbourne simply felt dull and uneasy, tongue-tied. He was saying farewell, perhaps for the last time, to the only two human beings he had really loved, and found he had nothing to say. He just felt dull and uneasy, dully remote from them. He noticed they were both wearing new hats he hadn't seen, and that skirts were being worn much shorter. He wished the train would go. Interminable waiting. What was Elizabeth saying ? He interrupted her :

' Is that the new fashion ? '

' What ? '

' Shorter skirts.'

' Why, yes, of course, and not so very new. Where have your eyes been ? '

' Oh, there were only village women where I 've been. I haven't seen a properly dressed woman since my firing leave.'

Tactless ! He had spent those few days with Fanny. Dear Fanny ! A good sort. She had thought it an awful lark to go on a week-end with a Tommy. She was dreadfully sick of the Staff. Still, it was inconvenient that the only decent hotels and restaurants were out of bounds to Tommies. Fanny felt quite democratic about it. Elizabeth hadn't cared. She lived with a kind of inner intensity which kept her from noticing such things.

They were silent for seconds which dragged like minutes. Then they all began to say something together, interrupted themselves. ' Sorry, I didn't mean to interrupt.' ' What were you going to say ? ' ' Oh, nothing, I forget.' And then relapsed into silence again.

Winterbourne found he was slightly intimidated by the presence of these two well-dressed ladies. What on earth were they doing at two o'clock in the morning, talking to a Tommy ? He tried to hide his dirty hands.

Damn the train ! Won't it ever go ? He felt uncomfortably hot in his greatcoat and began to unbutton it. The engine whistled.

' All aboard ! ' shouted the R.T.O.

Winterbourne hastily kissed Fanny and then Elizabeth.

' Good-bye, good-bye ; don't forget to write. We'll send you parcels.'

' Thanks, ever so. Good-bye.'

He made for the compartment where a door had been left open for him, but found it full. The luggage-van, piled with the men's rations, was next door. Winterbourne jumped in.

' You'll have to stand ! ' exclaimed Fanny.

' Why, no. There's plenty of room on the floor.'

The train moved.

' Good-bye.'

Winterbourne waved his hand. He felt no particular emotion, merely an intensifying of the general depressingness of things. He watched them receding, as they waved their hands.   Beautiful girls, both of them, and so smartly dressed.

' Be happy ! ' he shouted as a valediction, in a sudden gust of disinterested affection for them.   And then lost sight of them.

Fanny and Elizabeth were both crying.

' What did he shout ? ' asked Elizabeth through her sobs.

' " Be happy ! " '

' How curious of him ! And how like him ! Oh, I know I shall never see him again ! '

Fanny tried to comfort her.   But Elizabeth somehow felt it was all Fanny's fault.

Winterbourne sat on his pack in the joggling van for about ten minutes.   It was almost dark.   The guard was trying to read a newspaper by the light of a dim oil-lamp. The soldiers who had to see that the rations weren't stolen were already lying on the floor.   Winterbourne buttoned up his coat, turned up the collar, arranged a woollen scarf on his pack to make a pillow, and lay down on the dirty floor beside them.   In five minutes he was asleep.

IT was not nearly dawn when they reached Folkestone. The drafts from various units were now amalgamated, but still remained under their own officers. They were marched through the dull little town and bivouacked in a row of large empty houses, probably evacuated boarding-houses, fitted up with the usual inconveniences of small English hotels. They washed and had some breakfast. All rather dismal.

At seven they were marched to the quay, and then marched back. The officer had mistaken the word 'eleven' for 'seven.' So they had to wait again. It was their first introduction to the curious fact that much of the War consisted in waiting about and in undoing things which somebody had ordered in error or through mistaken zeal. The men, sitting on their packs in the empty room, were eagerly and vainly discussing their immediate future—which Base Camp would they go to, which unit would they be drafted to, what part of the line? Winterbourne went over to the uncurtained window and looked out. Drifting heavy clouds, a moderately rough, dirty-looking sea. The Esplanade was practically deserted. The shelters looked dilapidated ; most of the glass in them was smashed. The unused gas-lamps looked somehow desolate on their rusting standards. Another wounded town—dying, perhaps. Depression, monotony, boredom. He looked at his wrist-watch. Still more than two hours to wait. Now that the inevitable had occurred, he was very impatient to get into the front line. The only interest he had left was a consuming curiosity to see what the War was really like.

Curse this hanging about ! He drummed his fingers

on the window-pane.   The men in the room went on
talking, aimlessly, foolishly, talking to no purpose.
Winterbourne wondered at his own lack of emotion.
All his past life seemed a dream, all his vital interests had
become utterly indifferent, his ambitions were dissolved,
his old friends seemed incredibly remote and unimportant ; even Fanny and Elizabeth were unsubstantial,
graceful ghosts.   Depression, monotony, boredom—but
a peculiar sort, a strained, worried, exasperated sort.
For God's sake get a move on.   It 'll never end, so for
the love of Mike let 's get it over.   Let 's catch our little
packet.   We know our numbers are up, so let 's get them
quickly.

One of the men was whistling :

'*What 's the use of worry-ing?*'

What indeed ?   But can you help it ?   You, cheery
idiot, are worrying just as much as any one else.   Villiers'
torture by hope.   If you were *quite* certain that your
number was up, you 'd have at least the tranquillity of
resignation.   But you 're not quite certain.   Even in the
infantry men come back.   With a really healthy wound
you might be out of the line for six or nine months.   That
was called 'getting a blighty one,' if you were lucky
enough to get sent back to England—'Blighty.'   The
men were discussing blighties.   Which was the most
convenient blighty ?   Arm or leg ?   Most agreed that
if you lost your left hand or a foot, you were damned
lucky—you were out of the bloody War for good and you
got a pension and a wound-gratuity.   Winterbourne
stood with his back to them, looking out of the window ;
the ghosts of past summer visitors thronged the Esplanade.
Left hand or a foot.   Live a cripple.   No, not that, not
that, my God !   Come back whole, or not at all.   But

how those men love life, how blindly they cling to their
poor existences ! You wouldn't think they 'd much to
live for. No beautiful and smartly-dressed Fannies and
Elizabeths. Oh, they have their ' tarts,' they 've all got
a girl's ' photo ' in their pay-books—and what girls !
Tarts for Tommies. Cream tarts for Tommies.

He turned away abruptly from the window and sat
down to clean his buttons. Always keep yourself clean
and smart, and walk about in a soldierly way. . . .

His mood changed and his spirits rose as they marched
down to the docks. Only twelve hours had passed since
they left, and yet it seemed a tremendously long time.
Winterbourne realised that the monotony, the imbecile
restrictions, the incredible nagging of military pedants,
had been crushing him into a condition of utter stupidity.
He regretted deeply that he had been kept in England so
long. At least you were doing something real in France,
and there was movement. . . .

Troops were pouring along the quay, and mounting
the gangways on to three black-painted troopships.
Winterbourne recognised the ships as old friends—they
were pre-war Channel packet-boats transformed. Huge
notices were displayed on the quays : ' No. 1 Ship, 33rd
Div., 19th Div., 42nd Div., 118th Brigade.' An officer
with a megaphone shouted : ' Leave Men to the Right,
Drafts to the Left.' Another megaphone shouted :
' First Army Men, Number 1 Ship.' ' Third and Fourth
Armies, Number 3 Ship.' ' Captain Swanson, 11th Seaforth Highlanders, report to R.T.O.'s office immediately.'
It was rather stirring—animated and efficient as well as
bustling.

The draft went on board, and were shepherded to one
end of the upper deck. The whole ship was swarming

with leave men returning to France. Winterbourne
gazed at them fascinatedly—these were the real war
soldiers, fragments of the first half-million volunteers, the
men who had believed in the War and wanted to fight.
They made a kind of epitome of the whole army. Every
arm of the service was represented—Field Artillery,
Heavies, dismounted Cavalry, Gunners, Sappers, R.E.
Sigs., Army Service Corps, Army Medical Corps, and
infantry everywhere. He recognised some of the infantry badges, the bursting grenade of the Northumber-
land Fusiliers, the tiger of the Leicesters, the Middlesex,
the Bedfords, Seaforth Highlanders, Notts. and Jocks, the
Buffs. He was immediately struck by their motley and
picturesque appearance. He and the other draft troops
were all spick-and-span—buttons bright, puttees minutely
adjusted, boots polished, peaked cap stiffened with wire,
pack mathematically squared, overcoat buttoned up to
the throat. The leave men were dressed anyhow.
Some had leather equipment, some webbing. They put
their equipment together as it suited them, and none of it
had been shined or polished for months. Some wore
overcoats, some shaggy goatskin or rough sheepskin
jackets. The skirts of some overcoats had been roughly
hacked off with jack-knives—not to trail in the deep mud,
Winterbourne guessed. The equipment which still
weighed so heavily on the shoulders of the draft seemed
to give the real soldiers no concern at all—they either
wore it unconcernedly or chucked it carelessly on the
deck with their rifles. Winterbourne was charmed. He
noticed with amused scandal that the bolts and muzzles
of their rifles were generally tightly bound with oiled
rags. Winterbourne looked more carefully at their faces.
They were lean and still curiously drawn although the
men had been out of the line for a fortnight ; the eyes

had a peculiar look. They seemed strangely worn and mature, but filled with energy, a kind of slow, enduring energy. In comparison the fresh faces of the new drafts seemed babyish—rounded and rather feminine.

For the first time since the declaration of War, Winterbourne felt almost happy. These men were men. There was something intensely masculine about them, something very pure and immensely friendly and stimulating. They had been where no woman and no half-man had ever been, could endure to be. There was something timeless and remote about them, as if (so Winterbourne thought) they had been Roman legionaries or the men of Austerlitz or even the invaders of the Empire. They looked barbaric, but not brutal ; determined, but not cruel. Under their grotesque wrappings their bodies looked lean and hard and tireless. They were Men. With a start Winterbourne realised that in two or three months, if he were not hit, he would be one of them, indistinguishable from them, whereas now, in the ridiculous jackanapes get-up of the peace-time soldier, he felt humiliated and ashamed beside them.

' By God ! ' he said to himself, ' you 're men, not boudoir rabbits and lounge lizards. I don't care a damn what your cause is—it 's almost certainly a foully rotten one. But I do know you 're the first real men I 've looked upon. I swear you 're better than the women and the half-men, and by God ! I swear I 'll die with you rather than live in a world without you.'

Winterbourne moved a short distance away from the draft and watched a small group of leave men. One, a Scotsman in the uniform of an English line regiment, was still wearing his full equipment. He was leaning on his rifle, talking to two other infantrymen, who were sitting

on their packs.   One of them, a Corporal with scandal-
ously untrimmed hair and a dirty sheepskin jacket, was
lighting a pipe.

' An' wha' y' think ? ' said the Scot in his sharp-clipped
speech : ' when ah got hame, they wan'ed me ta gae and
tak' tea wi' th' Meenister and than gie a speech at a
Bazaar for Warr Worrkers.'

' Ah ! ' said the Corporal, ' did you tell 'em—puff—all
about the wicked Huns—puff—and say that what we
want in the line is more tiled bathrooms and girls and
not so many woollen mufflers and whizz-bangs ? '

' Ah did not ; ah said, " Gie me over that bottle o'
whisky, wumman, and haud y' whist." '

' What Division are you, Jock ? ' said the other man.

' Thirrty-thirrd. We 've bin spendin' a pleasant
summer on th' Somme, and we 're now winterrin' at the
Health-resorrts o' Ypres.'

' We 're forty-first Division.   Just on your left in the
Salient.   We came up there a month ago from Bullycourt.'

' Bullycourt 's a verry guid place to get away from. . . .'

Winterbourne could not listen any further—a zealous
N.C.O. herded him back to the draft. He went unwillingly. He had been waiting eagerly for the men to
get away from their time-honoured jests and speak of their
real experiences. He was disappointed that these men
talked in such a trivial and uninteresting way. He felt
they ought to be saying important things in Shakespearean
blank verse.   Something adequate to their experience, to
the intensity of manhood he instinctively felt in them and
admired so humbly. But, of course, that was ridiculous
of him. He felt that at once. Part of their impressive-
ness was this very triviality, their complete unconscious-
ness that there was anything extraordinary or striking
about them. They would have been offended at the

suggestion. They were ignorant of their own qualities.
As Winterbourne himself rapidly merged with these men
and became one of them, he lost entirely this first sharp
impression of meeting a new, curious race of men, the
masculine men. It was then the other people who became
curious to him. He found that the real soldiers, the front-
line troops, had no more delusions about the War than he
had. They hadn't his feeling of protest and agony over
it all, they hadn't tried to think it out. They went on
with the business, hating it, because they had been told
it had to be done and believed what they had been told.
They wanted the War to end, they wanted to get away
from it, and they had no feeling of hatred for their enemies
on the other side of No Man's Land. In fact, they were
almost sympathetic to them. They also were soldiers,
men segregated from the world in this immense barbaric
tumult. The fighting was so impersonal as a rule that it
seemed rather a conflict with dreadful hostile forces of
Nature than with other men. You did not see the men
who fired the ceaseless hail of shells on you, nor the
machine-gunners who swept away twenty men to death
in one zip of their murderous bullets, nor the hands which
projected trench-mortars that shook the earth with awful
detonations, nor even the invisible sniper who picked you
off mysteriously with the sudden impersonal ' ping ! ' of
his bullet. Even in the perpetual trench raids you only
caught a glimpse of a few differently-shaped steel helmets
a couple of traverses away ; and either their bombs got
you, or yours got them. Actual hand-to-hand fighting
occurred, but it was comparatively rare. It was a war of
missiles, murderous and soul-shaking explosives, not a
war of hand-weapons. The sentry gazed at dawn over a
desolate flat landscape, seamed with irregular trenches and
infinitely pitted and scarred with shell-holes, thorny with

wire, littered with debris.   Five to ten thousand enemies
were within range of his vision, and not one would be
visible.   For days on end he might strain his eyes, and not
see one of them.   He would hear them at night—clink
of shovels and picks, the scream of a wounded man, even
their coughing if there happened to be a cessation of
artillery and machine-gun fire.   But not see them.   In
the two hours following dawn in ' quiet ' sectors there was
sometimes a kind of truce after the feverish work and
perpetual firing during the night.   After morning stand-
down the front-line troops snatched a little sleep.   At
such a time the silence was eerie.   Twenty thousand men
within a mile, and not a sound.   Or so it seemed.   But
that was by contrast.   In fact, there was always some
shelling going on—heavies firing on back areas—and
generally in the distance the long rumble which meant a
general engagement. . . .

The soldiers, then, were not vindictive.   Nor, in
general, were they long duped by the War talk.   They
laughed at the newspapers.   Any new-comer who tried
to be a bit high-falutin was at once snubbed with ' Fer
Christ's sake don't talk patriotic ! '   They went on with
a sort of stubborn despair—why, they didn't quite know.
The authorities obviously mistrusted them, and forbade
them to read the pacific *Nation* while allowing them to
read the infamies of ' **** ****.'   The mistrust was
unnecessary.   They went on in their stubborn despair,
with their sentimental songs and cynical talk and perpetual
grousing ; and it 's my belief that if they 'd been asked
to do so, they 'd still be carrying on now.   They weren't
crushed by defeat or elated by victory—their stubborn
despair had taken them far beyond that point.   They
carried on.   People sneer at the War slang.   I, myself,
have heard intellectual ' objectors ' very witty at the

expense of ' carry on.' So like carrion, you know. All right, let them sneer.

The troopships crossing the Channel were escorted by four plunging little black torpedo-boats. Submarines in the Channel. A merchant-ship had been sunk that morning. Winterbourne had thought he would be apprehensive—on the contrary, he found that he scarcely thought about it. Nobody bothered about a little risk like that. They made for Boulogne, and the soldiers cheered the torpedo-boats as they turned back from the harbour entrance.

In his inexperience Winterbourne had assumed that they would at once entrain for the front, and that he would spend that night in the trenches. He had forgotten the element of waiting, the deliberation necessary in moving vast masses of men about, which made the slow, ruthless movement of the huge war-machine so inexorable. You hung about, but inevitably you moved, your tiny little cog was brought into action. And this, too, was strangely impersonal, confirmed the feeling of fatalism. It seemed insane to think that you had any individual importance.

The docks at Boulogne were crowded with materials of war, and the whole place seemed English. Notices all in English, the Union Jack, British officers and troops everywhere, even British engines for the trains. The leave men were roughly formed into columns and marched off to entrain. Every one wanted to know where his Division was. The R.T.O.'s dealt with them swiftly and efficiently. The drafts were also formed into a column and marched up the hill to the rest camp. They were in good spirits, and the inevitable Cockney humorist was in action. As they went up the hill, a poor old Frenchwoman came out of her cottage and began rheumatically and wearily to

pump water.   She did not even look at the passing troops
—much too accustomed to them.   The Cockney shouted
to her :

' 'Ere we are !   War 'll soon be over now ;   keep yer
pecker up, Ma ! '

They spent the night under canvas at the Boulogne rest
camp.   From his tent Winterbourne had an excellent
view of the Channel and the camp incinerator.   His first
duty on active service was picking up dirty paper and
other rubbish, and dumping it in the incinerator.   They
were told nothing about their future ;   the Army theory
being that your business is to obey orders, not to ask
questions.   Winterbourne fumed and fretted at the
inaction.   The other men speculated interminably as to
where they were going.

The tents had wooden floors.   The men drew a blanket
and waterproof ground-sheet each, and slept twelve to a
tent.   It was a bit hard, but not impossible to sleep.
Winterbourne lay awake for a long time, trying to get
some order into his reflections.   His attitude was plainly
modified by that day's experience.   Was there a contra-
diction in it ?   Did it imply that he now supported the
War and the War partisans ?   On the contrary.   He
hated the War as much as ever, hated all the blather about
it, profoundly distrusted the motives of the War partisans,
and hated the Army.   But he liked the soldiers, the War
soldiers, not as soldiers but as men.   He respected them.
If the German soldiers were like the men he had seen on
the boat that morning, then he liked and respected them
too.   He was with them.   With them, yes, but against
whom and what ?   He reflected.   With them, because
they were men with fine qualities, because they had
endured great hardships and dangers with simplicity,

because they had parried those hardships and dangers not by hating the men who were supposed to be their enemies, but by developing a comradeship among themselves. They had every excuse for turning into brutes, and they hadn't done it. True, they were degenerating in certain ways, they were getting coarse and rough and a bit animal, but with amazing simplicity and unpretentiousness they had retained and developed a certain essential humanity and manhood. With them, then, to the end, because of their manhood and humanity. With them, too, because that manhood and humanity existed in spite of the War and not because of it. They had saved something from a gigantic wreck, and what they had saved was immensely important—manhood and comradeship, their essential integrity as men, their essential brotherhood as men.

But what were they really against ? who were their real enemies ? He saw the answer with a flood of bitterness and clarity. Their enemies—the enemies of German and English alike—were the fools who had sent them to kill each other instead of help each other. Their enemies were the sneaks and the unscrupulous ; the false ideals, the unintelligent ideas imposed on them, the humbug, the hypocrisy, the stupidity. If those men were typical, then there was nothing essentially wrong with common humanity, at least so far as the men were concerned. It was the leadership that was wrong—not the war leadership, but the peace leadership. The nations were governed by bunk and sacrificed to false ideals and stupid ideas. It was assumed that they *had* to be governed by bunk—but if they were never given anything else, how could you tell ? De-bunk the World. Hopeless, hopeless. . . .

He sighed deeply, and turned in his blanket wrapping. One man was snoring. Another moaned in his sleep.

Like corpses they lay there, human rejects chucked into
a bell-tent on the hill above Boulogne.   The pack made a
hard pillow.   Maybe he was all wrong, maybe it was
' right ' for men to be begotten only to murder each other
in huge, senseless combats.   He wondered if he were not
getting a little insane through this persistent brooding
over the murders, by striving so desperately and earnestly
to find out why it had happened, by agonising over it all,
by trying to think how it could be prevented from occur-
ring again.   After all, did it matter so much ?   Yes, did
it matter ?   What were a few million human animals
more or less ?   Why agonise about it ?   The most he
could do was die.   Well, die, then.   But O God ! O God !
is that all ?   To be born against your will, to feel that life
might in its brief passing be so lovely and so divine, and
yet to have nothing but opposition and betrayal and
hatred and death forced upon you !   To be born for the
slaughter like a calf or a pig !   To be violently cast back
into nothing—for what ?   My God ! for what ?   Is there
nothing but despair and death ?   Is life vain, beauty vain,
love vain, hope vain, happiness vain ?   ' The war to end
wars ! '   Is any one so asinine as to believe that ?   A war
to breed wars, rather. . . .

He sighed and turned again.   It 's all useless, useless,
to flog one's brain and nerves over it all, useless to waste
the night hours in silent agonies when he might lie in the
oblivion of sleep.   Or the better oblivion of death.   After
all, there were plenty of children, plenty of war babies—
why should one agonise for their future, any more than
the Victorians thought about ours ?   The children will
grow up, the war babies will grow up.   Maybe they 'll
have their war, maybe they won't.   In any case they
won't care a hang about us.   Why should they ?   What
do we care about the men of Albuera, except that the

charge of the Fusiliers decorates a page of rhetorical prose? Four thousand dead—and the only permanent result a page of Napier's prose. We have Bairnsfather. . . .

He gave it up. Time after time he reverted to the whole gigantic tragedy, and time after time he gave it up. Two solutions. Just drift and let come what may ; or get yourself killed in the line. And much any one would care whichever he did.

THEY paraded at nine next morning, were casually inspected by an officer they did not know, and told to stand by. At eleven they drew bully beef and biscuits, and were ordered to parade again in half an hour, ready to move off. Winterbourne's spirits rose. At last they were getting somewhere. He would be in the trenches that night, and take his chance with the rest. No more fiddle-faddle.

He was mistaken. They entrained at Boulogne in a train which crawled interminably, and they detrained at Calais. They were simply transferred to another base.

The Base Camp at Calais was desperately overcrowded. It was filled with new drafts sent over to make up the losses on the Somme, and new columns of men kept pouring in daily from England, faster than the overworked Staff could allot them to units. They were crowded into hastily-erected bell-tents, twenty-two to a tent, which is closer than you can squeeze animals, and about as close as you can squeeze men. There was just room to lie down, and no more. Nothing to do after parade, except to moon about in the frosty darkness or lie down in one's little slice of space, or play crown-and-anchor and drink coffee-and-rum while the estaminets were open. The town of Calais was out of bounds, except to men with passes. And not many passes were granted.

The weather grew daily colder. The misery of the interminable waiting and the overcrowded tents and the lack of anything to do, was not thereby alleviated. Every morning huge greyish columns of men undulated over the sandy soil, and were drawn up in long lines. An officer on horseback shouted orders through a megaphone. Nothing much happened, and they raggedly undulated back again. Yet they drew nearer to the mysterious 'line.' They were given large jack-knives on lanyards. They were given gas-masks and steel helmets. They were given service rifles and bayonets.

The gas-masks were still the old flannel diving-bell variety soaked in chemicals. They had a sharp, acrid, inhuman taste, and if worn too long had been known to produce skin eruptions. The drafts were given constant gas-drill, and had to pass five minutes in a gas-chamber containing a concentration of the old chlorine gas sufficient to kill in five seconds. One man in Winterbourne's lot lost his head and tried to tear off his mask. The instructor leapt at him, shouting curses through his own mask, and with the help of two of the men held him until the doors were opened. Winterbourne noticed that the gas had tarnished his bright brass buttons and the metal on his equipment. Their clothes reeked of the gas for a couple of hours.

They carefully cleaned the long steel bayonets, and examined the short wood-enclosed rifles. Winterbourne's had a long groove cut by a bullet on the butt, and the bolt showed signs of considerable rust—obviously a rifle picked up on the battlefield and re-conditioned. Winterbourne wondered who was the man from whom he inherited it, and who would inherit it from him.

The days and nights grew colder and colder. Morning and evening rose and sank in blood-red mists, and at noon the sun was a cold, bloody smear in a misty sky. Ice formed on the dykes and the water-taps froze. It became more and more difficult to wash, and shaving and washing in the ice-cold water became an agony. Their skins chapped as the light north wind breathed sharper and sharper cold.   There appeared to be no baths, and they could not remove their clothes at night.   To sleep, they took off their boots, wrapped themselves in an overcoat and blanket, and shivered asleep, huddling together like sheep in a snowstorm.   Most of them caught colds and began to cough ; one man of the draft was taken to hospital with pleurisy.

And still day after day passed and they were not sent to their units.   Monotony, depression, boredom.   By four it was dark, and there was nothing to do until dawn.   The canteens and estaminets were thronged.   Winterbourne luckily discovered that the pickets could be bribed, and several evenings went into Calais to dine.   He bought a couple of French books and tried to read—in vain.   He found he was unable to concentrate his mind, and fell into a deeper depression.   There were few parades, and he had plenty of time for brooding.

They passed Christmas Day at the Base.   The English newspapers, which they easily obtained a day or two late, were filled with glowing accounts of the efforts and expense made to give the troops a real hearty Christmas dinner. The men had looked forward to this.   They ate their meals in huts which were decorated with holly for the occasion.   The Christmas dinner turned out to be stewed bully beef and about two square inches of cold Christmas pudding per man.   The other men in Winterbourne's tent were furious.   Their perpetual grumbling annoyed him, and he attacked them :

' Why fuss so much over a little charity ?   Why let them salve their consciences so easily ?   In any case, they probably meant well.   Can't you see that drafts at the Base are nobody's children ?   The stuff 's gone to the men in the line, who deserve it far more than we do.   We haven't done anything yet.   Or it 's been embezzled.

Anyway, what does it matter? You didn't join the Army for a bit of pudding and a Christmas cracker, did you?'

They were silent, unable to understand his contempt. Of course, he was unjust. They were simply grown children, angry at being defrauded of a promised treat. They could not understand his deeper rage. Any more than they could have understood his emotion each night when ' Last Post ' was blown. The bugler was an artist and produced the most wonderful effect of melancholy as he blew the call—which in the Army serves for sleep and death—over the immense silent camp. Forty thousand men lying down to sleep—and in six months how many would be alive? The bugler seemed to know it, and prolonged the shrill, melancholy notes—' last post ! last post ! '—with an extraordinary effect of pathos. ' Last post ! Last post ! ' Winterbourne listened for it each night. Sometimes the melancholy was almost soothing, sometimes it was intolerable. He wrote to Elizabeth and Fanny about the bugler, as well as about the leave men he had seen on the boat. They felt he was getting hopelessly sentimental.

' Un peu gaga ? ' Elizabeth suggested.

Fanny shrugged her shoulders.

Two days after Christmas their orders came. They were taking off their equipment after morning parade when the Orderly Corporal pushed his head through the tent flap :

' You 've clicked ! '

' What? How? What y' mean?' said several voices.

' Goin' up the line. Parade at one-thirty ready to move off immediate. Over you go, an' the best of luck ! '

' What part of the line ? '

'Dunno; you 'll find that when y' get there.'

'What unit?'

'Dunno. Some o' you 's clicked for a Pioneer Batt.'

'What 's that?'

'Muckin well find out. Don't f'get I warned yer for p'rade.'

And he was off to the next tent. The men began talking excitedly, 'wondering' this and 'wondering' that, futilely as usual. Winterbourne walked away from the tent lines, and stood looking over the desolate winter landscape. Half a mile away the tent lines of another huge camp began. Army lorries lumbered along a flat, straight road in the distance. It was beginning to snow from a hard, grey sky. He wondered vaguely how you slept in the line when there was snow. His breath formed little clouds of vapour in the freezing air. He pulled his muffler closer round his neck, and stamped on the ground to warm his icy feet. He felt as if his faculties were slowly running down, as if his whole mental power were concentrated upon mere physical endurance, a dull keeping alive. Time, like a torture, seemed infinitely prolonged. It seemed years since he left England, years of discomfort and depression and boredom. If the mere 'cushy' beginning were like that, how endure the months, perhaps years, of war to come?

He experienced a rapid fall of spirits to a depth of depression he had never before experienced. Hitherto, mere young vitality had buoyed him up, the *élan* of his former life had carried him along through the days. In spite of his rages and his worryings and the complications and boredoms, he had really remained hopeful. He had wanted to go on living, because he had always unconsciously believed that life was good. Now something within him was just beginning to give way, now for the first time the last faint hues of the lovely iris of youth faded, and in horror he faced the grey realities. He was surprised and a little alarmed at his own listlessness and despair. He felt like a sheet of paper dropping in jerks and waverings through grey air into an abyss.

The dinner bugle-call sounded. He turned mechanically and joined the men thronging towards the eating-huts. The snow was falling faster, and the men stamped their feet as they waited for the doors to open, cursing the cook's delay. There was the usual animal stampede for the best platefuls when the door opened. Winterbourne stood aside and let them struggle. The expressions on their faces were not pretty. He was practically the last in, and did not fare well. He ate the stewed bully, hunk of bread, and soap-like cheese with a sort of dog gratitude for the warmth, which was humiliating. He scarcely even resented the humiliation.

The train taking them to rail-head crawled interminably through a frozen landscape thinly sprinkled with snow. The light was beginning to wane. The skeleton outlines of dwarf trees, twisted by the wind, loomed faintly past the window. It was bitterly cold in the unwarmed third-class French carriage ; one of the windows was smashed, and the bitter air and snow swept in. The men sat in silence, wrapped in their greatcoats and stamping their feet rhythmically on the floor in vain efforts to keep warm. Winterbourne was cold to the knees, and yet felt feverish. His cough had grown worse, and he realised he had a temperature. He felt dirtily uncomfortable, because he had not taken his clothes off for days. The water at the camp had all frozen, and it had been impossible to get a bath.

Darkness slowly intensified.   Slowly, more slowly, the train crawled along.   Winterbourne was in that section of the draft going to the Pioneer Battalion.   He had asked the Sergeant what that meant :

' Oh, it 's cushy, much better than the ordinary infantry.'

' Why, what do they do ? '

' Workin' parties in No Man's Land,' said the Sergeant with a grin, ' an' go over the top when there 's a show.'

The train slightly increased its speed as they passed through a large junction.   Somebody said it was St. Omer, somebody else said St. Pol, some one else suggested Bethune.   They did not know where they were, or where they were going.   About two miles outside the junction the train came to a stop.   Winterbourne peered into the thick darkness.   Nothing.   He leaned out the glassless window and heard only the hissing steam from the stationary train, saw only the faint glow of the furnace. Suddenly, far away in front and to the left, a quick flash of light pierced the blackness and Winterbourne heard a faint boom.   The guns !   He waited, straining eyes and ears, in the freezing darkness.   Silence.   Then again— flash.   Boom.   Flash.   Boom.   Very distant, very faint, but unmistakable.   The guns.   They must be getting near the line.

Once again the train started and crawled interminably once more.   For about half an hour they passed through a series of deep cuttings.   Then, from the right this time, came a much nearer and brighter flash, followed almost at once by a deep boom audible above the noise of the train.   The other men heard it this time :

' The guns ! '

The train crept on stealthily for another couple of

minutes through the gloom. The men were all crowded round the window. Flash. Boom. Another two minutes. Flash. Boom.

Three-quarters of an hour later, they detrained at rail-head in complete darkness.

WINTERBOURNE had an easy initiation into trench warfare. The cold was so intense that the troops on both sides were chiefly occupied in having pneumonia and trying to keep warm. He found himself in a quiet sector which had been fought over by the French in 1914 and had been the scene of a fierce and prolonged battle in 1915 after the British took over the sector. During 1916, when the main fighting shifted to the Somme, the sector had settled down to ordinary trench warfare. Trench raids had not then been much developed, but constant local attacks were made on battalion or brigade fronts. A little later the sector atoned for this calm.

To Winterbourne, as to so many others, the time element was of extreme importance during the war years. The hour-goddesses who had danced along so gaily before, and have fled from us since with such mocking swiftness, then paced by in a slow, monotonous file as if intolerably burdened. People at a distance thought of the fighting as heroic and exciting, in terms of cheering bayonet charges or little knots of determined men holding out to the last Lewis gun. That is rather like counting life by its champagne suppers and forgetting all the rest. The qualities needed were determination and endurance, inhuman endurance. It would be much more practical to fight modern wars with mechanical robots than with men. But then, men are cheaper, although in a long war the initial outlay on the robots might be compensated by the fact that the quality of the men deteriorates, while they cost more in upkeep. But that is a question for the War Departments. From the point of view of efficiency in war, the trouble is that men have feelings ; to attain the perfect soldier, we must eliminate feelings. To the human robots of the last war, time seemed indefinitely and most unpleasantly prolonged. The dimension then measured as a ' day ' in its apparent duration approached what we now call a ' month.' And the long series of violent stalemates on the Western front made any decision seem impossible. In 1916 it looked as if no line could be broken, because so long as enough new troops were hurried to threatened points the attacker was bound to be held up ; and the supplies of new troops seemed endless. It became a matter of which side could wear down the other's man-power and moral endurance. So there also was the interminable. The only alternatives seemed an indefinite prolongation of misery, or death or mutilation, or collapse of some sort. Even a wound was a doubtful blessing, a mere holiday, for wounded men had to be returned again and again to the line.

For the first six or eight ' weeks,' Winterbourne, like all his companions, was occupied in fighting the cold. The Pioneer Company to which he was attached were digging a sap out into No Man's Land and making trench-mortar emplacements just behind the front line. They worked on these most of the night, and slept during the day. But the ground was frozen so hard that progress was tediously slow.

The Company were billeted in the ruins of a village behind the reserve trenches, over a mile from the front line. The landscape was flat, almost treeless except for a few shell-blasted stumps, and covered with snow frozen hard. Every building in sight had been smashed, in many cases almost level with the ground. It was a mining country with great queer hills of slag and strange pit-head machinery in steel, reduced by shell-fire to huge masses

of twisted rusting metal.   They were in a salient, with the
half-destroyed, evacuated town of M——— in the elbow-
crook on the extreme right.   The village churchyard was
filled with graves of French soldiers ; there were graves
inside any of the houses which had no cellars, and graves
flourished over the bare landscape.   In all directions
were crosses, little wooden crosses, in ones and twos and
threes, emerging blackly from the frozen snow.   Some
were already askew ; one just outside the ruined village
had been snapped short by a shell-burst.   The dead men's
caps, mouldering and falling to pieces, were hooked on to
the tops of the crosses—the grey German round cap, the
French blue-and-red kepi, the English khaki.   There
were also two large British cemeteries in sight—rect-
angular plantations of wooden crosses.   It was like living
in the graveyard of the world—dead trees, dead houses,
dead mines, dead villages, dead men.   Only the long
steel guns and the transport waggons seemed alive.
There were no civilians, but one of the mines was still
worked about a mile and a half further from the line.

Behind Winterbourne's billet were hidden two large
howitzers.   They fired with a reverberating crash which
shook the ruined houses, and the diminishing scream of
the departing shells was strangely melancholy in the frost-
silent air.   The Germans rarely returned the fire—they
were saving their ammunition.   Occasionally a shell
screamed over and crashed sharply among the ruins ; the
huge detonation spouted up black earth or rattling bricks
and tiles.   Fragments of the burst shell-case hummed
through the air.

But it was the cold that mattered.   In his efforts to
defend himself against it, Winterbourne, like the other
men, was strangely and wonderfully garbed.   Round his
belly, next the skin, he wore a flannel belt.   Over that a

thick woollen vest, grey flannel shirt, knitted cardigan jacket, long woollen under-pants and thick socks. Over that, service jacket, trousers, puttees, and boots; then a sheepskin coat, two mufflers round his neck, two pairs of woollen gloves and over them trench gloves. In addition came equipment—box respirator on the chest, steel helmet, rifle and bayonet. The only clothes he took off at night were his boots. With his legs wrapped in a greatcoat, his body in a grey blanket, a ground-sheet underneath, pack for pillow, and a dixie of hot tea-and-rum inside him, he just got warm enough to fall asleep when very tired.

Through the broken roof of his billet Winterbourne could see the frosty glitter of the stars and the white rime. In the morning, when he awoke, he found his breath frozen on the blanket. In the line his short moustache formed icicles. The boots beside him froze hard, and it was agony to struggle into them. The bread in his haversack froze greyly; and the taste of frozen bread is horrid. Little spikes of ice formed in the cheese. The tins of jam froze and had to be thawed before they could be eaten. The bully beef froze in the tins and came out like chunks of reddish ice. Washing was a torment. They had three tubs of water between about forty of them each day. With this they shaved and washed— about ten or fifteen to a tub. Since Winterbourne was a latecomer to the battalion, he had to wait until the others had finished. The water was cold and utterly filthy. He plunged his dirty hands into it with disgust, and shut his eyes when he washed his face. This humiliation, too, he accepted.

He always remembered his first night in the line. They paraded in the ruined village street about four o'clock.

The air seemed crackling with frost, and the now familiar bloody smear of red sunset was dying away in the southwest. The men were muffled up to the ears, and looked grotesquely bulky in their sheep- or goat-skin coats, with the hump of box respirators on their chests. Most of them had sacking covers on their steel helmets to prevent reflection, and sacks tied round their legs for warmth. The muffled officer came shivering from his billet, as the men stamped their feet on the hard, frost-bound road. They drew picks and shovels from a dump, and filed silently through the ruined street behind the officer. Their bayonets were silhouetted against the cold sky. The man in front of Winterbourne turned abruptly left into a ruined house. Winterbourne followed, descended four rough steps, and found himself in a trench. A notice said :

HINTON ALLEY

To the Front Line.

To be out of the piercing cold wind in the shelter of walls of earth was an immediate relief. Overhead shone the beautiful ironic stars.

A field-gun behind them started to crash out shells. Winterbourne listened to the long-drawn wail as they sped away and finally crashed faintly in the distance. He followed the man ahead of him blindly. Word kept coming down : ' Hole here, look out.' ' Wire overhead.' ' Mind your head—bridge.' He passed the messages on, after tripping in the holes, catching his bayonet in the field telephone wires, and knocking his helmet on the low bridge. They passed the Reserve line, then the Support, with the motionless sentries on the fire-step, and the peculiar smell of burnt wood and foul air coming from the dug-outs. A minute later came the sharp message :

'Stop talking—don't clink your shovels.' They were now only a few hundred yards from the German front line. A few guns were firing in a desultory way. A shell crashed outside the parapet about five yards from Winterbourne's head. It was only a whizz-bang, but to his unpractised ears it sounded like a heavy. The shells came in fours—crump, Crump, CRUMP, CRRUMP—the Boche was bracketing. Every minute or so came a sharp 'ping!'—fixed rifles firing at a latrine or an unprotected piece of trench. The duck-boards were more broken. Winterbourne stumbled over an unexploded shell, then had to clamber over a heap of earth where the side of the trench had been smashed in, a few minutes earlier. The trench made another sharp turn, and he saw the bayonet and helmet of a sentry silhouetted against the sky. They were in the front line.

They turned sharp left. To their right were the fire-steps, with a sentry about every fifty yards. In between came traverses and dug-out entrances, with their rolled-up blanket gas-curtains. Winterbourne peered down them —there was a faint glow of light, a distant mutter of talk, and a heavy stench of wood smoke and foul air. The man in front stopped and turned to Winterbourne :

'Halt — password to-night's "Lantern."'' Winterbourne halted, and passed the message on. They waited. He was standing almost immediately behind a sentry, and got on the fire-step beside the man to take his first look at No Man's Land.

''Oo are you ? ' asked the sentry in low tones.

'Pioneers.'

'Got a bit o' candle to give us, chum ? '

'Awfully sorry, chum, I haven't.'

'Them muckin' R.E.'s gets 'em all.'

'I 've got a packet of chocolate, if you 'd like it.'

' Ah !   Thanks, chum.'

The sentry broke a bit of chocolate and began to munch.

' Muckin' cold up here, it is.   Me feet 's fair froze. Muckin' dreary, too.   I can 'ear ole Fritz coughin' over there in 'is listenin' post—don't 'arf sound 'ollow. Listen.'

Winterbourne listened, and heard a dull, hollow sound of coughing.

' Fritz's sentry,' whispered the man.   ' Pore ole ******
—needs some liquorice.'

' Move on,' came the word from the man in front. Winterbourne jumped down from the fire-step and passed on the word.

' Good-night, chum,' said the sentry.

' Good-night, chum.'

Winterbourne was put on the party digging the sap out into No Man's Land.   The officer stopped him as he was entering the sap.

' You 're one of the new draft, aren't you ? '

' Yes, sir.'

' Wait a minute.'

' Very good, sir.'

The other men filed into the sap.   The officer spoke in low tones :

' You can take sentry for the first hour.   Come along, and don't stand up.'

The young crescent moon had risen and poured down cold, faint light.   Every now and then a Verey light was fired from the German or English lines, brilliantly illumin- ating the desolate landscape of torn, irregular wire and jagged shell-holes.   They climbed over the parapet and crawled over the broken ground past the end of the sap.

x

The officer made for a shell-hole just inside the English wire, and Winterbourne followed him.

'Lie here,' whispered the officer, 'and keep a sharp look-out for German patrols. Fire if you see them and give the alarm. There's a patrol of our own out on the right, so make sure before you fire. There's a couple of bombs somewhere in the shell-hole. You'll be relieved in an hour.'

'Very good, sir.'

The officer crawled away, and Winterbourne remained alone in No Man's Land, about twenty-five yards in front of the British line. He could hear the soft, dull thuds of picks and shovels from the men working the sap, and a very faint murmur as they talked in whispers. A Verey light hissed up from the English lines, and he strained his eyes for the possible enemy patrol. In the brief light he saw nothing but the irregular masses of German wire, the broken line of their parapet, shell-holes and debris, and the large stump of a dead tree. Just as the bright magnesium turned in its luminous parabola, a hidden machine-gun, not thirty yards from Winterbourne, went off with a loud crackle of bullets like the engine of a motor-bicycle. He started, and nearly pulled the trigger of his rifle. Then silence. A British sentry coughed with a deep hacking sound ; then from the distance came the hollow coughing of a German sentry. Eerie sounds in the pallid moonlight. 'Ping!' went a sniper's rifle. It was horribly cold. Winterbourne was shivering, partly from cold, partly from excitement.

Interminable minutes passed. He grew colder and colder. Occasionally a few shells from one side or the other went wailing overhead and crashed somewhere in the back areas. About four hundred yards away to his left began a series of loud, shattering detonations. He strained his eyes, and could just see the flash of the explosion and the dark column of smoke and debris. These were German trench-mortars, the dreaded ' minnies,' although he did not know it.

Nothing different happened until about three-quarters of an hour had passed. Winterbourne got colder and colder, felt he had been out there at least three hours, and thought he must have been forgotten. He shivered with cold. Suddenly he thought he saw something move to his right, just outside the wire. He gazed intently, all tense and alert. Yes, a dark something was moving. It stopped, and seemed to vanish. Then near it another dark figure moved, and then a third. It was a patrol, making for the gap in the wire in front of Winterbourne. Were they Germans or British ? He pointed his rifle towards them, got the bombs ready, and waited. They came nearer and nearer. Just before they got to the wire, Winterbourne challenged in a loud whisper :

' Halt, who are you ? '

All three figures instantly disappeared.

' Halt, who are you ? '

' Friend,' came a low answer.

' Give the word or I fire.'

' Lantern.'

' All right.'

One of the men crawled through the wire to Winterbourne, followed by the other two. They wore balaclava helmets, and carried revolvers.

' Are you the patrol ? ' whispered Winterbourne.

' Who the muckin' hell d' you think we are ? Father Christmas ? What are you doin' out here ? '

' Pioneers digging a sap about fifteen yards behind.'

' Are you Pioneers ? '

' Yes.'

' Got a bit o' candle, chum ? '

' Sorry, I haven't ; we don't get them issued.'

The patrol crawled off, and Winterbourne heard an alarmed challenge from the men working in the sap, and the word ' Lantern.' A Verey light went up from the German lines just as the patrol were crawling over the parapet. A German sentry fired his rifle and a machine-gun started up. The patrol dropped hastily into the trench. The machine-gun bullets whistled cruelly past Winterbourne's head—zwiss, zwiss, zwiss. He crouched down in the hole. Zwiss, zwiss, zwiss. Then silence. He lifted his head, and continued to watch. For two or three minutes there was complete silence. The men in the sap seemed to have knocked off work, and made no sound. Winterbourne listened intently. No sound. It was the most ghostly, desolate, deathly silence he had ever experienced. He had never imagined that death could be so deathly. The feeling of annihilation, of the end of existence, of a dead planet of the dead arrested in a dead time and space, penetrated his flesh along with the cold. He shuddered. So frozen, so desolate, so dead a world —everything smashed and lying inertly broken. Then ' crack—ping ! ' went a sniper's rifle, and a battery of field-guns opened out with salvoes about half a mile to his right. The machine-guns began again. The noise was a relief after that ghastly dead silence.

At last the N.C.O. came crawling out from the sap with another man to relieve him. A Verey light shot up from the German line in their direction, just as the two men reached him. All three crouched motionless, as the accurate German machine-gun fire swept the British trench parapet—zwiss, zwiss, zwiss, the flights of bullets went over them. Winterbourne saw a strand of wire just in front of him suddenly flip up in the air where a low bullet had struck it.   Quite near enough—not six inches above his head.

They crawled back to the sap, and Winterbourne tumbled in. He found himself face to face with the platoon officer, Lieutenant Evans. Winterbourne was shivering uncontrollably ; he felt utterly chilled. His whole body was numb, his hands stiff, his legs one ache of cold from the knees down. He realised the cogency of the Adjutant's farewell hint about looking after feet, and decided to drop his indifference to goose grease and neat's-foot oil.

'Cold ? ' asked the officer.

'It 's bitterly cold out there, sir,' said Winterbourne through chattering teeth.

'Here, take a drink of this,' and Evans held out a small flask.

Winterbourne took the flask in his cold-shaken hand. It chinked roughly against his teeth as he took a gulp of the terrifically-potent Army rum. The strong liquor half-choked him, burned his throat, and made his eyes water. Almost immediately he felt the deadly chill beginning to lessen. But he still shivered.

'Good Lord, man, you 're frozen,' said Evans. 'I thought it was colder than ever to-night. It 's no weather for lying in No Man's Land. Corporal, you 'll have to change that sentry every half-hour—an hour 's too long in this frost.'

'Very good, sir.'

'Have some more rum ? ' asked Evans.

'No, thanks, sir,' replied Winterbourne; 'I 'm quite all right now. I can warm up with some digging.'

'No ; get your rifle and come with me.'

Evans started off briskly down the trench to visit the other working parties. About a hundred yards from the

sap he climbed out of the trench over the parados ;
Winterbourne scrambled after, more impeded by his
chilled limbs, his rifle and heavier equipment. Evans
gave him a hand up. They walked about another
hundred yards over the top, and then reached the place
where several parties were digging trench-mortar emplacements. The N.C.O. saw them coming and climbed out
of one of the holes to meet them.

' Getting on all right, Sergeant ? '

' Ground 's very hard, sir.'

' I know, but—— '

Zwiss, zwiss, zwiss, zwiss came a rush of bullets, following the rapid tat-tat-tat-tat-tat-tat-tat of a machine-gun.
The Sergeant ducked double. Evans remained calmly
standing. Seeing his unconcern, Winterbourne also
remained upright.

' I know the ground 's hard,' said Evans, ' but those
emplacements are urgently needed. Headquarters were
at us again to-day about them. I 'll see how you 're
getting on.'

The Sergeant hastily scuttled into one of the deep emplacements, followed in a more leisurely way by the
officer. Winterbourne remained standing on top, and
listened to Evans as he urged the men to get a move on.
Tat-tat-tat-tat-tat. Zwiss, zwiss, zwiss, very close this
time. Winterbourne felt a slight creep in his spine ; but
since Evans had not moved before, he decided that the
right thing was to stand still. Evans visited each of the
four emplacements, and then made straight for the front
line. He paused at the parados.

' We 're pretty close to the Boche front line here. He 's
got a machine-gun post about a hundred and fifty yards
over there.'

Tat-tat-tat-tat-tat-tat. Zwiss, zwiss, zwiss.

' Look ! Over there.'

Winterbourne just caught a glimpse of the quick flashes.

' Damn ! ' said Evans, ' I forgot to bring my prismatic compass to-night. We might have taken a bearing on them, and got the artillery to turf them out.'

He jumped carelessly into the trench, and Winterbourne dutifully followed. About fifty yards further on, he stopped.

' I see from your pay-book that you 're an artist in civil life.'

' Yes, sir.'

' Paint pictures, and draw ? '

' Yes, sir.'

' Why don't you apply for a draughtsman's job at Division ? They need them.'

' Well, sir, I don't particularly covet a hero's grave, but I feel very strongly I ought to take my chance in the line along with the rest.'   •

' Ah ! Of course. Are you a pretty good walker ? '

' I used to go on walking tours in peace time, sir.'

Well, there 's an order that every officer is to have a runner. Would you like the job of Platoon Runner ? You 'd have to accompany me, and you 're supposed to take my last dying orders ! You 'd have to learn the lie of the trenches, so as to act as guide ; take my orders to N.C.O.'s ; know enough about what 's going on to help them if I 'm knocked out ; and carry messages. It 's perhaps a bit more dangerous than the ordinary work, and you may have to turn out at odd hours, but it 'll get you off a certain amount of digging.'

' I 'd like it very much, sir.'

' All right, I 'll speak to the Major about it.'

' It 's very good of you, sir.'

' Can you find your way back to the sap ?   It 's about
two hundred yards along this trench '

' I 'm sure I can, sir.'

' All right.   Go back and report to the Corporal, and
carry on.'

' Very good, sir.'

' You haven't forgotten the password ? '

' No, sir—" Lantern." '

About thirty yards along the trench, there was a rattle
of equipment, and Winterbourne found a bayonet about
two feet from his chest.   It was a gas-sentry outside a
Company H.Q. dug-out.

' Halt !   Who are yer ? '

' Lantern.'

The sentry languidly lowered his rifle.

' Muckin' cold to-night, mate.'

' Bloody cold.'

' What are you—Bedfords or Essex ? '

' No ; Pioneers.'

' Got a bit of candle to give us, mate ? it 's muckin'
dark in them dug-outs.'

' Very sorry, chum, I haven't.'

Rather trying, this constant demand for candle-ends
from the Pioneers, who were popularly supposed by the
infantry to receive immense ' issues ' of candles.   But
without candles the dug-outs were merely black holes,
even in the daytime, if they were any depth.   They were
deep on this front, since the line was a captured German
trench reorganised.   Hence the dug-outs faced the
enemy, instead of being turned away from them.

' Oh, all right ; good-night.'

' Good-night.'

Winterbourne returned to the sap, and did two more

half-hour turns as sentry, and for the rest of the time picked, or shovelled the hard clods of earth into sandbags. The sandbags were then carried back to the front line and piled there to raise the parapet. It was a slow business. The sap itself was camouflaged to avoid observation. Winterbourne hadn't the slightest idea what its object was. He was very weary and sleepy when they finally knocked off work about one in the morning. An eight-hour shift, exclusive of time taken in getting to and from the work. The men filed wearily along the trench, rifles slung on the left shoulder, picks and shovels carried on the right. Winterbourne stumbled along half-asleep with the cold and the fatigue of unaccustomed labour. He felt he didn't mind how dangerous it was—if it was dangerous—to be a runner, provided he got some change from the dreariness of digging, and filling and carrying sandbags.

After they passed the Support line, the hitherto silent men began to talk occasionally. At Reserve they got permission to smoke. Each grabbed in his pockets for a fag, and lighted it as he stumbled along the uneven duckboards. After what seemed an endless journey to Winterbourne, they reached the four steps, climbed up, and emerged into the now familiar ruined street. It was silent and rather ghostly in the very pale light of the new moon. They dumped their picks and shovels, went to the cook to draw their ration of hot tea, which was served from a large black dixie and tasted unpleasantly of stew. They filed past the officer, who gave each of them a rum ration.

Winterbourne drank some of the tea in his billet, then took off his boots, wrapped himself up, and drank the rest. Some real warmth flushed into his chilled body. He was angry with himself for being so tired, after a cushy night on a cushy front. He wondered what

Elizabeth and Fanny would say if they saw his animal gratitude for tea and rum. Fanny ? Elizabeth ? They had receded far from him; not so far as all the other people he knew, who had receded to several light years, but very far. ' Elizabeth ' and ' Fanny ' were now memories and names at the foot of sympathetic but rather remote letters. Drowsiness came rapidly upon him, and he fell asleep as he was thinking of the curious ' zwiss, zwiss ' made by machine-gun bullets passing overhead. He did not hear the two howitzers when they fired a dozen rounds before dawn.

EXCEPT for the episode with the officer, this specimen night may stand as a type of Winterbourne's life in the next eight or ten days. They went up the line at dusk; they were shot at, worked, and shivered with cold; went down the line, slept, tried to clean themselves, and paraded again. Four or five times they passed corpses being carried down the trenches as they went up. There was, of course, nothing to report on the Western front.

Then, just as the monotony was becoming almost as intolerable as drilling to the home-service R.S.M.'s 'Stand still, there, stand *steady* !' they had a night off, and were transferred to the day-shift. But this was even more tedious. They paraded soon after dawn, and worked in Hinton Alley, about two hundred yards from the Front line. Their job was to hack up the frozen mud—which was about as malleable as marble—extricate the worn duck-boards, dig 'sump-holes,' and re-lay new duck-boards. A job which in moist weather might have occupied two men for half an hour, in that frost occupied four men all day.

A Lieutenant-General came along while Winterbourne was laboriously jarring his wrists, trying to hack up the marble-like mud.

' Well, and what are you doing, my man ? '

' Replacing duck-boards, sir,' said Winterbourne, bringing his pick smartly to his side, and standing to attention, toes at an angle of forty-five degrees.

' Well, get on with it, my man, get on with it.'

Vive l'Empereur !

Diversions were few, but existed. There were, for

instance, the rats. Winterbourne had been too much absorbed by other new experiences to pay much attention to them at first. And during the day they kept rather out of sight. One evening, just about sunset, as they were returning down Hinton Alley, there was a block in the trench. Winterbourne happened to be just at the corner of the Support line, with its damaged, revetted traverses, and piles of sandbags on the parapet. The Germans were sending up some rather fancy signal-rockets from their front line, and he was vaguely wondering what they meant, when a huge rat darted, or rather scrambled, impudently just past his head. Then he noticed that a legion of the fattest and longest rats he had ever seen were popping in and out the crevices between the sandbags. As far as he could see down the trench in the dusk, they were swarming over parapet and parados. Such well-fed rats! He shuddered, thinking of what they had probably fed upon.

In a very short time he had become perfectly accustomed to the very mild artillery fire, sniping, and machine-gunning. No casualties had occurred in his own company, and he began to think that the dangers of the War had been exaggerated, while its physical discomforts and tedium had been greatly underestimated. The intense frost prevented his shaking off the heavy cold he had caught at Calais, and at the same time had given him a chill on the liver. The same thing had happened to half the men in the company, whether newcomers or old stagers; and all suffered from diarrhœa due to the cold. There was thus the added diversion of frequent visits to the latrine. Those in the line were primitive affairs of a couple of biscuit-boxes and buckets, interesting from the fact that the Germans had fixed rifles trained on most of them and might get you if you happened to stand up inopportunely. If you had any sense you waited until the bullet ping-ed over, and then calmly walked out ; for lack of which elementary precaution somebody occasionally was popped off. The Pioneers' latrine, just behind their billet, was a more elaborate six-seater (without separate compartments) built over a deep trench and surrounded with sacking on posts. One of the posts had been damaged by a shell, and there were numerous rents in the sacking from shell splinters. Here Winterbourne was forced to spend a larger portion of his spare time than was pleasant in cold weather. One day when he entered he found another occupant, an artilleryman. This person was carefully examining his grey flannel shirt ; and such portions of his body as were exposed to view were covered with small bloody blotches. Some horrid skin disease, Winterbourne surmised. He attended to his own urgent private affairs.

' Still terribly cold,' he ventured.

' Muckin' cold,' said the artilleryman, continuing absorbedly the mysterious search in his shirt.

' Those are nasty skin eruptions you have.'

' It 's them muckin' chats. Billet 's fair lousy with 'em.'

Chats ? Lousy ? Ah, of course, the artilleryman was lousy. So lousy that he had been bitten all over, and had scratched himself raw. Winterbourne felt uncomfortable. He detested the idea of vermin.

' How d' you get them ? Can't you get rid of them ? '

' Get 'em ? Everybody gets 'em. Ain't you chatty ? And there ain't no gettin' rid of 'em. The clothes they gives you at the baths is as chatty as those you 'ands in. Where there 's dug-out and billets, there 's chats ; and where there 's chats, they cops yer.'

Winterbourne departed from the lousy artilleryman with a new preoccupation in life—to remain one of the chatless as long as possible. It was not many weeks, however, before he too became resigned to the louse as an inevitable war comrade.

Like a good many recruits, when first in the line he was inclined to be foolhardy rather than timorous. When a shell exploded near the trench, he popped his head up to have a look at it ; and listened to the machine-gun bullets swishing past with great interest. The older hands reproved him :

‘ Don't be so muckin’ anxious to look at whizz-bangs. You ’ll get a damn sight too many pretty soon. And don't keep shovin’ yer ’ead over the top. *We* don't care a muck if ole Fritz gets yer, but if he sees yer he might put his artillery on *us*.’

Winterbourne rather haughtily decided they were timorous, an impression confirmed by the manner they instantly ducked and crouched when a shell came whistling towards them. So many shells exploded harmlessly that he wondered at their inefficiency. Late one afternoon the Germans began firing on Hinton Alley—little salvoes of four whizz-bangs at a time. The men went on with their work, but a little apprehensively. Winterbourne clambered partly up the side of the trench and watched the shells bursting—crump, Crump, CRUMP, CRRUMP. The splinters hummed harmoniously through the air. Suddenly he heard a loud whizz, and zip-phut, a large piece of metal hurtled just past his head and half-buried itself in the hard chalk of the trench. More surprised than scared, he jumped down and levered the metal up with his pick. It was a brass nose-cap, still warm from the heat of the explosion. He held it in his hand, gazing with curiosity at the German lettering. The other men jeered and scolded him in a friendly way. He felt they exaggerated—his nerves were still so much fresher than theirs.

That night, just after he had got down into kip, the night silence was abruptly broken by a discharge of artillery. Gun after gun, whose existence he had never suspected, opened out all round, and in half a minute fifty or sixty were in action. From the line came the long rattle of a dozen or more machine-guns, with the funny little pops of distant hand-grenades. He got up and went to the door. Ruins interrupted a direct view, but he saw the flashes of the guns, a sort of glow over a short part of the Front line, and Verey lights and rockets flying up continually. A Corporal came unconcernedly into the billet.

' What is it ? ' asked Winterbourne ; ' an attack ? '

' Attack be jiggered. Identification raid, I reckon.'

The German artillery had now opened up, and a shell dropped in the village street. Winterbourne retired to his earth floor. In about three-quarters of an hour the firing quieted down ; only one German battery of five-nines kept dropping shells in and about the village. Winterbourne began to reflect that shell-fire in gross might be more deadly than the few odd retail discharges he had hitherto experienced.

Next morning, the Corporal's diagnosis proved correct. As they went up Hinton Alley soon after dawn, they met a British Tommy escorting six lugubrious personages in field grey, whose faces were almost concealed in large white bandages swathed all round their heads.

' Who are they ? ' he asked.

' Fritzes. Prisoners.'

' I wonder why they are all wounded in the head.'

' Koshed on the napper with trench clubs. I reckon they 've got narsty 'eadaches, pore old barstards.'

About a week after that, they had a day off, and were warned to parade at five p.m. to begin another night-shift. (Each platoon in turn did a week's day-shift and three weeks' night-work.) The Sergeant turned to Winterbourne :

' And you 're to report at the Officers' Mess fifteen minutes before p'rade.'

Winterbourne duly reported, wondering uneasily what breach of military discipline he had committed. He was met on the doorstep by Evans, who was just coming out, all muffled up.

' Ah, there you are, Winterbourne. Major Thorpe says you may act as my runner, so hereafter you 'll parade here fifteen minutes earlier than the rest each night.'

' Very good, sir.'

All this time Winterbourne was rather wretchedly ill, and remained so for weeks. He had a permanent cough and cold, and was weakened by the prolonged diarrhœa. Every night he felt feverish, passing rapidly from a cold shivering to a high temperature. On the day after his arrival in the line, he had ' gone sick ' to get something to relieve his hard cough. Major Thorpe had chosen to consider this as an attempt to evade duty, and had promptly insulted him. Whereupon Winterbourne had decided that so long as he could stand he would never ' go sick ' again. So he carried on. The stretcher-bearer in his platoon had a clinical thermometer. One night, just before going up the line, Winterbourne got the man to take his temperature. It was 102.

' You didn't ought to go up the line like that, mate,' said the man, with a sort of coarse kindness Winterbourne liked. ' I 'll tell the orfficer you ain't fit for service, an' make it all right with the M.O. to-morrer.'

Winterbourne laughed :

' That 's decent of you, but I shan't go sick. I only wanted to see if I were imagining things.'

' You 're a bloody fool. You c'd get a cushy night in kip.'

It was a relief, therefore, to act as Evans's runner. On the nights when Evans was on duty Winterbourne did not carry a pick and shovel, and did no manual labour. He simply followed Evans about on his rounds, and carried messages to the N.C.O.'s for him. It was undoubtedly cushy. Almost an officer's job.

Winterbourne was brought into much closer intimacy with Evans, and had some opportunity to observe him. The officer was distinctly friendly, and they talked a good deal in the long hours of hanging about in the Front line. Evans brought sandwiches and a flask of rum with him, and invariably shared them with his runner—a kindness which touched Winterbourne profoundly. Usually about ten o'clock they sat on a fire-step under the frosty stars, and ate and talked. Occasionally a few shells would go whining overhead, or a burst of machine-gun fire would interrupt them. Their low voices sounded strangely muffled in the cold, dead silence.

Evans was the usual English public-school boy, amazingly ignorant, amazingly inhibited, and yet ' decent ' and good-humoured. He had a strength of character which enabled him to carry out what he had been taught was his duty to do. He accepted and obeyed every English middle-class prejudice and taboo. What the English

middle classes thought and did was right, and what anybody else thought and did was wrong. He was contemptuous of all foreigners. He appeared to have read
nothing but Kipling, Jeffery Farnol, Elinor Glyn, and the
daily newspapers. He disapproved of Elinor Glyn, as
too ' advanced.' He didn't care about Shakespeare, had
never heard of the Russian Ballets, but liked to ' see a good
show.' He thought *Chu Chin Chow* was the greatest play
ever produced, and the Indian Love Lyrics the most
beautiful songs in the world. He thought that Parisians
lived by keeping brothels, and spent most of their time in
them. He thought that all Chinamen took opium, then
got drunk, and ravished white slaves abducted from
England. He thought Americans were a sort of inferior
Colonials, regrettably divorced from that finest of all
institutions, the British Empire. He rather disapproved
of ' Society,' which he considered ' fast,' but he held that
Englishmen should never mention the fastness of Society,
since it might ' lower our prestige ' in the eyes of ' all these
messy foreigners.' He was ineradicably convinced of his
superiority to the ' lower classes,' but where that superiority lay Winterbourne failed to discover. Evans was an
' educated ' pre-War public-school boy, which means that
he remembered half a dozen Latin tags, could mumble a
few ungrammatical phrases in French, knew a little of the
history of England, and had a 'correct' accent. He had
been taught to respect all women as if they were his
mother ; would therefore have fallen an easy prey to the
first tart who came along, and probably have married her.
He was a good runner, had played at stand-off half for his
school and won his colours at cricket. He could play fives,
squash rackets, golf, tennis, water-polo, bridge, and
vingt-et-un, which he called ' pontoon.' He disapproved
of baccarat, roulette, and *petits chevaux*, but always went in

for the Derby sweepstake. He could ride a horse, drive a motor-car, and regretted that he had been rejected by the Flying Corps.

He had no doubts whatever about the War. What England did must be right, and England had declared war on Germany. Therefore, Germany must be wrong. Evans propounded this somewhat primitive argument to Winterbourne with a condescending air, as if he were imparting some irrefutable piece of knowledge to a regrettably ignorant inferior. Of course, after ten minutes' conversation with Evans, Winterbourne saw the kind of man he was, and realised that he must continue to dissimulate with him as with every one else in the Army. However, he could not resist the temptation to bewilder him a little sometimes. It was quite impossible to do anything more. Evans possessed that British rhinoceros equipment of mingled ignorance, self-confidence, and complacency which is triple-armed against all the shafts of the mind. And yet Winterbourne could not help liking the man. He was exasperatingly stupid, but he was honest, he was kindly, he was conscientious, he could obey orders and command obedience in others, he took pains to look after his men. He could be implicitly relied upon to lead a hopeless attack and to maintain a desperate defence to the very end. There were thousands and tens of thousands like him.

Winterbourne noticed that when they were in the line at night, Evans made a point of walking over the top, instead of in the trenches, even when it was plainly far more inconvenient and slower to do so, on account of the wire and shell-holes and other obstacles. At the time, he paid little attention to this, thinking either that it was expected of an officer, or that Evans did it to encourage the men.

Evans rather deliberately exposed himself, and always maintained complete calm. If the two men were exposed to shells or machine-gun fire, Evans walked more slowly, spoke more deliberately, seemed intentionally to linger. It was not until months afterwards that Winterbourne suddenly realised from his own experience that Evans had been reassuring, not his men, but himself. He had been deliberately trying to prove to himself that he did not mind being under fire.

Any man who spent six months in the line (which almost inevitably meant taking part in a big battle) and then claimed that he had never felt fear, never received any shock to his nerves, never had his heart thumping and his throat dry with apprehension, was either super-human, subnormal, or a liar. The newest troops were nearly always the least affected. They were not braver, they were merely fresher. There were very few—were there any ?—who could resist week after week, month after month of the physical and mental strain. It is absurd to talk about men being brave or cowards. There were greater or less degrees of sensibility, more or less self-control. The longer the strain on the finer sensibility, the greater the self-control needed. But this continual neurosis steadily became worse and required a greater effort of repression.

Winterbourne at this time was in the state when danger —and that was slight in these first weeks—was almost entirely a matter of curiosity, rather stimulating than otherwise. Evans, on the other hand, had been in two big battles, had spent eleven months in the line, and had reached the stage when conscious self-control was needed. When a shell exploded near them, both men appeared equally unmoved. Winterbourne was really so, because he was fresh, and had no months of war neurosis to control.

Evans only appeared so, because he was awkwardly and with shame struggling to control a completely sub-conscious reflex action of terror. He thought it was his ' fault,' that he was ' getting windy,' and was desperately ashamed in consequence. And that, of course, made him worse. Winterbourne, on the other hand, was obviously a man who would develop the neurosis rapidly. He had a far more delicate sensibility. He had already reached a state of acute ' worry ' over Fanny and Elizabeth and the War and his own relation to it. And yet his pride would compel him to urge himself far beyond the point where another man would merely have collapsed. He endured a triple strain—that of his personal life, that of exaspera-tion with Army routine, and that of battle.

Perhaps it was through the implicit if unexpressed attitude of the women that Winterbourne also endured the strain of feeling a degradation to mind and body in the hardships he endured in common, after all, with millions of other men. It was a fact that his mind degenerated ; slowly at first, then more and more rapidly. This could scarcely have been otherwise. Long hours of manual labour under strict discipline must inevitably degrade a man's intelligence. Winterbourne found that he was less and less able to enjoy subtleties of beauty and anything intellectually abstruse. He came to want common amuse-ments in place of the intense joy he had felt in beauty and thought. He watched his mind degenerating with horror, wondering if one day it would suddenly crumble away like the body of Mr. Valdemar. He was bitterly humiliated to find that he could neither concentrate nor achieve as he had done in the past. The *élan* of his former life had carried him through a good many months of the Army ; but after about two months in the line, he saw that intellectually he was slowly slipping backwards. Slipping backwards, too, in the years which should have been the most energetic and formative and creative of his whole life. He saw that even if he escaped the War he would be hopelessly handicapped in comparison with those who had not served and the new generation which would be on his heels. It was pretty bitter. He had been forced to smash through obstacles and to triumph over handicaps enough already. These lost War months, now mounting to years, were a knock-out blow from which he could not possibly recover.

And he felt a degradation, a humiliation, in the dirt, the lice, the communal life in holes and ruins, the innumerable deprivations and hardships. He suffered at feeling that his body had become worthless, condemned to a sort of kept tramp's standard of living, and ruthlessly treated as cannon-fodder. He suffered for other men too, that they should be condemned to this ; but since it was the common fate of the men of his generation, he determined he must endure it. His face lost its fineness and took on the mask of ' a red-faced Tommy,' as he was politely told later by a genial American friend. His hands seemed permanently coarsened, his feet deformed by heavy army boots. His body, which had been un-blemished when he joined, was already infested with lice, and his back began to break out in little boils—a thing which had never happened to him—either from impure drinking-water or because the clothes issued from the baths were infected.

No doubt it was the painter's sense of plastic beauty which made him feel this as something so humiliating and degrading. How else account for the feelings of shame and horror he felt at an occurrence which most men would have promptly forgotten ? He had been in the line about a month, and his diarrhœa had got steadily worse. One night, when accompanying Evans on his rounds, Winterbourne felt a physical necessity, and asked permission to go to a latrine. They were about two hundred yards away, and before Winterbourne got there the contents of his bowels were irresistibly evacuated in spite of his desperate efforts to control them. It was one of the coldest nights of that long, bitter winter—the thermometer was below zero Fahrenheit. Winterbourne halted in horror and disgust with himself. What on earth was he to do ? How return to Evans ? He listened. It was one of the quietest nights he ever experienced in the line, hardly a shot fired. Nobody was coming along the trench. He rapidly undressed, shivering with cold, stripped off his under-pants, cleaned himself as well as he could, and hurled the soiled clothes into No Man's Land. He dressed again and rushed back to meet Evans, who asked him a little sharply why he had been so long about it. The discomfort passed ; but the humiliation remained.

January slowly disappeared ; they were half-way through February, and still the frost held. It was a dreary experience. Each day was practically the replica of that before and after—up the line, down the line, sleep, attempt to get a little clean in the morning, inspection parade, dinner, an hour or two to write letters, then parade again for the line. Towards the end of February, the welcome news came that they were going out of the line for four days' rest. On the last night before they went out, Evans and Winterbourne were watching the men working, when they heard a series of rapid, sharp explosions. They looked over and could see the dull red flashes of bombs or small trench-mortars bursting about three hundred yards away. Simultaneously they exclaimed :

' It 's on our sap ! '

Evans jumped into the trench and rushed toward the sap, followed by Winterbourne, who tore the bolt-cover from his rifle and stuffed it in his pocket as he ran. They could hear the ' crash, crash, crash-crash, crash ' of the small mortars, which abruptly ceased when they were about forty yards short. Verey lights were shooting up in all directions, and the British machine-guns were rattling away. Evans dashed round a traverse and went plump into two of his own men who were staggering away from the sap, half-dazed and silly with the shock of explosions.

' What 's happened ? '

They were incoherent, and Evans and Winterbourne rushed on to the sap. Dimming down his torch with his left hand, Evans peered in ; and Winterbourne behind him saw two bodies splashed with blood. The head of one man was smashed into his steel helmet and lay a sticky mess of blood and hair half-severed from his body. The other man, the Corporal, was badly wounded, but still groaning. Obviously, one of the mortars had dropped plump in the sap. Another discharge came crashing on either side. Evans shoved his haversack under the Corporal's head, and shouted to make himself heard over the explosions :

' Get the stretcher-bearer, and send those windy ******* back here.'

' What about the sentry ? ' bawled Winterbourne.

' I 'll get him in. Off with you.'

Evans began to unbutton the Corporal's tunic, to bind his wounds, as Winterbourne left. The man was bleeding badly. Three hundred yards to the stretcher-bearer and three hundred yards back. Winterbourne raced, knowing that a matter of seconds may save the life of a man with a severed artery. He was too late, however. The Corporal was dead when he and the stretcher-bearer rushed panting into the sap.

They got the sentry's body later.

NEXT day they marched back about four miles to another village, half-destroyed but still partly inhabited. For the first time in two months Winterbourne sheathed his bayonet. It seemed symbolical of the four days' rest they were promised. Four days! An immense respite. The men were cheery, and sang all the war songs as they marched off in platoons : ' Where are the boys of the village to-night ? ' ' There 's a long, long trail a-winding.' ' I 'm so happy, oh, so happy, don't you envy me ? ' ' Pack up your troubles in your old kit-bag.' ' If you 're going back to Blighty.' ' I want to go home.' ' Rolling home.' But not ' Tipperary.' So far as Winterbourne knew, none of the troops in France ever sang ' Tipperary.'

He had not slept well, haunted by the vision of the dead man's smashed, bloody head, and the groaning Corporal. Evans looked a little pale. But they said nothing to each other. And after all, they were going on rest, four days' rest. Winterbourne tried to join in the singing. Major Thorpe trotted past them on his horse. They marched to attention, and ceremonially saluted. That also seemed peaceful.

In the village they were billeted in large barns. A thaw set in, so rapid that they started out on frozen ground and arrived in a village street deep in slushy mud. The nights were still cold, and old broken-down barns and earthen floors made chilly bedrooms. There seemed to be no water supply in the village, and they had to wash in thawing flood-pools, breaking the new thin ice with tingling fingers. But they went to the baths and changed their underclothes. The baths were in a shell-smashed brewery. Thirty or forty men stripped in one room and then went into another which had rows of iron pipes running across it, about eight feet from the ground. Small holes were punched in the pipes at intervals of about six feet. A man stood under each hole, and then a little trickle of warm water began to fall on his head and body. They had about five minutes to soap themselves and get clean. Winterbourne went back there alone the next day. By judicious bribing he managed to get an officer's bath and a new set of underclothes. It was delicious to be clean and de-loused again.

The four days passed very quickly. They paraded in the morning, did a little drill, played football or ran in the afternoons, and went to the estaminets in the evening. Winterbourne treated his section to beer, and drank half a bottle of Barsac himself. The men, all beer and spirit drinkers, despised the finer flavour of French wines and called them ' vinegar.' After dark, they sneaked out and stole sandbags of ' boulets '—coal-dust made into large pellets with tar—and burned them in a brazier to warm the chilly barn. Winterbourne protested against this thievery. But since the others went anyhow, and he benefited by the theft, he thought he might as well share the crime too. True, it was French Government property ; and nobody minds stealing from governments. But still, he hated to be a thief. The men called it ' scrounging.' Under pressure of necessity, every man in the line became a more or less unscrupulous scrounger.

On the third night Winterbourne ' clicked unlucky.' He was on Gas and Fire Picket. They sat all night round the Company field kitchen and drank tea, while one man was always on guard. The tin hat and the fixed bayonet were unwelcome reminders that they were soon returning to the line. The men talked of their homes in England, wished the War would end, hoped anyway they 'd get leave or a blighty soon, and envied the officers sleeping in beds. One man grumbled because there was no 'red lamp' in the village. Winterbourne felt glad there wasn't. Not that he would have been tempted, for he was quite fiercely chaste unless in love, but he hated the thought of these men giving their lean, sinewy bodies to the miserable French whores in the war-area bawdy-houses.

' It 's all right in Bethune,' said the grumbler. ' You can see 'em lining up outside the red lamps after dark under a Sergeant.'

* * * * * * * * * *

Winterbourne got up and walked out to the muddy road. The stars were faint and dim and lovely in the soft, misty night sky ; there seemed to be a first quiver of Spring in the scentless pure air. O Andromeda, O Paphian !

At dawn the birds twittered and sang, a little hesitantly in the cold morning mist. The sun rose in a golden haze, behind rows of poplars, over the flat dark earth.

They went into the line again, three miles to the right of their former positions. Their billets were about a mile and a quarter behind the town of M——, right in the crook of the salient. They lived in cellars in a small mining village, badly smashed, and entirely evacuated of civilians. A long, treeless road led straight up to M—— and Hill 91, one of the most fought-over places in the line, seamed with trenches, pitted with shell-holes, honey-combed with galleries, eviscerated with huge mine-craters, blasted bare of all vegetation. At Hill 91 the German line turned sharply left and linked up with a long slag-hill, about five hundred yards from the Pioneers' billets. Consequently, although they were a long way from Hill 91, their billets were under observation and within machine-gun range, while the road to M—— was constantly shelled, and enfiladed by machine-guns. It was a rotten position, and would have been evacuated but for the 'prestige' of keeping M——. A costly bit of prestige. It was estimated that venereal disease held continually a division of troops immobilised at Base Hospitals, to keep up the prestige of British purity : and another division must have been obliterated to retain that barren prestige of holding M——.

They arrived about eleven, and almost immediately Evans's servant came and told Winterbourne to report at the Officers' Mess cellar, in fighting order. Evans was waiting for him.

Hitherto the Company had been under strength, and officered by Major Thorpe and the two subalterns, Evans and Pemberton, who took duty alternately. While on rest, they had been made up to full strength, and were joined by three other subalterns, Franklin, Hume, and Thompson. They thus went up the line one hundred and twenty strong, with six officers, one of whom was supernumerary. Evans had been made a sort of unofficial second-in-command, while continuing to act as platoon officer. Since he was the most experienced of the subalterns, he was to overlook the new officers until they knew their jobs. He explained all this to Winterbourne as they went along.

'You must give me your word not to mention it to the other men, but there is almost certainly a show coming off on this front. Probably in about four weeks. You mustn't let the men know.'

'Of course not, sir.'

'We shall have twelve-hour shifts up here, I 'm afraid.

I 've got to take three platoons up to Hill 91, over there, at five to-night; and I want to reconnoitre. We 've got to repair and revet the front communication trenches, clear away some of our wire, and fill the gaps with knife-rests. We 've also got to repair Southampton Row, the main communication trench to your left. Every time we go up we 've got to take Mills bombs or trench-mortars or S.A.A. I think we 're going to have a lively time. I rode out about ten miles yesterday and saw fifteen batteries of heavies and a lot of tanks camouflaged by the road. The officers said they were booked for this sector or a little south.'

They were walking up the narrow, straight road to M——. About every minute a heavy shell—or a salvo of heavy shells—plonked into M——. There was a sudden spout of black smoke and debris, a heavy, sullen reverberating CLAANG as the loud detonation shook the twisted steel mining machinery and re-echoed from the chalky slopes of Hill 91. To their right was a long slag-hill, mangled with shell-holes. Evans pointed to it.

' The Boche front line runs just in front of that, about four hundred yards away. At some points our own front line is only twenty yards from theirs. It 's a rummy and awkward position. Most of the transport for M—— has to come up this road, and the poor devils are shelled and machine-gunned wickedly every night. All troops on foot have to use Southampton Row, the communication trench to your left. You see it 's got fire-steps and a parapet—it 's also a Reserve line which we have to man in case of necessity.'

They got into the ruined streets of M—— and were promptly lost. The town was blasted to about three feet of indistinguishable ruins. A wooden notice-board over a mass of broken stones, said : ' CHURCH.' Another further on said : ' POST OFFICE.' Evans got his map, and they stood together trying to make out the direct way to the section of trench they wanted. ZwiiING, CRASH, CLAANG !—four heavy shells screamed towards them and detonated with awful force within a hundred yards. The nearest swished over their heads and exploded twenty yards away. Four great columns of black smoke leaped up like miniature volcanoes ; broken bricks and fragments of shell-case clattered in the empty street. The reverberating echoes seemed like a groan from the agonising town. The explosions seemed to hit Winterbourne in the chest.

' Heavies,' said Evans very calmly ; ' eight-inch, probably.'

ZwiiiING, crash, CRASH ! CLAAANG ! Four more.

' Seems a bit unhealthy here. We 'd better push on.'

Winterbourne was silent. For the first time he began to realise the terrific inhuman strength of heavy artillery. Whizz-bangs and even five-nines were one thing, but these eight- or ten-inch high-explosive monsters were a very different matter.

ZwiiiING, CRASH, CLAAANG !

Minute after minute, hour after hour, day and night, week after week, those merciless heavies pounded the groaning town.

ZWIING, CRASH ! CRAASH ! CLAAANG !

It was too violent a thing to get accustomed to. The mere physical shock, the slap in the chest, of the great shells exploding close at hand, forbade that. They became a torment, an obsession, an exasperation, a nervous nightmare. Unintentionally, as a man walked through M——, he found himself tense and strained, waiting for that warning 'zwiing' of the approaching shell, trying to determine by the sound whether it was

coming straight at him or not. Winterbourne's duties
during the next two and a half months necessitated his
walking through M——, often alone, twice or four times
every twenty-four hours.

The real nightmare was only just beginning. There
had been the torment of frost and cold ; now came the
torments of mud, of gas, of incessant artillery, of fatigue
and lack of sleep.

Under the swift thaw the whole battered countryside
seemed to turn from ice to mud. It was deep on the *pavé*
roads, deeper round the billets, deeper still on the un-
paved tracks, and deepest of all in the trenches. In
Winterbourne's hallucinated memories, where images and
episodes met and collided like superimposed films, that
Spring was mud. He seemed to spend his time plodging
through interminable muddy trenches, up to the ankles,
up to the calves, up to the knees ; shovelling mud frantically out of trenches on to the berm, and then by night
from the berm over the parapets, while the shells crashed
and the machine-gun bullets struck gold sparks from the
road stones. When he was not doing that, he was scrap-
ing mud with a knife from his boots and clothes, trying
to dry socks and puttees and to rub some warmth into his
livid, aching feet. He had not known that wet cold could
keep one's legs so achingly dead for so long. He had not
known how wearisome it could be to drag tired legs and
carry burdens through deep, sticky chalk mud, where
each step was an effort, where each leg stuck deep as the
other was laboriously pulled from the sucking mud. He
had not known that one could hate an inert thing so much.
Overhead it might be sunny, with innumerable little
fleecy puffs of exploded shrapnel pursuing a darting white
airplane high in the misty blue March sky. Underfoot

it was mud.   They had no time to look at the sky as they
dragged along, toiling their bent way along those muddy
ditches.

He remembered a week of blessed respite which he
spent in an underground gallery, squatting twelve hours
a day by a winch and interminably winding sandbags of
chalk to men in the trench.   These galleries—which were
never used—were being dug to conceal two or three
divisions before a surprise attack.   They seemed to
extend for miles.   The cutting and picking at the advancing end was done by R.E.'s, skilled miners who cut with
astonishing rapidity and accuracy.   The Pioneers filled
the chalk into sacks and dragged them along the galleries,
where Winterbourne incessantly wound them to the top.
The Engineers had better rations than the infantry and
the Pioneers, whose lunch was bread-and-cheese.   They
had huge cold beefsteaks and bottles of strong tea-and-
rum for their lunch.   Winterbourne, during his half-
hour's midday rest, one day wandered up to their end of
the gallery, just as they were eating.   He could not help
glancing rather wolfishly at their meal.   One of them
noticed it, and, pointing to his steak, said with his mouth
full :

' Ah reckon tha doesn't get groob the likes o' this in thy
lot, lad.'

' No, but the stew's very good—only, you get a bit tired
of it every day.'

' Ay, that tha does.   But we 're skilled men, we are,
traade union.   They 're got to feed oos well, they 'ave.'

Half-kindly, half-contemptuously, the miner cut off a
hunk of his steak and held it out to Winterbourne in his
large dirty hand.

' Here tha art, lad, tak a bite at that.

' Oh no, thanks, it 's very kind of you, but . . .'

z

' Nay, lad, tha 's welcome ; tak it, tak it. Tha looks fair fammelled and wore out. Tha 's na workin' chap, ah knows.'

Torn between his feeling of humiliation, his desire not to reject the man's kindly-meant offer, and his hungry belly, Winterbourne hesitated. He finally took it, with a rather ghastly feeling of animal humiliation. The cold, tender meat tasted delicious. It was the first unsodden meat he had eaten for weeks. He gave them his last cigarettes, and returned to his winch.

Winterbourne detested ' berming.' Hour after hour standing in wet, chilly mud, shovelling the stuff away to prevent its sliding back into the trench from which it had been laboriously thrown, and widening the space between the top of the trench and the parapet. The machine-guns from the slag-hill constantly rattled away at them. One night Winterbourne and the man next him dug up the bones, tunic, equipment, and rifle of a French soldier, who had been hastily buried in the parapet many months before. His cartridges fell from the mouldering pouches and still looked bright in the dim star-dusk. Winterbourne dug up the skull ; it was large and dome-shaped, a typical Frenchman's head. They tried to find his identity disc, but failed. Pemberton, who was on duty that night, made them rebury what was left in a shell-hole. They stuck a cross over it next day, marked ' UNKNOWN FRENCH SOLDIER.'

The best nights were those when Evans was on duty, but often the urgency was so great that the officers' runners and the officers themselves worked and carried burdens. The most awkward burdens were the long sheets of corrugated iron used for revetting. They had to carry these along the road, since they were too large to get round the traverses. It was impossible to keep the metal sheets from clanking against rifles or the sheet of the man in front in the darkness. The machine-guns from the slag-hill opened out, and they could see the spurts of gold sparks on the road come towards them. Winterbourne felt his piece of corrugated iron violently hit and half-wrenched from his hand ; the man in front went down with a clatter. Somebody yelled ' Stretcher-bearer ! ' The men dumped their burdens and cowered on the ground. It was an awful confusion. Only Evans and Winterbourne were left standing on the road. Evans cursed the N.C.O.'s, and made the men form up again behind Winterbourne. It took a long time to find all the sheets of metal in the darkness, and the machine-guns went on rattling pitilessly. They were hours late in getting back to billets.

As March dragged on, more and more heavy guns arrived, clattering up behind their tractors in the darkness. A tank and its crew were hidden not far from the Pioneers' billets, and there were others further from the line. A new infantry division was pushed into the line on their right. Other divisions were said to be in readiness close behind. The sector became more and more lively, but no big attack was made. Winterbourne questioned Evans, who said it had been postponed to give the mud a chance to dry. What hopes !

The Germans had excellent observation posts on Hill 91, and their aircraft were constantly over the British lines and back areas. They were perfectly aware that an attack was being prepared. Every night they shelled M——, shelled the cross-roads leading to M——, shelled any artillery positions they had spotted, shelled the wrecked village where the Pioneers were billeted. The cellars were good enough protection against shell splinters, but far too flimsy to resist a direct hit. Every day or night huge crumps were flung at them, exploding with concussions which shook the ground and made sleep impossible. In the daytime Winterbourne sometimes crouched at his cellar-entrance and watched the explosions within his view. If one of these big shells hit a half-ruined house, almost every vestige disappeared in a cloud of black smoke and rosy brick-dust.

And there was gas, a good deal of gas. It was the beginning of the intensive use of gas projectiles, which later became so greatly perfected. Their experience of it began one March night on Hill 91. A smart local attack had driven the Germans out of their advance positions and carried the British line forward—at a cost— about two hundred and fifty yards on a front of eight hundred. Evans explained to Winterbourne that these local attacks were being made all along the line to deceive the Germans as to the exact position of the coming offensive. Since the Germans would have needed to be blind or lunatic not to see where the guns and troops were being massed, Winterbourne thought this an over-subtle and over-costly bit of policy. However, his not to reason why.

The Pioneers—three platoons of them—under Evans, Pemberton, and Hume, were to dig a new communication trench from the former British Front line to their present Outpost line of hastily-interlinked shell-holes. Evans told Winterbourne not to carry any tools :

' I expect it 'll be rather a sticky do. The old Boche is pooping off whizz-bangs all day and night up there. And I 'm hanged if I can find out exactly where our new Front line is supposed to be. It 's a network of Boche trenches up there, and we don't want to go barging into their line.'

They struggled up Southampton Row and skirted M——, which was being shelled heavily and reverberantly. They got into another trench on the fringe of Hill 91. Whizz-bangs kept cracking all round them, in little masses of about a dozen—several batteries firing together. Evans and Winterbourne were leading. Winterbourne paused :

'There's a curious smell about here, sir' (sniff, sniff), 'like pineapple or pear-drops.'

Evans sniffed the air.

'So there is.'

The smell rapidly became stronger after another salvo of whizz-bangs.

'By Jove, it's tear-gas!' said Evans. 'Pass the word along to put on gas-goggles.'

The line halted, while the men fumbled in the darkness for their goggles, and then slowly stumbled on. Winterbourne found he was practically blinded by his goggles in the darkness ; they kept going dim with perspiration. He took them off.

'We shall be here all night at this rate, sir. May as well be blinded with tear-gas as goggles. I'll keep mine off and reconnoitre.'

Evans pulled off his goggles, and the two went on ahead, telling the Sergeant to follow straight on until he came up with them. Tears poured from the two men's eyes as they toiled up the muddy trench. They kept dabbing their eyes with pocket handkerchiefs, like a couple of mutes at their own funerals.

Crash, crash-crash, crash, crash-crash-crash-crash, came the whizz-bangs ; and the pineapple smell became stronger than ever.

'It'll be a jolly look-out for us,' said Evans, 'if they

poop over poison gas too.   We shan't be able to smell it
with all this stink of pear-drops.   Peuh !   It 's like being
in a sweet factory.'

They laughed.   And then dabbed their streaming eyes
again.

In ten minutes they came up to the largest of the mine-
craters.   The wind was fresh on the hill-crest and there
was no gas.   Their smarting eyes began to recover.

' Here we are,' said Evans, ' and there 's the old
No Man's Land ; but where in hell our Front line is,
I don't know.   You stay here, Winterbourne, and tell
Sergeant Perkins to halt until I come back.   I 'll go
and reconnoitre.'

' I 'll go back, sir, and bring them up.'

' All right,' and Evans vanished in the darkness.
Winterbourne returned to the line of men, dismally
groping their way through the gassy trench.   They waited
for Evans, who led them over the old No Man's Land to
a very deep trench.   They turned to the left.   Evans
whispered to Winterbourne :

' There 's nothing here but a network of Boche
trenches ; look how deep they are.   I couldn't see a soul,
and there are still Boche trench-notices up.   I 'm hanged
if I know where we are.   For all I know we 're in the
Boche lines.'

Winterbourne unslung his rifle and bayonet, and walked
in front of Evans.   Verey lights went up occasionally,
but most mysteriously seemed to come from all sides,
behind them as well as in front and to the flanks.   The
trenches were immensely deep and dark, except when lit
dimly by the glow of Verey lights or the abrupt flashes of
whizz-bangs.   They went on and on, constantly passing
cross-trenches, completely lost, probably returning on
their footsteps.   They could hear the men muttering and

cursing behind them.   At another cross-trench they
halted in despair.   Winterbourne stood on a large
hummock in the middle of the wide trench, peering ahead
through the gloom.   Evans looked at his luminous
wrist-watch.

‘ Good Lord !   We ’ve been wandering in these blasted
trenches for nearly three hours.   It ’ll be too late to do
any work unless we get there at once.’

Winterbourne grabbed his arm :

‘ Look ! ’

Several shadowy figures were silhouetted against the
skyline, coming along the trench toward them.   Too
dark to distinguish the helmets.   English or German ?

‘ Challenge them,’ whispered Evans.   Winterbourne
threw his rifle forward :

‘ Halt !   Who are you ! ’

‘ Frontshires,’ said a weary voice.

‘ Ask which company.’

‘ Which company ? ’

‘ A, B, C, D—what ’s left of ’em.’

They were now close enough for Evans and Winterbourne to see they were in British uniform.   Evans passed
down word to his men to stand to the left and let the out-
going party pass.   The Frontshires staggered rather than
walked down the bumpy trench.

‘ We ’ung on until nearly all of us was killed, sir,’ said
one man huskily to Evans, as if apologising.

‘ When the Springshires were wiped out, we got enfiladed, sir,’ said another ;   ‘ there ’s on’y one of our
officers left.’

About fifty men, the flotsam of the wrecked battalion,
stumbled past them.   Then came the Sergeant-Major and
a young subaltern.   Evans stopped him, and asked the
way to the front line, explaining briefly their job.   The

subaltern seemed dazed with weariness. He kept swaying in the darkness.

' It 's up there . . . up there . . . somewhere. . . .'

' But how far ? '

' I don't know . . . not far. . . . I can't stop . . . mustn't leave the men.'

And he stumbled on again. Evans turned to Winterbourne :

' Well, Winterbourne, you might as well get off the body of that dead Boche you 're standing on, and we 'll push along.'

Winterbourne sprang away with a sensation of horror, and saw that he had indeed unconsciously been standing on a dead German.

They wandered about until nearly dawn, without finding the Front line. They came on a couple of wounded Germans, whom Evans put into stretchers. Just about dawn they found themselves back at the point where they had entered the old German trenches, and recrossed to familiar ground. The wounded Germans groaned as the stretcher-bearers stumbled and bumped them on the ground.

The remnant of the battalion of the Frontshires very slowly made their way into M——. Zwiiing, CRASH ! CLAANG ! went the great crumps, but they hardly heard them. They were too tired. They went through the town in single file. On the straight road the subaltern halted them, formed them roughly into fours, and took his place at their head. They shambled heavily along, not keeping step or attempting to, bent wearily forward under the weight of their equipment, their unseeing eyes turned to the muddy ground. They stumbled over inequalities ; several times one or other of them fell, and had to be dragged laboriously to his feet.   Others lagged hopelessly behind.   Time and again the young subaltern and the R.S.M. paused to allow the little group to re-form. Hardly a word was spoken.   They went very slowly, past the slag-hill, past the ruined village, past the Pioneers' billets, past the soldiers' cemetery, past the ruined château, past the closed Y.M.C.A. canteen ; and just as the fresh clear Spring dawn lightened the sky they came to the village where they had their rest billets.   The firing had quieted down, and the larks were singing overhead in the pure, exquisite sky.   In the pale light the men's unshaven faces looked grim and strangely old, grey-green, haggard, inexpressibly weary.   They shambled on.

Outside of Divisional Headquarters a smart sentry was on duty.   He saw the little party wearily stumbling down the village street, and thought they were walking wounded. The young subaltern stopped about thirty yards from the sentry, and once more re-formed his men.   The sentry heard him say, ' Stick it, Frontshires.'

Already the news had reached the back areas that the Frontshires had been nearly wiped out in a desperate defence—fifty of them and one officer left, out of twenty officers and seven hundred and fifty men.

The sentry sprang to attention and took one pace forward.   Sloped arms—one, two, three, as if on parade —and remained rigid.   As the little group drew level, he sharply brought his rifle and fixed bayonet to the ' present arms.'

The young officer wearily touched the brim of his steel helmet.   The men scarcely saw, and did not comprehend, the gesture.   The sentry watched them pass, with a lump in his throat.

There was still nothing to report on the Western front.

AFTER a few hours' sleep and a hasty meal, Evans and Winterbourne started for the Front line again. Evans was very much ashamed at having lost his way the night before, and the Major had strafed him for incompetence. Evans had not replied, as he might have done, that since the Major knew so well where they ought to have gone, he might have taken the trouble to lead them there.

It was about two on a sunny, cold afternoon. They skirted M—— with its everlasting, maddening Zwiiing, CRASH! CLAAAANG! In the trenches on the edge of Hill 91 they met two walking wounded, unshaved, muddy to the waist. One had his head bandaged and was carrying his steel helmet; the other had his tunic half off, and his left hand and arm were bandaged in several places. They were talking with great gravity and earnestness, and hardly saw Evans and his runner. Winterbourne heard one of them say:

' I told that muckin' new orfficer twice that some mucker 'd get hit if he muckin' well took us up that muckin' trench.'

' Ah,' said the other, ' moock 'im.'

Evans and Winterbourne paused at the old Front line on the crest of the hill to take breath, and looked back. The blue sky was speckled all over with the little fleecy shrapnel bursts from Archies, pursuing three different enemy planes. The heavy shells fell reverberantly into M—— at their feet. They looked over a broad, flat, grey-green plain, dotted with ruined villages, seamed with the long, irregular lines of trenches. The wavering broad ribbon of No Man's Land was clearly visible, blasted to the white chalk. They could see the flash of the heavies,

and enemy shells bursting on cross-roads and round
artillery emplacements. A Red Cross car of wounded
bumping its way from the Advanced Dressing Station in
M—— was shelled all down the road by field artillery.
They watched it eagerly, hoping it would escape. Once
or twice it disappeared in the smoke of the shell-burst and
they felt certain it was done for ; but the car bumpingly
reappeared, and finally vanished from sight in the direction of Rail Head.

'God ! What a dirty trick ! I 'm glad they didn't get
it,' said Winterbourne, as they scrambled out of the trench.

'Ah, well,' said Evans, 'Red Cross cars have been used
as camouflage before now.'

They easily found the new Front line in the daylight.
Directions in English had been hastily scrawled on the
old German trench notices, and they wondered how on
earth they could have missed the way the night before.
The Front line was full of infantry : some on sentry duty,
some sitting hunched up on the fire-steps ; many lying in
long, narrow holes like graves, scooped in the side of the
trench. They found an officer, who took them along to
show them where the new communication trench was
wanted. Winterbourne, turning to answer a question
from Evans, struck the butt of his rifle sharply against a
sleeping man in one of the holes. The man did not stir.

'Your fellows are sleeping soundly,' said Evans.

'Yes,' said the officer tonelessly ; 'but he may be dead
for all I know. Stretcher-bearers too tired to take down
all the bodies. Some of 'em are dead, and some asleep.
We have to go round and kick 'em to find which is which.'

The new trench they were to dig had been roughly
marked out, and ran from the old German front line
to the lip of Congreve's Mine-crater, now used as an

ammunition dump.   A salvo of whizz-bangs greeted them
as they went out to look at it.

'I don't altogether envy you this job,' said the Infantry
officer ; ' this is about the most unhealthy spot on Hill 91.
The Boche shells it day and night.   Your Colonel had a
hell of a row about it with the Brigadier, but our fellows
are too whacked to do any more digging.'

Over came another little bunch of whizz-bangs, in cor-
roboration—crash, crash-crash, crash.   The grey-green,
acrid smoke smelt foul.

'They're going to call it Nero Trench,' he added, as
they left him, ' because the ground's so black with coal-
dust and slag.   Well, good-bye, best of luck.   And, by
the by, look out for gas.'

The Nero Trench job was an intensified nightmare.
The Germans had it 'taped' with exactitude, and shelled
it ruthlessly.   Five minutes was the longest period that
ever passed without salvoes of whizz-bangs.   Evans and
Winterbourne, Hume and his runner, walked continually
up and down the line of men, who toiled hastily and
nervously in the darkness to make themselves a little
cover.   When the shells came crashing near them, they
crouched down on the ground.   It was found after the
first night that each man had simply dug a hole for himself instead of regularly excavating his three yards of
trench.   On some nights the shelling was so intense that
Evans withdrew the men for a time to the shelter of a
trench.   They had several casualties.

And then the Germans began a steady, systematic gas
bombardment of all the ruined villages in the advanced
area.   It began on the second night of the Nero Trench
job.   They had noticed on Hill 91 that a pretty heavy
bombardment was proceeding from the German lines,

and all the way down from M—— they heard the shells
continuously shrilling overhead. It puzzled them that
they could not hear them exploding.

' Must be bombarding the back areas,' said Evans.
' Let 's hope it gives 'em something to think about besides
sending us up tons of silly papers.'

But as they came nearer their village they could tell by
the sound in the air that the shells must be falling close
ahead of them. Soon they heard them falling with the
customary zwiiING, followed by a very unaccustomed soft
PHUT.

' They can't all be duds,' said Winterbourne.

A shell dropped short, just outside the parapet, with
the same curious PHUT. Immediately a strange smell,
rather like new-mown hay gone acrid, filled the air.
They sniffed, and both men exclaimed simultaneously :

' Phosgene ! Gas ! '

They all fumblingly and hastily put on their gas-masks,
and stumbled on blindly down the trench. Winterbourne
and Evans scrambled out on to the road and got into the
edge of the village. A rain of gas shells was falling on it
and all round their billets—zwiing, zwiing, zwiing, zwiing,
PHUT PHUT PHUT PHUT. Each took off his mask a second
and gave one sniff—the air reeked with phosgene.

Evans and Winterbourne stood at the end of the trench
to help out the groping, half-blinded men. As they filed
by, grotesques with indiarubber faces, great, dead-looking
goggles, and a long tube from their mouths to the box
respirators, Winterbourne thought they looked like lost
souls expiating some horrible sin in a new Inferno. The
rolled gas-blankets were pulled down tightly over the
cellar entrances, but the gas leaked through. Two men
were gassed and taken off in stretchers, foaming rather
horribly at the mouth.

The gas bombardment went on until dawn, and then ceased. Winterbourne fell asleep, with his gas-mask just off his face. Hitherto they had slept with the box respirator slung on a nail or piled with the other equipment ; after the experience of this and the subsequent nights, they always slept with the respirator on their chests and the mask ready to slip on immediately.

The heavies began again soon after it was light. Winterbourne was awakened by one which crashed just outside his cellar. He lay on the floor for a long time listening to the zwiiiING, CRASH, of the shells. He heard two ruined houses clatter to the ground under direct hits, and wondered if the cellars had held firm. They hadn't. But fortunately they happened to be unoccupied. Presently the German batteries switched off and began bombarding some artillery about five hundred yards to the left. Winterbourne profited by the lull to wash. He ran out of the cellar in his shirt-sleeves and gas-mask, with the canvas bucket in which he washed ; and found that a shell had smashed the pump outside his billet. He knew there was another about three hundred yards to the right, although he had never been there.

It was another cold but sunny morning, with the inevitable white shrapnel bursts all over the sky. He was now so accustomed to them that he scarcely noticed their existence. Occasionally a very faint rattle of machine-gun fire came from the war in the air, of which he was nearly as ignorant as people in England of the war on land.

He took off his mask and sniffed. A fresh wind was blowing, and, although there was plenty of phosgene in the air, it was not in any deadly concentration. He decided to risk leaving the mask off. The ground was deeply delved with the conical holes made by the big shells thrown over, and pitted everywhere by the smaller holes of the gas shells. He found a dud, and examined it with interest. A brownish-looking shell, about the size of a five-nine.

The cottages were rather scattered, and unused as cellar-billets in this direction. The top storeys had gone from nearly all, but in several the ground floor was fairly intact. He looked into each as he passed. The wall-paper had long ago fallen and lay in mouldering heaps. The floors were covered with broken bricks, tiles, smashed beams, laths, and disintegrating plaster. Odd pieces of broken furniture, twisted iron beds, large rags which had once been clothes and sheets, protruded from the mass. He poked about and found photographs, letters in faded ink on damp paper, broken toys, bits of smashed vases, a soiled satin wedding-gown with its veil and wreath of artificial orange-blossom. He stood, with his head bent, looking at this pathetic debris of ruined lives, and absent-mindedly lit a cigarette, which he immediately threw away —it tasted of phosgene. ' La Gloire,' he murmured, ' Deutschland über alles, God save the King.'

The next cottage was less damaged than the others, and its rough wooden shutters were still on their hinges. Winterbourne peered through, and saw that the whole of the inside had been cleared of debris, and was stacked with quantities of wooden objects. He shaded his eyes more carefully, and saw they were ranks and ranks of wooden crosses. Those he could see had painted on them R.I.P. ; then underneath was a blank space for the name ; underneath was the name of one or other of the battalions in his division, and then the present month and year, with a blank space for the day. Excellent fore-thought, he reflected, as he filled his bucket and water-bottle. How well this War is organised !

About nine, Evans's servant told him to report immediately in fighting order. Wearily and sleepily he threw on his equipment, re-tied the string of his box respirator, and slung his rifle and bayonet over his left shoulder. He waited with the officers' servants, who gave him a piece of bread dipped in bacon grease to eat. Presently Evans came out and they started off.

' I 've got to see an R.E. officer,' said Evans, ' about a new job on Hill 91. It 's a bit further to the left of where we 've been working, and it 'll take us half an hour longer to get there.'

Winterbourne seized the opportunity to put foward one or two ideas he had been thinking over :

' I hope you won't mind, sir, if I say something—it 's not an official complaint at all, you understand, only what I 've been personally thinking.'

' Go ahead.'

' Well, sir, I assume that the reason we are kept in billets instead of in the line is to give us more rest so that we come fresh to work. But here it doesn't work out that way, especially in the past fortnight ; and it 's likely to get worse instead of better. It seems to me that we should be much better off if we were in dug-outs in the reserve line. We have that long walk through the mud twice a day ; we get all the shells meant for the transport and ration parties ; we get an all-night strafing in the line ; we 're shelled all the way down ; we come back to gassy billets, which are shelled with heavies twenty hours out of twenty-four. The cellars are no real protection against a direct hit. They 're damper than dug-outs, and just as dark and ratty. There are far more whizz-bangs and light stuff in the line, but far fewer heavies ; and if we had even fifteen-foot dug-outs, we 'd get some sleep, instead of starting awake every ten minutes with a crump

outside the cellar entrance. We 're getting a lot of useless casualties, sir. I passed the cook-house as I came
along, and the cook told me one of his mates had just gone
down with gas from last night. And the S.M. looks as
green as grass. Can't you get us put in the line, sir ? '

Evans cogitated a moment or two :

' Yes, I think you 're right. No, I can't get us moved.
I haven't the authority. I wish I had. I 'll ask the
Major to put it before the Colonel. It 's quite true what
you say. In the past week we 've had eight casualties in
the line, and twelve here or going up and down. But
with this show coming off I expect every trench and dug-
out will be packed.'

Winterbourne felt enormously proud that Evans had
not snubbed his suggestion. Evans went on, after a
pause :

' By the way, Winterbourne, have you ever thought of
taking a commission ? '

' Why yes, sir ; it was suggested by the Adjutant of my
battalion in England. I believe my father wrote to him
about it. He, my father, was very keen about it.'

' Well, why don't you apply ? '

It was now Winterbourne's turn to cogitate :

' I find it rather hard to explain, sir. For many
reasons, which you might think far-fetched, I had and still
have a feeling that I ought to spend the War in the ranks
and in the line. I should prefer to be in the Infantry, but
I think the Pioneers are quite near enough.'

' They often come round for volunteers, you know.
If you like, I 'll put you down next time and the Major
will recommend you to the Colonel.'

' It 's kind of you, sir. I 'll think about it.'

One night, two nights, three nights, four nights passed,

and still there was no big battle. And they were not
moved. Every night they were shelled up the line, shelled
in the line, shelled on the way back, and arrived in a hail-
storm of gas shells. They had to wear their gas-masks
for hours every day. And sleep became more and more
difficult and precarious.

Winterbourne's intimacy with Evans and his own
' education ' put him in rather an ambiguous position.
Evans trusted him more and more to do things which
would normally have been done by an N.C.O. And
Winterbourne's feeling of responsibility led him to take
on and conscientiously carry out everything of the kind.
One night there was supposed to be a gas-discharger
attack by the British in retaliation for the heavy German
gas bombardments. All the officers wanted to see it ;
and since it was staged for an hour before dawn, that
meant either that one officer had to take the Company
down or that the men had to be kept up two hours longer,
exposed to artillery retaliation. Evans solved the problem. He sent for Winterbourne :

' Winterbourne, we want to stop and see the fun up
here. Now, you can take the Company down, can't you ?
I 'll tell Sergeant Perkins that you 're in charge ; but of
course you 'll give orders through him. Come back here
and report after you get them back.'

' Very good, sir.'

There was no British gas attack, but the Germans put
up what was then a considerable gas bombardment.
They sent over approximately thirty thousand gas shells
that night, most of them in and around the village where
the Pioneers were billeted. The Company had to wear
gas-masks over the last half-mile, and Winterbourne had
a very anxious time getting them along. He had discovered a disused but quite deep trench running through

the village almost to their billets, and he took the men
along there instead of through the village street.   It was
a little longer, but far safer.   The shells were hailing
all round them, and Winterbourne didn't want any
casualties.   Sergeant Perkins and he managed to get
the men safely into billets.   Winterbourne turned and
said :

'Well, good-night, Sergeant ; I must go up the line
again and report to Mr. Evans.'

'You ain't going up agen, are you ? '

'Yes, Mr. Evans told me to.'

''Struth !   Well, I 'd rather it was you than me.'

Winterbourne fitted on his gas-mask, and groped his
way out of the Sergeants' cellar.   The night was muggy,
a bit drizzly, windless and very dark—the ideal conditions
for a gas bombardment.   What little wind there was came
from the German lines.   He hesitated between taking the
long muddy trench or the more open road ; but since he
was practically blinded in the darkness with his goggles, he
decided to take the trench, for fear of losing his way.   It
was rather eerie, groping his way alone up the trench,
with the legions of gas shells shrilling and phutting all
round him.   They fell with a terrific ' flop ' when they
came within a few yards.   He stumbled badly two or
three times in holes they had made in the trench since he
had come down.   For nearly half a mile he had to go
through the gas barrage, and it was slow work indeed,
with the mud and the darkness and the groping and the
stumbling.   Interminable.   He thought of nothing in
the darkness but keeping his left hand on the side of the
trench to guide him and holding his right hand raised in
front to prevent his bumping into something.

At last he got clear of the falling gas shells, and ventured a peep outside his mask. One sniff showed him the air was deadly with phosgene. He groped on another two hundred yards and tried again. There was still a lot of gas, but he decided to risk it, and took off his mask. With the mask off he could see comparatively well, and travelled quite rapidly. About an hour before dawn he reported to Evans.

' There is a devil of a gas bombardment going on round the billets and for half a mile round, sir,' said Winterbourne ; ' that 's why I 'm so late. The whole country reeks of gas.'

Evans whistled.

' Whew ! As a matter of fact, we 've been drinking a bit in the dug-out with some Infantry officers, and one or two are a bit groggy in consequence.'

' Better wait till dawn, then, sir. If you 'll come up into the trench you 'll hear the shells going over.'

' Oh, I take your word for it. But the Major insists on going down at once. We 've just heard that there isn't going to be a gas attack. You 'll have to help me get them down.'

' Very good, sir.'

The Major was entirely sober ; Evans was perfectly self-controlled ; but the other four were all a little too merry. It was a perfect nightmare getting them through the gas barrage. They would insist there was no danger, that the gas was all a wash-out ; and kept taking off their masks. They disregarded the Major's peremptory orders, and Evans and Winterbourne had constantly to take off their own masks to argue with the subalterns and make them put on theirs. Winterbourne could feel the deadly phosgene at his lungs.

Just after dawn they reached the Officers' Mess cellar, fortunately without a casualty. Winterbourne felt hor-

ribly sick with the gas he had swallowed. The Major
took off his gas-mask, and picked up a water-jug.

' Those confounded servants have forgotten to leave
any water,' exclaimed the Major angrily. ' Winterbourne, take that tin jug and go and get some water from
the cook-house.'

' Very good, sir.'

The shells were still pitilessly hailing down through
the dawn. It was a hundred yards to the cook-house, and
Winterbourne three times just escaped being directly hit
by one of the ceaselessly falling shells. He returned to
the Mess, and left the water.

' Thanks very much,' said Evans ; ' you may go now,
Winterbourne. Good-night.'

' Good-night, sir.'

' Good-night,' said the Major ; ' thank you for getting
that water, Winterbourne ; I oughtn't to have sent you.'

' Thank you, sir ; good-night, sir.'

Outside the Major's and Evans's part of the cellar the
other officers were sitting round a deal table by the light
of a candle stuck in a bottle, which looked dim and ghastly.
The place was practically gas-proof, with tightly-drawn
blankets over every crevice.

' Win'erbourne,' said one of them.

' Sir ? '

' Run along to the Quar'master-Sergeant and bring us
a bottle of whisky.'

' Very good, sir.'

Winterbourne climbed the cellar steps, lifted the outer
gas-curtain rapidly, and stepped out. There was such a
stench of phosgene that he snapped his mask on at once.
The shells were falling thicker than ever. One hit the
wall of the house, and Winterbourne felt bricks and dust
drop on his steel helmet and shoulders. He shrank

against what was left of the wall. Two hundred yards
to the Q.M.S.'s billet. That meant nearly a quarter of a
mile through that deadly storm—for a half-drunken man
to get a few more whiskies. Winterbourne hesitated. It
was disobeying orders if he didn't go. He turned resolutely and went to his own billet : nothing was ever said
of this refusal to obey an officer's orders in the face of
the enemy.

Winterbourne stood outside the entrance to his cellar,
took off his steel helmet and folded down the top part of
his gas-mask so that he could see, while still keeping the
nose-clip on and the large rubber mouthpiece in his teeth.
The whitish morning light looked cold and misty, and the
PHUT PHUT PHUT PHUT of the bursting gas shells continued
with ruthless iteration. He watched them exploding ; a
little curling cloud of yellow gas rose from each shell-hole.
The ground was pitted with these new shell-holes, and
newly-broken bricks and debris lay about everywhere. A
dead rat lay in a gas-shell hole just outside the entrance—
so the War caught even the rats ! There had been a
young, slender ash-tree in what had once been the cottage
garden. A heavy explosive had fallen just at its roots,
splintered the slim stem, and dashed it prone with broken
branches. The young leaves were still green, except on
one side where they were curled and withered by gas.
The grass, so tender a Spring green a week before, was
yellow, sickly, and withered. As he turned to lift the gas-
blanket he heard the whizz and crash of the first heavy of
the day bombardment. But the gas shells continued.
    Inside the cellar was complete darkness. He took off
his mask and fumbled his way down the broken stairs,
trying not to wake the other runners. It was important
to use only one match, because matches were scarce and

precious. The air inside was foul and heavy, but only slightly tainted with phosgene. Winterbourne half-smiled as he thought how furiously he had contended for ' fresh air ' in huts and barrack-rooms, and how gladly he now welcomed any foul air which was not full of poison gas. He lighted his stub of candle, and slowly took off his equipment, replacing the box respirator immediately. His boots were thick with mud, his puttees and trousers torn with wire and stained with mud and grease. A bullet had torn a hole in his leather jerkin, and his steel helmet was marked by a long, deep dint, where it had been struck by a flying splinter of shell. He felt amazingly weary, and rather sick. He had known the fatigue of long walks and strenuous Rugby football matches and cross-country runs, but nothing like this continual, cumulative weariness. He moved with the slow, almost pottering movements of agricultural labourers and old men. The feeling of sickness became worse, and he wanted to vomit out the smell of gas which seemed to permeate him. He heaved over his empty canvas bucket until the water started to his eyes, but vomited nothing. He noticed how filthy his hands were.

He was just going to sit down on his blanket and pack, covered by the neatly-folded ground-sheet, when he saw a parcel and some letters for him lying on them. The other runners had brought them over for him. Decent of them. The parcel was from Elizabeth—how sweet of her to remember ! And yes, she had sent all the things he had asked for and left out all the useless things people would send to the troops. He mustn't touch anything except the candles, though, until to-morrow, when the parcel would be carefully divided among everybody in the cellar. It was one of the good unwritten rules—all parcels strictly divided between each section, so that every one got something, even and especially the men who were too poor or too lonely to receive anything from England. Dear Elizabeth! how sweet of her to remember!

He opened her envelope with hands which shook slightly with fatigue and the shock of explosions. Then he stopped, lighted a new candle from the stub of the old one, blew out the stub, and carefully put it away to give to one of the infantry. The letter was unexpectedly tender and charming. She had just been to Hampton Court to look at the flowers. The gardens were rather neglected, she said, and no flowers in the Long Border—the gardeners were at the War, and there was no money in England now for flowers. Did he remember how they had walked there in April five years ago? Yes, he remembered, and thought too with a pang of surprise that this was the first Spring he had ever spent without seeing a flower, not even a primrose. The little yellow coltsfoot he had liked so much were all dead with phosgene. Elizabeth went on:

'I saw Fanny last week. She looked more charming and delicate than ever—and such a marvellous hat! I hear she is *much* attached to a brilliant young scientist, a chemist, who does the most *peculiar* things. He mixes up all sorts of chemicals and then experiments with the fumes and kills dozens of poor little monkeys with them. Isn't it wicked? But Fanny says it's most *important* war work.'

The sickness came on him again. He turned sideways and heaved silently, but could not vomit. He felt thirsty, and drank a little stale-tasting water from his water-bottle. Dear Elizabeth! how sweet of her to remember!

Fanny's letter was very rattling and gay. She had been there, she had done this, she had seen so-and-so. How

was darling George getting along ? She was so glad to
see that there had been no fighting yet on the Western
front. She added :

' I saw Elizabeth recently. She looked a little worried,
but *very* sweet. She was with such a charming young
man—a young American who ran away from Yale to join
our Flying Corps.'

The heavy shells outside were falling nearer and nearer.
They came over in fours, each shell a little in front of the
others—bracketing. Through the gas-curtain he heard
the remains of a ruined house collapse across the street
under a direct hit. Each crash made the cellar tremble
slightly, and the candle flame jumped.

Well, it was nice of Fanny to write. Very nice. She
was a thoroughly decent sort. He picked up the other
envelopes. One came from Paris, and contained the
Bulletin des Écrivains—names of French writers and
artists killed or wounded, and news of those in the armies.
He was horrified to see how many of his friends in Paris
had been killed. A passage had been marked in blue
pencil—it contained the somewhat belated news that
M. Georges Winterbourne, *le jeune peintre anglais*, was
in camp in England.

Another letter, forwarded by Elizabeth, came from a
London art-dealer. It said that an American had bought
one of Winterbourne's sketches for five pounds, and that
when he heard that Winterbourne was in the trenches he
had insisted upon making it twenty-five pounds. The
dealer therefore enclosed a cheque for twenty-two pounds
ten, being twenty-five pounds less commission at ten per
centum. Winterbourne thought it rather cheek to take
commission on the money which was a gift ; but still—
Business As Usual. But how generous of the American !
How amazingly kind ! His pay was five francs a week, so

the money was most welcome. He must write and thank . . .

The last letter was from Mr. Upjohn, from whom Winterbourne had not heard for over a year. Elizabeth, it appeared, had asked him to write and send news. Mr. Upjohn wrote a chatty letter. He himself had a job in Whitehall, 'of national importance.' Winterbourne rejoiced to think that Mr. Upjohn's importance was now recognised by the nation. Mr. Shobbe had been to France, had stayed in the line three weeks, and was now permanently at the base. Comrade Bobbe had come out very strong as a conscientious objector. He had been put in prison for six weeks. His friends had 'got at' somebody influential, who had 'got at' the secretary of somebody in authority, and Mr. Bobbe had been released as an agricultural worker. He was now 'working' on a farm run by a philanthropic lady for conscientious objectors of the intellectual class. Mr. Waldo Tubbe had found his vocation in the Post Office Censorship Bureau, where he was very happy—if he could not force people to say what he wanted, he could at least prevent them from writing anything derogatory to his Adopted Empire. . . .

George laughed silently to himself. Amusing chap, Upjohn. He got out his jack-knife and scraped away the mud so that he could unlace his boots. Outside the shells crashed. One burst just behind the cellar. The roof seemed to give a jump, something seemed to smack Winterbourne on the top of the head, and the candle went out. He laboriously re-lit it. The other runners woke up.

'Anything up?'

'No, only a crump outside. I'm just getting into kip.'

'Where 've you been?'

' Up the line again, for the officers.'

' Get back all right ? '

' Yes, nobody hit.   But there 's a hell of a lot of gas about.   Don't go out without putting on your gas-bag.'

' Good-night, old man.'

' Good-night, old boy.'

THREE more nights passed rather more tranquilly. There was comparatively little gas, but the German heavies were persistent. They, too, quieted down on the third night, and Winterbourne got to bed fairly early and fell into a deep sleep.

Suddenly he was wide awake and sitting up. What on earth or hell was happening? From outside came a terrific rumble and roaring, as if three volcanoes and ten thunderstorms were in action simultaneously. The whole earth was shaking as if beaten by a multitude of flying hoofs, and the cellar walls vibrated. He seized his helmet, dashed past the other runners, who were starting up and exclaiming, rushed through the gas-curtain; and recoiled. It was still night, but the whole sky was brilliant with hundreds of flashing lights. Two thousand British guns were in action, and heaven and earth were filled with the roar and flame. From about half a mile to the north, southwards as far as he could see, the whole front was a dazzling flicker of gun-flashes. It was as if giant hands covered with huge rings set with searchlights were being shaken in the darkness, as if innumerable brilliant diamonds were flashing great rays of light. There was not a fraction of a second without its flash and roar. Only the great boom of a twelve- or fourteen-inch naval gun just behind them punctured the general pandemonium at regular intervals.

Winterbourne ran stumbling forwards to get a view clear of the ruins. He crouched by a piece of broken house and looked towards the German lines. They were a long, irregular wall of smoke, torn everywhere with the dull red flashes of bursting shells. Behind their lines their artillery was flickering brighter and brighter as battery after battery came into action, making a crescendo of noise and flame when the limits of both seemed to have been reached. Winterbourne saw but could not hear the first of their shells as it exploded short of the village. The great clouds of smoke over the German trenches were darkly visible in the first very pallid light of dawn. It was the preliminary bombardment of the long-expected battle. Winterbourne felt his heart shake with the shaking earth and vibrating air.

The whole thing was indescribable—a terrific spectacle, a stupendous symphony of sound. The devil-artist who had staged it was a master, in comparison with whom all other artists of the sublime and terrible were babies. The roar of the guns was beyond clamour—it was an immense rhythmic harmony, a super-jazz of tremendous drums, a ride of the Walkyrie played by three thousand cannon. The intense rattle of the machine-guns played a minor motif of terror. It was too dark to see the attacking troops, but Winterbourne thought with agony how every one of those dreadful vibrations of sound meant death or mutilation. He thought of the ragged lines of British troops stumbling forward in smoke and flame and a chaos of sound, crumbling away before the German protective barrage and the Reserve line machine-guns. He thought of the German front lines, already obliterated under that ruthless tempest of explosions and flying metal. Nothing could live within the area of that storm except by a miraculous hazard. Already in this first half-hour of bombardment hundreds upon hundreds of men would have been violently slain, smashed, torn, gouged, crushed, mutilated. The colossal harmony seemed to roar louder as the drum-fire lifted from the Front line to the Reserve. The battle was begun. They would be mopping-up soon—throwing bombs and explosives down the dug-out entrances on the men cowering inside.

The German heavies were pounding M—— with their shells, smashing at the communication trenches and cross-roads, hurling masses of metal at their own ruined village. Winterbourne saw the half-ruined factory chimney totter and crash to the ground. Two shells pitched on either side of him, and flung earth, stones, and broken bricks all round him. He turned and ran back to his cellar, stumbling over shell-holes. He saw an isolated house disappear in the united explosion of two huge shells.

He clutched his hands together as he ran, with tears in his eyes.

WINTERBOURNE found the other runners buckling up their packs and fastening their equipment with that febrile haste which comes with great excitement. Even in the cellar the roar of the artillery made it necessary for them almost to shout to each other.

' What are the orders ? '

' Stand by in fighting order, ready to move off at once. Dump packs outside billets.'

Winterbourne in his turn feverishly put on his equipment, buckled his pack, and cleaned his rifle. They stood, rifles and bayonets ready, in the low cellar, ready to spring up the broken stairs as soon as they were warned. In a moment such as this, a kind of paroxysm of humanity, the most difficult thing is to wait. They dreaded the awful storm thundering above them, but they were irresistibly hallucinated by it, eager to plunge in and be done with it. The German shells thudded continuously all round them, muted by the vaster clamour of the attacking artillery. No orders came. They fidgeted, exclaimed, and finally one by one sat silent on their packs, listening. A large rat ran down the cellar stairs and began to nibble something. The beast was exactly level with Winterbourne's head. He shoved a cartridge into the breech of his rifle, murmuring, ' Why should a dog, a horse, a rat have life, and they no breath at all ? ' He aimed very carefully and pulled the trigger ; there was a terrific bang in the confined cellar, and the rat was smashed dead in the air. Not ten seconds later a red, perspiring face under a steel helmet was anxiously poked through the cellar entrance. It was the Orderly Sergeant.

' What the muckin' hell are you doing, down there ? '

' Having a spree—didn't you hear the champagne cork ? '

' Spree be mucked—one of you ******* fired his rifle and muckin' near copped me.   Mucked if I don't report the muckin' lot of yer.'

' Wow !   Put a sock in it ! '

' Muck off ! '

' Ord'ly sergeants are cheap to-day ! '

' Well, you muckers got to report to yer officers at once 'Op it.'

They ran up the broken stairs, pretending to poke their bayonets at him, and laughing, perhaps a little hysterically.   The fat, good-natured little Sergeant went off, shaking his fist at them, shouting awful threats about the punishment awaiting them, with a broad affectionate grin on his face.

For Winterbourne the battle was a timeless confusion, a chaos of noise, fatigue, anxiety, and horror.   He did not know how many days and nights it lasted, lost completely the sequence of events, found great gaps in his conscious memory.   He did know that he was profoundly affected by it, that it made a cut in his life and personality.   You couldn't say there was anything melodramatically startling, no hair going grey in a night, or never smiling again.   He looked unaltered ; he behaved in exactly the same way. But, in fact, he was a little mad.   We talk of shell-shock, but who wasn't shell-shocked, more or less ?   The change in him was psychological, and showed itself in two ways. He was left with an anxiety complex, a sense of fear he had never experienced, the necessity to use great and greater efforts to force himself to face artillery, anything explosive.   Curiously enough, he scarcely minded machine-gun fire, which was really more deadly, and completely

disregarded rifle-fire.   And he was also left with a profound and cynical discouragement, a shrinking horror of
the human race. . . .

A timeless confusion.   The runners scattered outside
their billet and made for the officers' cellar through the
falling shells, dodging from one broken house or shell-
hole to another.   Winterbourne, not yet unnerved,
calmly walked straight across and arrived first.   Evans
took him aside :
'We 're going up as a company, with orders to support
and co-operate with the Infantry.   Try to nab me a rifle
and bayonet before we go over.'
'Very good, sir.'
Outside was an open box of S.A.A., and they each drew
two extra bandoliers of cartridges, which they slung round
their necks.

They moved off in sections, filing along the village
street, which was filled with fresh debris and ruins re-
ruined.   It was snowing.   They came on two freshly-
killed horses.   Their close-cropped necks were bent
under them, with great glassy eyeballs starting with
agony.   A little further on was a smashed limber with the
driver dead beside it.

In the trench they passed a batch of about forty German
prisoners, unarmed, in steel helmets.   They looked
green-pale, and were trembling.   They shrank against
the side of the trench as the English soldiers passed, but
not a word was said to them.

The snowstorm and the smoke drifting back from the
barrage made the air as murky as a November fog in
London.   They saw little, did not know where they were
going, what they were doing or why.   They lined a trench
and waited.   Nothing happened.   They saw nothing but

wire and snowflakes and drifting smoke, heard only the roar of the guns and the now sharper rattle of machine-guns. Shells dropped around them. Evans was looking through his glasses, and cursing the lack of visibility. Winterbourne stood beside him, with his rifle still slung on his left shoulder.

They waited. Then Major Thorpe's runner came with a message. Apparently he had mistaken a map reference and brought them to the wrong place.

They plodged off through the mud, and lined another trench. They waited.

Winterbourne found himself following Evans across what had been No Man's Land for months. He noticed a skeleton in British uniform, caught sprawling in the German wire. The skull still wore a sodden cap and not a steel helmet. They passed the bodies of British soldiers killed that morning. Their faces were strangely pale, their limbs oddly bulging with strange fractures. One had vomited blood.

They were in the German trenches, with many dead bodies in field grey. Winterbourne and Evans went down into a German dug-out. Nobody was there, but it was littered with straw, torn paper, portable cookers, oddments of forgotten equipment, and cigars. There were French tables and chairs with human excrement on them.

They went on. A little knot of Germans came toward them holding up their shaking hands. They took no notice of them, but let them pass through.

The barrage continued. Their first casualty was caused by their own shells dropping short.

Major Thorpe sent Winterbourne and another man with a written duplicate message to Battalion Head-

quarters. They went back over the top, trying to run.
It was impossible. Their hearts beat too fast, and their
throats were parched. They went blindly at a jog-trot,
slower in fact than a brisk walk. They seemed to be
tossed violently by the bursting shells. The acrid smoke
was choking. A heavy roared down beside Winterbourne
and made him stagger with its concussion. He could not
control the resultant shaking of his flesh. His teeth
chattered very slightly as he clenched them desperately.
They got back to familiar land and finally to Southampton
Row. It was a long way to Battalion Headquarters. The
men in the orderly-room eagerly questioned them about
the battle, but they knew less than they did.

Winterbourne asked for water and drank thirstily. He
and the other runner were dazed and incoherent. They
were given another written message, and elaborate directions which they promptly forgot.

The drum-fire had died down to an ordinary heavy
bombardment as they started back. Already it was late
afternoon. They wandered for hours in unfamiliar
trenches before they found the Company.

They slept that night in a large German dug-out,
swarming with rats. Winterbourne in his sleep felt them
jump on his chest and face.

The drum-fire began again next morning. Again they
lined a trench and advanced through smoke over torn
wire and shell-tormented ground. Prisoners passed
through. At night they struggled for hours, carrying
down wounded men in stretchers through the mud and
clamour. Major Thorpe was mortally wounded and his
runner killed ; Hume and his runner were killed ;
Franklin was wounded ; Pemberton was killed ; Sergeant

Perkins was killed; the stretcher-bearers were killed. Men seemed to drop away continually.

Three days later Evans and Thompson led back forty-five men to the old billets in the ruined village. The attack on their part of the front had failed. Further south a considerable advance had been made and several thousand prisoners taken, but the German line was unbroken and stronger than ever in its new positions. Therefore that also was a failure.

Winterbourne and Henderson were the only two runners left; and since Evans was in command, Winterbourne was now company runner. The two men sat on their packs in the cellar without a word. Both shook very slightly but continuously with fatigue and shock. Outside the vicious heavies crashed eternally. They started wildly to their feet as a terrific smash overhead brought down what was left of the house above them and crashed into the duplicate cellar next door. A moment later there was another enormous crash and one end of the cellar broke in with falling bricks and a cloud of dust. They rushed out by the steps at the other end, and were sent reeling and choking by another huge black explosion.

They stumbled across to another cellar occupied by what was left of a section, and asked to sleep there since their own cellar was wrecked. Six of them and a corporal sat in silence by the light of a candle, dully listening to the crash of shells.

In a lull they heard a strange noise outside the cellar, first like wheels and then like a human voice calling for help. No one moved. The voice called again. The Corporal spoke :

' Who 's going up ? '

' Mucked if I am,' said somebody ; ' I 've 'ad enough.'

Winterbourne and Henderson simultaneously struggled to their feet. The change from candle-light to darkness blinded them as they peered out from the ruined doorway. They could just see a confused dark mass. The voice came again :

' Help ! for Christ's sake come and help ! '

A transport limber had been smashed by a shell. The wounded horses had dragged it along and fallen outside the cellar entrance. One man had both legs cut short at the knees. He was still alive, but evidently dying. They left him, lifted down the other man and carried him into the cellar. A large shell splinter had smashed his right knee. He was conscious, but weak. They got out his field-dressing and iodine and dripped iodine on the wound. At the pain of burning disinfectant the man turned deadly pale and nearly fainted. Winterbourne found that his hands and clothes were smeared with blood.

Then came the problem of getting the man away to a dressing-station. The Corporal and the four men refused to budge. The shells were crashing continuously outside. Winterbourne started out to get a stretcher and the new stretcher-bearer, groping his way through the darkness. Outside their billet he tripped and fell into a deep shell-hole, just as a heavy exploded with terrific force at his side. But for the fall he must have been blown to pieces. He scrambled to his feet, breathless and shaken, and tumbled down the cellar stairs. He noticed scared faces looking at him in the candle-light. He explained what had happened. The stretcher-bearer jumped up, got his stretcher and satchel of dressings, and they started back. Every shell which exploded near seemed to shake Winterbourne's flesh from his bones.

He was dazed and half-frantic with the physical shock of concussion after concussion. When he got back in the cellar he collapsed into a kind of stupor. The stretcher-bearer dressed the man's wound, and then looked at Winterbourne, felt his pulse, gave him a sip of rum and told him to lie still. He tried to explain that he must help carry the wounded man, and struggled to get to his feet. The stretcher-bearer pushed him back :

'You lie still, mate ; you 've done enough for to-day.'

THE battle on their part of the Front died down into long snarling artillery duels, gas bombardments, fierce local attacks and counter-attacks. Further south it flamed up again with intense preludes of drum-fire. What was left of the Pioneer Company returned to more normal occupations. So far as they were concerned, one great advantage of the battle was that the Germans had been driven from the long slag-hill, and from a large portion of Hill 91. By fierce counter-attacks the Germans regained much of the lost ground on Hill 91, but they never came anywhere near recovering the slag-hill. The ground they had lost further south made that impossible. Consequently, some of the worst features of the salient were at last obliterated, and they were no longer under such close observation or enfiladed by machine-guns.

They had a day's rest, and were then put on the cushy job of building a new track up to the southern fringe of Hill 91 across the old Front lines and No Man's Land. They were outside the range of vision of the German observation posts, and it was two days before the German airplanes discovered them—two days of comparative quiet. Then, of course, they got it hot and strong.

In clearing away the wire they made a number of gruesome discoveries, and examined with great interest the primitive hand-grenades and other weapons of 1914-15 which were lying rusting there in great quantities. Winterbourne took an immense interest in building this track, an interest which puzzled and amused Evans, especially since this was the first time he had ever seen Winterbourne show any enthusiasm for their labours.

' I can't see why you 're so keen on this bally old track,

Winterbourne. It's one of the dullest jobs we've ever had.'

' But surely you can see, sir. We're making something, not destroying things. We're taking down wire, not putting it up ; filling in shell-holes, not desecrating the earth.'

Evans frowned at the phrase ' desecrating the earth.' He thought it pretentious, and with all his obtuseness he had an instinctive resentment against Winterbourne's unspoken but unwavering and profound condemnation of War. Evans had a superstitious reverence for War. He believed in the Empire ; the Empire was symbolised by the King-Emperor ; and the King—poor man !—is always having to dress up as an Admiral or a Field-marshal or a brass-hat of some kind. Navydom and Armydom thereby acquired a mystic importance ; and since armies and navies are obviously meant for War, it was plain that War was an integral part of Empire-worship. More than once he clumsily tried to trap Winterbourne into expressing unorthodox opinions. But, of course, Winterbourne saw him coming miles away, and easily evaded his awkward booby-traps.

' I suppose you're a *republican*,' he said to Winterbourne, who was innocently humming the Marseillaise. ' I don't believe in Republics. Why, Presidents wear evening dress in the middle of the morning.'

Winterbourne nearly burst into a cackle of laughter, but managed to restrain himself. He denied that he was a republican, and admitted with mock gravity that Evans had put his finger on a serious flaw in Republican institutions.

But his joy in constructing the track was short-lived. As they were finishing their second day's work he saw a battery of Field Artillery cross the old No Man's Land

by the road they had built, and then bump its way over
shell-holes to a new position. So even this little bit of
construction was only for further destruction.

They went on to night-work again, and Winterbourne
distinguished himself by pulling out of the ground a dud
shell which the other men refused to touch, in case it went
off. They crouched on the ground while Winterbourne
tugged and strained to get it out, and Evans stood beside
him urging him to go easy. Suddenly Winterbourne
went into a series of gasping chuckles, and in answer to
Evans's questions managed to jerk out that the alleged
shell was a stump of wood with an iron ring round it. The
men returned sheepishly to their work. In reward for his
heroic conduct Winterbourne was allowed to join a gang
who were pulling up real duds embedded in the *pavé* of
the main road, which had become available through the
German retirement. They levered and tugged the shells
up very gingerly, since the oldest duds are liable to
explode if treated roughly. Winterbourne was glad when
that little job was done.

The nightly gas bombardments became worse than
ever, and Winterbourne sometimes spent twelve hours a
day in his gas-mask. They used their respirators so
frequently that a new set had to be issued.

Since Evans was now temporarily in command and had
only Thompson to help him and about forty men available for work, they did only one shift, which Evans
and Thompson took on alternate nights. As company
runner, Winterbourne carried all messages between the
Company and Battalion H.Q. On the other hand, Evans
always let him rest on the nights when he himself was not
on duty. Winterbourne was profoundly thankful for
these nights off. His winter cough, aided perhaps by

microbes communicated by lice, had evolved into a sort of tertian ague. Every third night he had alternate fits of sweating and shivering. It was much pleasanter to lie down even in a damp cellar than to go up the line feeling utterly weak and feverish.

He was sleeping soundly alone in the runners' cellar, oblivious to the zwiing, PHUT, of the gas shells outside, when he was awakened by Henderson, the other surviving runner, who came stumbling down the cellar stairs in the darkness. Winterbourne lit a candle for him. Henderson had just taken off his gas-mask, and stood with rumpled hair and a pale, scared look.

'What's up?' said Winterbourne; 'what's the matter?'

'Thompson's killed.'

'Good Lord! The only other officer! How?'

'Whizz-bang.'

'How did it happen?'

'The Boche put up an attack to-night. Thompson took us off work, and told us to line a trench. He was standing on top, and told me to get into the trench. A whizz-bang burst just beside him. He died in five minutes.'

'O God! Did he say anything?'

'Yes, he was perfectly conscious and calm. He told me how to get the men back. He sent best of luck to Evans and you and the S.M. And he made me take a couple of letters from his pocket to send to his wife and mother. He was horribly mangled—right arm and right leg smashed, ribs broken, and a great tear in the side of his face. He made me promise to make Evans write home that he was shot through the heart and died instantaneously and painlessly.'

'Damn! He was a nice chap. One of the best officers we had.'

The inner gas-curtain was lifted, and Evans's servant stumbled in, taking off his mask.

' Report at once, fighting order, Winterbourne.'

Winterbourne hurriedly put on his boots and puttees, struggled into his equipment, snapped on his mask, and jog-trotted over to the officers' cellar through the now familiar hail of gas shells. He was amazed and distressed and ashamed to find how much his flesh instinctively shrank when a shell dropped close at hand, how great an effort he now needed to refrain from ducking or cowering. He raged at himself, called himself coward, poltroon, sissy, anything abusive he could think of. But still his body instinctively shrank. He had passed into the final period of War strain, when even an air-raid became a terror.

Evans was laboriously writing. The large cellar looked very cellar-like and empty, with one man in place of the six who had lived there less than a fortnight before.

' You know Mr. Thompson 's killed ? '

' Yes, sir. Henderson told me.'

' I can't carry on as a Company by myself with less than forty available men.' Evans spoke bitterly. ' There 's a chit from Division complaining that we are doing far less work than a month ago. They don't seem to know there 's been a battle, and that we 're worn out and reduced to a third our strength.'

He was silent, re-read his despatch, folded it, and handed it to Winterbourne.

' Take this down to Batt. H.Q. I 've marked it Special Urgency. Make them get the Colonel up if he 's asleep. If he questions you, tell him our position. I haven't seen him for three weeks. And refuse to leave without an answer.'

' Very good, sir.'

'And, Winterbourne.'

'Sir?'

'There's another chit here somewhere urging us to get two volunteers for Infantry commissions in each Company. Henderson's going—he's a stout little tyke. The other volunteers are that filthy cook's-mate and the sanitary man. Idiotic. I won't recommend them. But I want you to volunteer. Will you?'

Winterbourne hesitated. He didn't want the responsibility; it was contrary to his notion that he ought to stay in the ranks and in the line, take the worst and humblest jobs, share the common fate of common men. But then, he had consented to be a runner. And then, he was sorely tempted. It meant several months in England, it meant seeing Fanny and Elizabeth again, it meant a respite. He was amazed to find that he didn't want to leave Evans, and suddenly saw that what he had done in the past months had been chiefly done from personal attachment to a rather common and ignorant man of the kind he most despised, the grown-up public-school boy.

'What are you hesitating about?'

'Well, sir,' said Winterbourne whimsically, 'I was wondering how you'd get on without me.'

'*****!' said Evans. 'Besides, at this rate I shan't last much longer. Now, shall I put your name down?'

'Yes, sir.'

He afterwards regretted that 'Yes.'

Evans's sharp note brought an abrupt change in their lives. They exchanged places with one of the other Pioneer companies in a quieter section of the line. Evans marched his forty men down as one platoon, and they passed successively the four platoons of the relieving Company. The men exchanged ironical jibes as they passed.

Their new quarters were a great improvement. They were joined by a Captain, who took nominal command, and two subalterns. But no men. There appeared to be no men available. They lived in shelters and dug-outs in the Reserve line. Winterbourne, Henderson, and two other runners lived in a two-foot shelter just outside the officers' dug-out. Winterbourne was now officially Company runner. He lived one fortnight in the line, and one at Battalion H.Q. The sacking bed at H.Q., the comparative absence of shelling, the better food, the rest, made it seem like paradise. He did not know that his application for a commission had been passed at once, and that he was being looked after.

Two days after they got to their new quarters, in the line, Evans's servant poked his head excitedly into the runners' shelter.

' Winterbourne ! '

' Yes.'

' You 're to come at once. Mr. Evans is sick.'

' Sick ! '

Winterbourne found Evans leaning against the side of the trench, a ghastly green pallor on his face.

' Whatever 's the matter, sir ? '

' Gas. I 've swallowed too much of the beastly stuff. I can't stand it any longer. I 'm going to the dressing-station.'

' Shall I get a stretcher, sir ? '

' No, damn it, I 'll walk down. I can still stand. Take my pack and come along.'

Every few yards Evans had to stop and lean against the trench wall. He heaved, but did not vomit. Winter-bourne offered his arm, but he wouldn't take it. They passed two corpses, rather horribly mutilated, lying on stretchers at the end of the communication trench.

Neither said anything, but Evans was thinking, ' Well, gas is better than that,' and Winterbourne thought, ' How long will it be before some one puts me there ? '

He finally got Evans to the dressing-station, supporting him with his right arm. They shook hands outside.

' You 'll get your commission, Winterbourne.'

' Thanks. Are you all right, sir ? Shall I come down with you further ? '

' No ; go back and report that you left me here.'

' Very good, sir.'

They shook hands again.

' Well, good-bye, old man ; best of luck to you.'

' Good-bye, sir, good-bye.'

He never saw Evans again.

When Evans had gone, Winterbourne's interest in the Company suddenly evaporated. He did not know the new officers, rather disliked the Captain, and of course was not on the same footing with them as he had been with Evans. Henderson left for England to be trained as an officer. Winterbourne felt lonelier than ever. And he realised with disgust and horror that his nerve was gone. His daily trips were really very easy—about a mile and a half, a few gusts of machine-gun bullets and about thirty or forty crumps on the road each way. The Germans had discovered some tanks hidden behind a slag-hill round which he had to pass. They shelled it with heavies. Winterbourne now found that he had to force himself to walk forward to them and through the area where they were bursting. It was worse at night. One night he did what he had never done before when carrying a message —waited ten minutes for the shelling to quiet down.

That ten minutes, curiously enough, saved his life. He heard several shells fall in and around Company H.Q. just

as he came along the trench. One of them had fallen
plump on their fragile shelter and blown it to pieces,
instantly killing the runner, Jenkins, a boy of nineteen,
who was lying there. If Winterbourne had not lingered
that ten minutes on the road, he would inevitably have
been killed too. He felt very guilty about it. Perhaps if
he had come back the boy would have been sent back
with a return message. But no, if there had been a return
message it would have been his job.

He lost his blanket, ground-sheet, and pack. The
runners were transferred to a similar shelter twenty yards
further on. Winterbourne hated to pass the smashed
shelter. He always thought of Jenkins and his absurd
boyish grin. Jenkins had been errand-boy and then
assistant to a grocer in a small provincial town. A most
undistinguished person. He had a solemn respect for
John Bull and its opinions. Otherwise he wasn't solemn
at all, always cracking rather pointless jests, and grinning
his boyish grin, and hardly ever grousing. Winterbourne
regretted him.

At Battalion Headquarters, Winterbourne tried to read,
and found it impossible. He discovered an old number of
The Spectator with an article on Porson, written by a man
he had known. He had to read the article before he
remembered who Porson was, and found himself puzzling
over quite ordinary sentences like a ploughman. He
threw the paper down in despair, and got permission to go
to an estaminet. They had no wine, and spirits were forbidden. He sat there drinking the infamous and harmless French beer, and droning out sentimental songs with
the other Tommies. He got into the habit of bribing
the Q.M.S.'s clerk to give him extra rum. Anything to
forget.

At the end of one of his fortnightly periods at Battalion
H.Q., Winterbourne went as usual to the R.S.M. :

' Winterbourne, D Company runner, returning for
service in the line, sir.'

The R.S.M. turned over some papers, pursing up his
lips :

' Let me see, let me *seeee*. Yes, yes. Yes, yes. Here
we are: 31819 Private Winterbourne, G. Yes. You're
returning to England on Friday for the purpose of proceeding to an Officer Cadet Corps. Report to the Orderly-
room at four (pip emma) on Thursday for your papers,
and draw iron rations from the Q.M.S. Will report to
R.T.O. at Rail Head before eight (ack emma) on Friday,
and will be struck off the strength. Got that ? '

' Yes, sir. Will you give me a chit to show them in the
line, please ? '

' No. To-day 's Wednesday. You 'd better stay here,
and I 'll send up the runner who is taking your place.'

' Very good, sir.'

The boy who was taking Winterbourne's place was
delighted to get the job. He was a quick-witted youth
who had been trained as an elementary-school teacher,
and thanked Winterbourne as if the new job had been his
gift. He was killed by a bullet as he climbed out of the
communication trench with his first message. Winterbourne began to feel as if he had made a pact with the
Devil, so that other men were always being killed in his
stead.

For the remaining two days he was virtually excused
duty. He was allowed to go to the baths each day, and
got himself clean and free from lice. He received
absolutely new underclothes, not the worn, soiled gar-
ments full of dead lice usually issued at the baths ; was
given new puttees and trousers in place of his soiled, torn

ones, and handed in his rent leather jerkin. He had a
sacking bed, and slept twelve hours a night. Already he
was a different being from the dazed and haggard man
of the Hill 91 days.

He wanted very much to go to England, and yet his
chief feeling was that of apathy. Now that his orders
had come, he felt he would just as soon have stopped
where he was. Why prolong the agony? If he
stayed, he would either be hit sooner or later, or
become a battalion runner, a much better and less
anxious job than that of an Infantry subaltern. Still,
it might be worth while, just to see Elizabeth and
Fanny again. . . .

It was hot midsummer weather. He wandered out
along the straight French road, with its ceaseless up and
down of mechanical transport and military traffic. The
Military Police and armed pickets suspiciously turned him
back. He found a little hedgeless field of poppies and
yellow daisies, and sat down there. The heavies were
firing with regular deliberation ; overhead the white
shrapnel bursts pursued an enemy plane ; from the far
distance came a very faint ' claaang ! ' as a shell smashed
into M——. It was so strange to have unmuddy boots,
to sit on grass in the sun and look at wild flowers, to see
one or two undamaged houses, not to be continually on
the alert. He sat with his elbows on his knees and his
doubled fists under his chin, staring in front of him. His
body was rested, but he felt such an apathetic weariness
of mind that he would have been glad to die painlessly
there and then, without ever going back to England,
without ever seeing Elizabeth and Fanny again. His
mind no longer wandered off in long coherent reveries,
but was either vaguely empty or thronged with too vivid
memories. It seemed incredible that only seven months

or so had passed since he had left England—more like
seven years. He felt, not so much self-contempt as self-
indifference. He did not despise George Winterbourne ;
he merely wasn't interested in him. Once he had been
extremely interested in himself and the things he wanted
to do ; now he didn't care, he didn't want to do anything
in particular. Directly the military yoke was lightened
and he was left to himself for a few hours, he was aimless,
apathetic, listless. If he had been told there and then
that he was discharged from the Army and could go, he
wouldn't have known what to do except to stay there and
stare at the poppies and daisies.

The night before he left, the runners and officers'
servants got rum and beer and champagne and made him
drink with them. They exhorted him not to forget his
old pals, and not to be a swine to his men when he was
an officer. He promised, regretting all the time the
subtle difference which was already dividing him from
them. ' Fancy 'avin' to salute old George!' said one of
them. Fancy indeed! He wished so much he had
stayed with them. He drank a good deal, and for the
first time in his life went to bed tight.

He got to Rail Head just before eight, hot and perspiring from a rapid walk in full kit under a July sun.
An immense drum-fire was thundering from the north.
The Division was under orders to proceed there in two
days. There was to be another great offensive at Ypres.
He shuddered, thinking of the showers of bursting metal,
flogging and churning the ground, shearing and rending
human flesh ; the immense concourse of detonations
hammering on human nerves.

The R.T.O. gave him directions and he got into a
waiting train. It was empty, except for a small group of

leave men at the other end.   Glad of a little solitude, he
did not join them.

The German heavies gave him a last amiable farewell.
They began dropping shells on Rail Head.   That sicken-
ing apprehension of the explosion came on him, and he
felt sure that a shell would fall on his carriage before the
train left.   He fought the apprehension savagely, as if the
only thing he wanted to do in life was to repress his fear
reflex.   The shells came over, one at a time, at regular
intervals of a minute.   He listened for them, sweating,
and gripping his rifle.   Either let the train start or get it
over.   The train waited interminably.   ZwiiING, CRASH !
to the right ;   ZwiiING, CRASH !   to the left ;   ZwiiING,
CRASH !   to the right ;   ZwiiING, CRASH !   to the left.   He
sat there alone for thirty-five minutes—thirty-five ZwiiING,
CRASH !   It was somehow more awful than drum-fire, a
more penetrating torture.

At last the train started and puffed slowly out of the
station.   Winterbourne sat quite still, listening to the
crashes growing fainter and fainter as the train gathered
speed.   At last they disappeared altogether in the rattle
of wheels.   In place of the long, slow crawl coming up,
the train clattered along at great speed.   He passed undamaged stations, thronged with French peasants, French
soldiers on leave, and British troops ;   he saw the lovely
Corot poplars and willows shimmering in the sun as they
wavered in the light breeze ;   there were cows in the fields,
and he noticed yellow iris in the wet ditches, and tall,
white hog's-parsley.   A field of red clover and white
daisies made him think of the old days at Martin's Point.
An immense effort of imagination was needed to link
himself now with himself then.   He looked almost with
curiosity at his familiar khaki and rifle—so strange that
ten years later that boy should be a soldier.   Then he

noticed that he had forgotten to sheath his bayonet. It had been fixed so long that he had to wrench it off. There was a little ring of rust round the bayonet boss. He got out his oily rag and anxiously cleaned it. The bayonet sheath was so full of dried mud that he had to clean that too.

At Boulogne he sent a telegram to Elizabeth. The R.T.O. told him to leave all his kit on the quay, and to take only his personal belongings. He slipped off his equipment and laid his rifle beside his dinted helmet, feeling as if he were carrying out some strange valedictory rite. He went on board ship, holding his razor, soap, tooth-brush, comb, and some letters, wrapped in a clean khaki handkerchief. He managed to scrounge a haversack and strap on board.

The troop train from Folkestone to London was filled with leave men and others returned from France. As the train puffed up to the junction, the men crowded to the windows. Girls and women walking in the parallel street, standing in the doorways, leaning out the window, waved pocket-handkerchiefs, cheered shrilly, and threw them kisses. The excited men waved and shouted to them. Winterbourne was amazed at the beauty, the almost angelic beauty, of women. He had not seen a woman for seven months.

It was dark when they got to Victoria, but the station was brilliantly lighted. A long barrier separated a crowd from the soldiers, who thronged out at one end. Here and there a woman threw her arms about the neck of a soldier in a close embrace which at least at that moment was sincere. The women's shoulders trembled with their sobs ; the men stood very still, holding them close a moment, and then drew them away. At once the women made an effort and seemed gay and unconcerned.

Many of the men were proceeding elsewhere, and were not met.

Winterbourne saw Elizabeth standing, in a wide-brimmed hat, at the end of the barrier. Again he was amazed at the beauty of women. Could it be that he knew, that he had dared to touch, so beautiful a creature ? She looked so slender, so young, so exquisite. And so elegant. He was intimidated, and hung back in the crowd of passing soldiers, watching her. She was scanning the faces as they passed ; twice she looked at him, and looked away. He made his way through the throng toward her. She looked at him again carefully, and once more began scanning the passing faces. He walked straight up to her and held out his hands :

' Elizabeth ! '

She started violently, stared at him, and then kissed him with the barrier between them :

' Why, George ! How you 've altered ! I didn't recognise you ! '

WINTERBOURNE had a fortnight's leave before reporting
to his Regimental Depot. He came in for two or three
air raids, and lay awake listening to the familiar bark of
Archies. The bombs crashed heavily. It was very mild
—all over in half an hour. Still, the raids affected him
unpleasantly ; he had not expected them.

He spent his first morning wandering about London by
himself. He was still amazed at the beauty of women,
and was afraid they would be offended by his staring at
them. Prostitutes twice spoke to him, offering him
' Oriental attractions.' He saluted them, and passed on.
The second girl muttered insults, which he scarcely heard.
There seemed to be a great many more prostitutes in
London.

The street paving was badly worn, but looked mar-
vellously smooth and kempt to Winterbourne, accustomed
to roads worn into deep ruts and reft with shell-holes.
He was charmed to see so many houses—all unbroken.
And buses going up and down. And people carrying
umbrellas—of course, people had umbrellas. There was
khaki everywhere. Every third man was a soldier. He
passed some American marines, the advance-guard of the
great armies being prepared across the Atlantic. They
had wide shoulders and narrow hips, strong-looking men ;
each of them had picked up a girl. They walked in
London with the same proprietary swagger that the
English used in France.

A military policeman stopped and roughly asked him
what he was doing. Winterbourne produced his pass.

' Sorry ; thought you was a deserter, old man. Don't
go out without yer pass.'

The second night after his arrival Elizabeth took him
to a Soho restaurant to dine with some of her friends.
Fanny was not there, but the party included Mr. Upjohn,
Mr. Waldo Tubbe, and Reggie Burnside. There were
several people Winterbourne had never met, including a
man who had made a great hit by translating Armenian
poetry—from the French versions of Archag Tchobanian.
He was extremely intellectual and weary in manner, and
took Winterbourne's hand in a very limp way, turning
his head aside with an air of elegant contempt as he
did so.

Winterbourne sat very silent through the meal, nervously rolling bread pills. He was amazed to find how
remote he felt, how completely he had nothing to say.
They talked about various topics he didn't quite follow,
and titteringly gossiped about people he didn't know.
Elizabeth got on wonderfully, chattered with every one,
laughed, and was a great success. He felt very uncomfortable, like a death's-head at a feast. He caught a glimpse
of himself in one of the restaurant mirrors, and thought
he looked ludicrously solemn and distressed.

Over coffee they shifted seats, and one or two people
came and talked to him. Mr. Upjohn dropped clumsily
into the next chair, thrust out his chin, and coughed.

' Are you back in London for good now ? '

' No. I 've a fortnight's leave, and then go to an
Officers' Training Corps.'

' And then will you be in London ? '

' No ; I shall have to go back to France again.'

Mr. Upjohn irritatedly clucked his tongue—tch, tch !

' I mildly supposed you 'd finished soldiering. You
look most grotesque in those clothes.'

' Yes, but they 're practical, you know.'

' What I mean to say is that the most important thing

is that the processes of civilisation shouldn't be interrupted by all this war business.'

' I quite agree. I——'

' What I mean to say is, if you get time, come round to my studio and have a look at my new pictures. Are you still writing for periodicals ? '

Winterbourne smiled.

' No. I 've been rather busy, you know, and in the trenches one—— '

' What I mean to say is, I 'd like you to do an article on my Latest Development.'

' Suprematism ? '

' Good Lord, NO ! I finished with *that* long ago. How extraordinarily ignorant you are, Winterbourne ! No, no. I 'm working at Concavism now. It 's by far the greatest contribution that 's been made to twentieth-century civilisation. What I mean is . . .'

Winterbourne ceased to listen and drank off a full glass of wine. Why hadn't Evans written to him ? Died of the effects of gas, probably. He beckoned to the waiter.

' Bring me another bottle of wine.'

' Yessir.'

' George ! ' came Elizabeth's voice, warning and slightly reproving. ' Don't drink too much ! '

He made no answer, but sat looking heavily at his coffee-cup. Blast her. Blast Upjohn. Blast the lot of them. He drank off another glass of wine, and felt the singing dazzle of intoxication, its comforting oblivion, stealing into him. Blast them.

Mr. Upjohn grew tired of improving the mind of a cretin who hadn't even the wits to listen to him, and slid away. Presently Mr. Waldo Tubbe took his place.

' Well, my dear Winterbourne, I am very happy to see you again, looking so well. The military life has set you

up splendidly.   And Mrs. Winterbourne tells me that at
last you have received a commission.   I congratulate you
—better late than never.'

'Thanks.   But I may not get it, you know.   I 've got
to pass the training-school.'

'Oh, that 'll do you a world of good, a world of good.'

'I hope so.'

'And how did you spend your leisure in France—still
reading and painting ? '

Winterbourne gave a little hard laugh.

'No, mostly lying about, sleeping.'

'I 'm sorry to hear that.   But, you know, if you will
forgive my saying so, I always doubted whether your
Vocation were really toward the arts.   I felt you were
more fitted for an open-air life.   Of course, you 're doing
splendid work now, splendid.   The Empire needs every
man.   When you come back after the Victory, as I trust
you will return safe and sound, why don't you take up life
in one of our colonies, Australia or Canada ?   There 's
a great opening for men there.'

Winterbourne laughed again.

'Wait till I get back, and then we 'll see.   Have a glass
of wine ? '

'No-oeh, thank you, no-oeh.   By the way, what is that
red ribbon on your arm ?   Vaccination ? '

'No ; company runner.'

'A company runner ?   What is that ?   Not runner
away, I hope ? '

And Mr. Tubbe laughed silently, nodding his head up
and down in appreciation of his jest.   Winterbourne did
not smile.

'Well, it might be under some circumstances, if you
knew which way to run.'

'Oh, but our men are so splendid, so splendid, so

unlike the Germans, you know. Haven't you found the Germans mean-spirited ? They have to be chained to their machine-guns, you know.'

' I hadn't observed it. In fact, they 're fighting with wonderful courage and persistence. It 's not much of a compliment to our men to suggest otherwise, is it ? We haven't managed to shift 'em far yet.'

' Ah ! but you must not allow your own labours to distort your perspective. The Navy is the important arm in the War ; that and the marvellous home organisation, of which you, of course, can know nothing.'

' Of course, but still . . .'

Mr. Tubbe rose to move away.

' Delighted to have seen you, my dear Winterbourne. And thank you for all your interesting news from the Front. *Most* stimulating. *Most* stimulating.'

Winterbourne signed to his wife to go, but she ignored the signal, and went on talking earnestly and attentively with Reggie Burnside. He drank another glass of wine, and stretched his legs. His heavy hobnailed boots came in contact with the shins of the man opposite.

' Sorry. Hope I didn't hurt you. Sorry to be so clumsy.'

' Oh, not at all, nothing, nothing,' said the man, rubbing his bruised shin with a look of furious anguish. Elizabeth frowned at Winterbourne, and leaned across to get the bottle. He grabbed it first, poured himself another glass, and then gave it to her. She looked angry at his rudeness. He felt pleasantly drunk, and cared not a damn for any one.

Coming home in the taxi she reproved him with gentle dignity for drinking too much.

' Remember, dear, you 're not with a lot of rough soldiers now. And, please forgive me for mentioning it, but your hands and fingers are terribly dirty—did you forget to wash them ? And you were rather rude to everybody.'

He was silent, staring listlessly out the taxi-cab window. She sighed, and slightly shrugged her shoulders. They did not sleep together that night.

Next morning at breakfast they were both preoccupied and silent. Suddenly George emerged from his reverie.

' I say, what 's happened to Fanny ? She 's not out of town, is she ? '

' No, I don't think so.'

' Why wasn't she at dinner with us last night ? '

' I didn't ask her.'

' You didn't ask her ! Why ever not ? '

Elizabeth looked annoyed at the question, but tried to pass it off lightly.

' I don't see much of her now—Fanny 's so popular, you know.'

' But why don't you see her ? ' Winterbourne pursued clumsily. ' Is anything wrong ? '

' I don't see her because I don't choose to,' replied Elizabeth tartly and decisively.

He made no reply. So, owing to him there was fixed enmity between Fanny and Elizabeth ! His mood of depression deepened, and he went to his room. He picked a book from the shelves at random and opened it— De Quincey's *Murder Considered as One of the Fine Arts*. He had entirely forgotten the existence of that piece of macabre irony, and gazed stupidly at the large-type title. Murder Considered as One of the Fine Arts. How damned appropriate ! He put it down and began to look over his painting materials. Elizabeth had taken his sketching-blocks and paper and all his unused canvases except one. The tubes of paint had gone hard and dry, and his palette was covered with shrunken hard blobs of paint just as he had left it fifteen months before. He carefully cleaned it, as if he might be sent before his Company officer on the charge of having a dirty palette.

He turned up some of his old sketches and looked through them. Could it be that he had composed them? They were undoubtedly signed ' G. Winterbourne.' He looked at them critically, and then slowly tore them up, threw them in the empty fire-grate, struck a match and set fire to them. He watched the paper curl up under the creeping flame, glow dull red, and shrink to black fragile ash. Numbers of his canvases were stacked in little neat piles against the wall. He ran through them rapidly, letting them fall back into place as if they had been cards. He paused when he came upon a forgotten portrait of himself. Had he painted that? Yes, it was signed with his name. Now, when and where had he done it? He held the small canvas in his hands, gazing intently at it with a prodigious effort of memory, but simply could not remember anything about it. The picture was undated, and he could not even remember in which year he had done it. He deliberately put his foot through it, tore away the strips of canvas from the frame and burned them. It was the only portrait of him in existence, since he had always refused to be photographed.

In the line they had been forbidden to keep diaries or to make sketches, since either might be of use to the enemy if they got possession of them. He shut his eyes. In a flash he saw vividly the ruined village, the road leading to M——, the broken desecrated ground, the long slag-hill, and heard the ' claaang ' of the heavies

dropping reverberantly into M——. He went to Elizabeth's room to get a sheet of paper and a soft pencil to
make a sketch of the scene. She had gone out. As he
rummaged at her table, he turned over and could not help
seeing the first lines of a letter in a handwriting unknown
to him. The date was that of the day on which he had
returned to England, and the words he could not help
seeing were : ' DARLING,—What a bore, as you say !
Never mind, the visitation can't last long, and . . .'
Winterbourne hastily covered the letter up to avoid
reading any more.

He went back to his room with paper and pencil and
began to sketch. He was astonished to find that his hand,
once as steady as the table itself, shook very slightly but
perceptibly. The drink last night, or shell-shock ? He
persisted with his sketch, but the whole thing went wrong.
He got tired of blocking lines in and irritatedly rubbing
them out. And yet that scene existed so vividly in his
memory, and he could see exactly how it could be formal-
ised into an effective pattern. But his hand and brain
failed him—he had even forgotten how to draw rapidly
and accurately.

He dropped the pencil and rubber on the half-erased
sketch and went back to Elizabeth's room. She was still
out. The room was very quiet and sunny. The old
orange-striped curtains had gone and were replaced by
long, ample curtains of thick green serge, to comply with
the regulations about lights. There were summer
flowers in the large blue bowl, and fruit on the beautiful
Spanish plate. He remembered how the wasp had come
through the window, like a tiny Fokker plane, almost
exactly three years ago. To his surprise he felt a lump in
his throat and tears coming to his eyes.

A church clock outside chimed three-quarters. He

looked at his wrist-watch—a quarter to one. Better go somewhere and have lunch. He dropped into the first Lyons' Restaurant he came to. The waitress asked if he would like cold corned beef—thanks, he 'd had enough bully beef for the time being. After lunch, he rang up Fanny's flat, but got no reply. He walked in her direction, strolling, to give her time to return home. She was not in. He scribbled a note, asking her to meet him as soon as she could, and then took a bus back to Chelsea, lay down on his bed and fell asleep. Elizabeth came into the room about six and tiptoed out. At seven she woke him. He started up, fully awake at once, mechanically grabbing for his rifle.

' What 's up ? '

Elizabeth was startled by this sudden leap awake, and he had unconsciously jostled her roughly as she bent over him.

' I 'm so sorry. How you started ! I didn't mean to *frighten* you.'

' Oh, it 's all right. I wasn't frightened—used to jumping up in a hurry, you know   What time is it ? '

' Seven.'

' Good Lord ! I wonder what made me sleep that long ! '

' I came to know if you 'd dine with me and Reggie to-night.'

' Is he coming here afterwards ? '

' Of course not.'

' I think I 'll have dinner with Fanny.'

' All right ; just as you please.'

' Can I have the other key to the flat ? '

Elizabeth lied :

' I 'm afraid it 's lost.   But I 'll leave the door unlocked as I did to-day.'

' All right.   Thanks.'

' Au revoir.'

' Au revoir.'

Winterbourne washed, and worked desperately hard
with a nail-brush to get out the dirt deeply and apparently
ineradicably engrained in his roughened hands.   He got
a little more off, but his fingers were still striated with lines
of dirt which made them look coarse and horrible.   He
rang Fanny up from a call-box.

' Hullo.   That you, Fanny ?   George speaking.'

' *Darling !*   How are you ?   When did you get back ? '

' Two or three days ago.   Didn't you get my letter ? '

Fanny lied :

' I 've been away, and only found it when I got back
just now.'

' It doesn't matter.   Listen :   will you dine with me
to-night ? '

' Darling, I 'm *so* sorry, but I simply can't.   I 've an
appointment I simply must keep.   *Such* a bore ! '

Such a bore, as you say !   Never mind ; the visitation
can't last long, and . . .

' It doesn't matter, darling.   When can we meet ? '

' Just a moment : let me look at my memorandum-
book.'

A brief silence.   He could hear a faint voice from
another line crossing his : 'My God!   you say he 's killed !
And he only went back last week ! '

Fanny's voice again :

' Hullo.   Are you there, George ? '

' Yes.'

' To-day 's Wednesday.   I 'm awfully busy for some
reason this week.   Can you see me on Saturday for
dinner ? '

' Must it be as late as Saturday ?   I 've only a fortnight,
you know.'

' Well, you can make it lunch on Friday, if you prefer.
I 'm lunching with somebody, but you can come along.
It 'd be nicer to dine alone together, though, wouldn't it ? '

' Yes, of course.   Saturday, then.   What time ? '

' Seven-thirty, the usual place.'

' All right.'

' Good-bye, darling.'

' Good-bye, Fanny dear.'

He dined alone, and then went to a Circassian Café,
which he had been told was the new haunt of the intelligentsia.   It was very crowded, but he knew nobody
there.   He found a seat, and sat by himself.   Opposite
him at a couple of tables was a brilliant bevy of elegant
young homosexuals, two of them in Staff Officer's
uniform.   They paid no attention to him, after a
supercilious stare, followed by a sneer.   He felt uneasy,
and wondered if he ought to be there in his Tommy's
uniform.   Perhaps the Café was out of bounds.   He
paid for his coffee and left.   After wandering about the
streets for a time, he dropped into a pub in the Charing
Cross Road, and stood beside a couple of Tommies drinking beer.   They were home-service N.C.O.'s—instructors,
he gathered from their conversation, which was all about
some petty way in which they had scored off an officer
who did not know his drill.   Winterbourne thought he
would stand them a drink and get into talk with them, but
his eye fell on a notice which forbade ' treating.'   He
paid and left.

He dropped into a music-hall.   There were numbers
of War songs, very patriotic, and patriotic War scenes with
the women dressed in the flags of the allied nations.   All

references to the superiority of the Allies and the inferiority of the Germans were heartily applauded. A particularly witty scene showed a Tommy capturing several Germans by attracting them with a sausage tied to the end of his bayonet. A chorus of girls in red pre-War military tunics sang a song about how all the girls love Tommy, kicking up their trousered legs in unison, and saluting very much out of unison. There was a Grand Finale of Victory to the tune of :

' When we 've wound up the watch on the Rhine,
Everything will be Potsdam fine.'

At the end of the performance the orchestra played ' God Save the King.' Winterbourne stood rigidly to attention with the other soldiers in the audience.

Eleven o'clock. He thought he would go and sleep at his Club. The place was dimly lighted and empty, except for three or four elderly men, who were earnestly discussing what ought to have been done in the hand of bridge they had just played. There were notices everywhere urging members to be economical with light. The servants were women except the head waiter, a pale little spectacled man of forty-five, who informed Winterbourne that no Club bedrooms were available. They had all been commandeered for War purposes. Winterbourne found it odd to be addressed as ' sir ' again.

' I 've got me papers too, sir,' said the waiter ; ' expect to be called up any day, sir.'

' What category are you ? '

' B 1, sir.'

' Oh, you 'll be all right. Keep telling them you 're a skilled club steward, and you 'll get an Officers' Mess job.'

' Do you really think so, sir ?   My wife worries about
me something dreadful, sir.   She says she 's sure I 'll
catch my death of cold in the trenches.   I 've a very
weak chest, sir, if you 'll pardon me mentionin' it, sir.'

' I 'm sure they won't send you out.'

The little waiter died of double pneumonia in a Base
Hospital early in 1918.   The Club Committee made a
grant of ten pounds to his widow, and agreed that his
name should appear on the Club War Memorial.

Winterbourne felt sleepless.   He was so much accustomed to being alert and awake at night and sleeping by
day, that he found a difficulty in breaking the habit.   He
spent the night aimlessly wandering about the streets and
sitting on Embankment benches.   He noticed that there
were very few occupants of the benches—the War found
work for every one.   Odd, he reflected, that in War-time
the country could spend five million pounds sterling a
day in trying to kill Germans, and that in peace-time it
couldn't afford five million a year to attack its own desti-
tution.   Policemen spoke to him twice, quite decently,
under the impression that he was a leave man without
a bed.   He tried to explain.   One of them was very
fatherly :

' You take my advice, my boy, and go to the Y.M.C.A.
They 'll give yer a bed cheap.   I 've got a boy your age
in the trenches meself.   Now, say you was my boy.   I
wouldn't 'ave 'im goin' with none of these London street
women.   'E 's a good boy, 'e is.   An' they 've treated 'im
cruel, they 'ave.   'E 's been in France nearly two year,
and never 'ad any leave.'

' No leave in nearly two years !   How extraordinary ! '

' No, not even after 'e was in orspital.'

' What was he in hospital with ? '

' 'E wrote us it was pneumonia, but we believe 'e was wounded and didn't want to fret us, because he wrote afterwards it was pleurisy.'

' Do you happen to know the number of his Base Hospital ? '

' Yes, Number XP.'

Winterbourne smiled sadly and cynically ; he knew that was a venereal disease hospital. Pay was stopped while a man was under treatment, and he lost his right to leave. Winterbourne determined not to undeceive the policeman.

' How long is it since he came out of hospital ? '

' Ten months or more.'

' Oh, well, he 'll certainly get leave before Christmas.'

' D' you think so ? Reely ? 'E 's such a good boy, good-lookin' and well set-up. P'raps you 'll see 'im when you go back. Tom Jones. Gunner Tom Jones.'

Winterbourne smiled again at the thought of looking for Tom Jones in the swarming and scattered thousands of the Artillery. But he said :

' If I meet him, I 'll tell him how much you 're looking forward to seeing him.'

He pressed half a crown in the policeman's hand, to drink the health of Tom and himself. The policeman touched his helmet and called him ' sir.'

He had breakfast at a Lockhart's—kippers and tea—and washed in an underground lavatory. He got back to the flat about ten. Unthinkingly he went into Elizabeth's room. She and Reggie were having breakfast in dressing-gowns. Winterbourne apologised almost abjectly, and went to his own room. He threw off the boots from his aching feet and lay down clothed. In ten minutes he was fast asleep.

The meeting with Fanny was somehow a failure.   She
was extremely gay and pretty and well-dressed and charming, and talked cheerily at first, and then valiantly against
his awkward silences.   Winterbourne did not know why
he felt so awkward and silent.   He seemed to have nothing
to say to Fanny, and his mind appeared to have become
sluggish—he missed half her witty sayings and clever
allusions.   It was like being up for oral examination and
continually making silly mistakes.   Yet he was very fond
of Fanny, very fond of her, just as he was very fond of
Elizabeth.   And yet he seemed to have so little to say to
them, and found it so hard to follow their careless intellectual chatter.   He had tried to tell Elizabeth some
of his War experiences.   Just as he was describing the
gas bombardment and the awful look on the faces of men
gassed, he noticed her delicate mouth was wried by a
suppressed yawn.   He stopped abruptly, and tried to
talk of something else.   Fanny was sympathetic, but he
could see he was boring her too.   Of course he was
boring her.   She and other people got more than enough
of the War from the newspapers and everything about
them ; they wanted to forget it, of course, they wanted
to forget it.   And there was he, dumb and dreary and
khakied, only awaking to any appearance of animation
when he talked of the line after drinking a good deal.

He took Fanny home in a taxi, and held her hand,
gazing silently in front of him.   At the door of her flat he
kissed her :

' Good-night, Fanny dearest.   Thank you so much for
having dinner with me.'

' Aren't you coming in ? '

' Not to-night, dear.   I'm dreadfully sleepy—bit tired,
you know.'

' Oh, all right.   Good-night.'

' Good-night, darl—— '

The last syllable was cut off by the sharp closing of the flat door.

Winterbourne walked back to Chelsea. The street lamps were very dim. For the first time in his life he saw the stars plainly above Piccadilly. In the King's Road he heard the warning bugles for an air raid. He got into bed, extinguished the light, and lay there listening, wide awake. To his shame he found the shell-fear come back as the Archies opened up, and he started each time he heard the thud of a bomb. They came closer, and one crashed in the next street. He found he was sweating.

Elizabeth did not get back until three. Reggie and she had taken shelter in the Piccadilly Hotel. Winterbourne was still awake when she came in, but did not call to her.

His leave came to an end, and he spent five weeks of vague routine at his depot. He hated coming back to barrack-room life, and did not like the men he was with. They were all Expeditionary men, but strangely different from what they were in the line. Most of the comradeship had gone ; they were selfish, rather malicious to each other, and servilely flattered the N.C.O.'s who could get them passes. They seemed to think about nothing except getting passes out, so that they could meet girls or go to pubs. They grumbled ceaselessly. Some of them occasionally told hair-raising War stories, which Winterbourne thought quite probable, though he refused to accept their evidence as conclusive. He always remembered one story, or rather episode, related by a Sergeant in the Light Infantry :

' We 'ad a bloody awful time on the Somme. I shan't forget some of the things I saw there.'

' What things ? ' asked Winterbourne.

' Well, one of our orfficers laid out there wounded, and we see a German run up with one of those stick-bombs, pull the string, and stick it under the orfficer's head. 'E was wounded in both arms, and couldn't move. So 'e 'ad five seconds waitin' for his 'ead to be blowed off by that bomb sizzlin' under 'is ear. We 'adn't time to get to 'im. Some one shot the German, and then some o' our chaps picked up a wounded German orfficer and threw 'im alive into a burning ammunition dump. 'E screamed something 'orrible.'

From the depot he was sent to the Officers' Training Camp with two days' leave. He managed to get Fanny and Elizabeth to meet and lunch with him on the day he left. They both saw him off from Waterloo, and then parted outside the station.

The months of dreary training in the cold, dreary camp dragged by. He had two days' leave in the middle of the course, then ' passed out ' as an officer, and was sent on leave again, with orders to wait until he received official notice of his appointment.

Elizabeth and Fanny both admired the cut and material of his cadet's uniform, which was exactly like an officer's except that it bore no badges of rank and that he did not wear the shoulder-strap of his Sam Browne belt. He looked ever so much smarter in his new officer's clothes, with the little blue chevron, marking service overseas, sewed on his left sleeve. They both quite took to him again, and during his month's leave gave him a good time. Fanny thought him still an excellent lover. Only, instead of gay and amusing talk ' in between,' he sat heavily silent, or drank and talked about that boring, awful War. It was such a pity—he used to be such a charming companion.

This leave came to an end too. He was gazetted, and went to his new regimental depot, situated in wooden huts on a desolate heath in the North of England, a place swept by rain and wind, and deadeningly chill in the wet winter days. The other officers were sharply divided into two sections or sects. Wounded survivors from the early days of the War, now on Permanent Home Service; and the newly-gazetted officers, with a sprinkling of wounded on Temporary Home Service. They ate in one large mess-room, but had two common rooms, which seemed to be tacitly reserved for each of the two groups, who scarcely ever mingled. Only the cadets from Sandhurst were admitted into the more exclusive room.

There was very little to do—parading with the Company, inspection, a little drill, orderly officer occasionally. There were so many new officers waiting to go overseas that the quarters were uncomfortably crowded, and there seemed to be almost as many officers as men on parade. He got the impression that infantry subalterns were cheap as stinking fish.

At last he got his orders to proceed overseas—France again, though he had hoped for Egypt or Salonika. He had two more days of leave and a quarrel with Elizabeth, who found him writing a loving note to Fanny on the morning he arrived. He went off in dudgeon and spent the time with Fanny. He saw Elizabeth again on the afternoon of the day before he left, and patched matters up with her. She was now furiously jealous of his spending nights with Fanny, but 'forgave' him. She said that the War had affected his mind so much that he did not know what he was doing; and anyway, as he was going out

again at once, they might as well be friends. They
kissed, and he went off to keep a dinner engagement
with Fanny.

His train left at seven the next morning. He got up at
five-thirty, and kissed Fanny, who woke up and sleepily
offered to get him coffee. But he made her lie still,
dressed hastily, made himself some coffee, found he could
not eat anything, and went back to the bedroom. Fanny
had fallen asleep again. He kissed her very tenderly and
gently, not to wake her ; and softly let himself out of
the flat. He had difficulty in finding a taxi, and was
horribly worried lest he should miss his train and be
suspected of overstaying leave. He got to the platform
one minute before the train started. There was no
porter to carry his large valise, but he managed to get
into a carriage just as the train started. It was a
Pullman, so crowded with officers that he hadn't room
to sit down, and had to stand all the way to Dover.
Most of them had newspapers. The news of the crushing defeat of the Fifth Army was just coming through.
They were being sent out to replace losses. He
thought of something which had happened the night
before. . . .

Fanny had insisted on his coming with her for a couple
of hours to a party of the intelligentsia given by some one
with chambers near the Temple. As they passed
Charing Cross Station, Winterbourne bumped into a man
from his own Company who had just arrived by the
leave train.

' Go on with the others, Fanny dear. I 'll catch you
up. Anyway, I 've got the address.'

He turned to Corporal Hobbs, and said :

' Are you still with the old lot ? '

' No ; I left 'em in November. Got trench feet at

Ypres. I was supposed to be court-martialled, but that was washed out. I 've got a job at the Base now.'

' You 're lucky.'

' You 've heard the news, I s'pose ? '

' No ; what ? '

' Well, we heard there 's a big surprise attack on the Somme. We 're retiring, and our old Division is s'posed to have copped it badly—smashed to pieces, the R.T.O. said.'

' Good God ! '

' I think it must be true. All leave 's stopped. I just managed to get away before the order came. There were only about ten men on the boat. Lucky for me I went down early.'

' Well, so long, old man.'

' I see you 're an officer now.'

' Yes, I 'm just going out again.'

' Best of luck to you.'

' Best of luck.'

He found the man's chambers. There were about ten people present. Winterbourne knew some of them. They had also heard the news of the battle through a man in Whitehall, and were discussing it.

' It 's a bad defeat,' he said. ' I 'm told that the highest authorities think it adds another year to the war and will cost at least three hundred thousand men.'

He said it carelessly, as if it were a matter of casual importance. Winterbourne heard them constantly using the phrase ' three hundred thousand men,' as if they were cows or pence or radishes. He walked up and down the large room apart from the others, thinking, no longer listening to their chatter. The phrase ' Division smashed to pieces' rang in his brain. He wanted to seize the people in the room, the people in authority, every one not directly in the War, and shout to them : ' Division smashed to pieces ! Do you know what that means ? You must stop it, you 've got to stop it ! Division smashed to pieces ! ' . . .

WINTERBOURNE listened intently. Yes, it was! He turned to his runner :

'Did you hear that, Baker ? '

'Hear what, sir ? '

'Listen.'

A plane droned gently and distantly in the still air, and then very faintly but distinctly :

Claaang !

'There ! Did you hear it ? '

'No, sir.'

'It was one of the heavies falling into M——. You 'll hear them soon enough. But come on, we must hurry. We 've a long way to go if we 're to get back before dark.'

A year, almost to the day, after he had gone into M—— for the first time, Winterbourne was returning to it as an officer in command of a company.

From London he had proceeded direct to Etaples, where he remained for several days under canvas on the sandy slopes among the pines. Large numbers of officers were being sent out, and they had to sleep four to a tent. Winterbourne thought this a luxurious allotment of space, but the other three subalterns, who had never been to France before, complained that there was not enough room for their camp-beds and that they had to sleep in their flea-bags. Winterbourne had not troubled to bring a camp-bed, knowing how few opportunities there would be to use it.

There was very little to do in Etaples, even with the more extended opportunities of an officer. They messed in a large, draughty marquee, but there was a camp cinema where he spent part of each evening. There were numbers of women at the Base, and he noticed that some of them were pregnant. Apparently there was no attempt at concealment ; but then the birth-rate was declining rapidly in England, and babies were urgently needed for the Next War. He observed that the cemetery had doubled in size since he had last seen it from the train a few months before. That Ypres offensive must have been very costly. Such acres of wooden crosses, the old ones already battered and weather-stained, the new ones steadily gaining on the dunes. And now there was this smashing defeat on the Somme. Haig had issued his back-to-the-wall Order, there was unity of Allied command under Foch, and America had been frantically petitioned to send reinforcements immediately. And still the front daily yielded under the pressure of repeated German attacks. It looked like being a longer War than ever.

At Etaples he was allotted to the 2/9th Battalion of the Foddershires, and left to join them with about fifteen other subalterns, most of whom had never been in the line. He found the battalion on rest in a small village about twenty miles behind M——. They belonged to one of the Divisions which had been smashed to pieces, and the battalion had suffered severely, losing most of its officers (including the Colonel) and the greater part of its effectives. The new Colonel was an ex-regular Corporal who had obtained a commission early in the War, and by dexterity and martinet methods had risen to the rank of Acting Lieutenant-Colonel. He was not a fighting soldier, but an expert trainer. He had the bullying manner of the barrack-square drill-instructor, and his method of ' training' was to harass every officer and man under his command from morning to night. After a week's 'rest' under this commander, Winterbourne felt nearly as tired as if he had been in the line. The subalterns who had never been under fire were exhausted and dismayed.

However, it must in justice be admitted that Colonel Straker was faced with appalling difficulties, and Winterbourne would have sympathised with the man if he had not so obviously been trying to push his own professional career in the Army at the expense of every one he commanded. The old battalion was a wreck. It had four of its officers left, one of whom was the Adjutant ; a few of its old N.C.O.'s and a sprinkling of men were there, mostly signallers and headquarters men. Not a single one of the Lewis gunners remained. Two companies had been captured, and the remainder had fought a way out with terrific losses. The gaps had been filled chiefly by raw, half-trained boys of eighteen and a half, many of whom were scared stiff by the mere thought of going into the trenches. To secure an adequate number of N.C.O.'s the Colonel had to promote nearly every man who had any experience of the War, even transport drivers who could scarcely write their names.

Winterbourne had expected to go into the line at first as a supernumerary officer under instruction, and to pick up his duties by watching others and always going about with them. To his dismay, but also a certain amount of flattered vanity, he found himself immediately appointed as acting commander of B Company. But it was inevitable. Several of the new officers were mere boys ; others volunteers from the Army Service Corps—perfectly competent at their own job but quite ignorant of trench warfare ; and others again were 'keymen' from business houses, reluctantly yielded to the 'combings out' of 1917. Winterbourne had four subalterns under him—

Hutchison, Cobbold, Paine, and Rushton. They were all good fellows, but three of them had seen no service whatever, and the fourth had been in Egypt only.

When Winterbourne inspected his company on the first day, his heart sank within him. He felt it was monstrous to send these scared-looking boys into the line without a proper stiffening of more experienced men. It would have been far better to spread them out. They cleaned their buttons perfectly, drilled very neatly, turned right or left with an imitation Guards stamp, and trembled when an officer spoke to them. But they were mighty raw stuff for the job ahead of them. Winterbourne thought of his own greenness when he had first gone into the line, and his heart sank lower as he thought of his own utter inexperience as an officer. He had a very sketchy idea of how a company was run in the line. Of course, he had heard and carried orders, and had been roughly schooled in company organisation—on paper— at the Cadet School. But that was very different from assuming the responsibility for a hundred-odd men, most of them frightened boys who had never seen any but practice trenches and never heard a shell burst. Well, the only thing was to carry on, and do his best. . . .

The Division was to take over part of the M——— sector from the Canadian Army Corps. Winterbourne had to occupy part of the Reserve line just to the left of M———. The four company commanders with their runners were sent on ahead in a lorry to reconnoitre the positions and arrange details of 'taking over.' The Colonel particularly impressed upon Winterbourne the necessity for obtaining and carefully reading the written instructions for defence which would be with the officer he was relieving.

They were to have met Canadian guides at a given rendezvous, but the guides were not there. Winterbourne, who could have found his way to M—— in the blackest darkness, and who had twenty times passed up and down the trench he was to occupy, decided to push on. The other three, mistrusting him, stayed. He set out with Baker, his servant and runner. Owing to the shortage of men, the officers' servants had to act as runners, with the result that they performed both jobs abominably. Baker had been allotted to Winterbourne by the despotic Colonel, who interfered in the minutest details and then held the company commander responsible for everything which went wrong. Thus he was in a position to take credit for every success and push off the responsibility for failure on some one else.

Winterbourne would certainly not have chosen Baker for himself, and wondered what possible caprice of the Colonel had forced the boy on him. He was a decent enough lad—a milliner's delivery boy—but timid, unintelligent, and lazy. Baker seemed to think that he had performed all his duties as a runner if he followed Winterbourne so closely that he continually trod on his officer's heels.

They passed many places familiar to Winterbourne—the cemetery (now much enlarged), the ruined village (now still more ruined), the long slag-hill, Southampton Row. Nothing had changed, except to become a little more desolate and smashed. He noticed that several large shells had fallen in the cemetery that morning or the night before, digging up the graves violently, scattering bones and torn blankets and broken crosses over the other graves. He turned in for five minutes, and walked down the long row containing the graves of his Pioneer companions. He stood a couple of minutes at Thompson's grave. A shell splinter had knocked the cross crooked. He set it straight.

Winterbourne found the trench easily enough, and asked the first Canadian sentry for Company Head-quarters. The man was leaning very negligently on the parapet, chewing gum. Winterbourne, accustomed to perpetual ' sir-ing ' and heel-clicking and general ser-vility, was almost shocked when the man very casually jerked his thumb over his left shoulder without saying a word, and returned thoughtfully to his gum-chewing. He found the company commander, a Major, demo-cratically sitting in the trench on a double-seated latrine, talking humorously to one of his men. The British always had separate latrines for officers.

Winterbourne enjoyed this hugely, and liked the Canadians. They at once invited him to whisky high-balls and bridge. He managed to evade this, and then explained his own situation ; asked for the written orders of defence and to see all the positions. The Canadian officer stared and said they had no written instructions.

' Well, what do you do if you 're attacked ? '

' I guess you 'd form a defensive flank—if they ever got past the machine-gunners in M——.'

The Canadian officer walked Winterbourne round the positions. He was bareheaded—strictly against orders —and his men greeted him as he passed with friendly nods and an occasional brief remark. Winterbourne noticed that they did not wait for him to speak first, and did not call him ' sir.' He reflected with amuse-ment that the Canadians were easily the crack troops of the British armies, and were sent into all the hardest fighting. And yet they didn't even say ' sir ' to an officer !

This meeting with the Canadians was probably the
last piece of enjoyment or tranquillity that Winterbourne
ever had.   From the moment he went back to his own
battalion his life became one long harassed nightmare.
He was deluged with all sorts of documents requiring
information and statistics he was totally unable to furnish.
The blunders, the mistakes, the negligences of his inexperienced men were legion, and all were visited upon
him by the martinet Colonel.   For days and weeks he
got scarcely any sleep, and never once even took his boots
off.   He had continually to be up and down the trench,
especially during the periodic six days in the Front line,
and even in Support.   He spent hours a day answering
idiotic written questions brought by weary runners, and
trying to puzzle out minute and unnecessary orders.   He
was always being told to report to Battalion Headquarters,
where he was savagely attacked and reprimanded for the
most piffling and unimportant errors.   He went on patrol
himself, contrary to orders, to make sure that at least one
patrol a night was properly done—and was severely
reprimanded for that.   The boys, suddenly released from
button-polishing and saluting and drill (which they had
been taught to consider all-important), became deplorably
slack in important matters.   They lost portions of their
equipment, dropped their ammunition, never knew their
orders as sentries, went to sleep on sentry duty, shivered
when ordered to go on patrol, cried when put in listening-
posts in No Man's Land, littered up the trench with
paper, bully-beef tins, and fragments of food, urinated in
the trenches, and ' forgot ' perpetually everything they
were told.   While Winterbourne was at one end of his
section of trench, desperately and sweatingly trying to get
some sort of order and sense into them, others were
committing all sorts of military abominations at the other

end. It was useless to 'take their names' for punishment,
especially as there aren't many punishments as bad as
being in the line. One day he did exasperatedly make
the Sergeant-major 'take their names,' and by night-fall
found he had collected forty-two. Ludicrous. The
N.C.O.'s gave the job up in despair and let things drift.

He found most of the recruits were hopelessly slow in
getting on their gas-masks, and appeared to be in such a
state of hebetude that they did not realise that gas was
dangerous. They did preposterous things. They would,
for instance, entirely abandon a Lewis-gun post to get
their dinners. It was ten days before Winterbourne
discovered this. The subalterns had seen it, of course,
but had not known that they ought to report it. Winterbourne 'ran' the responsible N.C.O. as an example. He
'ran' a boy for sleeping on sentry duty, and then washed
out the charge when he reflected that the poor wretch
might be shot for so serious a military crime. His Front
line positions were an exhausting nightmare, too. His
front was over five hundred yards. He had an outpost
line of four listening and observation posts with a section
in each. Three hundred yards further back he had his
main defence line and his own headquarters. Behind
that he had various isolated Lewis-gun positions. All
these were imposed upon him in spite of his protests.
The defence scheme might be all very well on paper, and
might have worked out with experienced troops, but it
was hopeless under these peculiar circumstances. He
realised after a couple of nights in the Front line that
under any determined attack it would be impossible for
him to hold his positions for ten minutes. He urged this
on the Colonel, begging that the dispositions might be
temporarily revised and the men brought more closely
together under his own eyes. He was told that he was

incompetent and not fit to be a lance-corporal. Winterbourne sarcastically replied that some people are born
corporals and some are not. He offered to resign his
command, and was ordered to continue it under threat of
immediate arrest and court-martial for negligence and
disobeying orders in the face of the enemy. Knowing
how easily a court-martial can be 'cooked,' Winterbourne
unwillingly carried on.

Most fortunately, he was not at first attacked, but he
lost several men. Two were wounded on a ration party,
having lost contact and wandered about half the night.
One was shot through the neck by a fixed rifle, although
Winterbourne had thrice ordered every N.C.O. to warn
the men about it. At stand-to one morning the Germans bombarded them with mustard-gas shells. Winterbourne had warned them of the gas until he was sick
of doing so. Two mustard shells fell just outside the
parapet of a fire-step with six men on it. They ducked
down when the shells burst, and then stood stupidly
looking at the bright yellow shell-hole, wondering what
the funny smell was. Three of them were gassed, and
two died.

Winterbourne spent most of each night plodding up
and down his immense area of trenches to see that every
one was at his post. After dawn one morning, instead of
trying to snatch an hour's sleep, he went up to inspect his
listening-posts, feeling an uneasy intuition about them.
There were four, about a hundred yards apart, isolated
in what had once been the Front line. At the third
listening-post he found six rifles leaning against the trench
and no men. They had been captured by a silent raiding
party in broad daylight ! Probably all asleep. Winterbourne was furious, sent his runner back for another
section, and remained on guard himself. The runner

came back timidly after an interminable time, and said the Sergeant wouldn't come. Winterbourne didn't want the other posts to know that one had been captured, fearing a panic. It was useless to leave the runner on guard ; he would simply have waited until Winterbourne's back was turned and have run to the other posts and spread an alarmist report. Winterbourne hurried back, and found that the runner had delivered such a garbled and incoherent message that the Sergeant had been utterly unable to understand, and had sent him back for precise orders. Of course, the Colonel put all the responsibility upon Winterbourne, and threatened him again with a court-martial. Winterbourne protested and they had a furious row ; after which the Colonel redoubled his persecutions. When they went out for four days' 'rest' after their first three weeks in the line, Winterbourne felt more exhausted and depressed than he would have believed possible. He saw that the men got into their billets, after infinite tramplings and shoutings in the darkness, and fell on to a sacking bed. He slept for fourteen hours.

Of course, Winterbourne had taken all this far too tragically and responsibly. The situation happened to be one which most disastrously fed his 'worry' neurosis. A bitterly humorous destiny seemed intentionally to involve him in circumstances which rent his mind to pieces and exhausted his body—unnecessarily. It was a misfortune, due possibly to the fact that the initial of his name made him come towards the end of a list, that he was sent to a battalion so raggedly composed and so naggingly commanded. We passed out almost together at the Cadet School ; but where everything ran comparatively easily and smoothly for me, all went wrong with

him.   He brooded incessantly and saw all things in terms
of the bleakest despair—the collapse of his own life, his
present situation, the continued retirement of the Allied
Armies which seemed to promise an indefinite continua-
tion of the War, his feeling that even if he came out alive
he would never be able to rebuild his life.   It was unlucky to go straight back to M——, which had such tragic
associations for him and made it doubly hard to repress
shell-shocked nerves.   His state of mind, what with
sleeplessness and worry and shock and ague—which came
back as soon as he was in the line again—and physical
exhaustion and inhibited fear, almost fringed dementia,
and he would have collapsed but for his strength of will
and pride.   He was a wrecked man, swept along in the
swirling cataracts of the War.

The days passed into weeks, the weeks into months.
He moved through impressions like a man hallucinated.
And every incident seemed to beat on his brain Death,
Death, Death.   All the decay and death of battlefields
entered his blood and seemed to poison him.   He lived
among smashed bodies and human remains in an infernal
cemetery.   If he scratched his stick idly and nervously
in the side of a trench, he pulled out human ribs.   He
ordered a new latrine to be dug out from the trench, and
thrice the digging had to be abandoned because they came
upon terrible black masses of decomposing bodies.   At
dawn one morning when it was misty he walked over the
top of Hill 91, where probably nobody had been by day
since its capture.   The heavy mist brooded about him
in a strange stillness.   Scarcely a sound on their immediate front, though from north and south came the
vibration of furious drum-fire.   The ground was a desert
of shell-holes and torn rusty wire, and everywhere lay

skeletons in steel helmets, still clothed in the rags of sodden khaki or field grey. Here a fleshless hand still clutched a broken rusty rifle; there a gaping, decaying boot showed the thin, knotty foot-bones. He came on a skeleton violently dismembered by a shell explosion; the skull was split open and the teeth lay scattered on the bare chalk; the force of the explosion had driven coins and a metal pencil right into the hip-bones and femurs. In a concrete pill-box three German skeletons lay across their machine-gun with its silent nozzle still pointing at the loop-hole. They had been attacked from the rear with phosphorus grenades, which burn their way into the flesh, and for which there is no possible remedy. A shrunken leather strap still held a battered wrist-watch on a fleshless wrist-bone. Alone in the white curling mist, drifting slowly past like wraiths of the slain, with the far-off thunder of drum-fire beating the air, Winterbourne stood in frozen silence and contemplated the last achievements of civilised men.

A raiding party was sent out from his front. He watched the box barrage from the Front line. The Germans filled the night with Verey lights and coloured rockets. Their artillery and trench-mortars and machine-guns retaliated fiercely. Smoke and gas drifted across. After interminable waiting the officer and three of the men staggered back, bleeding, blackened with smoke, their clothes torn to pieces on the wire. The raid had failed.

A company of gas experts came up from the Base, and sent over some thousands of Stokes mortars loaded with a heavy concentration of poison gas. As soon as the last mortar was fired they were in a fearful hurry to get away. The German artillery retaliation smashed their trenches.

Next morning, Winterbourne watched through glasses the Germans carrying out their dead on stretchers.

A British airplane fell in No Man's Land. Winterbourne saw the pilot, who was still alive, struggle to get from the wreckage. An enemy machine-gun was turned on him, and he fell limp across the side of the cockpit. The plane was smashed to pieces by British heavies to prevent the Germans from obtaining the model.

They shifted to another part of the line. The company were out in No Man's Land in the darkness strengthening their shattered wire against a threatened attack. Suddenly half a mile of German front leaped into a line of flame. There was a whistling roar of projectiles, and a thousand gas-containers crashed to the ground all about them. Men were killed outright by direct hits, and wounded by pieces of flying metal. Every man who took more than two breaths of the deadly concentration was doomed. All that night and far into the misty dawn the stretchers went down the communication trench carrying inert figures with horrible foam on their mouths.

The German attacks spent their force, and the huge Allied counter-attacks began. The starving German armies were hurled back to the Hindenburg Line, their impregnable defence. The Canadians miraculously stormed the Drocourt-Quéant switch line.

Winterbourne was back on the Somme, that incredible desert, pursuing the retreating enemy. They came up the Bapaume-Cambrai road by night, and bivouacked in holes scratched with entrenching tools in the side of a sandy bank. The wrecked countryside in the pale moonlight was a frigid and motionless image of Death. They spoke in whispers, awed by the immensity of desolation. By day the whole landscape was covered with the debris left by the broken German armies. Smashed tanks, guns with their wheels broken, stood out like fixed wrecks in the unmoving ocean of shell-holes. The whole earth seemed a litter of overcoats, shaggy leather packs, rifles, water-bottles, gas-masks, steel helmets, bombs, entrenching tools, cast away in the panic of flight. By night the sky glowed with the flames of burning Cambrai, with the black hump of Bourlon Hill silhouetted against them.

They drove the Germans from Cambrai, and pressed on from village to village, constantly shelled and harassed by machine-gun fire from their rearguard. The German machine-gunners, fragments of the magnificent armies of the early War years, died at their posts. The demoralised German infantry surrendered wholesale.

For three days in succession Winterbourne's company formed the advance-guard, and he led it in the darkness over unknown ground, by compass-bearing, in a kind of dazed delirium. Pressing on through falling shells in the blank night, with the ever-present dread of falling into a machine-gun ambush, became an agony. They fought their way into inhabited villages, which had been held by the Germans for over four years. The terrified people crouched in cellars or ran distractedly into the fields. They took the village of F——, after a brief but fierce bombardment, an hour after dawn. The roads leading in and out were encumbered with dead Germans, smashed transport, the contorted bodies of dead horses. Dead German soldiers lay about the village street, which was cluttered with fallen tiles and bricks. In a garden a war-demented peasant was digging a grave to bury his wife, who had been killed by a shell-burst. In the ruined village school. Winterbourne picked up a book—it was Pascal's *Thoughts on Christianity*.

Part of Cambrai had been levelled to the ground in 1914, and stood a melancholy monument of neatly-piled wreckage. Part of the remainder was burned. In the undestroyed streets many houses had been looted. The furniture had been smashed, pictures and photographs torn from the walls, cushions ripped open with bayonets, curtains slashed down, carpets gashed into rags. The whole mass of desecrated objects had been flung into the centre of the floor, after which the Germans had urinated and dropped their excrement upon it. Winterbourne gazed into a dozen houses which had been treated in this way. The villages beyond Cambrai had not been sacked, but were utterly filthy and swarming with buzzing legions of flies. Isolated cottages had sometimes been completely gutted of their contents. In one place Winterbourne found an emaciated Frenchwoman and two starved children living in a cottage with nothing but straw— literally nothing but straw—in the place. He gave them his iron rations and twenty francs. The woman took them with a dull hopelessness.

They were approaching the Belgian border. On the evening of the 3rd of November, Winterbourne with about twenty men rushed into the village of K——, just as the Germans hastily retreated from the other end. He had been ordered to occupy the place if possible, and to arrange billets. He lodged his Company, placed guards and pickets, and then went through the cellars. The Germans were experts in placing booby-traps which would explode if carelessly moved, and Winterbourne did not know whether there might not be men concealed in the cellars to take them unawares. He went down into cellar after cellar with his electric torch, and was soon reassured. The Germans had fled in such haste that they had left their rifles and equipment in several cellars. The floors were strewn with straw. On a table he found a half-finished letter, abandoned in the middle of a sentence. In another a large black dog lay dead—its owner had killed it with a bullet rather than leave it to possible ill-treatment.

The Colonel explained over a map the dispositions for the coming battle. The conference of officers took notes of the orders, which were very elaborate, but precise and clear. It was nearly half-past three when they had finished, and zero hour was six thirty. Winterbourne had been on foot since five the morning before. His eyes smarted with lack of sleep, and his mind was so dulled that he could scarcely comprehend and write down his orders. He mis-spelled words as he scrawled down notes in shaking, deformed handwriting. He puzzled a long time over map-references, and irritated the Colonel by repeatedly asking questions.

They had an hour or so before they moved out to their battle positions. The other officers hurried away to snatch a little sleep. Winterbourne felt utterly sleepy, but quite unable to sleep. The thought of another battle, even with the dispirited and defeated German rearguard, filled him with shrinking dread. How face another barrage ? He tried to write letters to Fanny and Elizabeth, but his mind kept wandering away and he could not collect his thoughts sufficiently to string together a few banal sentences. He sat on a chair brought him by his servant, with his head in his hands, staring at the straw and the dead black dog. He had only one thought—

peace.   He must at least have peace.   He was at the very
end of his endurance, had used up the last fraction of his
energy and strength.   He wished he was one of the
skeletons lying on Hill 91, an anonymous body among
the corpses lying outside in the street.   He had not even
the courage to shoot himself with his revolver ;   and
added that last grain of self-contempt to his despair.

They assembled by platoons in the village street, and
each officer marched off in silence to his allotted position.
Winterbourne followed with his little knot of Company
Headquarters, and saw that each platoon was in its proper
place.   He shook hands with each officer.

' Quite sure about your orders and objective ? '

' Yes.'

' Good-bye.'

' Oh, make it *au revoir.*'

' Good-bye.'

Winterbourne returned to his own position and waited.
He looked at his luminous wrist-watch.   Six twenty-five.
Five minutes to zero hour.   The cold November night
was utterly silent.   Thousands of men and hundreds of
guns were facing each other on the verge of battle, and
there seemed not a sound.   He listened.   Nothing.   His
runner whispered something to a signaller, who whispered
a reply.   Three more minutes.   Silence.   He could feel
the beating of his heart, more rapid than the tick of seconds
as he held his watch to his ear.

CRASH !   Like an orchestra at the signal of a baton the
thousands of guns north and south opened up.   The
night sprang to flickering daylight with the gun-flashes,
the earth trembled with the shock, the air roared and
screamed with shells.   Lights rushed up from the
German line, and their artillery in turn flamed into action.

Winterbourne could just see a couple of his sections advancing as he started off himself, and then everything was blotted out in a confusion of smoke and bursting shells. He saw his runner stagger and fall as a shell burst between them; then his corporal disappeared, blown to pieces by a direct hit. He came to a sunken road, and lay on the verge, trying to see what was happening in the faint light of dawn. He saw only smoke, and pushed on. Suddenly German helmets were all round him. He clutched at his revolver. Then he saw they were unarmed, holding shaking hands above their heads.

The German machine-guns were tat-tat-tatting at them, and there was a ceaseless swish of bullets. He passed the bodies of several of his men. One section wiped out by a single heavy shell. Other men lay singly. There was Jameson, dead; Halliwell, dead; Sergeant Morton, Taylor and Fish, dead in a little group. He came to the main road, which was three hundred yards short of his objective. A deadly machine-gun fire was holding up his Company. The officers and men were lying down, the men firing rifles, and the Lewis guns ripping off drums of bullets. Winterbourne's second runner was hit, and lay groaning: 'Oh, for God's sake kill me, *kill* me. I can't stand it. The agony. *Kill* me.'

Something seemed to break in Winterbourne's head. He felt he was going mad, and sprang to his feet. The line of bullets smashed across his chest like a savage steel whip. The universe exploded darkly into oblivion.

RÉPUBLIQUE FRANÇAISE

COMMANDEMENT EN CHEF DES ARMÉES ALLIÉES

Quartier Général.

G.Q.G.A., 12. 11. 1918.

OFFICERS, NON-COMMISSIONED OFFICERS, AND
MEN OF THE ALLIED ARMIES

After resolutely holding the enemy in check, for months you have repeatedly attacked with unwearied energy and confidence.

You have won the greatest battle in history and saved the most sacred of all causes : the liberty of the world.

You may well be proud.

You have wreathed your colours with immortal fame.
Posterity is grateful to you.

(Signed)   F. FOCH,
Marshal of France,
Commander-in-Chief of the Allied Armies.

END OF PART III

EPILOGUE

ELEVEN years after the fall of Troy,
We, the old men—some of us nearly forty—
Met and talked on the sunny rampart
Over our wine, while the lizards scuttled
In dusty grass, and the crickets chirred.

Some bared their wounds ;
Some spoke of the thirst, dry in the throat,
And the heart-beat, in the din of battle ;
Some spoke of intolerable sufferings,
The brightness gone from their eyes
And the grey already thick in their hair.

And I sat a little apart
From the garrulous talk and old memories,
And I heard a boy of twenty
Say petulantly to a girl, seizing her arm :
' Oh, come away ; why do you stand there
Listening open-mouthed to the talk of old men ?
Haven't you heard enough of Troy and Achilles ?
Why should they bore us for ever
With an old quarrel and the names of dead men
We never knew, and dull forgotten battles ? '

And he drew her away,
And she looked back and laughed
As he spoke more contempt of us,
Being now out of hearing.

And I thought of the graves by desolate Troy
And the beauty of many young men now dust,

And the long agony, and how useless it all was.
And the talk still clashed about me
Like the meeting of blade and blade.

And as they two moved further away
He put an arm about her, and kissed her ;
And afterwards I heard their gay distant laughter.

And I looked at the hollow cheeks
And the weary eyes and the grey-streaked heads
Of the old men—nearly forty—about me ;
And I too walked away
In an agony of helpless grief and pity.

THE END

Printed in Great Britain by T. and A. Constable Ltd.
at the University Press, Edinburgh

THE PHOENIX LIBRARY

Pocket size, 3s. 6d. net per volume

2

4

THE CENTAUR LIBRARY

Cr. 8vo.   3s. 6d. net per volume

6

THE ST. JAMES'S LIBRARY

Demy 8vo.   Mostly illustrated.   5s. net